RECIPROCITY

D.C. Gilbert

DEDICATION

I am dedicating this book to the memory of my good friend, Joe Palazzolo. I met Joe at Godbold Dog Park in Cary, North Carolina. He had just moved down from New York State and would come to the park with his rescued Greyhound, Silver City Lou. Lou and Sophie, my German Shepherd, became good friends, as did Joe and I. Eventually, Joe became the man behind the character "Pallie" in the second installment of the JD Cordell Action Series titled Montagnard. Pallie is a member of my fictional Golf Platoon, SEAL Team 5.

Pallie's character is a fun-loving but tough-as-nails Sicilian American with Joe's somewhat gruff exterior, personality, sense of humor, and huge heart.

Sadly, Joe lost his battle with cancer on June 30, 2021. But, as Joe still lives in the hearts of family and friends, Pallie will carry on in this next tale. I believe Joe will be proud of his part in the story.

ACKNOWLEDGMENTS

I want to thank my father, Curtiss Gilbert, for his help reviewing this work and for giving me his thoughts and great feedback on the storyline. I also want to thank Beth Kallman Werner at Author Connections for her excellent work as my editor. Lastly, I thank all my readers, friends, and family who have supported me on this journey. You are all greatly appreciated.

PROLOGUE

Damn, it's hot!

Taylor wiped sweat from his forehead with a towel, then glanced at his opponent across the makeshift ring. The man was huge, definitely not Filipino.

Must be Samoan, Taylor thought. He'd seen a few Samoans during his time in the special forces and respected them. Solid operators.

Taylor stood just under six feet in his socks and weighed a solid one hundred and ninety-five pounds. His opponent was a bit taller and heavier; he could also hit. The big man had trained, probably Muay Thai. While the Samoan's technique was a bit sloppy, he moved like a Thai boxer, and his elbows and knees were wicked. A punishing knee to Taylor's ribs had prompted the end of the first round.

These local, unsanctioned fights typically were scheduled for three rounds. However, there was no timer, bell, or anything you could call rules. If a fighter got injured, the center referee would pause the fight long enough to ensure the fighter could continue. That pause effectively ended the round. While a few fights Taylor had fought in had gone two rounds, he'd yet to see one make it to three. They were too brutal for that. Tonight was Taylor's twelfth such fight.

A few weeks back, broke and badly in need of a drink, he'd stumbled into a bar playing host to a local "fight night." After watching the first two amateurs go at it, Taylor, unimpressed, started to leave. Then he saw the winner being handed five thousand Philippine pesos—roughly the equivalent of one hundred and fifty American dollars. So, when the promoter called for two more volunteers, Taylor made his way out onto the dance floor.

The fight was short, despite, or maybe because of Taylor's dire need for a drink. His training saw to that. Collecting his winnings, he'd headed straight to the bar and, after a few shots, felt steady enough to venture down the street to the liquor store, where he picked up a bottle of his self-prescribed medication. From there, he'd stumbled back to his apartment.

Since that night, Taylor had participated in eleven more human cockfights. He'd lost the next two simply because he was too drunk to stand, never mind defend himself. However, the instinct for self-preservation combined with a need for cash made Taylor modify his drinking habit just enough to fit his fight schedule. Then he began to win, quickly becoming a favorite with several locals who started betting on him instead of the Filipino fighters.

As his winnings grew, those betting on Taylor began to win a lot of money. His fans were happy, but not all were pleased. Some of the local gangs began to take notice. After all, they had their favorite fighters and did not like constantly losing to an American drunkard.

Tonight's opponent was the toughest Taylor had faced so far. Although they were matched in size, this man was tough as nails and knew how to fight.

Lucky I don't have a few broken ribs, Taylor thought.

He took a swallow from the beer he'd left sitting on a stack of crates when his name was called to fight. The venue tonight was an old warehouse along the Pasig River, in the Tondo district of Manila. Tondo is the largest district in area and population; it also had the highest crime rate in the Philippines. Taylor figured there had to be at least one murder per week. Fortunately, most of the killings were drug-related and did not involve foreigners or tourists. Still, he knew some extremely dangerous men and women who lived there.

While not exactly Madison Square Garden, someone had set up the warehouse nicely. Chairs and tables circled a marked-off fight ring, and a makeshift but well-stocked bar ran along one side of the building.

A pungent blend of cigar, cigarette, and marijuana smoke filled the air; alcohol flowed freely. A sizable crowd had shown up for tonight's event. Taylor noticed that the clientele attending his fights was improving as he continued to win. More affluent spectators were now in the crowd. Taylor saw some successful businesspeople, and recognized a few leaders of some prominent local gangs. He saw fewer of the societal dregs who'd frequented his earlier fights in local dives. More women were now in attendance, which did not escape Taylor's eyes. They were typically attractive, often on the arms of well-dressed men. There were also a few women who seemed to be alone. Two caught his eye, especially since both had been present at his last two fights. They looked to be twin sisters, and both were stunningly beautiful.

The referee called. Wiping his forehead and taking one last slug from his beer, Taylor returned to the center of the ring.

Time to end this, before I screw around and get hurt.

His opponent, confident he'd hurt Taylor badly with that last knee to the ribs, came on strong, pressing his advantage. He fired a hard cutting kick at Taylor's right leg, which Taylor narrowly avoided; he immediately followed with a left jab, then a hard right elbow strike toward the temple. Taylor slipped the jab and raised his left forearm to deflect the elbow. It was what the other fighter was waiting for, and he launched a brutal shin kick at Taylor's battered ribs.

Taylor shifted slightly to his right as his left arm dropped suddenly, hooking around his opponent's kicking leg and trapping it against his left side. Ignoring the screaming pain from his badly bruised ribs, Taylor shifted, taking his opponent off balance. Grabbing the fighter's windpipe in a vise-like grip, he swept the bigger man's left leg out from under him, driving his opponent to the floor. The big man hit hard. Taylor followed him down while maintaining control of the leg. He dropped his right knee into the man's groin and a loud groan escaped the Samoan's clenched teeth. Taylor reached down and grabbed a handful of hair, jerking the man's head around, and slammed his fist into the right side of the man's massive jaw, which must have been chiseled from granite because, somehow, it did not shatter. Even so, the Samoan collapsed to the floor. He was out cold; the fight was over.

Taylor released his grip on his opponent's hair and stood up. Swaying just a bit, he paused and looked down at the unmoving form. Then, he abruptly turned and walked over to the stack of crates to finish his beer.

Okay, time to collect my money and get the hell out of here.

Sensing a presence behind him, Taylor turned to find a woman looking up at him. She was one of the twins he'd spotted earlier, even more breathtaking up close. She smiled.

"That was a great fight. You are an excellent fighter." Her eyes boldly roamed over his six-foot frame. "I have made good money from your last two fights."

Taylor nodded. "Glad to hear that, ma'am. Excuse me, I have to collect my winnings and then go get cleaned up. It was nice talking to you." He turned to walk away.

"Wait."

Taylor paused and looked back.

"There's a shower here at the warehouse you can use if you like. I can ensure your money is safe until you're ready to leave."

Taylor frowned, then chuckled. "Why would I do that … trust you to keep my money safe?"

"I like you, and let's just say I want to … buy you a drink. After that, who knows?" She smiled again, then shrugged, leaving the possibilities hanging.

Taylor's mind began to consider those possibilities.

I could use a drink, he thought.

This lady was damn pretty, even if she only came up to his chest. "You don't think the warehouse owner would object to me using the shower?"

Again, the woman smiled. "I can guarantee it. My sister and I own the warehouse. So, Taylor? Can I call you Taylor? What do you say? Or would you prefer I call you something else?"

"Sure, Taylor will do. And what should I call you?"

"My name is Blessica, Blessica Baguinda."

Taylor knew the name. Everyone in the Tondo district and probably throughout the entire city of Manila knew it. Blessica and her sister, Mahalia, ran the Dalawang Mga Ate Na Mafia, or Two Sisters Mafia.

Blessica saw the surprise and recognition register on his face. "I see you have heard of me."

Taylor nodded. "I have. You and your sister are, shall we say, well-known in some circles."

"Does it matter?"

Taylor considered that and then shook his head. After all, he was not exactly a model citizen himself. "I guess not."

Blessica smiled widely. "Great. Let me show you to the shower."

CHAPTER 1
Vietnam

Lt. Colonel Fong pushed open the door and strutted into the recently opened Phuc Loc Tu Pawnshop in District 1 of Ho Chi Minh City. Fong had visited the establishment the previous week, informing the owner of the community protection plan for which he collected monthly donations. Not unexpectedly, the owner was hesitant to contribute. After having a good week collection-wise, Fong felt uncharacteristically generous and gave the man a week to think it over.

Now, a week later, collections had gone exceedingly well, and Fong's mind had already turned toward the evening's entertainment. Collecting a protection payment from one reluctant pawnshop owner would not get in the way of those plans.

When Fong confronted the pawnshop owner again, the man stood his ground, still finding no reason to pay for protection.

"My business does not need protection from young thugs. I can handle any punks who try to hustle me. And besides, there are also the police. So, I see no reason I must pay."

Fong smiled. "Ah... yes. Sadly, the local police are worthless. You will get no help from them. The fee covers my protection, and I am with the Mobile Police Force. Everyone contributes. It would be best for you to consider supporting safety in our community. It is a small price to pay to stay in business. We would not want anything to happen to you and your little business here, would we?"

The pawnshop owner shook his head. "Twenty percent is too much. I do not scare so easily. I am not afraid of you or your threats."

Fong frowned. *I do not have time for this nonsense.*

Deciding to take a more direct approach, Fong escalated his game. "Ahh! But you have a lovely daughter, such a pretty young thing. We certainly would not want anything to happen to her, now would we? Are you beginning to understand me?"

For the first time, a flicker of fear appeared in the pawnshop owner's eyes. Fong knew he had him.

"If you do not pay, I cannot guarantee your daughter's safety." Fong shrugged with a deliberately troubled look on his face. "She might disappear. Or worse, she could even find herself working in one of the brothels."

The pawnshop owner's eyes grew wide. "You would not do that…"

Fong shrugged and smiled. "Of course not. But I cannot control all the unsavory characters in District 1 without proper funding. I must answer to my boss, too. He is high up in the government. So, I do what I must to keep him happy. So should you."

The pawnshop owner felt sick; he knew he had no choice. Although he was tough and used to shady deals, he treasured his fourteen-year-old daughter. She was the center of his world. Excusing himself, the man went to his cash box and counted the money. Then, placing it into an envelope, he handed it to Fong, who smiled.

"That is a sound decision. I knew you would make the right choice. Your daughter is such a sweet young girl. We must keep her safe at any cost." Again, Fong smiled. "See you next month." Pocketing the envelope, Fong turned and walked out the door into the street.

Feeling pleased after the successful conclusion of his business at the pawnshop, Fong found himself with a good appetite and decided to have dinner at Chanh Bistro. Ordering the crispy skin duck breast served with grilled cauliflower and sourdough bread, he decided that a chilled bottle of Allan Scott

Sauvignon Blanc from New Zealand would complement his meal perfectly.

And after dinner, I will spend the evening with Ahn. Fong grew excited at the thought. She was his most prized possession, and her apartment was just a few minutes away. He'd rented the place for her a few blocks from Bui Vien walking street.

An hour and a half later, Fong paid the taxi driver and climbed the stairs to the apartment building's entrance. Entering the security code on the keypad, he opened the door and went in. Then, opting for the stairs over the elevator, he ascended to the third floor and used his key to enter the apartment. Wrapped in a silk robe, Ahn sat on the couch, legs curled under her, looking at pictures in a Western travel magazine.

"And how is my little bird tonight?" Fong asked with a smile. He slid off his loafers and moved toward the couch. "What are you looking at, Ahn?"

Ahn looked up. "Just a magazine my friend let me borrow. She is planning to go to America for a job."

Fong laughed. "Good luck to her. You are lucky that you have a good job already. You don't need to go to America." He reached out to take Ahn's hand. "You take good care of me, and I take good care of you."

Ahn allowed Fong to help her up and followed him into the bedroom. As Ahn headed toward the bed, Fong took off his jacket and laid it on a chair in the corner. He watched as Ahn slid out of the silk robe.

11

Quickly removing the rest of his clothing, Fong joined her on the bed. She was a flawless beauty and all his, which was just how he wanted it; he owned her. Beginning to explore her exquisite body, he felt his excitement grow. The sound of his cell phone chirping brought the moment to a halt. Fong frowned.

Damn!

From the ringtone, he knew it was a call he could not safely ignore. Fong did not fool with many different ringtones, but he'd given one to his most important contact, the one he certainly did not want to anger. So, pleasure would have to wait.

Sliding out of bed, Fong walked to the chair over which he'd laid his suit jacket and extracted his phone from its inner breast pocket.

"Xin chào."

The voice at the other end was quiet but commanding, leaving no room for discussion. "You will fly to Hanoi tonight and report to me first thing in the morning. Is that understood, Fong?"

"Yes, I understand."

"Good. Nine o'clock, do not be late."

That was it. The call ended. Looking at the watch on his left wrist, Fong considered his options. He certainly had to be in Hanoi in the morning. There was no avoiding that. However, flights to Hanoi left nearly every hour, and it was still early.

"Are you coming back to bed?" Ahn inquired, adding a slightly pouting tone to her voice. She could be tough to resist, and she knew it. Ahn had learned to accept this arrangement, at least for now. Besides, she had little choice. It was certainly better than working at one of the nightclubs, or worse, out on the streets. While she was still young and pretty, a few more years on the streets and she'd become just another used-up old whore. Ahn was terrified of ending up like that. And, despite being in his mid-fifties, Fong exercised daily, keeping himself in good physical condition. Ahn had to admit she got great pleasure from Fong's regular visits. He was a good lover and couldn't get enough of her.

That was precisely why Fong, after a few early dalliances, had moved Ahn out of the club where she worked and set her up in this plush apartment. Ahn did not mind one bit. It was much easier and safer now that she only had one man with which to contend. For Fong, it was a matter of convenience. He wanted Ahn all to himself and had the means to afford such a luxury.

It took Fong only a moment to reach a decision. Being a corrupt high-level police officer, while very lucrative, involved some risk. He knew the odds were excellent that he would survive the visit to Hanoi. His boss seemed pleased with his work now. But Fong held no illusions; he knew there were no guarantees.

Sometimes, you must take your pleasures where you can find them.

Fong tossed the phone onto the chair and crossed to the bed where Ahn waited. He'd catch a later flight. There was no hurry.

CHAPTER 2
Knoxville, Tennessee

JD and Ellen scheduled their wedding soon after JD returned from Vietnam with his mother. Much to Mai's dismay, the young couple was adamant about their preference for a small reception, with just family and a few close friends. Mai only came around once JD reminded her that she and his father had married in an olive-drab canvas, general-purpose, large US Army tent on a small military base in the Vietnamese central highlands. And their marriage seemed to stick just fine.

Once his mother admitted the truth in her son's observation, she took immediate control of preparations, declaring that even if it had to be a small wedding, she could at least make the arrangements.

Annie, JD's sister, was delighted when Ellen asked her to serve as her maid of honor. Annie and Robert's two young boys, Jimmy and Allen, would handle the all-important task of co-ring bearers.

JD called Vivas a few weeks before the wedding, to tell him the news and inquire if he might be interested in serving as his best man.

"Hell, man. I'd be honored. There's no way I won't be there. I'll go AWOL if I have to. What are they going to do to me—send me to Vietnam? I've been there, done that." Both he and JD laughed. "I've only got a few months left in the Navy anyway."

Fortunately, Vivas didn't have to go AWOL. He simply requested and received a week's leave time to fly out from San Diego and attend. To everyone's surprise and delight, he showed up the day before the wedding with Hana at his side.

"Hana flew into San Diego and then we flew here to Knoxville together," Vivas explained with a huge grin. "There was no way she would miss your wedding, JD."

JD turned red when Hana threw her arms around him and planted a huge kiss on his cheek.

"Carlos is right. There's no way I'd miss your wedding. Besides, I want to meet the woman who has captured your heart. She must be something."

Releasing Vivas from a huge, heart-felt hug, Ellen laughed and turned, greeting Hana with a smile and a welcoming embrace.

"It is so nice to finally meet you, Hana. JD has told me so much about you. I am so grateful he had your help in Thailand and Vietnam. You are an amazing woman yourself."

Hana stepped back to give Ellen an appraising look. "It's nice to finally meet you too, Ellen. I must confess that I was quite smitten by JD when I first got to know him, so I was disappointed to learn he was already taken. Then I heard you were the lady doctor al Qaeda kidnapped in Niger." She paused. "My father, Rick, told me what you did for Ajax during your rescue. That was something, considering what you'd just been through."

Leaning in, Hana lowered her voice. "I can see why JD loves you. You have a good man, Ellen." Hana glanced over to where JD and Carlos were talking to Annie's husband, Robert, who laughed at something Carlos had just said. "And now I have Carlos, and I couldn't be happier."

Ellen smiled. "You certainly do, Hana. And Carlos is a good man."

Ellen's parents and her two brothers had flown in from Chicago to attend. Henry and Grace Chang were delighted to meet the man who'd helped rescue their daughter from terrorists. Henry immediately embraced JD, and there were tears in Grace's eyes when she rose to kiss his cheek. JD was uncomfortable at first, but then relaxed. He understood what it meant to the older couple. He remembered what it felt like to learn someone had kidnapped his mother on the other side of the world. It was not a good feeling.

After everyone got acquainted, Henry and Grace took quite a shine to Annie's two little boys. They were probably anticipating grandchildren of their own in the not-too-distant future. Grace took the boys under her kind but firm wing, giving the other women a much-needed break as they continued to work on preparations for the next day's wedding ceremony.

JD spotted Ellen's two brothers standing shyly in a corner, and headed over to welcome them to the family.

The weather the following day could not have been more perfect. It was a beautiful afternoon in East Tennessee. The sky was a brilliant blue, the sun was shining, and a light breeze made the sun's warmth pleasant.

The service began promptly at 2:00 p.m., with Father Joe Patterson officiating the traditional Episcopalian ceremony using the 1928 Book of Common Prayer. It had always been a Cordell family favorite, the classic old English verse sounding like poetry.

People seated on white folding chairs waited quietly for Henry Chang to escort his daughter to the small, slightly raised platform where the groom waited.

Hana leaned into Vivas and whispered that JD looked quite dashing in his tan dress slacks, navy blue sport coat, and light blue checkered shirt open at the collar. On the invitation, Ellen and JD had suggested guests dress comfortably.

"What about me?" Vivas inquired, a poorly feigned look of crushed feelings on his face.

"You look positively dashing, my love."

Vivas had dressed in his Navy Summer Whites. Jimmy and Allen thought that was cool, eyeing all the ribbons and the SEAL trident. A few minutes earlier, the two boys had been asking what each ribbon was for. Vivas patiently answered each query until it was time for the boys to prepare for their ring-bearer responsibilities.

A couple of Ellen's colleagues from her job at the University of Tennessee Medical Center were in attendance. She worked at the internal medicine practice and her co-workers were happy for her and JD. Along with a few old friends and Sophie, they were the only guests.

Unfortunately, Pallie was at sea on a training exercise and could not attend the wedding. Still, he relayed his blessing and some sage advice to JD through Vivas, who'd shared Pallie's words of wisdom to everyone's amusement and delight during the previous evening's welcome dinner.

Standing on the platform with Father Joe, JD had to admit—at least to himself—that he was nervous. He had to laugh over that.

It's one thing to clear a house of terrorists in some remote village in Iraq, or take out a drug smuggler in Vietnam—but marriage? JD could feel his palms sweating. *This is uncharted water… and one hell of a big step.*

JD felt somebody move to stand beside him. It was Vivas.

"You alright, buddy?"

A flash of color caught JD's eye and he turned to see Henry Chang leading his daughter Ellen toward the platform, with Annie following slightly behind. Ellen was positively radiant in her blue and white floral print summer dress.

My God, I love that woman. Suddenly, JD felt calm. He turned slightly toward Vivas. "I'm fine, thanks!"

Vivas chuckled and whispered, "Good. I'd hate to report to Pallie that his hero got KO'd by a pretty face."

JD grinned and turned to meet his bride.

Mai invited everyone to a reception at her home in Knoxville, three hours after the ceremony ended. The timing allowed people to explore the old grist mill or the dam and then drive from Norris Dam State Park to her home. It was too wonderful a day to rush things.

Everything was perfect. Mai was an excellent hostess, providing a simple but delicious buffet with finger foods from several cuisines. There were platters of grilled marinated pork on little skewers, a large bowl of sticky rice, Vietnamese shrimp and crab summer rolls, Chinese steamed dumplings, and a variety of dim sum, all sitting on the long dining room table. There was also a platter of tiny lamb chops with several dipping sauces, and a platter of jumbo peel-and-eat shrimp with cocktail sauce. In a large cooler, there was a great selection of ice-cold craft beers and various chilled wines. There was iced tea, sprite, or ginger ale for the younger and non-alcohol-drinking guests. A Keurig machine was standing by with various coffees and teas for those who wanted a hot beverage. Mai had thought of every detail.

JD introduced Vivas to Tokumura Sensei, and they enjoyed discussing various martial arts concepts before Henry and Grace approached and stood waiting a few feet away. JD sensed that Ellen's parents wanted to talk to him.

Leaving Vivas and Tokumura to continue the discussion without him, the groom stepped off with the Changs. They exchanged pleasantries about the wedding for a few minutes, but it was clear that both of his new in-laws had something on their minds. Finally, Grace hesitantly broached the subject.

"I am sorry to ask you this on your wedding day, JD, but I am so worried. Ellen hasn't told us much, and we don't want to press her too hard. We are both worried about her. It must have been terrible in Africa for her and that poor young man, her assistant, Norman. But she has said nothing to us, nothing at all. Is this normal? You know about these things. Will she be okay? We want her – both of you – to be happy together."

JD stood quietly for a moment, deciding how to answer best. He knew what he could not tell them; that was part of his job. At least, it had been at the time. He was unsure what to say to them about the rest. It was no surprise they wanted to know. They loved their daughter and were concerned about her. What caring parent wouldn't be? But JD knew some things they did not need to know. It wouldn't help anything to tell them, and would only make them worry more. He needed to quickly filter the facts, to be honest with the Changs while protecting everyone involved, especially Ellen.

After a slight hesitation, JD began to answer their questions the best he could, deciding to focus on Ellen. Leaving out the worst details, he described the rescue, her bravery, and what she had done for Ajax despite what she had endured. Grace teared up at the mention of the dog.

"I was so sorry to hear that you lost Ajax. Ellen told us what happened in Vietnam. He must have been such a brave dog, an amazing dog."

Henry nodded.

JD felt a tug in his heart. "Yes, he was. He was a great dog, a fearless warrior, and a loyal partner. And your daughter, despite being terrified plus physically and emotionally exhausted, stopped Ajax from bleeding out in the Humvee while it was racing across the desert. She then performed emergency surgery on Ajax on a folding table in our cobbled-together quarters using little more than a tactical first aid kit." JD smiled. "And, of course, Sweeney's beard trimmer."

Henry Chang smiled at that.

"Ellen would not rest until she had Ajax stable, on intravenous fluids and antibiotics." JD paused, and Grace noticed the strong feelings carried in his voice as he continued. "I know a lot of men who could not have done what she did. Your daughter will forever have my profound respect and admiration, as well as my love. She will be fine. I promise."

Grace suddenly gave JD a warm hug, speaking softly. "I think our daughter has found a wonderful husband."

Henry nodded and smiled again.

That evening, while JD brushed his teeth, he thought about his earlier discussion with Ellen's parents. He hoped he'd said the right things. He was pretty sure, from their reaction, that he had. In a way, Henry and Grace Chang reminded him of his own parents. It must have taken a lot of courage to leave all they knew behind and start a new life in a foreign country. He knew they'd come separately, meeting later in Chicago. JD sensed a quiet strength in his new in-laws, a strength that did not boast, or demand recognition. It was a regal determination that allowed them to do what they must. His mother had that same kind of unassuming power.

JD rinsed his mouth with some water and turned off the bathroom light, then walked into the bedroom where Ellen was waiting. The soft glow of the single lamp on the bedside table shrouded Ellen's face in a faint shadow. The effect took JD's breath away. The two had begun living together in Ellen's loft on Gay Street. While technically less square footage than JD's condo, the layout made it seem more spacious. Sophie was quite satisfied with her over-stuffed chair downstairs. Her keen German Shepherd's nose detected the scent of the chair's previous occupant. She'd encountered that scent at the condo where she'd come to live with JD and gotten used to it. It was a comforting smell.

Crawling into bed, JD commented, "Well, I think your parents like me."

"I saw you were talking to them earlier; my mom was in tears. What was that about?"

"Your mom and dad asked about Niger. I didn't know what to tell them, so I just told them how amazing you were and what you did for Ajax."

Ellen smiled. "Well, I don't know about me being amazing, but that explains Mom's crying. We never had pets other than goldfish when I was growing up, but my mom always loved dogs. I think she always wanted one. My dad's being so frugal kept us from getting a dog." JD settled in and adjusted the covers. Ellen continued, "I told Mom what Ajax did when you guys were in Vietnam and how he saved your mother. She cried then, too."

JD reached over and gently placed his hand on Ellen's cheek. He loved the feel of her skin.

"I'm just happy they both like me."

"You know what?"

"What?"

"I like you too. Now, come over here." Ellen opened her arms as JD closed the distance between them.

CHAPTER 3
Vietnam

The early morning flight to Hanoi had been uneventful. After ordering the driver to wait, Lt. Colonel Fong clambered out of the taxi's back seat. The driver pulled away, looking for a place to park. Fong was nervous. He worked to calm himself, or at least to appear so. He saw himself as an influential and dangerous man, and he was, in certain circles, such as his district of Ho Chi Minh City. But this was an entirely different league. The man who had summoned him to his office in Hanoi could make Fong disappear with a word, and no one would even consider asking any questions.

Trán Ngô Sang leaned back into the leather chair behind his desk. His office was lavishly furnished as befitting a senior colonel with the Ministry of Public Security. Trán contemplated the dusty ceiling fan blades slowly turning overhead as his brain processed Fong's report.

Somebody needs to clean those fan blades immediately after this meeting.

Fong's report had infuriated him. Trán prided himself on his ability to remain calm under pressure, but Fong's news of his cousin's death had severely tested Trán's self-control. Not that he and his cousin were particularly close. It was more that his cousin had helped make him a wealthy man. Trán had provided his cousin with protection and access to powerful people in the communist government in exchange for compensation. It had been a lucrative arrangement. Trán would miss that income and now would have to find a way to replace it. His standard of living, as well as his reputation, had to be maintained.

The minutes spent contemplating the fan's blades allowed Trán to regain composure. Finally, he directed his gaze back to the man across from him.

"So, you are quite certain of all this?" It was more a statement than a question.

"Yes," Fong replied. "My investigation has been exhaustive, and while parts are still ongoing, we have learned a great deal."

Trán nodded. Fong was a corrupt police officer, but he hadn't gotten to where he was by being incompetent at his job.

"We found your cousin's body close to the tree line at the old Michelin plantation house, near Lai Khe. He was shot twice through the heart with a large caliber pistol, a .45 favored by the American military. We identified several other bodies at the plantation house as members of his security team. The charred remains of your cousin's head of security, Huýnh, were inside the house with several additional security team members. Someone carved out Huýnh's throat with a large combat knife."

This bit of information surprised Trán. Huýnh had been very good with a knife.

"This was the work of professionals," Fong continued. "There was quite a firefight. We found brass casings scattered all over the grounds. It also looks like whoever assaulted the compound suffered no casualties, but there were signs indicating a few may have been injured."

"What of my cousin's business ledgers—his accounts?"

Fong shrugged. "The plantation house burned to the ground, probably set on fire by the attackers. There was no sign of your cousin's business accounts or any cash. Any books or money were either taken by those who killed him or burned up in the house."

Trán accepted this other bit of bad news and again kept from losing his temper. Any missing cash would be a minor loss, but those business ledgers would be worth a fortune to whoever possessed them.

Who would dare to do such a thing? Anyone who knew his cousin would know how well-connected and protected he was. Trán decided whoever did this was either insane or suicidal.

"Do we know yet who killed my cousin and why? I am thinking perhaps a rival drug lord?" Trán knew of his cousin's efforts to eliminate opium smuggling competitors in the region and had been aiding him in those efforts.

"No," Fong shook his head. "I do not think a rival drug boss did this. I am sure this was a rescue mission."

"A rescue?"

"Shortly before this attack, your cousin ordered me to arrest a Vietnamese American woman named Mai Cordell, traveling in the country. The woman was staying at the Park Hyatt in Ho Chi Minh City. I arrested her and took her to the plantation house. At the time, I had no idea who she was. Of course, the arrest was unofficial; there is no record of it. It is not a coincidence that the woman's arrest happened about a week before the attack on your cousin's plantation house."

"Who was this woman? What did he want with her?"

"I have since learned that during the war, your cousin had her family executed as punishment for supporting the Americans. Her father was the mayor of a small village in an area where your cousin commanded a battalion of Viet Cong freedom fighters." Fong paused, checking his notepad. "When the VC executed her family, Mai somehow survived, fleeing to a nearby Jarai village where the village elder took her in. It appears her father was friendly with the Jarai chief. She later married an American officer and left Vietnam with him."

"That does not adequately explain his interest in her today. Why did he have you arrest her?"

"You know of your cousin's history with the Jarai criminal named Dish?"

"Of course." Most Vietnamese government officials knew of the savage Jarai criminal who sold guns to outlaw rebels. There was still a reward on his head. However, not many knew of his cousin's long-standing feud with this criminal who'd fought with the Americans.

"Mai Cordell is the criminal's adopted sister. Dish's father adopted her and she grew up in his village. She moved to America before your cousin also ordered that Jarai village be destroyed as punishment for helping the Americans."

"That was many years ago. So why was she here now?"

"It seems she returned to Vietnam to find her adopted brother. One of your cousin's spies overheard her talking to a Jarai whore, asking about the criminal in a bar. So, I believe your cousin had me arrest her so he could use her as bait to trap his old enemy."

Trán sat back in his chair, stunned.

"There is more," Fong went on. "I am certain that Dish rescued his sister and used the opportunity to settle his old score with your cousin. But I also know he had help. There were some interesting discoveries at the crime scene. For instance, a trained attack dog was working with the rescue team. I have rounded up and interrogated most of the security team members who survived the attack. Several claimed they saw a large dog enter the house with three men, and one of the charred bodies in the house looked to have bite wounds from a large dog on his arm. A few reported that the two men they saw looked like Westerners, certainly not Vietnamese. Someone shot several of your cousin's men inside the house with a .50 caliber rifle. We found the slugs in the burned rubble and later located the sniper's shooting position. It appears that the sniper shot them through a window to keep them from killing the woman before the two Westerners with the dog could get to her. The rescue was very well planned. I think Dish had professional help. It looks like a team of foreign professionals, probably American, helped rescue Mai Cordell."

Trán Ngô Sang leaned forward, resting his palms flat on his desk. "How could that be? How would they get into the country without our knowing?"

Fong chuckled. "That would be relatively simple, Colonel. They could easily travel here from Thailand. They would only have to cross through Laos or

Cambodia and enter Vietnam almost anywhere in the border region. That's a very mountainous area riddled with old smuggling trails. It has recently become quite popular with Western tourists who now bicycle between these border countries to take photographs. Anyone attempting to sneak in could easily blend in if they were smart. And show any border guard a passport with fifty American dollars in it, and…" Fong shrugged, letting his voice trail off.

Trán digested this new information slowly. Finally, he sat back, fingers absentmindedly toying with the tip of his white goatee. "Of course, the American government will deny any involvement."

"Of course. And the American government may not have been involved. They could have been private contractors, associates of the Jarai criminal."

Trán's eyes again focused on the ceiling fan. Fong waited for what seemed like several minutes. Then, finally, Colonel Trán stood. "You are to continue your investigation. I want to know where Dish is now, and you will find out who helped him. I want to know who is responsible for my cousin's death, and I want them dealt with severely. Do you understand?"

"Of course, Colonel. I will see to it." Fong got up from his chair and turned to leave.

"Do this for me, Fong, and I will be greatly pleased. But do not fail me; I am not in a forgiving mood."

Fong nodded, then turned quickly and exited through the office door.

CHAPTER 4
The Philippines

Bill Taylor felt his six-foot frame relax, sinking into the mattress. His gaze wandered over the beautiful Filipina sitting astride him. They had just finished round two. Taylor could not see her face; her long, dark brown hair hid it from his view. She had a lovely face, but too often—in fact, more often than not—it was a sad face. Blessica's smile rarely seemed to reach her eyes. He'd noticed when she first selected him for a night of sex after one of his fights. The fighting excited her; she had a "thing" for winners. Of course, Taylor hadn't turned her down even though he knew Blessica was using him.

Hell, I'm using her too. There was no pretense of a relationship beyond satisfying a physical need.

Taylor suppressed what would have been a bitter laugh. *I'm her stress relief. She'll tire of me soon enough. Then, I'll be discarded like an old, worn-out shoe.*

As far as Taylor was concerned, that was fine with him. He figured his days were numbered anyway. In the meantime, he'd enjoy her while he still could.

What kind of man would turn down great sex with a woman who looks like her? Taylor's damaged psyche ignored the sad emptiness of that last thought.

He knew that Blessica and her sister, Mahalia, called the shots for one of the most feared gangs in Tondo. The two were twins, but Blessica was outgoing and personable. Mahalia was quiet and reserved, bordering on sullen. *And maybe just a little scary.*

On one or two occasions, Taylor had let his mind entertain the thought of spending a night with Mahalia. However, that was not likely to happen. He'd heard that she batted for the other side.

Blessica rolled off him and spread out on her side of the king-sized bed. "You can go now."

"I was hoping you'd let me spend the night. This bed is big enough, and I'm tired after the fight, not to mention our… activities."

Blessica laughed. "Are you joking? I got what I needed. I think you enjoyed it also. Now you must go."

"Can I at least take a quick shower?"

"Of course, as soon as you get home."

"I don't know why I put up with this shit."

"Because the sex is outstanding. You like screwing me."

She sure has that right. Taylor climbed out of bed and began pulling on his clothes.

"Will I see you again?"

"You fight again next Friday, I think?"

"I reckon so."

"Well, perhaps if you survive that fight, I will see you again." For a moment, Blessica's face showed a sad smile. Then she laughed. "Perhaps then, you can stay the night and even shower."

As she put it, staying the night somehow seemed less inviting.

Taylor thought as he pulled his running shoes on and tied them up, *I need to meet a better class of people.*

But that was not very likely, either. Taylor was self-aware enough to know that in trying to escape his demons, he'd sunk to a point where no decent person would likely give him a second thought.

So, what kind of a woman would want me?

"Okay, Blessica, I guess I'll see you later."

"Perhaps." Blessica headed toward the bathroom and its colossal walk-in shower. "You know the way out."

As they neared his apartment, Taylor told the cab driver to let him out. He paid the fare and walked the last four blocks to his residence, looking around and occasionally checking his surroundings.

He laughed at himself. *Old habits die hard.*

Very few people knew where he lived, and he preferred to keep it that way. Besides, it wasn't exactly the kind of place you'd want to entertain guests. Taylor rented a single room at the back side of a large building that housed a small bar on the ground floor. The bar was frequented by local toughs; not at all a destination that might attract tourists. The building's first floor also had a pawnshop and a tattoo parlor. Both establishments had seen better days. Most of their customers were now young Filipino gangsters with cash to burn. The second floor consisted of several low-rent apartments occupied by women who entertained a steady stream of different men.

Taylor's room had once served as a storeroom, but it was now furnished with a cot, table, chair, and a small refrigerator. In the corner, an old water hose and drain that were probably used at one time to clean mops, now served as his shower—at least when the water worked. There was also a small sink below a cheap square mirror hanging from a nail. Tonight, thankfully, the water was working.

Taylor took a cold shower and brushed his teeth. The brown eyes staring at him from the mirror looked sad and tired. He ran his hand through the short, dirty blond hair on his head and then turned to survey his meager quarters.

The room was cheap. Taylor got a good discount for keeping troublemakers in the bar at a minimum, and occasionally rousting a drunken john out of one of the upstairs apartments. Word slowly got around that this was not a good place to cause a disturbance. Taylor kept his "apartment" clean and orderly; some might call it spartan. The neatness was simply the result of habit, ingrained from years of military service.

Grabbing a whiskey bottle from the low shelf near the refrigerator, Taylor opened it and took a long swig. Sleep, when necessary, was rarely pleasant. Alcohol didn't always keep away the demons that came in the night, but sometimes, it helped.

Taking a second swig from the bottle, Taylor set it down on the old crate he used as a nightstand and, bending over, removed his running shoes. He sat down on the cot. Retrieving the bottle, he took another long pull, then stretched out on the thin mattress. His mind returned to the evening's pleasant exertions with Blessica. He knew, of course, that she only used him. He told himself he didn't mind. The sex was great, after all. And, since she didn't care about him, there was no worry about emotional entanglements. Besides, she and her sister were gang leaders. He didn't need to get involved in their world. Taylor didn't know exactly what they were into, but he didn't care either. At least, that's what he told himself.

He knew about the prostitution. *Maybe drugs and some protection rackets as well. I should break it the fuck off...*

He took another drink from the whiskey bottle.

The bitch doesn't deserve me.

Taylor shuddered suddenly. *But then again, I don't deserve any better, do I?*

Another swig from the bottle. He could feel the alcohol working now.

I gave up any claim to a righteous life back in Afghanistan. I am where I should be, where I deserve to be.

Returning the bottle to his lips, Taylor tilted it up and drained it.

Fuck it!

He tossed the empty bottle to the floor, where it miraculously didn't break. Instead, it rolled into a corner near the refrigerator. Getting to his feet, he stumbled just a bit as he crossed to the shelf, where he grabbed a second bottle before returning to the cot. The self-prescribed medication was beginning to work.

Taylor glanced at the one picture he had hanging on the wall near his cot. It was a photograph of some old special forces buddies back in Afghanistan. He missed those days.

Another shiver passed through his body, and opening it, he took a long pull from the bottle.

Here's to the good life.

He'd be out like a light with a few more good slugs. Then, hopefully, his sleep would be undisturbed.

Across town, now wrapped in a silk bathrobe, Blessica entered the luxury condo's kitchen. Mahalia sat at the breakfast bar, sipping from a steaming cup of green tea.

"Did you get rid of him?"

Grabbing a mug from the cupboard, Blessica tossed a tea bag into it and filled it with boiling water from the kettle. She leaned back against the counter.

"He's gone."

"I don't know what you see in him."

Blessica laughed. "If you liked men, you certainly would."

"Men are filthy animals." Mahalia hadn't looked at a man since a gang kidnapped her and Blessica several years ago. When the thugs took the two girls to a nearby island to work as prostitutes, they were both young teens. They'd been fortunate and, after a few weeks, had managed to escape by killing one of the gang members and fleeing into the jungle at night. But the experience had forever changed their lives - Mahalia, perhaps more so.

Blessica shrugged. "He doesn't matter. He will be killed or crippled in this next fight. I heard that it's all arranged. Someone is bringing that brute, Garcia, from Mindanao. So, I doubt you'll have to suffer seeing Taylor again after that monster gets his hands on him."

"Well, that's good news!" Mahalia poured the remainder of her tea into the sink. "I am going to bed. We have a new shipment coming in tomorrow; remember that."

Blessica nodded, taking another sip of her tea. "I'll be there."

Blessica moved over to the barstool her sister had vacated and sat down.

It's too bad about Taylor. She'd made a lot of money betting on him in the fights. *And he was great in bed.*

That was as close to feeling regret as Blessica would ever allow herself to get. The man was a loser, a nobody. And besides, in the world where she and Mahalia existed, love didn't count for much. You took whatever you could get.

Life is short; you could be dead tomorrow. She could not afford to let her guard down, even for a second. Blessica drained the rest of her tea.

I'd better get some sleep. I wonder what the new shipment will look like.

CHAPTER 5
Coronado Naval Base

Vivas took a sip of the ice-cold Corona. The Little Club, located beside the ferry landing on Coronado, was a favorite with Golf Platoon. Pallie, Maddux, Jackson, and Sweeney were with him, and it was Sweeney's turn to buy the next round.

Vivas glanced around the bar and sighed. It was the typical nightly mix of Navy SEALS, loud country music, and several middle-aged couples drunkenly clutching each other as they swayed on the dance floor. Vivas would miss this place.

Jeannie, the waitress, distributed the next round of beers and deftly avoided Jackson's attempt to swat her on the butt.

"Too slow, old man."

"So, Vivas, you are going to Thailand and marrying that Hana chick?" Sweeney asked, shaking his head in disbelief.

Vivas nodded after setting the beer back down on the table. "I fly out the day after tomorrow."

"Damn," Maddux added. "She must be something."

"You don't know the half of it," Pallie replied. "We couldn't have gotten JD's mom out of there without her. She even stood side-by-side with us in that gunfight with those drug smugglers. She took out at least one of those assholes herself with an M4. Besides that, she is smarter than all you goombahs put together, and I might add, a lot prettier."

Vivas laughed. "That's for damn sure, Pallie."

"Yeah, but she's not even American," Sweeney persisted.

"Well, fuck, neither is Vivas! He's a damned Puerto Rican!" Jackson laughed.

"You're just jealous, Jackson, 'cause Puerto Ricans are so handsome, we get all the pretty girls."

"Shit!" Jackson muttered.

Pallie slapped Vivas on the back. "You're doing the right thing, buddy, trust me. I mean, shit, if I weren't marrying Kathy, I'd probably fly back to Bangkok and hook up with Hana myself. She only went for you because I was already taken."

"Thanks, Pallie, I think …"

"Too many damn weddings are going on here, Sweeney," Jackson remarked. "First, JD up and marries

41

the doc we rescued in Niger. Then Pallie gets himself engaged to some Swedish girl. Now, Vivas is running off to marry some chick way the fuck over in Thailand. It's freaking crazy."

"Yep. It's a good thing I'm married to the Navy," Sweeney laughed. "If the Navy wants me to have a wife, they can issue me one. Until then, I consider it my patriotic duty to share my magnificent self with as many women as possible. You know, share the love."

Vivas drained the last of his beer. "Sweeney, you're so full of shit you're starting to sound like Jackson."

"Speaking of… time for another round." Jackson held his arm up to catch Jeannie's eye, and she headed toward their table. "Get us another round, would you, Jeannie?"

"Coming right up." She headed back toward the bar.

"At least Pallie will be happy." Maddux reached over and punched Pallie in the shoulder. "Once Vivas' replacement gets here, he won't be the new guy anymore."

Pallie laughed. "You're damn straight. Somebody else can have the shit details back." The truth was that Pallie hadn't been the new guy for some time. When JD left, the team had gotten a new sailor, a squared-away SEAL named Blake Gardinier. Unfortunately, Blake's mother had suddenly become seriously ill, and Gardinier was now on emergency leave as her only living relative. There was no telling how soon he'd be back, so at least temporarily, Pallie was back to being the new guy.

Jeanie arrived with the fresh draft beers and set them on the table. "We're going to miss you here, Vivas."

Vivas grinned over at Jackson. "See …" He took a big gulp of the frosty cold Corona and sat back. "Last one for me, guys. I've got a lot of shit to get squared away before I fly out."

"Lightweight," Maddux quipped.

"Anything I can do, Vivas?" Pallie asked.

'Well, since you volunteered, I could use a ride to the airport. I'm selling my truck."

"Done."

CHAPTER 6
Thailand

The tuk-tuk dropped Dish off at a small office building a few blocks from the nightclub, Obsession. Hana had leased the small office building to house the new charitable enterprise she'd named Spring Lotus Foundation. The lotus flower is regarded as a symbol of rebirth and spiritual enlightenment. It has a life cycle unlike any other plant, rooting itself in the muddy river bottom and submerging each night into the water, then miraculously resurfacing each morning to bloom fresh with the new day. The lotus flower also possesses an incredible will to live. Its seeds can go years without water and still germinate to create a new life. Thus, it was the perfect symbol for Hana's latest project.

Hana had recently purchased an old hotel. It was a small, three-story structure with ten rooms, a shared bathroom on each floor, and a creaky old elevator. There was a small lobby with a front desk and a small office connected to a manager's living quarters with a private bathroom. While dated, the hotel had solid bones and was located in a reasonably nice neighborhood just a few blocks from the club. It only needed a facelift and a few upgrades. Hana planned to use the hotel to house the young women or occasional young men who entered her program.

So far, she had footed all the start-up costs herself. However, JD's mother, Mai, had taken a keen interest in the project and was working to establish the foundation as a registered international charity, opening gateways to possible additional funding. Dish, with Chanmali's help, was overseeing the hotel renovations. Later, he would use his connections to help safely shuttle young Montagnard and other Asian kids trapped in bad situations into Thailand.

The work on the hotel was progressing nicely, and Dish was pleased. One of the rooms where renovations were already completed housed two young ladies he had grown quite fond of. The first girl, Jum Y, he and Chanmali had brought to Thailand with them. Jum Y was a young Jarai woman who had helped his sister when a drug smuggler kidnapped her in Vietnam. The other girl, Xuan, was the daughter of Mai's distant cousin. Mai met Xuan while searching for her brother when she visited her father's old village. After Mai's kidnapping and subsequent rescue, Xuan's father decided that his daughter might be safer in America if he could arrange it. Naturally, Mai was delighted to help.

Dish and Chanmali now lived in the hotel manager's apartment. At seventy-plus years old, Dish found the new space pleasant, especially after living for years in a longhouse on a remote ridge in the Vietnamese highlands. Chanmali, Dish's common-law wife, was also pleased with their new quarters. After all, it had hot and cold running water, something she had lived most of her life without. Chanmali was hard at work making their new accommodation home.

As Dish entered the office building, he saw a Vietnamese man standing in the entranceway of an alley across the street. The man was doing nothing.

That's odd, Dish thought. The man looked out of place. *He does not belong there.*

The man stood between two buildings, an apartment dwelling and an upscale restaurant frequented by young customers, primarily tourists with money to spend. There was no reason for the man to be standing where he was. Poorly dressed, he would be unwelcome in either establishment. The bench down the street would make more sense if he planned to meet someone. Dish had long ago learned to listen to his gut instincts.

That man is watching us.

Entering the office building, Dish passed by the reception desk, where Benh greeted him with a pleasant smile and nod. Benh, a former dancer at Obsession, jumped at the opportunity to do something meaningful

46

outside the club. She had become the Spring Lotus Foundation receptionist, a job she took very seriously.

Dish did not understand what drove these young men to want to be young ladies. He found it quite sad. Still, he couldn't help but like Benh. She was a helpful and pleasant kid, even if she was a little mixed up.

"Benh, have you seen Quan this morning?"

"Yes, Mr. Dish. He is in his office. Hung took Hana to the airport. Carlos is flying in today. It is all so exciting." Benh was gushing with exuberance.

Dish couldn't help smiling. He had to admit Benh acted just like a happy, animated young lady. "Thank you, Benh. I am sure Hana is excited, also. It is good."

Dish continued across the reception area and entered a short hall leading to four small offices, two on each side. At the end of the hall was an elevator to the upper floors. Quan's office was the first door on the right. Dish poked his head in.

"Quan, have you noticed the man standing outside the alley entrance?"

Quan looked up from his desk. "Yes. Three different men over the last three days. They watch while we are open and leave when we close. They are also watching the club."

That is not good. "It could be trouble from Vietnam."

Quan shrugged. "Yes, it could be. We will know tonight."

Dish nodded, reassured that Quan knew his job. *That was also good.*

The Boeing 787 Dreamliner taxied toward the terminal at Bangkok's Suvarnabhumi Airport. Vivas could barely keep himself in his seat. It'd been a long flight, and he was anxious to see Hana. While they'd stayed in constant contact, it had been more than six weeks since he and Hana had last been together at JD and Ellen's wedding. Suddenly, he felt as nervous as a schoolboy on a first date.

That is just crazy, he thought. *But it feels nice.*

After meeting Hana in Thailand, Vivas returned to the States and finished the last three months of his enlistment contract. He loved being a SEAL and planned on making a career out of the Navy, but events sometimes transpire that change life's priorities.

During his five years of active service in the teams, he'd seen a lot of horrible situations, especially for kids. SEALs don't typically get deployed to the vacation hubs of the world. When he and Pallie volunteered to go with JD on an off-the-books mission to help him rescue his mother in Vietnam, Vivas gained an insider's glimpse of a part of the world he'd never seen before. It shook him to his core. Then he met Hana and learned about her club, Obsession, and how she tried to do what she could for her employees. Soon after, Jum Y entered the story, and Vivas learned that Jum Y had been sold to a brothel by her father to pay off his gambling debts. His reaction had been identical to that of Dish.

How in the hell could a father do that to his daughter? There was something dark and rotten at work in some parts of the world.

Vivas was impressed by Hana. She was young but sharp and astute—a successful businesswoman in an environment populated with high-rollers, criminals, and low-life thugs. As her story came out, his respect grew. He admired that even though she could not control the world in which she lived, she did protect those who worked for her to the best of her ability. His mind briefly flashed to Quan and Hung, two of her security people he'd gotten to know.

She certainly had some ability. Vivas smiled to himself.

Hana was tough. The trip from Bangkok to Dish's hideout in the mountains along the Vietnamese Laotian border had made that fact evident. Vivas was unsure at what point he'd fallen in love with her. JD had seen it, though. He and Hana had been sitting together, talking about her plans to help Jum Y, when she'd turned to him and blurted out, "JD says you are in love with me." Just like that. And it hit him like a ton of bricks. JD was right, and Vivas knew then that his life would take on a new direction. Nothing from that moment forward would ever be the same again. Point in fact, here he was now, back in Thailand.

The big jet stopped and the seatbelt light finally blinked off. As the flight attendant opened the hatch, Vivas quickly got to his feet and grabbed his carry-on bag from the overhead compartment. He wasn't bringing much with him. He had some clothes and a few assorted Flesheater knives in his checked luggage; that was about it. He'd sold his pick-up truck, and his apartment on Coronado had come furnished.

Not much to show for almost seven years in the Navy. Well, at least I have some money in the bank.

Hana had said not to worry about anything and to "get your ass over here." The thought made him smile again. He was smiling a lot more these days.

Carrying his bag and strolling through the gate, Vivas spotted her immediately and felt his face light up. Hana, dressed in a black business suit trimmed with white, waited for him at the gate.

Holy smokes. The sight of her standing at the gate left Vivas suddenly finding it difficult to breathe.

Then his eyes narrowed, noticing two men standing several meters behind Hana. They were easy for his trained eye to spot: two men alone in the crowd. They were not here to catch a flight. While not an expert, Vivas was sure the two men were Vietnamese.

Approaching Hana, he could see the joy shining in her eyes and it made him feel wonderful. He swept her into his arms.

"Oh my God, it is so good to see…"

"Shut up and kiss me, Carlos." Vivas was happy to comply.

After embracing for a few happy moments, Hana pulled away. "You spotted those two Vietnamese men. I saw it in your eyes."

"Yes, you should not be here alone."

"I am not alone, Carlos." Hana indicated a man standing against the wall near some vending machines a few yards away. The man's focus was clearly on the two Vietnamese men, but he took a moment to nod to Carlos. It was Hung.

Carlos nodded back. "You brought Hung? He's getting old, and what about his bad back?"

Hana laughed at that. "Today, his back is fine. You know Hung is a damn good bodyguard, and he has his old Tokarev with him. His age has not yet affected his aim in any way I can see. And besides, now you are here."

Carlos accepted that. "Okay, Hana. But I'll feel better when we get you on safer ground. I have two checked bags. Let's get them and get out of here."

"Of course, Carlos. Hung will get the car and meet us outside baggage claim." Hana signaled to Hung, who nodded, turned, and walked off.

Two hours later, a group gathered in the small conference room at the Spring Lotus Foundation's headquarters. Hana sat in one chair at the small conference table with Vivas beside her. Dish sat across from Hana while Quan stood leaning against the wall near the door.

Hung had opted to station himself in one of the comfortable lobby chairs to keep an eye on things out front. He was currently sipping with appreciation the cup of hot jasmine tea Benh had set down next to him. Quan would fill him in later if there was something he needed to know.

Vivas finished describing the two men at the airport. Those men had followed them by car back to the office building before turning down a side street one block away. Hung had made no effort to lose them.

"Either they are not very good at their jobs, they don't care about being spotted, or they are trying to intimidate us," Vivas offered.

"I think they are not so good," Dish commented. "Remember Trán's men at the plantation? They were street thugs, not soldiers. I think they are—what is the word—beginners?"

Quan laughed and spoke in English. "I don't think any of us are intimidated by that bunch, but it is important not to be overconfident."

He paused. "A couple of my men will grab whoever is watching from the alley this evening. They will take him to the basement at Obsession and we will see what he can tell us."

Vivas looked up. "He may not tell us anything."

Quan shrugged.

Dish glanced over at Quan standing by the door, then turned to Vivas. "I think he will talk. And I agree, there are too many coincidences here. It is not good. I think someone in Vietnam is planning revenge for taking Mai and killing Trán."

Hana sighed. "That makes sense. I'd hoped this would not happen."

Vivas looked over at Quan. "If the guy you grab is, as you say, just a thug, he may talk, and maybe we will find out what is behind this. But, if he is a pro, he may not."

Hana shrugged. "Quan can be very persuasive. The man will talk." She shuddered. "I don't like it, but sometimes it is necessary. Sadly, it is the world in which we live. Rick occasionally got information for the CIA in Obsession's basement and other places. He didn't enjoy doing it, but it was his job. I believe it has saved many lives over the years."

Vivas understood. "Okay. We need to be prepared if they are planning something. It will certainly be helpful if we can learn something from whomever Quan's men grab tonight. I do not think anyone should be isolated. We need a central location we can defend. Is that here, at the hotel, or at the club?"

"We should all stay at the club," Quan replied. Security is better there. Covering the main entrance and the two other exits to protect people will be much easier. There is plenty of room and it's an old building—some walls are very thick."

Both Dish and Hana agreed.

Vivas looked over at Hana. "We should probably not all go at once. We need to space it out. If we can make it look like normal daily activity, maybe those watching won't suspect what we are up to."

"That's a good idea," Hana agreed. "You and I can leave soon. It would seem normal under the circumstances. The rest can wait and make their way to the club a few at a time. Dish and Hung could go about lunchtime. We can send someone to the hotel to pick up Chanmali, Xuan, and Jum Y. Quan can bring Benh."

"Benh?" Vivas inquired. "Who is Benh?"

"You've met Benh. She's the waitress who got Pallie all worked up when we met that first night in the club."

"Really? Well, Benh will be disappointed to learn Pallie is getting married in a few months."

"Let me guess, to a tall Swedish blond?"

"Exactly."

Quan broke in. "Okay. My men will get the man from the alley tonight. Then we shall see. Grabbing their spy might end up forcing their hand."

"We shall see," Vivas agreed.

CHAPTER 7
The Philippines

Bill Taylor was in the fight of his life. Right now, he just hoped he could get out of it alive, or at least not seriously crippled. His opponent, who went by the name Garcia, was a dangerous fighter. He was big for a Filipino, and built like a fire hydrant. So far, Garcia had absorbed everything Taylor dished out with no discernible effect. Taylor, on the other hand, was hurting.

Damn it! Taylor thought. *Fuck!*

It was painfully evident that he'd spent way too much time drinking and not enough time training. It looked like all Garcia ever did was train. The guy was an indestructible fighting machine and damn good at blending Yaw-Yan, which resembles Muay Thai, with Dumog, a Filipino grappling art. One round into the three-round fight, Taylor was concerned about surviving the next.

To make matters worse, he was aware of a different atmosphere in the bar—it was hostile. Unsanctioned fights are brutal, but this was different. This man was seriously trying to take him out, maybe permanently.

If I can't outfight him, I will have to outthink him. But shit, I must have pissed somebody off.

The fight was being held on the dance floor of a seedy little bar in the Mabini area of the Manila waterfront. The promoters acquired the bar, which closed over a lease dispute with the landlord, as the venue for this night's extravaganza. Taylor's fight was the third and final fight of the evening.

The air was dense with smoke from cigarettes and cigars. The pungent aroma of cannabis filled the air as well. Leaning against the bar, attempting to suck air into his aching lungs, Taylor was not quite ready when the center referee called him back onto the dance floor. The two combatants met in the middle of the makeshift ring; the referee nodded and yelled, "Mag away." Round two began.

Garcia came on strong. Like a shark sensing blood in the water, he moved in for the kill. Taylor circled right, trying to avoid closing for the moment. An idea was forming in his head. It might work, if he didn't lose a knee.

Garcia advanced quickly, wanting to end the match once and for all. The lady was paying him a lot of money to ensure this American asshole never fought again. The American won too much, and many Filipino gang members lost a lot of money betting against him. There was national pride, after all, and now they were pissed.

Garcia saw his opponent's right foot slip on the sweat and beer-covered floor, and the American lurched to his right, trying to recover his balance. It was just what Garcia was waiting for. Seizing the opportunity, he aimed a wicked downward-cutting kick at the American's extended and vulnerable left leg, its knee momentarily exposed and locked out.

If I could destroy the American's knee …

Then, suddenly, the knee was gone. Taylor had faked the slip and left his left leg extended purposefully. He was not off-balance. As soon as Garcia's leg started down into the kick, Taylor shifted, driving a one-knuckle punch into Garcia's floating ribs. Immediately retracting the strike, he drove his fist upward, smashing it into Garcia's exposed chin. There was a loud crack as Taylor felt the man's jaw shatter and collapse upward, lifting Garcia off his feet. The Filipino fighter rocked up and back on his heels before collapsing onto the floor, where he lay still. The crowd was silent.

Taylor staggered to the bar and, grabbing what remained of his last beer, poured it down his throat.

Screw this. I'm getting my money and getting out of here while I can.

Setting the empty beer mug down on the bar, Taylor scanned the room, spotting the fight promoter standing near the main entrance. He headed that way.

"Okay, kaibigan, I'll take my money now. I'm leaving. I've got a hot …" Taylor never finished the sentence. Too late, he sensed someone closing in behind him. There was a sharp pain in the back of his head, and the lights went out.

Taylor stirred. He desperately wanted to open his eyes and move, but could not. The pain caused by any attempt to move was too intense, and the reaction his eyes had to light was not any better. He lay still, eyes closed, attempting to take stock of his situation using his other senses. He could feel something soft beneath him, and a slight breeze was coming from somewhere; it tickled the skin of his chest and legs. He could smell something cooking; it smelled good. Finally, he drifted back into unconsciousness.

When Taylor came to again, he could tell it was dark even without being able to open his eyes. His entire body hurt. He didn't want to move, but he had to try. He gathered himself for the effort.

"Do not move. You are safe here." The voice was pleasant, gentle, female, and Filipino. It was calm, somehow reassuring.

His voice sounded raspy. "Where am I? Who are you?"

"My name is Ruby Damilo. You are at my house here in Tondo. You are badly hurt. You must not try to move."

"What happened to me?"

"I was riding my scooter home from work, and I saw many men beating someone very badly. They were kicking and hitting with sticks. I could do nothing to stop them, so I go on." The voice paused. "I don't know. I get almost home, and then something make me turn around and go back. The men are gone, but I find you. I think you are dead, but then you make a sound. I don't know what to do. So, finally, I go home and get my son. I borrow a cart from my neighbor. Then I come back and take you to my house. That was three days ago."

"Your son?"

"My son, Amado. He is fourteen and strong. Amado is a good boy."

"I guess I owe you thanks. My name is …"

"I know who you are. You are American fighter. My son sees you fight. I do not want him to see these fights, but he is a boy. I cannot watch him all the time. I must work." She paused momentarily, as if looking for something else to say. "Amado tells me some people like you, many do not. You win too many fights. Too many gangsters lose money betting against you."

"Three days?"

"Yes, you were hurt badly. You sleep like you are dead. But you are alive. Getting better now. You rest. Try

59

to eat a little. I will make you some soup." With that, she was gone.

A few minutes later, Taylor heard someone else quietly enter the room and stand there silently. Finally, after a minute, he asked, "You are Amado?"

"I am Amado."

"Thank you, Amado. Your mother told me you helped her bring me here."

There was silence for a moment. Then, "I did it because my mother asked, but it is dangerous to have you here. Many bad people do not like you. If they find you here, it will be bad for my mother. You must stay inside and stay quiet. When you can, you go."

Taylor managed a slight nod. It hurt. "You are fourteen, Amado?" There was no answer. "You have a good head on your shoulders. I appreciate what you and your mother have done for me, and I understand the difficult position this places you in." He paused. "There's no danger of me moving for a while. It hurts too much. I will stay inside and quiet, and I will leave as soon as I am able. I promise."

"Thank you," Amado replied just as his mother came back.

"Don't bother the man, Amado."

"He is not bothering me. You have a good son who is trying to look out for you. Amado and I have an agreement; right, Amado?"

"Yes." Amado left the room.

"He is a good boy. I am sorry if he bothered you."

"He's no bother. He is just concerned about you."

"I made you some chicken soup. It has noodles in it, but no meat. See if you can eat some of this. Then maybe more later if okay."

"I am not sure I can manage that yet."

"It is alright. I will help you. I hope you are not injured inside. I cannot take you to a doctor."

Taylor thought about that for a moment. "I don't think that is a problem. I have been beat up, blown up, and shot a few times. I am hurt, but I don't think there are any internal injuries to worry about." He smiled. "Time will tell."

Ruby carefully managed to pour a spoonful of the hot soup into his mouth. He couldn't even lift his head to help. It tasted delicious.

"That is good. Salamat. Thank you."

"Walang anuman, you are welcome. It is not too hot?"

"No, it's good."

Ruby filled the spoon again. "I know who you are but I do not know your name."

"My name is William Taylor. I am fortunate you turned your scooter around, Ruby. Thank you."

"It's okay. Now, you must stop talking and eat this soup."

Ruby managed to get all of the soup into the man on her couch before he drifted back to sleep. That was good. He needed to sleep.

She took the bowl and spoon to the kitchen, washed and dried them. Then, shifting from counter to table, she began packaging the sausages she had made earlier. Ruby supplemented her income by making pork sausages and pork and chicken barbeque, and selling them to local markets. She wanted a better life for her son.

Thirty minutes later, finished with her task, Ruby turned to look at the man sleeping on the couch near the open windows, the steady breeze helping cool the small apartment.

He seems like a good man; polite, even shy.

Bringing Taylor here in the cart had been hard work. Amado had helped her, albeit somewhat reluctantly. He told her he'd seen the man fight but would not tell her where or when. She would have to revisit that with Amado later. Ruby did not want her son hanging out in such places.

Amado said the American fought like a man possessed, without fear. Her son had warned her; he was a dangerous man.

I couldn't just leave him lying in the alley, could I? He was badly hurt and needed help. What kind of a person would that make me?

She'd gotten a good look at Taylor's eyes while spooning the soup into his mouth. He had troubled eyes.

This man has many ghosts.

But would an evil man be haunted by such ghosts? Ruby did not think so. You needed to have a good soul to be haunted by your past, didn't you?

Yes, Amado is right. He is probably a dangerous man, but dangerous does not necessarily mean evil.

Taylor awoke at four in the morning, shivering and bathed in a cold sweat. He'd heard a scream. As he struggled to get up, an intense wave of pain shot through his body. He paused, listening, waiting for the pain to subside.

Who the hell screamed?

Everything seemed perfectly quiet.

Maybe I imagined the scream.

But maybe not; it had happened before. Screams at night were not unusual in the neighborhoods he frequented these days.

Taylor glanced around the unfamiliar room, having no clue where he was. Moving was still too painful, but his eyes could finally open. This was not his cot or apartment; he was sleeping on somebody's couch. Then, finally, it dawned on him that he must have blacked out. But how in the hell did he get here? And where the fuck was here?

Trying again to sit up, it instantly became clear he wasn't going anywhere yet. He settled back on the strange couch. At least it was comfortable.

Where am I? What the fuck?

He suddenly remembered the lady; *what was her name?*

Ruby. Yes, that was it. *And the boy, Amado.* Then he remembered the soup.

Taylor settled back into the couch, trying to will his knotted muscles to relax. He was safe, for the moment. Ruby was helpful and friendly, and he could not see her posing any threat.

His mind shifted gears. He realized he'd been dreaming again. It was that same damn dream with those same damn eyes. They followed him everywhere, like a scene from an old horror movie repeatedly playing in his mind. Those eyes, accusing him, staring back at him, burning into his soul just before her head exploded into a sea of blood and brains that covered every inch of his tortured soul.

Fuck, I need a drink.

But there was nothing here to drink. Taylor's supply of cheap booze was all back at his apartment, wherever the hell that was. He was in no condition to attempt getting back to his little hole. Sighing, Taylor again sunk back into the couch.

Shit, he thought. *Maybe I should put an end to all this crap.*

He had considered it before. His life had devolved to a point where nobody would even notice he was gone. Even Blessica would not miss him.

Hell, she may have been behind that beating they gave me, although he did not want to think so.

Deep down inside, Taylor knew he wouldn't hurt himself. He couldn't. As fucked up as he was, he was not a quitter. And suicide had to be the biggest quit of all. Bill had never considered it a coward's way out. It took guts to put a pistol into your mouth and squeeze the trigger.

It was just that it was so damn final. There would never, ever be another chance.

Not that I deserve one. I would like to have a fucking drink, though.

He reminded himself that a drink was not happening and shifted his focus toward shutting down the conversation in his head. It had not been a particularly restful night so far; he needed to sleep.

Ruby lay very still in her bed, afraid to move, not wanting to make a sound. She did not want the injured man on the couch to know she was awake. Lying in bed, she'd been worrying about what to do about the American fighter when she heard him scream. It wasn't a scream of pain or fear. Instead, it was a horrible, desperate sound, like a primal scream of rage or the defiant roar of a mortally wounded beast. It frightened her.

What kind of dreams could cause a man like that to make such an awful sound? What could he have done to cause such pain?

Ruby wondered if Amado, too, had heard the man. Of course, there had been no sound from her son's tiny bedroom, but then Amado often fell asleep listening to music with the headphones she'd gotten for him last Christmas.

The man was quiet now. Hopefully, he'd gone back to sleep and would not have another bad dream. Ruby had seen the ghosts in the man's eyes. Now, she realized, she had also heard them.

CHAPTER 8
Thailand

The smell of fear was palpable. The terrified man sat blindfolded and strapped to a folding metal chair in the center of the room. He'd been there for several hours. It was all designed to let his imagination run wild. Then, finally, the door opened and the room's lights flipped on. Quan, followed by Dish, Vivas, and Hana, entered the room.

"Are you sure you want to go in there?" Vivas asked Hana before they opened the door.

"No, but I can't just sit and wait. I'll leave if things get too bad. This is my club, and I need to protect my people. It is my responsibility."

Vivas nodded.

The small room appeared to have once been a medical office. The dingy walls were painted white and the floor was covered with light gray tile, now stained with age. An old examination table stood against one wall and an old metal medicine cabinet stood against another, both covered in thick dust. The lighting system, however, was new and painfully bright.

The man in the chair desperately needed a drink. He was scared, soaked in sweat, and rank with the stale smell of old alcohol. Vivas almost felt sorry for him.

Quan wasted no time.

"I'm going to ask you some questions. I am not patient and we don't have much time, so here is how this will go. I will ask once nicely. If you tell me what I need to know, you will live, and once this is over, we will let you go. If you do not answer, I will get my knife and start cutting pieces of you off. In the end, you will talk. You can decide how much it will cost you."

The frightened man, trying to appear brave, shouted something in Vietnamese.

Hana turned to Vivas. "He said he will not talk."

"I gathered that," Vivas replied with a grimace. He didn't like this sort of thing either.

Quan continued. "You and several other men have been taking turns, watching and following us for several days."

The man started to deny the accusation.

"Don't waste my time. You are amateurs and were easily spotted. You will tell me what you are planning and who is giving the orders."

To his credit, the Vietnamese man remained silent.

"You understand that, even if you don't talk, your friends will kill you because they will think you did."

Looking down, the sweating man still refused to speak.

"Okay then." Quan walked over to the dust-covered medicine cabinet. He came back carrying an old wooden-handled butcher knife. Walking back to the man strapped to the chair, he removed the blindfold. Cursing in Vietnamese, the man blinked his eyes several times as they adjusted to the bright lights. Quan waited, then held the knife before the man's eyes. It had a rusty-looking blade.

"Now, one more chance. I will ask nicely for the last time. Why have you been following us? What are you planning? Who paid you to do this?"

The man's eyes grew large at the sight of the knife. Vivas was genuinely surprised when the man cursed again.

"Okay." Quan looked over at Dish. "I suppose we will have to do it the hard way. Should we start with an ear or a finger?"

Dish stepped up and examined the blade of the old knife in Quan's hand, reaching out to test its edge with his thumb.

"That knife is not sharp. Maybe you sharpen it first?"

"Oh no, it is very dull; I never sharpen it. The dull blade makes the pain much more intense."

That was all it took. The man in the chair let out a shrill wail. Then, between sobs, he blurted out the entire story.

"They come tonight just before the club begins to close. Ten bad men with guns. They come to kill him," indicating Dish, "and they come to kill her," indicating Hana, "the woman who helped." The man paused, catching his breath. "Lieutenant Colonel Li Fong of the Mobile Police Force hired us for the job, but I heard the orders are from Colonel Trán with the Ministry of Public Security."

"Trán?" Vivas queried. He and Dish both looked up upon hearing the name.

The man continued, "He is the cousin of the man they killed." He paused, glancing fearfully around the room. He did not find a sympathetic eye. "A powerful man."

Vivas nodded. "Well, that explains a lot."

Dish grunted in agreement.

"I am going to check on the club." Hana hurried through the door. Vivas moved to follow. "I'm okay, Carlos. I need some air. You guys finish up here, okay? I'll see you in a bit." Turning, she took the stairway that led back up to the main level.

Once Hana was gone, Vivas turned back to the other two. The man in the chair was now sobbing and muttering incoherently. Vivas spoke quietly.

"You know we can't just let him go. He will warn the rest that we are onto them. They will adjust their plans. They'll be more cautious, making them more dangerous. And they will probably kill him for talking," indicating the sobbing man, "but he may not realize that until it is too late."

Quan nodded.

"What do we do with him?" Dish asked. He knew what he would do under the circumstances, but he was no longer in charge.

Quan decided. "I'll have a couple of my men see he cleans himself up; he stinks. We can keep him tied up in this room under guard. Then we shall see, depending on how things go tonight. He might live through the night, or he might not."

Vivas and Dish both nodded. It was an unpleasant situation, but this man had put himself into it. After all, he had come after them.

When Quan's men arrived to take control of the wretched, still-sobbing spy, Vivas left to find Hana. Dish had already set off with Sirichai, a new security team member, to collect Chanmali, Jum Y, and Xuan and escort them to the club. They were taking no chances on leaving anyone isolated and vulnerable to attack.

Hana was not on the main floor or at the bar, so Vivas continued to her office. Obsession's office occupied the loft that overlooked most of the main floor.

He found Hana standing at the two-way mirrors, watching the dance floor.

"Hana, are you alright?"

She laughed but did not sound happy.

"I suppose I might as well be. I was just thinking, Carlos. I finally got things turned around. Jum Y and Xuan have sponsors and can now go to America. I have you with me, and we can be so happy together... And now, this happens."

He moved to stand behind her, placing his hands on her hips. "This is not your fault, Hana. You didn't cause this. Men like Trán and now this cousin of his are evil. They deal in drugs, slavery, and human misery. When Trán kidnapped Mai, we learned what his plans for her were and how he treated other women. Monsters like him use fear, degradation, and drugs to enslave their people. What we did to save JD's mother ... well, I would do again. It was the right thing to do, no matter how unpleasant."

Hana turned to face him, leaning her head against his chest. "What makes people like that poor man in the basement do what they do?"

"I don't know the answer to that. Greed, maybe? Desperation? If you work for an evil enough boss, maybe fear. But they've left us little choice. These men are coming to kill you and Dish tonight. And they'd kill anyone at the club who got in their way without a thought, including your dancers, Chanmali, the girls, or Hung."

"I know that, Carlos. I hoped we'd left all this behind when we rescued JD's mother and Dish killed Trán."

"Sadly, that is not the case, at least not right now. But it will stop."

"When? When will it stop?"

Vivas shrugged. "When it becomes too costly for them to continue, or we kill them."

Hana sighed. "If we close the club, they will know something is up and simply change their plans, won't they?"

"I would think so."

"And since we know they are coming, we can be ready, which gives us an advantage."

"Yep, unless they change plans because they are missing a man. I think they will decide he chickened out, got drunk, and passed out somewhere, especially if we stick with the club's normal routine. It looks like this Fong character hired street thugs who are hardly professionals. If we don't alter your routine, they won't be worried we are onto them."

"Not professionals?"

"Not by a long shot, not like Quan, myself, or Dish. These thugs will be anxious to get this done, get out of Thailand, and get paid. Fortunately for us, they don't have the patience it takes to be good at this."

Hana smiled just a little. "I hope you are right."

"That reminds me. I need a weapon. I had a few knives in my luggage, but that is it."

"Not a problem. I used to work with gun smugglers, remember? We have a healthy cache of weapons, and I am sure Quan has a few spare M16s or even an M4. Of course, we have quite a collection of handguns, too."

"Perfect. I'll go see if I can find Quan."

"Carlos?"

"Yes, Hana."

"Wait a bit. Stay with me. We have time. The club doesn't close until 2 a.m."

"Okay, sure." He raised his arms to encircle her waist and hugged her closer. Hana's lips met his. After a long moment, she pulled back.

"Carlos, you realize we haven't set our wedding date yet?"

"That's the first thing on my list after we get through tonight, I promise."

Hana looked up into his eyes with a mischievous smile on her face. "It is possible that we will not survive tonight."

"We will; I promise you that."

"That may be all well and good, but I don't want to take the chance. I want you now, right here."

"Here?"

Hana stepped back just a bit, laughing. "Well, maybe over there." She pointed to a couch that sat against the office wall. "Go lock the door."

"Yes, ma'am." He turned to lock the door and when he turned back, Hana was waiting on the couch.

CHAPTER 9
Knoxville, Tennessee

JD parked the new Jeep Wrangler Sport Unlimited to the left of a substantial steel gate. They'd bought the Jeep just two weeks earlier. Ellen suggested they get something roomier than his beloved old two-door Wrangler, which had accumulated a lot of mileage over the last few years.

"Maybe something less ... ah ... tactical," she'd suggested with a grin. "How about a Honda CRV or something cool, like a Camaro?"

JD did not look enthused. "I'm not getting a glorified minivan. Besides, you've got your Volvo. And where will Sophie ride?" After visiting several dealers and test-driving several vehicles, JD made a sensible compromise and chose the four-door Jeep Wrangler. Ellen just laughed.

It was a fantastic day for a walk. JD had taken this same walk countless times during his junior and senior years in high school.

"The last time I was here, this gate was just a steel cable," he observed.

The gate prevented vehicle access to the old road out to Point 19. JD turned to Ellen. "Are you sure you want to do this?"

"Of course I'm sure. I'm pregnant, not an invalid."

Ellen was just over five months along; her condition starting to be noticeable. They'd been planning this short hike for several days, looking forward to a relaxing stroll. Thankfully, it was a beautiful mid-November day, warm enough but cool enough. This late in the season, the couple had Loyston Point to themselves.

"Besides, Sophie will be distraught if we turn around now. It's only three miles." Sophie's keen German Shepherd nose was already working overtime, taking in the delightful woodsy smells carried on mid-morning breezes. She was ready to go.

"Okay then." JD got out of the Jeep and opened the passenger door for Ellen. When he opened the back gate, Sophie bounded out. She was just over seven in dog years, still filled with youthful canine enthusiasm. JD grabbed the carefully packed rucksack containing bottled water, snacks for humans and canines, mosquito repellent, ponchos, other emergency items, and Sophie's favorite ball. The three made their way around the gate and started down the road to the point.

Enjoying the outdoors on a fabulous, sunny day, they took their time as Sophie romped back and forth ahead of them, exploring everything but never straying too far.

After walking about a mile, Ellen paused. "It's pretty here. Did you come out here often when you were younger?"

"Yeah. Especially during the summers. Once I was old enough to drive, I practically lived out here when we were out of school."

"What did you do? Did you fish?"

"Some of my friends did. I mostly swam or, if by myself, practiced karate. Some kids would drink beer or smoke a little pot. Sometimes, there were fights." JD paused, laughing. "We used to jump off the rocks. I remember one girl ran and jumped before realizing how low the lake level was. It always depended on how much rain we got. Anyway, she did this magnificent bellyflop. It must have hurt. I bet it was thirty feet to the water. The front of her body was bright red. She lost her bikini top, too."

"That must have been embarrassing. What happened?"

JD shrugged. "I gave her my t-shirt."

"Always the gentleman."

JD stepped ahead to throw a stick Sophie had found in the woods and did not hear Ellen's comment. Quickly, she caught up to him on the trail.

"You didn't fight, did you?"

"No. Well, once, but it wasn't much."

"What happened?"

"It really wasn't that much. There was this little guy, Greg Martin, who everyone called Roach, who liked instigating trouble. He somehow learned that I studied karate and went around daring anyone to see what I could do. Finally, I guess one decided to try me."

"And?"

"Well, we were camping, and it was dark. I was sitting in a lawn chair watching the fire when someone pushed me hard from behind. I rolled right through the fire."

"Oh my gosh! What happened? Did you get burned?"

"No, I didn't get burned; it happened too fast. But I was pretty pissed off. I came up, brushing red coals out of my clothes, and the guy came at me again. I grabbed his left arm and shoulder and swept his feet from under him. He hit the ground hard. I followed him, stopping my fist about an inch from his chin. I told him we could end it there or continue; it was up to him. He opted to end it there."

"Wow! Then what?"

"Believe it or not, we were actually pretty good friends after that."

A short while later, the trail opened onto Point Nineteen, with rock ledges to the left and a sandy beach area to the right. The lake was calm, and nobody else was in sight. Ellen looked up and spotted a bald eagle soaring high overhead.

"Wow! Look at that." She pointed as JD looked up.

"I've heard they are making a comeback around here. Very cool."

Not minding that the temperature was a bit cool, Sophie plunged into the cold water and looked back at JD as if to say, "Are you going to throw my ball or not?"

Ellen sat down on the sand and leaned against a rock as JD began rummaging through the rucksack, looking for Sophie's ball.

CHAPTER 10
Thailand

Checking to see if Dish was back with the women, Vivas found Hana in her office. She was talking with Benh and Hung.

"Have you seen Dish? He should be back with the ladies by now."

"No, I haven't. Quan is on his way up. He should know."

Walking over to the refrigerator in the office's small kitchen area, Vivas retrieved a cold bottled water. Twisting the cap off, he took a long swallow, then turned around in time to see Quan enter the office. Hana, Benh, and Hung finished whatever they were discussing and turned to face the two men. Benh flashed Vivas a friendly smile as she stood to exit the room.

Quan motioned for Benh to wait. "Please stay, Benh. We must talk. I think we may need your help."

Benh slowly sat back down on the couch. It had not occurred to her that she might be included in their planning.

Hana spoke. "Quan has come up with a plan. First and foremost, I must protect my people. Second, I want us all to survive this attack on our club."

Vivas grinned. "Me too. We want to make sure nobody gets hurt. If things at the club do not appear normal, Fong's goons might change their plans, which would not be good for us. As it stands now, we have a slight edge since we have a general idea of their intentions."

"Yes, I agree," Quan replied. "Everything must look normal. My plan revolves around getting the dancers and wait staff off the floor quickly enough so they will be safe."

"How?" Vivas asked after taking another swallow from the water bottle.

Hana answered. "Several times each night, groups of our dancers perform on the stage together. Then, every night, we end the show with a big dance number with all the dancers. We announce it over the PA system. When all the dancers gather backstage, I go onstage for the introduction. The dancers then return to the stage for the closing act. We have done this for years. And, this would be their best opportunity for a shot at me."

Quan nodded.

"Tonight," Quan added, "when the dancers are called backstage, the other staff will follow quietly, and they won't return. I don't think any customers will notice for a few minutes."

Vivas thought about it for a moment. "That might work. Where would they go? I would guess to the basement?"

Quan nodded. "They go to the basement. Hung and two of my men can easily guard access to the basement stairway; they will be safe there."

Hung agreed. "That is a good idea. Access to the basement can be easily guarded."

"Will you go to the basement with the dancers, Hana?"

Vivas had phrased it as a question, but Hana knew Carlos meant it otherwise.

"No, I must be on stage, announcing the closing number. It is what I always do."

Vivas frowned. "That's not a good idea. You could get hurt, or worse."

"Not if you guys get them all first. Everything must appear normal, right?"

Before Vivas could argue, Quan cut in. "The man we captured said they will have ten armed men. I think they will be all, or mostly, Vietnamese. If carrying pistols, they will probably wear light jackets to cover them."

"It makes sense," Vivas observed. "A loose shirt would also work."

"That is possible, But I should still be able to spot them. A nervous Vietnamese man with a loose shirt is not much different than a nervous Vietnamese man in a jacket."

"I guess you are right about that. Where is Dish? Have you seen him and the girls?"

"They have just returned. Everyone is okay." Both Hana and Vivas showed expressions of relief on hearing this.

"Tonight, Dish will go to the basement with the dancers and everyone else."

Hana looked up, surprised. "He agreed to that?"

"Yes, but only after I promised him an M16 and showed him the tunnel. I told him I needed him to ensure everyone was safe if things went badly. I also asked him to ensure our visitors see him on the club floor before the final dance so they know he is there. Then, he and Benh will ensure everyone goes to the basement and out through the tunnel."

"Tunnel?" Vivas asked.

"Well, it's not really a tunnel," Hana answered. "It's just connected basements leading to the basement of a massage parlor three buildings down. The entrance is well hidden on our end. Rick made a deal with the other businesses shortly after buying Obsession. This club was not a venture without some real risk, and he wanted a way for people to get out discreetly if required."

Vivas was impressed. "Your dad is a pretty forward-thinking guy."

Hana smiled. "Yes, he is. It comes from years of working for the CIA."

Vivas continued, "Okay, what next? I agree these men will likely come into the club a little before closing time, probably in small groups of maybe two or three. They will try to position themselves to cover most of the club. As Quan said, they will probably be nervous and a little over-dressed. They should be easy enough to spot."

"I have called in my entire security team," Quan replied. "With Hung and the two men guarding the stairs to the basement, we will have twelve armed men in addition to you and me."

"How good are your men?"

Hana answered. "We only hire men who have served with the Royal Thai Army Rangers or the 1st Special Forces Group. I leave those decisions to Quan, who served with that same Special Forces Group. Quan has the final say on any security we hire."

Vivas nodded. "Okay, they're good."

Quan continued, "If we spot them as they arrive and ensure they are seated at specific tables, my men can cover them. If ten men arrive in twos and threes, as we suspect, that is no more than five or six tables. So, we ensure we position men to cover those tables."

Quan turned to Benh. "Benh, will you help us with this? If you are willing, I will be at the front door with you and try to spot them as they come in. I do not think it will be too hard. You can act as the hostess tonight, seating customers and seating those I indicate at the selected tables."

Benh was shocked. She glanced over at Hana, then turned back to Quan. It was clear the idea frightened her. After a few seconds, Benh spoke in a soft but determined voice. "This is my home. I will do what I can to protect those who are here."

Hana reached over and placed a reassuring hand on Benh's shoulder. "We will be fine. I have seen Quan and Carlos in action; we have very good men."

Quan nodded reassuringly.

"When Hana comes on stage to announce the closing dance, all the staff will go backstage. Benh, you will lead them to the basement. They will not understand what is happening, but they must go quickly. Do whatever you need to do. Dish will help you."

Benh nodded.

Quan turned to Hana. "Hana, I think you are right. They will make their move when you come out on stage, especially if they also see Dish on the floor. You will be alone on the stage, an easy target. I think that is when they will try to kill you. My men will stop them before they can shoot."

"Let us hope so." Hana forced a brave smile.

"Where do you want me?" Vivas asked. He did not like it, but there was little point in arguing.

"I would like you to be up in the office with a rifle. Would an M16 work for you? The mirrors are like sliding windows. We will open them enough so you can see clearly, but with the stage lights, they will not be able to see you. Does that work for you?"

"Yes. How will we communicate? We need radios or something."

"The club has four small radios, the same as most nightclubs use. I was thinking one for you, one for me, one for Hung, and one for Dish. Benh will be with me. Hung will be with Hana until she goes on stage to announce the final dance. We should be okay."

Vivas nodded. It would have to do.

Quan continued. "From the office, you will be able to see everything. Good position to protect Hana." Quan grinned. "Maybe you can protect all of us. You are a SEAL, correct? That means an excellent shot, yes?"

Vivas nodded, saying nothing.

By 10:00 p.m., Obsession was busy. Because it was a Tuesday night, the club was not as packed as it might have been on a Friday or Saturday. Vivas figured that was a good thing. It was probably also why Fong's men had chosen tonight for their attack.

Fortunately, the smaller crowd allowed them to reserve several strategically located tables for tonight's unwelcome visitors. Six tables in carefully selected spaces in the club now had Reserved signs. The plan was simple enough, and Vivas had a great view—with a clear shot—of all six tables from his position in the office.

Hopefully, if things go as planned and we catch them off guard, we may not have to fire a shot.

Hana had told Carlos that most customers would begin to leave at about 1:00 a.m. Those remaining would be the few trying to negotiate an after-hours dalliance with a ladyboy who'd caught their eye. Since returning from Vietnam, Hana strongly discouraged her dancers from participating in such activities. She hired them strictly as dancers and paid them quite well, but unfortunately, a few still could not resist the added income. Hana was realistic enough to know she could not control what they did off the clock, but she'd warned them they better keep such activity extremely discreet if they liked working at her club. Her dancers knew that if their after-hour actions caused the club the slightest problem, they would be seeking employment elsewhere.

Vivas had witnessed Hana's evolution since the night they listened to Jum Y tell her story on the veranda of Dish's longhouse in Vietnam.

This situation must be hard on her, he thought.

Fortunately, from what he'd seen, Hana had already accomplished much with her Spring Lotus Foundation. Good things were growing out of Hana's evolution.

Vivas checked his watch: 11:30 p.m. The hardest part of a situation like this was the waiting. He wasn't worried about himself, Dish, Hung, or Quan, for that matter. They all had a lot of experience waiting for violence to unfold. Instead, it was Hana, Benh, and maybe some of Quan's newer men he was most concerned about. Waiting like this could be dangerously hard on the nerves.

Quan and Hana thought Fong's hit squad would begin to appear between 11:30 and midnight, early enough not to attract attention. A few customers always came in later, hoping to find a date after the final stage show. They would attempt to blend into that group. It was a reasonably sound plan with a good chance of success had it not been uncovered.

We should be okay if they don't change their plan because of their missing man. That man was currently tied up and secured in the basement. As far as Vivas could see, that was the only unknown variable.

Suddenly, his eye caught Benh moving near the front entrance. He watched her move to one of the designated tables, where she removed the "Reserved" sign. If she was scared, she hid it well. Vivas noticed the two members of Quan's team positioned to cover that table suddenly shift more upright in their seats.

Easy, guys. Don't give anything away.

As if the two men read his mind, they seemed to relax and settle back into conversing with the two dancers sitting with them. A few seconds later, Benh reappeared, guiding two men to the table. She seemed to be doing fine. Seating them, she waved a waitress over and, after exchanging a few pleasantries with the two men, returned to her hostess station by the door.

Vivas found himself impressed with Benh's courage. *So, the killers decided not to cancel.*

He studied the two men from his vantage point. At this distance, he could not tell if they were Thai or Vietnamese, but they both were wearing light jackets, easily capable of concealing a weapon.

Ten minutes later, Benh again appeared and approached a second table. She removed the Reserved sign before returning to the club entrance, then led three men to the table. Two were wearing long, loose-fitting shirts, while the third wore a light jacket. Vivas immediately recognized two of them as the men he had spotted at the airport. These three men were seated a little closer to the club's stage. So far, Quan's hunches were right on target.

Almost twenty minutes passed before Benh reappeared. Quickly removing the Reserved signs from two tables, she promptly returned with two groups of two men, seating each pair at one of the tables. That was nine men. The poor man tied up in the basement had said ten were coming.

Where in the hell is the tenth man? Was he the one tied up in the basement?

Vivas scanned the entire club from table to table, then checked the dance floor. Nine men were at four tables; the fifth and sixth tables still had Reserved signs. Quan's men looked relaxed and casual, but he could tell they were watching and ready. Hana was right. They were good.

But was there a tenth man?

Had he somehow gotten by Quan and was already here in the club? If so, Vivas couldn't pick him out. He reached for the radio.

"Quan, I don't see the tenth man. What do you think?"

"I am not sure. Maybe he is not here yet. Maybe I missed one. It is not impossible. Hung and Dish are on the floor looking. It is almost time for the showcase. The three of you watch for him. If another man is in the club, we must spot him fast. My men will handle those at the tables, so there's no problem. I will help them protect Hana."

Vivas keyed the mike. "Hung, Dish, do you copy that?" Both men responded in the affirmative.

At 12:45 a.m., the music stopped, and the DJ's voice came over the PA system. "All dancers, please report backstage to prepare for Obsession's world-famous dance showcase extravaganza. Gentlemen, the show begins in five minutes."

Quan turned to Benh. "You go now; make sure everyone goes to the basement. The two men at the door will help. We must find the missing shooter if there is one."

Shaking slightly, Benh nodded and headed across the club toward the stage door. On cue, the dancers began leaving the dance floor or tables where they sat with customers and made their way toward the doorway to the stage's right. As instructed by Hana earlier, other club staff discreetly followed the dancers. Nobody seemed to notice; most customers were anticipating the upcoming show.

With the M16 ready, Vivas's eyes scanned the room through the partially opened mirror using the rifle's iron sights. With the lights off in the office and the stage lights shining in front of him, it was virtually impossible to see him. He, however, had a great view of the club.

Vivas watched Benh follow the last staff member through the stage door. He spotted Dish as the old warrior moved out and stood casually surveying the club. Vivas knew he was looking for anything out of place. Hung also studied the crowd from the opposite side of the stage.

The last staff member filed down the stairs to the basement; then Benh stopped. Quan's men motioned her to continue, but Benh shook her head. There was something off. A feeling? No, it was more like a voice telling her she needed to return.

Benh turned and started back toward the stage door.

Hana walked out onto the stage. She was stunning in a shimmering, silver-sequined gown split well up the left thigh and matching high-heeled shoes. Her black hair cascaded over her shoulders. Not a soul in the nightclub would have known she was frightened. In the office, Vivas suddenly felt proud of her courage. Then, he immediately squashed that feeling.

Stay icy! Now is not the time.

Hana's voice came over the PA system. "Gentleman, this is the event you have been anxiously waiting for! Tonight's showcase extravaganza features the loveliest dancers in Thailand. Please welcome the beautiful dancers of Club Obsession back to the stage."

At the last table Benh had seated, one man leaped to his feet. Screaming unintelligibly in Vietnamese, he raised his right arm. In his hand was a pistol. The man aimed the gun at Hana. The M-16 in Vivas' hands coughed twice, both bullets striking the man in the forehead, less than an inch apart.

All hell broke loose. Some customers hit the floor while others ran for the exit. Eight more men jumped to their feet, reaching for concealed guns. Several unexpectedly felt a gun forcibly pressed into their backs and were quickly shoved back into their chairs. Two men promptly discovered razor-sharp knives being held at their throats and decided it would be wiser to sit back down. Using the barrel of his Beretta M9, Quan pistol-whipped the stunned man still seated at the table where his comrade now lay dead. The man collapsed to the floor without a sound.

One man, lying on the floor near an unreserved table, spotted Dish at the stage door. Reaching back, he slowly eased an old Makarov from the waistband of his pants, bringing it around to line the sights up on Dish, who was scanning another section of the crowd. The reward would be great if he could kill this Jarai savage and survive this night. The man sighted the gun and began to take up the slack in the trigger.

"No!" It was Benh. She'd seen the man point the gun at Dish and bolted from the stage doorway, shoving Dish to the floor just as the Makarov barked. Immediately, two more shots rang out. Then it was quiet. Dish rolled over, looking up to see Hung standing on the stage, his old Tokarev still pointing at the man who'd fired the first shot. But Hung was no longer looking at the man, who was now dead. Instead, he was looking at something else. Dish turned to follow Hung's gaze, and his eyes fell on Benh. She was lying on the floor a few feet away. Quickly, Dish scrambled over to her.

"Benh? Benh? Oh no ..." She'd been shot. The gunman's bullet had struck her in the left side of her chest as she shoved Dish out of the way. Benh's eyes were closed. She was breathing, but just barely — shallow, rasping breaths. It did not sound good.

Dish rolled Benh up into his arms. The old warrior felt his eyes well up with tears.

"Benh ... what did you do? You crazy girl. What did you do? Why didn't you go to the basement?"

Benh's eyes opened. Slowly, she focused on Dish. Then, to his surprise, she smiled. "God ... told me ... come back. God told me ... save you."

"What? You crazy girl. God said… What are you saying? Why…?"

Benh looked up at Dish and saw the tears streaming down his face. "It's okay, Lung. You will help more people like me."

Benh sighed, and then she was gone.

Dish noticed the sudden silence. He looked up to see Hana standing beside Vivas. Tears were streaming down Hana's cheeks. Then Xuan appeared. Hung and Quan were standing there as well. The searing pain on both their faces was evident.

Jum Y knelt beside Dish, placing her arm around his shoulders. She remained silent, the look on her face saying it all.

Vivas leaned in toward Hana. "Lung?" he asked in a choked whisper.

Hana reached up to wipe the tears from her cheek before answering. "It means uncle. She called him uncle."

Vivas nodded, then leaned in once more. "I didn't know Benh was a Christian."

"She wasn't."

Vivas turned away, embarrassed to have anyone see the tears in his eyes. He walked over to where Sirichai had the eight surviving would-be killers laid out on their stomachs and hands zip-tied behind their backs. At that moment, Vivas could have killed every one of them. Benh, as mixed up a kid as she was, was worth more to the world than all eight of those assholes.

Hana turned and sat down at a table, covering her face with her hands. Quan approached and stood beside her, placing his hand on her shoulder. After several long seconds, Hana looked up at Quan.

"Would you mind getting me my phone, please? It is on the shelf just off the stage." Quan nodded and left her side.

A short while later, Hana ended a second call and walked over to where Vivas stood brooding over eight nervous-looking men. Two of Quan's men stood by as well. The eight men were trussed up too well to do anything, but nobody wanted to take chances.

"The police chief will be here with some of his men in a few minutes. They will collect these criminals, the two bodies, and the man in the basement. Benh's body, I will take care of myself. She had nobody but her family at Obsession."

Vivas nodded. "Dish is taking it hard. It's funny how you can care so much about people – she was a good kid."

"Yes ... Behn was. She didn't deserve to die like that. Listen, Carlos. I also called Rick. He is coming here, and Slim is coming with him. I told him everything is under control and that you are here, but he has something on his mind and wouldn't talk about it over the phone."

Vivas almost smiled. "Probably coming to kick my ass for messing around with his daughter."

"No, he knows about us. I told him shortly after we got back to Thailand from Vietnam. All he said was, and I quote, 'A damned SEAL?' Of course, I told him you are now an ex-SEAL."

"I bet it didn't help much. So, your police chief is going to ignore all this?"

"Well, not exactly. But the chief is an old friend of Rick's and an uncle to me. This attack will go down as an attempted robbery foiled by the superb security team at the club. But, of course, we will have to close for a few days while the investigation is ongoing."

Vivas shook his head in amazement. "That's neat and simple. All tied up in a nice package."

Hana looked down and nodded. When she looked back at Vivas, her face had an odd look.

"Carlos, I can't do this anymore. I have decided to sell the club once we end this mess. Rick and I have more money than we need, and selling the club will bring in more. I can't have a foot in both worlds anymore. I want to concentrate on Spring Lotus. I need to help more kids like Jum Y and Benh." Hana's voice broke.

"I think that is for the best, Hana. I love you, but I struggle with this club and what it means. I was willing to deal with it to be with you, especially knowing what is in your heart. But if you can leave the club behind, I think that would be, as we used to say in BUDS training, the next evolution. Come here, babe." Hana stepped in close, and Vivas wrapped his arms around her. She was crying.

Tough enough to stand her ground in a gun battle with drug dealers and still cry over losing one of her employees. That takes courage and one hell of a heart.

Vivas held her close for several minutes. "You're one hell of a woman, Hana."

Hana said nothing, remaining still a moment longer as if gathering strength to move. Then she stepped back. "I must call Mai. She will want to know what's happened. She is a partner in Spring Lotus, after all. And you should call JD."

"Why?"

"Do you want him to hear about this from his mother?"

"No, I guess not."

CHAPTER 11
Knoxville, Tennessee

After returning home from their lake outing, they decided to have dinner at the Downtown Grill and Brewery, just below their loft. JD was stepping out of the shower when Ellen yelled from the kitchen downstairs, where she'd been reading some reports in preparation for an upcoming medical association meeting.

"Hey honey, you have a phone call."

"Who is it?"

"It's Carlos. He's calling from Thailand."

"What the hell? Vivas? Ah … just a second. Tell him I'm coming. Let me get some shorts on."

"Not necessary on my account," Ellen laughed.

JD looked at the clock as he slipped into comfortable old jogging shorts. It was 6:30 p.m., which meant 6:30 a.m. in Thailand. JD came down the stairs a second later and scooped his phone from the kitchen table. "Vivas, what's up, buddy?"

Ellen watched JD's expression transition from excited kid to combat-hardened U.S. Navy SEAL. She dried her hands and went to stand next to him, patiently waiting as he asked Vivas a few questions. It was clear something terrible had happened. Finally, the call wrapped up.

"Listen, Vivas. If you or Hana need anything at all, call me. I can be on the next flight out." There was a pause. "I know that, Vivas. But you and Hana are family. If you need anything, you call. If you don't and I find out about it later, I'm going to hunt you down, okay? Call me right away if anything changes." JD set the phone down. "Shit…"

"What is it, baby?"

JD looked over at Ellen. "There was an attack on Hana's club … Obsession. It looks like some relative of the man who kidnapped Mom is behind it. Vivas says he's some big shot with the Vietnamese Ministry of Public Security."

"Oh my God! Is everyone all right?"

"Luckily, they got wind of it ahead of time, and they were ready. Vivas shot one of the assassins. One of Hana's security guys, named Hung, got another. They were able to capture the rest. Eleven men in total. Vivas said the survivors were all turned over to the Bangkok police."

Ellen shook her head anxiously. "No, JD, I mean, is everyone okay on our side?"

JD paused a minute. The words "our side" sunk in. "Hana, Vivas, and Dish are all okay. One of the dancers, her name was Benh, died. She got shot pushing Uncle Dish out of the line of fire."

"Oh no. Did you know her?"

"Well, not really. Benh was ... uh ... one of Hana's ladyboy dancers. I met Benh when we first met Hana." JD paused, remembering. A sad smile appeared on his face. "Pallie took a real liking to Benh until he learned she was a guy... Oh shit. I don't know. Maybe Benh was a girl, just with the wrong plumbing. Anyway, it sure caught Pallie off guard. He wasn't ready for that!"

JD sat down on the couch, and Ellen sat close to him. "Anyway, Benh saved Uncle Dish's life."

"She died saving your uncle. We will always remember and be grateful to her for that."

"Vivas said Hana was calling Mom. I guess I'll talk to Mom a little later."

Ellen could see the conflicting emotions churning across her husband's face. Gone was the happy, contented man of a moment ago, and it hit Ellen then.

She most certainly understood that she'd married a Navy SEAL and had even seen him in action once. She knew he was a good man—decent, kind, generous—but it hit her that her husband was a living paradox. JD was— a man intimately familiar with violence and its applications; he possessed the ability to use force effectively when the situation demanded.

While he did not like having to battle, JD lived for a good fight. Moreover, he was a man willing to put his life on the line to defend what he cared about; his code demanded it. Right now, all JD could do was sit helplessly and wait.

God, that must be so hard for a man like you, Ellen thought.

It frightened her a bit. She slid closer, wrapping both arms around him. She hoped this would be the end of it here, but a little voice whispered in her ear that it would not. And now, they both had a third little life to consider. They had their first child on the way.

CHAPTER 12
The Philippines

Taylor sat on the couch, enjoying the breeze from the open window. He was beginning to feel much better. It was now three days since Ruby had found him beaten half to death in the alleyway. By the end of the third day, he'd been able to sit up and feed himself. Ruby kept a big pot of homemade soup on the stove and encouraged him to eat whenever possible. That was becoming more frequent.

Yesterday was a tough day. Taylor wanted a drink badly and considered asking Amado if he would get him a bottle or two from his apartment. He fought hard against acting on that impulse, not wanting to do anything that might bring attention to where he was. Moreover, he did not want to create problems for Ruby or her son, and decided that necessitated staying sober.

They have both been very good to me.

Even Amado had warmed up despite his initial concerns. He seemed to enjoy asking Taylor endless questions, many of which Taylor would not answer. But there were a few he could and did.

Ruby appeared in her bedroom doorway, having changed out of her work clothes. For the first time, Taylor noticed she was quite pretty. Not in the classic sense, but he decided that she had a clean, wholesome look, a pleasant manner, and a great smile.

"I know how much you have wanted a drink," she said. "I have nothing here for you."

"It's true, I have wanted a drink. But I think it is better for all of us if I do not."

"Thank you."

She moved into the main room of the small apartment. It served as both the kitchen and the living room. "May I ask … why do you drink all the time? And why do you fight? Amado says you are skilled as a fighter, that you fight like a man with no fear, or perhaps a man who doesn't care if he lives or dies."

Taylor looked down, not wanting to meet her eyes. "I guess … I have not cared for some time."

Ruby sat down at the small kitchen table, turning in the chair to face him.

"Why would you not care? My son told me that you are a dangerous man. Based on how he says you fight, I think that is true. Are you a danger to Amado and me?"

Taylor looked up but said nothing.

She answered her question for him. "I do not think so. I think you are not a bad man. I think you have ghosts. Ghosts do not haunt bad men; they only trouble men with good souls. You must have a very good soul to be troubled so badly. I have thought about this very much over the last few days since I brought you here."

Taylor did not know what to say. What could he say? He was suddenly aware of several emotions colliding in his brain: guilt, anger, and yes … shame.

Shame? Damn!

He had not felt shame in a long time. Guilt, yes, every single damn day. But he had not felt ashamed until this moment.

I am ashamed.

That surprised Taylor. This woman was sitting here reading him like a book. What the hell did she know about what he'd been through? What he'd done? How the fuck would she have any idea about what he deserved or did not deserve? What gave her the right to judge him?

Taylor looked at Ruby again, ready to lash out. Then he saw her eyes, and again, he felt ashamed.

She isn't judging me.

There was no judgment in her eyes. Taylor only saw concern. Concern for herself and her son, indeed. But there was more. He also saw concern for himself in her eyes, and a simple honesty he had forgotten existed. Ruby spoke again.

"Will you tell me what haunts you so? I hear you fighting your demons at night when you sleep. I hear your screams. You have horrible dreams. It frightens me."

Taylor's brain was trying to process a mix of uncomfortable thoughts and emotions.

She's heard my screams?

Then it hit him. The screams that were waking him up night after night were his own.

Ruby spoke again. "It is okay if you do not…"

He heard his voice speaking in a detached whisper, as if coming from somewhere else. "I was with the 3rd Special Forces Group in Afghanistan. My team was embedded with Afghan soldiers battling the Taliban in the Hindu Kush mountains. We were clearing a small village of insurgents. I took an overwatch position to cover the team and our Afghan allies as they went from house to house.

"Everything was going fine until…"

Ruby sat quietly, waiting patiently for him to continue.

"…until, through my rifle scope, I saw a woman step out of a house down the street. She had a little girl with her—it must have been her daughter. Maybe the girl was nine or ten years old, I don't know."

Taylor couldn't stop now. It was like a dam had broken. It had to come out.

"I watched the woman place two Russian RGN hand grenades into that little girl's hands and pull the pins.

Then, she shoved her daughter toward the members of my team. The little girl started to run toward them."

Tears were running down Taylor's face. Ruby sat transfixed, watching as pain, guilt, sorrow, and horror featured simultaneously in Taylor's expression.

"Through my scope, I could see tears on that poor little girl's face, but she did what her mother told her to do. Those grenades had a three-and-a-half to four-second fuse. I waited, counting the seconds, praying to God for her to drop the grenades and run back. I waited for a miracle. I waited as long as possible, and then, God help me, I took the shot."

Taylor collapsed back onto the couch, exhaling with the weight of confession, finally relieved. Ruby waited, somehow sensing the story was not yet over.

"I don't know … I don't know how that little girl knew, but she knew. As my finger squeezed the trigger, she looked right at me. How could she even see me? I was far away, on a rooftop. But she saw me. Her little face, covered in tears, looked right up through the scope of my rifle and into my eyes. Her face, eyes, and tears seared into my brain and burned my soul. Ever since that day, they have always been with me."

Ruby felt her heart breaking. She felt this man's pain, his terrible anguish; a tear rolled down her cheek. Getting up, she moved to sit next to Taylor on the couch, placing her hand on his shoulder as Taylor's voice continued, seemingly unaware of her presence.

"How can I stand before God? How can I face anyone—my family, my brothers, my friends? Why do I even deserve to be here now?

That damn woman later went to the Afghan government and accused me of murdering her daughter. But there were too many witnesses when the grenades exploded, leaving little doubt. Of course, command cleared me officially, but I just can't seem to clear myself."

Taylor paused, suddenly aware of Ruby sitting beside him and her hand on his shoulder. Sitting up a bit, he wiped the tears from his face, and a sad smile appeared. "Some hero, huh? I'm sorry, Ruby. I shouldn't have dumped this on you. You don't even know me, and you have been so kind. Once it started pouring out of me, I couldn't stop it."

"It is okay, Bill. Do you mind if I call you Bill?"

Taylor shook his head to indicate he didn't mind.

"I think this needed to come out. It was like a poison, slowly killing you. You needed to tell someone, and I am here. And, too, I did ask you. It is okay."

"I guess I crawled into a bottle and never crawled out. Maybe I hoped somebody in one of these stupid fights would kill me. Unfortunately, I am damn good at fighting, even drunk. That's tough to beat when you mix it with not caring."

"Can I say something to you, Bill?"

"Sure. I'll listen. It seems only fair after what I just dumped on you."

"I may not have all the right words in English, but I will try."

She paused a few seconds before speaking. "As a mother, I don't understand how any mother could do that to her daughter or any child. That is an evil I have never seen. God did not do that, and you did not do that. You are not to blame. Only the poor little girl's mother is to blame. But I cannot begin to think how terrible that must be for you to bear, because you are a good man. That is why it hurts you so badly."

Ruby paused as Taylor leaned forward, his elbows on his knees, and buried his face in his hands, saying nothing.

"Like many Filipinas, I am a Christian woman. I do not believe that God blames you for what happened.

This is hard to explain in English, so I hope you understand my meaning. I think the little girl does not blame you. She was obeying her mother, but you say she was crying. Why? I think the little girl did not want to die. She did not want to kill those men who had never harmed her. She only obeyed her mother as a good girl should. That evil mother betrayed her daughter. How can a mother be so evil and filled with such hate? As a Christian, I believe there is only one God, the same God who created Christians and created people of all religions, including those people of no religion. That poor little girl was going to meet God that day. She almost met God with the blood of many men on her soul. Instead, she met him with a clean soul. You did that, Bill. As hard as it has been for you, you did that. God would not want that little girl to come to him with all that blood on her soul. He would not blame her, but still, it would be there. And I think, I know, maybe it sounds crazy, but if that little girl could talk to you now, she would be grateful for what you did."

Ruby kept her hand on his shoulder and fell silent.

Taylor slowly sat up straight. His face wore a confused expression.

Taken with a sudden urge, Ruby leaned over to kiss his cheek. "Bill Taylor, you are a decent man, a good man. That is why this has been so terrible for you. But you must live. The world needs good men like you. If they knew the truth, your family would be sad for you, but, I think, also very proud. And I know for certain that many good women want to find a good man like you." She stood. "Now, I must go to bed." She started for her bedroom.

"Ruby…?"

"Yes?" She paused near the door.

"Salamat, thank you."

"Walang anuman, you are welcome. Goodnight, Bill."

Taylor sat quietly for several minutes after Ruby went to bed. His brain repeatedly cycled through the things she had said. Too many thoughts were swirling in his mind to make sense of it all, but he kept returning to what Ruby had said about neither God nor the little girl blaming him.

It made no sense at all. But, of course, the girl would blame him; after all, he'd shot her.

He swiveled around and stretched out. It was comfortable for an old couch, and Taylor felt his eyes growing heavy.

Shit. I need to get some sleep, and shower in the morning. I must be getting quite rank. Taylor decided to ask Ruby about that in the morning. His badly beaten body was beginning to heal, and he figured he could handle bathing himself well enough on his own now. Rolling onto his right side, he fluffed the pillow and settled in.

Taylor woke to find Ruby cooking at the kitchen stove. His eyes went to a clock on the shelf across the room. It was 9:47 a.m.

"Oh, shit. Oops. Sorry, I overslept."

Ruby laughed. "It is okay. Today is Saturday. It is a free day for me, and you need to sleep."

"I'd like to shower, if that is okay. I think I can manage it on my own."

"That would be good. I was going to ask you if you are able. I put a towel in there for you. Also, there is a blanket you can use as a robe. Leave your clothes. I will wash them. They are beginning to smell very bad."

"I bet they are."

"I can send Amado to your apartment for more clothes, if you like. I think staying inside a while longer is safest until you can move better."

"We can talk about that later, I guess. But I don't want Amado getting into any trouble. We shall see."

"Okay."

He made his way to the bathroom slowly and carefully, still a bit unsteady on his feet.

Damn, they beat the shit out of me. I am lucky to be alive.

Taylor was soaping up his hair for the second time when he was struck with the sudden realization that, for some reason, his demons hadn't visited him during the night.

CHAPTER 13
Thailand

Vivas sat in the small lobby of the Spring Lotus offices. After the attack on the club, they had beefed up security. They were not taking any chances.

Sitting in a chair that faced the street, Vivas chatted quietly with Xuan, who had volunteered to help cover the front desk for the time being. Xuan enjoyed practicing her English and described her home near the village Mai had lived in until Dish led her to safety during the war in Vietnam. For his part, Vivas managed to pick up a smattering of Vietnamese while he kept a watchful eye on street traffic and anyone approaching Spring Lotus' entrance.

Two men approached the lobby's front door. Vivas immediately recognized both, and got to his feet as they drew near. The door opened, and the two men walked in.

Hana's father, Rick, was first to come through the door, followed by Slim, the quiet former Delta Force operator who'd led the team of contractors that helped to rescue Ellen Chang in Niger.

Rick Hahn grinned at Vivas. "Son of a bitch! A damn Navy SEAL. What the fuck is my daughter thinking?"

Hana stepped out of her office. "That you are damn lucky to have such a fine man for a son-in-law."

Vivas laughed. "Yeah, Dad."

Hahn extended his hand. "You can call me just about any damn thing you want, but if you call me dad again, I'll knock you out."

Grinning, Vivas took his hand and shook it. "Sure thing, pops."

Vivas turned to Slim. "How's it going? Been a while since Niger."

"Yep, it sure has. Good to see you, man." Slim offered his hand to Vivas while smiling at Hana. "Hi there, Hana. How are you holding up, honey?"

"Hey, Slim. I'm okay, I guess. Welcome back to Thailand."

"Beats the shit out of the Sahara Desert any day of the week."

Hahn walked over to his daughter and gave her a warm hug. After a few seconds, his face was suddenly all business. "Is Quan around, Hana? We all need to talk."

"He'll be back shortly." She beckoned everyone to follow her into the small conference room, then turned to leave. "I'll be right back. I'll get some drinks; is water okay?"

Everyone nodded.

"Quan called a few minutes ago. He and Dish were out making arrangements for Benh's funeral; it's the day after tomorrow. They are on their way back now."

After Hana left, Hahn turned to Slim. "Would you mind keeping an eye out front for a few minutes while I have a few words with my future son-in-law?"

'Sure thing, boss." Slim went back out to the lobby.

Hahn remained standing while Vivas sat at the conference table. "Think I'll stand a bit. I sat long enough on that damn plane."

Vivas laughed. "I know how that is. The flight from San Diego to Bangkok is a killer."

"Hana told me what happened the other night. From what I heard, you all handled it well. And I guess I owe you thanks. Hana told me she was about to be killed until you put two bullets in the asshole's forehead."

"Yeah, well … I couldn't very well let that happen. I am planning on marrying her."

"Yeah, well anyway, nice shooting. And … thanks."

"It was my pleasure."

Twenty minutes later, when Quan and Dish arrived, the entire group gathered around the table. Slim and Quan both opted to stand. Rick started right in.

"Hana, after you called, I got ahold of Major Anurat in Sisaket and asked him to see if he could dig up anything on a Senior Colonel Trán with the Vietnamese Ministry of Public Security. It turns out that Anurat already knew quite a bit about him. Essentially, this guy is as crooked as the Ho Chi Minh Trail. Trán is a common Vietnamese name, and he was unsure about him being a cousin to the Trán killed in Vietnam when you folks rescued JD's mom, but it would certainly make sense under the circumstances."

"Cousin, uncle, or great aunt; it doesn't matter now," Slim commented.

Hahn nodded. "Anurat said that this Senior Colonel Trán is eyeball-deep in protection rackets, drug smuggling, and human trafficking. So, if he is the cousin of the Trán Dish killed, this all begins to add up."

Vivas and Quan both agreed.

Dish spoke up. "Then also make sense that this Trán would know and use scum like Fong to carry out his plan for revenge."

"What do we do now?" Hana asked. "Xuan and Jum Y are ready to travel to the US. This other Trán shouldn't know about them, but we can't be sure. We've completed their arrangements to leave Thailand and fly to the US in three days. They both wanted to stay for Benh's funeral."

"We keep them safe for three days and then put them on the plane," Rick replied. "Somebody should probably go with them as a security escort. Trán could still have people watching us, but they should be safe enough when they get to the States. Where are they going?"

"I was able to keep them together, which will be great for them. Both girls are going to Knoxville, Tennessee. Xuan will be staying with Mai, of course. A very nice couple is sponsoring Jum Y. The woman's name is Vicky Davis. Her husband is Glen." Hana turned to Quan. "Do we have someone we can put on the flight with them, someone you recommend?"

Quan considered for a minute before answering. "I could send Sirichai. He is young but competent, a former member of the Thai Special Forces. Of course, he'll be unarmed, but Sirichai is a skilled Thai boxer. He was a Thai army champion before joining the special forces."

"Good. If you will talk to Sirichai, I will make the arrangements."

"I will see him right after we finish talking."

"It's good that they both will be in Knoxville," Vivas observed. "It will be a tough adjustment for a while, and they can support each other."

Hahn nodded. "Yes. It's great you were able to set this up that way." He paused. "Okay, let's see what other information Anurat comes up with. We can then decide on the best action plan."

"Perhaps the failure of this attempted hit might persuade this other Trán to back off," Hana suggested.

Quan spoke up. "I do not think so. The killing of his cousin cost Trán a lot of money and a loss of face. He must effectively re-establish control, or some will lose their fear of him."

"Yes," Dish added. "When we rescued Mai, I burned much cash and Trán's books. Replacing the cash is not too hard; it just takes a little time. But burning those books hurt him very badly. We must kill this other Trán and Fong before this will end."

Slim cut in. "I hate to say it, but Dish is right. Evil folks like this Trán character only understand one thing. Sadly, you must kill them before they figure it out."

"Okay," Vivas replied. "So, we keep our eyes peeled and get Xuan and Jum Y safely out of here. We gather what information we can and wait to see how things unfold. There's not much else we can do at this point."

Hana reached over to take Vivas's hand and nodded.

Rick stood. "That's pretty much how I see it." He moved around to stand near Hana, touching her shoulder.

"Hana, I am so sorry about Benh. I know she meant a lot to you. Vivas told me she had stopped dancing and worked as your receptionist. He also told me that Benh helped set your plan in motion the other night at the club. That took courage."

"She saved my life," Dish added, speaking softly. "She was too young…"

Hahn looked over at Dish. "I understand, old friend. We owe her a great deal. Both Trán and this Fong will be brought to justice. I promise."

Turning back to Hana, "Slim and I have rooms at the JW Marriott. We'll get settled in and then come back. Maybe we can get dinner. We need to catch up."

Hana stood, and Rick reached out to hug his daughter, speaking quietly into her ear. "I am so sorry about all this, Hana. I love you, and I am so damn proud of you. I want you to know that." He paused, then spoke again, a little louder this time. "And despite all the kidding you'll likely hear, I think you have a pretty damn good man there … for a SEAL."

With that, Rick turned and, nodding to Vivas, left the room.

With a quick wave to the group, Slim stood and moved to follow Rick out. "See y'all back here in a bit."

After Rick and Slim left, Dish and Quan excused themselves. Dish left to return to the hotel, where renovations were underway, and Quan mumbled something about talking to Sirichai. Hana and Vivas found themselves alone in the conference room.

Vivas spoke first. "Well, I hope we can bring this mess to a satisfactory ending soon."

"Me too, Carlos. During this meeting, it struck me again. I want out of this."

"What do you mean, babe?"

She turned to face him directly. "I want to get married now, as soon as possible."

Vivas grinned. "I'm okay with that. I can talk to the embassy and find out what's involved."

"And I will tell my father at dinner tonight that I want to sell Obsession."

"Are you sure? That is a big decision, Hana." Hana had mentioned selling the club to him before, on the night of the attack, but Vivas had figured it was the grief and shock of the moment.

"I am sure. I can't straddle this line anymore, especially after Benh's death. I can't get what she said to Dish right before she died out of my head. I know Dish will do whatever he can to live up to that. So, I will ask Quan if he is willing to run Spring Lotus here in Thailand with help from Dish and Chanmali. I think Quan will want to do it."

"And what will you do, babe?"

"I want to move to the U.S. and start a family with you. I can work with JD's mother and help with that side. I want out of Thailand, Vietnam, and the whole damn thing."

Vivas got out of his chair and moved closer to Hana, leaning in to kiss her. "Then that is what we will do."

"You're not mad?"

"Why would I be mad?"

"You left the Navy to come over here, and now I want to go there. You could have stayed in the Navy, Carlos."

"Hana, I chose YOU over the Navy, not Thailand. I can find work back home. That is not a problem."

"You know, you don't have to work at all, Carlos. I am very wealthy."

Carlos smiled. "Yeah, I figured that out. But I still must pull my weight, honey. I must do something."

"Maybe you could work for Spring Lotus."

"Maybe, but we don't have to decide that right this minute, do we?"

"What else can we do? I must get my mind off all this unpleasantness for a little while."

"Hmm. Maybe we could start working on that family."

Hana laughed. "You know, that might do the trick. Well, the apartment is right upstairs. What are we waiting for?"

Chanmali knocked on the door of Jum Y and Xuan's dormitory room. A few seconds later, Xuan opened the door, and her young face lit up at the sight of Chanmali. Both girls had come to consider the older woman family, often referring to her as "grandmother."

"Good morning, Xuan. I hope the two of you slept well last night."

"Yes, Grandmother. Very well, thank you."

"That's good because a young man named Sirichai— one of Quan's men—is here to take you shopping. He has a list of things Hana says you will need when you go to America."

"Sirichai?" Both girls had noticed the handsome young Thai who'd joined Quan's security team a few weeks before the attack at the club. Xuan thought that Jum Y was especially taken with him. They'd since learned that Chai, as Jum Y had taken to calling him, was a former soldier with the Thai Special Forces and a very skilled Thai boxer.

Jum Y will love this, Xuan thought. "Tell Sirichai we will be down in a few minutes. I must wake Jum Y. She is still sleeping."

"You two better hurry. Sirichai may not want to wait too long. I do not think he is so happy to, as he put it, 'babysit' two little girls on a shopping trip."

"Babysit?" Xuan's eyes flashed. Then she grinned. "Tell Sirichai we will be down in a bit. Jum Y and I must get ready to shop."

Chanmali chuckled and nodded. "I will let the young man know." She turned and headed down the hallway toward the stairs. Chanmali had still not grown accustomed to the creaky old elevator.

Xuan turned back into the room, closing the door behind her. There was a mischievous look on her pretty face.

"Jum Y! Jum Y! Wake up."

Jum Y groaned, covering her face with her pillow. "What is it, Xuan? Can't you see I'm trying to sleep?"

"You must wake up; Jum Y. Sirichai is downstairs waiting to babysit us on a shopping trip." Xuan emphasized "babysit" in mock anger.

"Babysit? Chai said that?"

"According to Grandmother, he did. Come on, Jum Y. Let's have some fun. It has been so sad lately. Let us prepare ourselves for our babysitter."

Jum Y sat up in her bed and grinned. "You are right, Xuan. We must get ready."

Throwing the covers back, Jum Y leaped out of bed and ran for the shower.

Just over an hour later, the two girls stepped off the old elevator and into the lobby, where Sirichai waited impatiently. He looked up when he heard the elevator slow to a clanky stop on the ground floor. When the two young ladies rounded the corner into the lobby, his eyes widened in shock.

Both girls had taken great pains in preparing for their shopping trip, each dressed in the very best outfits they had. They both wore Western-style jeans. In addition, Xuan added a jade green silk blouse, short white boots, and white hoop earrings. Jum Y wore a bright red sleeveless stretch blouse, new black running shoes, and a jade pendant on a black choker necklace. Jum Y had also used her prodigious skill with makeup on both Xuan and herself. To say both young ladies were now knockouts would have been an extreme understatement. With her delicate Vietnamese facial features, Xuan could have easily graced the cover of any young woman's favorite fashion magazine.

Sirichai attempted to appear stern and unaffected but found himself stunned and speechless.

Ignoring the dumbfounded young man, Jum Y spoke to Chanmali, who stood behind the front desk, trying desperately to contain the amused grin that threatened, despite her best efforts, to break out all over her typically inscrutable face.

"Good morning, Grandmother. Is our babysitter ready?"

Chanmali, still struggling to remain serious, answered. "Good morning to you, Jum Y. Sirichai is quite ready. He has been waiting very patiently."

Sirichai lurched clumsily toward the door. "I'll flag a taxi."

Once Sirichai was gone, both girls grinned at each other.

"That will show him," Xuan exclaimed happily. "Babysitter, indeed."

A sly smile formed on Jum Y's face. "Oh, we're not through with him yet."

"Don't be too hard on him, you two," Chanmali counseled. "He is just a young man and quite full of himself. I am sure he feels Quan assigned him this duty because he is new to the club. But it is quite serious. We don't know what bad people may still be around, and the fact that Quan chose him to escort you says much about him."

Xuan, considering Chanmali's words, nodded her head. "I think you are right, Grandmother. We will be careful."

"But still have a little fun," Jum Y added.

Xuan smiled. "Yes, maybe just a little."

CHAPTER 14
Washington, D.C.

President Steele looked across the desk at the three people he had summoned to the Oval Office. He'd called Mike Connors, Director of the CIA; Admiral Spence, the head of Special Operations Command; and Martha Knopp, the newly appointed Director of Homeland Security.

Surprisingly, President Steele had called the meeting himself and not gone through his chief of staff. That in itself was unusual. When the attendees arrived, none of the President's staff members were present, either. That was a sure sign that the topic of this meeting would be way off record.

It was evident from the look on the president's face that he had something weighing heavily on his mind. The three patiently waited for him to begin. Finally, unable to stand it any longer, Mike Conners broke the silence.

"What's up, Mr. President?"

Steele cleared his throat. "What we are about to discuss never leaves this room. If at any point you feel you cannot be a part of this discussion, you are free to leave. However, whatever we discussed before you left must never be mentioned. I will have the responsible party's head on a platter if I hear a whisper about this meeting anywhere. Is that understood?"

All three answered in the affirmative. They all knew and respected this man. If it had to be this way, he had a good reason.

"Good. Gentlemen, you both know Martha. She and I go back a long way. She was working with Army Intelligence when I still commanded troops in the field. She has also served as a prosecuting attorney for the state of Alabama. Martha has my utmost confidence and respect."

Connors nodded. "Martha and I have had some dealings in the past. Good to have you on the team, Martha."

"Thanks, Mike. Glad to be here."

Spence reached over to shake her hand. "We've never met, but your reputation precedes you. I think you'll make an excellent director of Homeland Security."

"Thank you, Admiral Spence. That means a lot coming from you."

Steele coughed. "Okay, let's dispense with the pleasantries. I am calling you here because I will authorize a covert operation within our borders. It will, I think, be within my legal authority, but it walks a thin line. I have a trusted staff lawyer looking into that right now. The operation will be way off the books, but it needs doing, and by God, I will do it."

"That sounds serious, Mr. President," Admiral Spence offered.

"You are correct, and I am deadly serious about it. You know that Mai Cordell and General Ellerson have been friends for several years, since her late husband's time in Vietnam. I have been talking to the two of them for some time now. After her return from Vietnam, I called to welcome her home and let her know how happy I was that everything worked out so well and everyone was home safe..."

The president paused.

"And then, I asked if there was anything I could do." Steele chuckled. "If you know Mai Cordell, you know she is formidable. She has a sharp mind and knows what she wants. Mrs. Cordell made it clear that there indeed was something I could do, and proceeded to fill me in on her rescue, what had happened, and the project she is currently involved in. To make a long story short, this operation directly results from what I have learned since Mai Cordell's rescue."

"What is Mrs. Cordell involved with?" Connors asked.

"It is currently a privately financed initiative called Spring Lotus. Their mission is to rescue and help Asian kids in horrible situations, such as forced servitude, sex trafficking, or prostitution." Steele frowned. "I'm afraid this trafficking is the newest form of slavery; God help us all. The Spring Lotus organization's mission is to help these poor kids start a new life where they have a chance of succeeding. It is in startup mode, with its first two kids in the pipeline. One is a young Montagnard woman who helped during Mai's rescue, and the second is a distant relative of Mai from her home village in Vietnam.

The Montagnard girl was sold into prostitution by her father. I understand that he owed a large gambling debt and could not pay it. The father of the other girl, the one related to Mai, felt she would not be safe there if the wrong people learned of her connection to Mai after Mai's rescue from Vietnam."

"Son of a bitch," Connors commented. "What kind of father would do that to his daughter?"

"It happens more often than you'd think, Mike," Martha responded. "And right here in the States, as well."

"Exactly," Steele confirmed. "After talking to Mai, I had some folks I trust dive deeply into trafficking in the US. I was horrified to learn how rampant sex trafficking is in our own country. I am not sure what I can do about that now. I am still thinking about that. But there is another aspect of this problem that I can do something about right now."

"That is?" Spence asked.

"More and more kids are being trafficked across our border with Mexico. Not just Hispanic kids, either. According to Border Patrol, we are experiencing a growing influx of Asian kids, African kids, Middle Eastern kids, and Filipino kids, mostly girls. Those who survive the journey live horrible, tragic lives of prostitution and sexual slavery. And kids from the US are being trafficked into Mexico the same way. It is an abomination. In my opinion, the animals trafficking these kids are not fit to walk the planet."

Connors and Spence nodded in silent agreement. Both men had daughters, and President Steele had two daughters himself.

Martha shook her head. "It is a real problem and proves, at least as far as I am concerned, that evil does exist. But these traffickers aren't just evil, sir; they're smart, ruthless, and dangerous. They have the backing of the cartels. We can't legally cross into Mexico without the Mexican government's permission. We all know you won't get that. What can we do?"

"I know," Steele responded. "That's why we're not crossing into Mexico. These traffickers are bringing those kids here, across the border. So, we deal with them here. They hold these kids until they can arrange to move them out or have buyers pick them up. It could be a few hours or a few days."

Connors shifted in his seat. "What do you propose we do, sir?"

"I am putting together a task force to find these locations, rescue these kids, and … uh … discourage these animals from doing it again. This operation will be without any official support or record. If the media gets wind of it, it will be all over the news and our delightful house speaker will launch one special investigation after another. I'm prepared for that, but I'd rather it doesn't happen. Call the operation what you want. As director of Homeland Security, Martha will have operational control. I want her to contact you two if she needs anything - anything at all."

Both Connors and Spence nodded. "She's got it," Spence agreed.

Martha, contemplating a spot on the wall over Connors' head, now looked at the president. "Discourage?"

"Well, if they surrender, they will be tried and, if found guilty, punished severely. We will go after the maximum penalties. However, we all know most will probably be set free by some addle-brained judge who thinks criminals have more rights than their victims."

"And what if they don't surrender?" Connors inquired.

Steele looked directly at Connors. There was no mistaking the look on his face. "I don't want these assholes going home to try again in a few weeks."

CHAPTER 15
Coronado Naval Base

Commander Elliot leaned back in his chair to stretch, glancing at the clock hanging to the left of his office door. He had a few more minutes.

Returning his attention to the operational readiness reports before him, it seemed at SOCOM (Special Operations Command), there was some concern that a shake-up was needed following specific events involving Navy SEALs that recently made media headlines. Elliot was inclined to blame the previous administration's policies—in particular, their penchant for relieving seasoned brass and replacing them with "more ideologically aligned" ass-kissers.

My men are world-class warriors. What the fuck did command expect? Too much downtime is not good for them. More importantly, they need leaders they can respect, not these damn paper tigers they've been recently serving under!

Despite his thoughts on where the blame lay, Elliott was a professional. He would do whatever it took to ensure the men under his command were highly motivated, fully operational, and damned professional. Leadership came naturally to him.

There was a knock at the door, and Elliot looked up from the reports. "Enter."

"Petty Officer Second Class Palazzolo, reporting as requested, sir."

"Ah, yes! Palazzolo. At ease. Take a seat, please." Commander Elliott indicated a chair just next to his desk.

"Thank you, sir." Pallie sat in the offered chair and waited for the commander to divulge the reason for his requested presence.

Swiveling around in his chair, Elliott faced Pallie and leaned back. Pausing for a moment, the commander collected his thoughts, then cleared his throat.

"Palazzolo, I have called you in because I need a volunteer, and I think you're the best man for the job."

"Sir?"

'What do you think about those who make their living trafficking human beings?"

"The truth, sir?"

Elliot nodded. "Speak freely, sailor."

"I'd love to get my hands on some of those scumbags and maybe even put a bullet between their eyeballs. Why, sir?"

"This doesn't leave the room, but the short version is the president has decided to do something about the human trafficking problem at our southern border. He is assembling a task force with orders to deal aggressively with human traffickers crossing into the USA. According to reports from the Border Patrol, they see a serious increase in young women smuggled into the States; many from Asia, the Philippines, and other countries. Many of these girls are forced into prostitution, ending up in massage parlors and brothels. The president has had enough. He wants these poor kids rescued and assisted in whatever way is most appropriate, and he wants to hit the traffickers … hard."

"I can understand that, sir."

"I thought you might." Commander Elliot paused, taking a moment to look out the window. "Shortly before he retired, Chief Whitley and I had a little 'off the record' chat about your involvement with a certain off-the-books rescue mission in Southeast Asia."

"Sir, I don't…"

"Relax, Palazzolo. Whitley and I go way back, and he didn't go into detail. Besides, the kidnapping eventually made the network news. Since then, Mrs. Cordell has been outspoken in her efforts to get help for some of these kids, although she focuses more on Southeast Asia."

Elliott paused, shifting in his chair. "Chief Whitley commented that you seemed different when you returned—a bit more seasoned, perhaps—since what you experienced."

"Okay, sir. Sure. What some of those kids go through hit me damn hard."

"I want you to volunteer to work with the president's task force. I think you will take it to heart and bring some insight that may prove useful. This mission is way off the books, and I think you know how to handle that as well."

Pallie didn't respond right away. He was thinking about Jum Y.

And what was that other girl's name, the one from the plantation who spotted JD's mother? Oh yeah. Hoa.

It only took a few seconds for Pallie to decide. "Okay, Commander. You've got yourself a volunteer."

"Thank you. I know I can count on you. I'll get the orders cut. They'll probably assign you to a potato peeling detail above the Arctic Circle. The truth will stay between you and me."

Pallie allowed himself to grin. "Is that all, sir?"

"For now, Palazzolo. You're dismissed."

Pallie stood and saluted. Once Commander Elliott returned the salute, Pallie left the office.

CHAPTER 16
Thailand

Xuan sat on her twin bed. She and Jum Y had spent many months in Thailand, the first two to pass through Hana's new Spring Lotus program. The two girls would board their flight to America later this evening. Xuan had just finished packing. She glanced at Jum Y, still trying to get herself packed, sensing something was wrong.

"What is wrong, Jum Y? You are having so much trouble packing, and we don't have that much to pack."

Jum Y glanced over her shoulder. "It is nothing, Xuan. I have something on my mind. That is all."

"Something … or someone?"

"What do you mean?" Jum Y turned to face Xuan, who sat on her bed, a knowing smile on her face.

"You are thinking of Sirichai."

Jum Y's eyes instantly turned toward the floor, and then she recovered and looked squarely at Xuan. "I don't know what you mean."

"Don't be silly, Jum Y. It is as clear as the nose on your face. I have seen it for some time now. I think you like him. He is easy to like. I think Benh liked him too."

The mention of Benh only added to Jum Y's sadness. Benh had always been friendly to her and Xuan; and chatted with them often. However, Benh never mentioned Sirichai to them, not that she could remember. But it was indeed possible.

Chai is so handsome, and when he is not trying to be serious, he is so much fun to be around.

Jum Y abruptly sat down on her bed. Her pretty face was suddenly sad, like she had just lost her best friend.

"You are crazy, Xuan. Besides, even if it were true, Sirichai would never look at me. You know what I was."

Xuan walked over to sit beside Jum Y and gave her friend a big hug.

"You mustn't think like that, Jum Y. I know what happened, but you were never bad. You were betrayed and you had no choice. That was then; this is now. You are a good person with a new life in front of you. Any man would be fortunate to have you in his life. You are decent, kind, and so brave. I admire you, Jum Y."

Jum Y buried her face against Xuan's shoulder.

"You are a good friend, Xuan. Thank you for your caring words."

"Words are easy to say when they are true."

Jum Y wiped tears from her face. "You believe that?"

"I do."

"You are right. Thanks to Dish, Hana, your Aunt Mai, and everyone here, I have a chance for a new life. But it will not matter much as far as Chai is concerned. I will be in America, and he will be here."

Xuan smiled a small, secret smile. "Do you not know, Jum Y? I heard Carlos and Hana talking yesterday. Sirichai is 'babysitting' us on our trip to America."

At 11:45 p.m., Hahn pulled the van over near the departure area doors at Bangkok's Suvarnabhumi Airport. Their flight was scheduled to take off at 1:00 a.m.; they were cutting it a bit close.

For security reasons, neither Hahn nor Vivas wanted them to hang around the airport longer than necessary. After checking the area, Vivas exited the passenger side and opened the sliding door. Sirichai got out first, followed by Hana, Xuan, and Jum Y. Hahn opened the rear hatch, then stood back as a porter loaded the two girls' luggage onto a cart. He scanned their surroundings, looking for anything out of place. Nothing appeared to be amiss. The group moved into the airport's main lobby and waited while Hahn parked the van.

Once Hahn returned, Vivas took the lead, and the group headed toward the check-in counter. The porter with the girls' luggage followed, with Sirichai and Hahn in the rear. No one in the group gave a thought to the older woman polishing a traveling businessman's shoes when she looked up at their entry and flashed a welcoming smile. After all, shoe shiners were always looking for their next client. The group quickly moved on.

Unfortunately, all three men missed the quick nod the older woman gave to a young boy loitering nearby. In his early teens, the boy sat in a chair, charging his phone at a convenient charging station. Unplugging the phone, he followed the group at a distance, seemingly intent on nothing.

The boy did not know them and did not care; he was a spotter. His job was to see what flight the passengers got on and then report back.

Twenty minutes later, the luggage was checked, and boarding passes were in hand.

Vivas looked over at Sirichai and grinned. "Damn, Chai. That's a long haul for a round-trip flight. It must be twenty-six or twenty-seven hours one way, not counting stopovers. But then, I guess it won't be too bad, at least not on the way there, with these two lovely ladies for company."

Xuan and Jum Y both giggled.

Sirichai blushed a bit. "Yes. We have stops in Manila and Detroit before reaching Knoxville. We have almost five hours in Manila, but the other stop is short, about an hour. Hana has given me five days to rest in Knoxville before I fly back."

"That's great, Chai. You should call JD and ask him to introduce you to southern-style barbeque. I've got his number here; hold on." Vivas reached for his phone and gave Sirichai a number, adding it to his contacts. "Make JD buy the beers."

"I do not drink."

"Damn, I knew there had to be something wrong with you. JD won't mind, though. It'll make you a cheap date."

A few minutes later, the Korean Air flight attendant at the desk called for first-class passengers to approach the gate. They all stood.

"That's us," Jum Y announced.

"What the heck?" Hahn exclaimed. "First class?"

Vivas laughed. "Hana is a first-class kind of gal. Besides, it's a painfully long flight to be cooped up in those little economy seats."

Xuan was quiet. Vivas turned to her. "Are you okay?"

"Yes, I'm just a little nervous. I have never been on a plane before."

"You'll be okay. I mean, look at me! I've flown around the world at least, oh, I don't know, twenty-five or thirty times. You can see that I'm fine!"

"Now you've done it, Vivas. We'll be lucky to get Xuan on the flight at all," Hahn joked. "Alright, ladies, let's get you loaded up."

Hana hugged both girls as they prepared to board the aircraft. "You will both be just fine. You've met Mai, she is a wonderful person. I know she will do everything she can to help you succeed in starting your new lives in

America." Vivas could tell both girls were scared, but he knew they would make it.

All they need is a fair chance.

Hahn came over and stood next to Vivas. "Now that's two brave young ladies."

"I know they're scared, but they are getting on the plane anyway. That takes courage."

Tears ran down Hana's cheeks when she came to stand with her fiancé and father. "Well, I guess that is that."

"You've done a good thing here, babe." Vivas put his arm around her. "Are you ready to go?"

"Affirmative."

"Okay, then, let's get out of here." Rick started back toward the terminal concourse.

As Hana and the two men made their way toward the terminal exit and departures parking lot, Hahn noticed a young boy standing near some vending machines. It was the same boy they'd seen at the charging station when they first got to the airport.

"Vivas, isn't that the same kid, the one charging his phone at the entrance when we came in?"

Vivas glanced over. "Yes, it is. But he's just a kid. Probably waiting for somebody."

"Maybe so," Hahn acknowledged. Still, Rick was never one to take chances. He took several seconds to give the kid a good look, wanting to be able to recognize him if it ever became necessary.

As the three walked along, Hana and Vivas discussed his plan to visit the embassy the next day to find out what the American embassy required for their upcoming marriage. Hahn pretended to be uninterested in their conversation.

Approaching the airport's main exit, Hahn looked around once more. That same boy was now talking to the old shoeshine lady who had greeted them as they had entered earlier.

That must be it, he thought. *The kid is probably hanging around while his grandmother works.* Still, there was a nagging doubt he couldn't seem to shake. *Damn, I've been in this line of work too long.*

As the big jet slowly taxied to the runway to take its place in line for takeoff, Xuan and Jum Y chattered excitedly. They had never seen such luxury. Their seats were huge and very comfortable; everything was new and fascinating. The girls glanced at Sirichai, who now sat next to an elderly Thai woman who had him engaged in a conversation about her beautiful grandchildren. Sirichai caught their glance and nodded back at them. He smiled bravely as the woman beside him discussed another granddaughter's many attributes. It was going to be a long flight.

Jum Y leaned back in her seat.

"Are you scared?" she asked, her voice quiet.

"A little. But my Aunt Mai will be there when we arrive. She is a wonderful lady."

"Yes, she is. I was lucky she spoke to me that day. And to think I almost walked away." She shuddered at the thought. "I would not be here now if I had not spoken with her."

The two girls had become great friends over their months together in Thailand, learning about life in America and its customs, and practicing English. Jum Y had been distant initially, but as trust and friendship grew, she'd told Xuan about how and where she'd met Mai and what had happened afterward.

Xuan was first horrified at Jum Y's story, then heartbroken, and finally, grateful.

"I would not be here either, Jum Y. You saved my Aunt Mai's life, and now we are both here for you today. Don't ever forget that."

Jum Y started to speak, but Xuan cut her off. "Besides, that is all over now. We are starting new lives and will always be best friends in America."

"Best friends in America," Jum Y repeated.

As the big jet accelerated to take off, Xuan reached for Jum Y's hand and grabbed it. Jum Y squeezed back reassuringly. Once the aircraft was airborne and the bumps smoothed out, Xuan relaxed but continued holding on to Jum Y for assurance. Glancing over at Sirichai, Xuan smiled. The elderly Thai woman had not slowed noticeably in bragging about her granddaughter. Sirichai was smiling bravely, dutifully nodding his head at the appropriate moments.

CHAPTER 17
The Philippines

Mahalia answered the phone on the second ring. "Kumusta?"

"Good day. I am talking to Mahalia, I believe?

She recognized the voice immediately. "Yes, Minister Trán. What a surprise to hear from you. It has been a long time."

Trán had been a highly reliable source of young Vietnamese girls for several years. Then suddenly, nothing for the last year or so. Mahalia and Blessica had discussed this fact just the previous week, wondering whether they should be concerned.

The girls Trán provided arrived in Manila loaded in shipping containers. Lured by job postings and recruiters advertising for nannies, bartenders, or waitresses, they quickly learned something different was in store for them.

"Yes, I must apologize for the period of inactivity. Unfortunately, I had to deal with a family member's tragic death, and it took some time to tie up a few loose ends. We will be back to our normal operations shortly."

Mahalia smiled. "I am happy to hear this, Minister. Our clients have very much missed the talent you provide."

"We are recruiting new girls right now. It will not be long. However, I have a favor to ask. It is one for which you would be well-compensated. I can assure you and your sister of that."

"How can we help you, Minister?"

"I am calling you from my office on a secured line so we can speak freely. Two young ladies will arrive at the airport in Manila in about two hours. As I understand, they will have five hours to stay at the Manila airport before continuing their flight. I am very interested in these girls and would owe you a great debt if the two do not leave the Philippines. The names on their tickets are Jum Y and Xuan Li. I would like you to hold them somewhere until I can arrange their return to Vietnam. They must not be harmed or touched, if you can get your hands on them. I have special plans for them."

"It is short notice, Minister, but you have been an excellent business associate. I will see what we can arrange. I think it may be difficult unless they leave the airport, but five hours is a long time. They might decide on a short trip into the city, to eat or check out some sights there. That is possible, even likely."

Trán considered this. "I understand. Kidnapping the two girls would certainly be my preference. However, if that is not possible, I want these two girls dead. A young man accompanies them. I know nothing about him. The man is of no concern to me. He is young and alone and should not be much trouble."

"Okay. I understand, Minister Trán. Let me discuss this with Blessica, and we shall see what we can do. Can you give me their flight number and arrival time?"

Trán quickly provided the requested information, which Mahalia jotted down on a pad near the phone in the kitchen. Then, she repeated it back to the colonel.

"That is correct."

"Okay, then. I can at least promise these girls will not leave Manila. If we cannot take them, we will make sure they are dead."

"Thank you, Mahalia. I knew I could count on you. I will contact you in two days to continue our discussion. I have some additional business to tend to. I will soon update you on the next shipment of girls I am assembling. Have a good day, my dear."

"You too, Minister Trán. And so nice to be back in business with you." Ending the call, Mahalia went in search of Blessica. They would need to move fast.

Tony Salonga sat in the driver's seat of the beat-up old Mitsubishi L300 van. He flicked the remainder of his cigarette out the window. Two of his crew sat in the back, discussing the attributes of Charmaigne Starling, a hot newcomer in the Pinay porn industry.

"Will you two mga tanga shut the hell up! Pay attention. Shit!"

The two men shut up. It was not a safe move to upset Salonga. The story was that he was somehow related to a notorious Tondo gang leader from the forties named Nicasio Salonga, also known as Asing Salonga. If true, a host of crimes, including several murders, had been attributed to Tony's ancestor before a rival gang member gunned him down at the ripe old age of twenty-seven. And, Tony did have a quick temper.

Three other members of Tony's crew were in the airport, watching for the arrival of the two girls and their escort. One of the three, a young man named Aldo, was young and clean-cut, a real lady's man. He always dressed sharply and had a way about him that made people want to trust him. Salonga regularly used that to his advantage. It was bonus luck that Aldo's mother was Thai, and he'd grown up speaking Thai as well as Tagalog. Because of this, Salonga had told him to hang out near the taxi stands and see what he could pick up if the girls decided to head into Manila.

The three watching the airport terminal had orders to check in every ten minutes, keeping Tony updated on the girls' activities once their flight landed. If they did not venture out of the airport, the two idiots in the van would go in. Both were armed. When they were all in place, on

Tony's signal, the three already in the terminal would create a distraction some distance from where the girls waited, drawing everyone's attention away. Then, the other two would shoot the girls and the guy escorting them. Finally, they would regroup in the van and get out of there. At least, that was the plan.

If the girls left the airport, they'd follow behind in the van, kill the guy, and grab the girls at the first opportunity. It was a simple plan, as far as plans go. That was how Salonga liked it. Complicated plans always got fucked up. The guys on his crew were tough and loyal; they would follow orders. But they were not noted for their ability to think on the fly.

Salonga looked at his watch. The girls' flight would land in about forty minutes.

"You mga asno stay here and stay sharp. I've got to piss. I'll be back in a minute."

The two men in the back of the van nodded.

As soon as Salonga was gone, the two thugs went back to discussing what amazing sexual feats they'd perform if they ever got lucky enough to hook up with Charmaigne Starling.

The girls' excitement grew as the Boeing 787 taxied toward the Ninoy Aquino International Airport gates.

"We have over five hours to wait here. Maybe we could go into Manila and get something to eat," Xuan suggested. "This is so exciting."

Sirichai shook his head. "I am not sure that would be a good idea."

Jum Y looked over at Sirichai and pouted. "I don't see why. We ask where a safe place with good food is, we take a taxi, eat, and return. How dangerous can that be?"

Sirichai needed more convincing. "I still do not like it. And I am responsible for taking you to America. If anything were to happen…"

Jum Y cut him off. "What could happen? Nobody knows we are here, and we have you to protect us. What could go wrong?"

Sirichai looked over at Xuan for support. He found none.

"I think it would be alright. We do have five hours, after all. We could get an airport taxi and ask where to go, somewhere in the city, and have something to eat. We'll be back in plenty of time."

Looking at his watch, Sirichai frowned. "It's almost four o'clock in the morning. I doubt anything is open, anyway. We'll be better off eating at the airport."

Both girls made gagging faces.

A few minutes later, the aircraft rolled to a stop at the gate and the seatbelt light went out. Since they were changing planes, they grabbed their carry-on bags and joined the other passengers, moving slowly toward the exit door. A few minutes later, they found themselves inside the terminal.

Sirichai scanned the surroundings. People milled about, waiting for flights, talking on cell phones, or sitting in uncomfortable seats, watching whatever was on the many TV screens throughout the terminal. He saw nothing that seemed out of place.

Jum Y had already located the sign for the taxi area and, grabbing Xuan, headed that way. Sirichai took off after them and quickly caught up.

"We can see what might be available, but I will decide what we do. Do you understand?"

Both girls nodded. "Sure," Jum Y replied.

Xuan looked at Jum Y. "I am sure they don't speak Thai or Vietnamese."

"I will try English," Jum Y replied. "I read that most Filipinos speak at least some English."

Jum Y approached the Yellow Taxi stand and spotted a nice-looking young man.

"Are you a taxi driver?"

The young man looked at her and smiled. "No, I'm just waiting for someone. The taxi queue starts right there." He pointed to a sign that read, 'Yellow Metered Taxi Entrance.' "Where are you girls going?"

Sirichai came up, speaking in Thai. "Jum Y, we do not know this guy."

The young man smiled. "Your friend is right. You do not know me. You should be careful." He spoke in Thai, then smiled again. "My mother was Thai. I speak Thai and Tagalog." The young man laughed. "And a little English."

Sirichai turned to face the young man. "They wanted to go and get something to eat, but I am sure nothing is open. We should eat here at the airport."

Jum Y frowned. "I am sure something must be open. It would be nice to see some of Manila while we're here. After all, we still have almost five hours left to wait."

Xuan nodded. "That should be enough time if there is somewhere we can go."

The young man seemed to give that some thought. "You know … there is Makchang's. It's a Korean BBQ place on Adriatico Street. It is open twenty-four hours; a nice place, and you would be safe if you take a Yellow Taxi; that's the official airport taxi company. There'll be no traffic now. This early in the morning, it's about a thirty-minute drive, and they have excellent food. They're famous. It's Korean, not Filipino, but it is good. I eat there occasionally - when I can afford it." He smiled again.

Xuan grinned. "That sounds good."

Sirichai hesitated, thinking.

"Come on, Chai." Jum Y added. "We can take a safe, official airport taxi to a nice restaurant only thirty minutes away. We can even ask the taxi to wait while we eat, and then thirty minutes back. So, we have plenty of time. Come on, Chai. Please? What could happen?"

Sirichai tossed the idea around in his head. *I can't see anything wrong with it. After all, we'll take an airport cab and go to a well-known restaurant. I won't let them out of my sight.*

He made his decision. "Alright. Why not? I guess we can do that. We do have the time. I can't see a problem with it."

The young man smiled again. "I think you will like Makchang's." A phone chirped, and he reached for his back pocket. He looked at the number. "Excuse me, please. I must take this call; it's my mother." The young man smiled and, turning away, began to walk off. Sirichai heard him say something in what must have been Tagalog as he walked away. Something tugged at his brain, but he could not nail it down. Finally, he let it go.

Forty-five minutes later, the three were seated at a table in Makchang's, looking over the menu. Because it was so early in the morning, there was little to see except city lights during the cab ride. However, the cab driver was happy to wait for them. The meter would be running; it was easy money.

After a brief discussion, Xuan decided on the egg ramen soup and Sirichai ordered bibimbap—a mixture of rice, vegetables, and a fried egg with beef. Jum Y ordered galbi, or BBQ beef short ribs. Their food soon arrived with its accompanying selection of pickled vegetables.

"It all looks so good!" Xuan realized how hungry she was after the long journey.

"It smells good, too," Jum Y added, grinning from ear to ear. "It's better than what we'd get at the airport at 4:00 a.m., that's for sure."

Sirichai had to agree with that. And they were fine. No problems. Maybe he had been a bit overcautious. He dug into his bibimbap.

Throughout their meal, Sirichai looked up and glanced out the window. He did this every few minutes, scanning the street outside as well as the door. While there was no trouble and things seemed quiet, he still had a job to do. This time, an old Mitsubishi van rolled past the restaurant and parked across from the entry. A man got out of the front passenger side and came around the vehicle. Sirichai recognized him immediately. It was the young man they had spoken to at the airport, and he was not alone. Two men were with him, and Sirichai recognized the type immediately.

Sirichai stood. "Go to the kitchen. GO, now! Ignore the cooks. Go straight back. These places always have a back door in the kitchen for deliveries."

Xuan looked up. "Chai, what do you mean? What is wrong?"

Looking up from her half-finished platter of ribs, Jum Y followed Sirichai's gaze. Immediately, she understood.

"Come on, Xuan. We must do as Chai says. Don't argue." Getting to her feet, she grabbed Xuan's wrist and began to pull her toward the kitchen.

"I'll be right behind you. Go!!" Chai stood between the two girls and the men coming through the door.

As the girls raced into the kitchen, the three men maneuvered to get around the bodyguard standing between them and their targets. They had orders to kill him. Grinning, the young man from the airport stayed in the center as his two companions shifted to either side.

Sirichai's job was to protect the girls, not get into a brawl. He turned to follow the girls into the kitchen when its swinging door flew back open. Two more thugs stepped into the dining area, one dragging Xuan with him. The other had Jum Y. They were followed closely by a third man carrying a semi-automatic pistol, which he now pointed at Sirichai.

Surveying the situation, the man with the gun barked out some orders in Tagalog. "Get the girls into the van."

As Jum Y began to struggle, the thug holding her slammed his fist into her abdomen. She doubled over, retched, and went limp. The thug lifted her over his shoulder and headed through the restaurant's front door to the van parked across the street. Xuan offered no more resistance and was quickly led out through the same door toward the van.

"I must get these girls to the boss. Are the keys in the van?"

Aldo nodded.

"Kill this asshole and get rid of the body. Use my truck out back." Salonga tossed Aldo the keys. "Call me once you have taken care of everything."

The good-looking young man from the airport grinned. "Yes, boss." He turned toward Sirichai and spoke in Thai.

"How was your dinner, asshole? I hope you enjoyed it. It's the last fucking meal you're going to eat."

Sirichai didn't answer. His mind was calmly analyzing the situation. The thug to his left, clearly younger, looked nervous and hesitant. In the center, the leader of the three, Aldo, was a talker and a pretty boy; he would not want to get his hands dirty. He relied on his buddies for that. However, the one to Chai's right looked aggressive and confident, a man prone to using violence. Sirichai focused on him and put a smile on his face. Anything to help unnerve his assailants.

"You may kill me, but I promise you, you three will not leave this restaurant in one piece."

Sirichai waited and watched as the thug he'd identified as the more dangerous of the three slid a wicked-looking butterfly knife from his hip pocket and flipped it open. The man was familiar with its use.

Sirichai shrugged. Taking a quick step to his left, he retrieved one of the wooden chopsticks he'd just been using to enjoy his bibimbap from the table. Shifting back to his right, the chopstick held loosely in his right hand, he waited.

Aldo laughed. "Hurry, Manny, kill this idiot with his little stick. After that, we'll dump his body in the river and find some girls. I'll call Salonga later."

Manny nodded and grinned wickedly.

The thug came in hard and fast, flicking the knife toward Sirichai's right arm, held up in a defensive posture. The thug might have been experienced in using violence, but he did not have the years of constant training Sirichai had undergone. Sirichai knew better than to underestimate his opponent. Angling slightly to avoid the slash, he stepped to the left to see how the thug responded.

Manny was quick. Sirichai had to give him that. The attacker pivoted on the balls of his feet and, stepping in, reversed the slash, this time aimed at Sirichai's face. Stepping inside the arc of the slash, Sirichai checked the swing with his right forearm, the chopstick still held in the grip of his right hand. His knee rose, driving powerfully into the thug's floating ribs. It was the brutal knee smash that made Thai boxers famous. The man grunted as the air exploded from his lungs. He felt his ribs crack, and his back arched in pain. It was all Sirichai needed. His right arm shot forward, then reversed, driving the chopstick into the thug's throat near the carotid artery.

Dropping the knife, the man clutched at the chopstick now protruding from both sides of his throat and collapsed to the floor, the gurgling sound emanating from him audible to the two other thugs, now standing in shocked silence.

Aldo recovered first. "What are you waiting for? Kill that son of a bitch!"

The younger thug hesitated. He was scared and wanted to run. But if he did and word got back to his gang, they would hunt him down and kill him. It would not be a pleasant death. So, sliding his knife from his hip pocket, he took a cautious step toward the man his boss had just ordered him to kill.

If I kill this asshole, I'll be in good with the boss, maybe even work for the sisters.

That was what he wanted, after all. Everyone knew how well the Baguinda sisters treated their top soldiers. He took another hesitant step forward, inching closer to his target. Then he paused. The man stood there, calm and relaxed; he seemed almost bored.

Almost like he already knew exactly what was going to…

The thug felt his knees grow weak as realization set in. He felt his bladder release. The wannabe soldier's face turned deathly white.

I don't stand a fucking chance. This man will—I'm already a dead man.

Dropping his knife, he turned and bolted from the restaurant. It's better to run away and hide on another island than die here.

Aldo also wanted to run, but for some reason, his legs would not cooperate. He stood frozen in fear as the man who'd been escorting the two girls walked over, bent down, and picked up the dropped knife. Aldo watched the man then approach to stand face-to-face with him.

Sirichai asked a question. "Who took the girls?"

157

Aldo hesitated. If he told this stranger who he worked for, the sisters would have him killed.

As if reading his thoughts, Sirichai spoke again. "Yes, whoever it was will kill you if they find out you talked. Tell me, quickly, or I will kill you here and now." There was no hesitation in Chai's words. Gone was the polite young man escorting two young women. In his place stood an angry and dangerous man.

There was no doubt in Aldo's mind that he had scant seconds to live. His mind began to race.

He'll kill me now if I don't tell, or even if he doesn't believe me. But if I tell him, I am dead anyway. Oh fuck. Shit!

But what if I tell him—and maybe I can get away, get to Thailand? There is a chance if I can get out of Manila.

Aldo made up his mind.

"The Baguinda sisters have them. Tony Salonga, the man with the gun, works for them. We were to grab them but not harm them. Somebody in Vietnam is planning to take them back, I think. I don't know for sure."

"Who in Vietnam ordered this kidnapping?"

"I do not know for certain, but a powerful man, a government official, sometimes sends shipments of young Vietnamese girls to Manila. The girls come on cargo ships in containers. Some go to work for the Baguinda sisters, and the sisters sell some to other countries—mostly the Middle East, South Korea, or Mexico. Sometimes, the US. But there hasn't been a shipment in a long time. There are some problems in Vietnam, I think. That is all I know; I swear."

"If anything happens to those two girls, I will hunt you down and kill you if it takes the rest of my life." Sirichai lowered the knife and turned to walk away.

Aldo's eyes grew wide as his mind processed those words. He remembered the stiletto in his hip pocket. He could still kill this man, and then he'd be set. Who'd fuck with him after killing such a formidable opponent? His right hand went for the knife and closed around the grip. His thumb hit the button.

The noise of the spring-loaded blade was loud in the charged atmosphere of the empty Korean restaurant. Sirichai pivoted on the balls of his feet as his right arm whipped back, the knife sliding smoothly from his grip to bury itself in the thug's abdomen with a quiet thud. Aldo dropped to his knees in shock, then slowly collapsed, rolling to his left side on the tile floor where he lay still.

Sirichai stood there momentarily gazing down at the dying man, and then his thoughts turned to Jum Y and Xuan. *They will be terrified.* He remembered that the man he just killed had said they were not to be harmed.

There is still a chance.

The sound of approaching police sirens interrupted his thoughts; it was time to disappear.

I need to call Quan.

Quickly, he ran out to the front of the restaurant and noted the van's tag number.

Probably stolen, but you never know.

159

Sirichai hurried back into the restaurant, passing through the kitchen and into the alley. Turning away from the main street, he continued down the alleyway and turned right at the next narrow street. He had no sense of where he was but needed to distance himself from the restaurant.

Walking a few more blocks, he turned left. Four blocks later, he came upon a small park with benches scattered among the trees and shrubs. Cutting through the park, he crossed to an intersection of several streets where a tuk-tuk driver sat in his three-wheeled taxi, eating a late dinner. Sirichai approached the driver and raised his hand questioningly. The man nodded. Sirichai climbed into the tuk-tuk and, speaking English, requested a nice hotel. The driver nodded and fired up his taxi.

Taking his cell phone out of his jacket pocket, Sirichai punched the speed dial button for the office back in Thailand. Quan would not be happy. He was furious with himself as well. He'd failed to protect the girls. But there was a chance, at least according to that thug he'd killed, if they acted quickly enough.

As the phone rang, Chai's mind returned to Jum Y and Xuan. He must get those poor girls back.

Ending the call with Salonga, Blessica set the phone on the kitchen table. She went to the coffee maker on the counter and freshened what remained in her mug. Salonga had relayed great news. They now had the two girls who would soon be at their warehouse on the river.

Trán would be happy, and it was good to keep him that way. He was a powerful man in their circles. Blessica would never admit to anyone that she feared Trán, preferring to say it was wise to have a healthy respect for him. On the other hand, Mahalia seemed, at least to Blessica, to be fearless, almost to the point of recklessness. That sometimes caused friction between the sisters, but neither of them ever let that show before their gang members. With coffee mug in hand, Blessica called for her sister.

She found Mahalia in bed with a Cambodian girl who'd ended up in Manila after answering a job advertisement for a nanny position in Dubai. The disillusioned girl quickly discovered that Dubai was not going to happen.

Blessica attributed her sister's preference to their short-lived period of captivity and forced prostitution as teenagers. Mahalia often chose one of the girls who caught her eye and kept her around for a few weeks. The girls, learning the alternative, never seemed to object too much.

Blessica had never felt an attraction for another woman, but she could understand how their captivity as young girls might have had a powerful, long-term effect on Mahalia.

The twin sisters were born in Marawi City on the island. While still in their early teens, they were both kidnapped by a gang of Muslim terrorists who tortured and sexually abused them, keeping them in their camp to serve as prostitutes. The terrorists, however, did not account for the fact that growing up in Marawi City, Blessica and Mahalia were no strangers to violence. Early one morning, they managed to kill their guard and escape into the jungle. Hiding there for several days, they both survived and eventually returned to Marawi City. Their family, fearing they would not be safe, helped them make their way to the island of Luzon, where they moved to the Tondo area of Manila, living with a distant cousin of their mother. Unfortunately, Tondo was rough, and their mother's cousin did not have much.

The sisters founded Dalawang Mga Ate Na Mafia during the late 1990s, in the Tondo area of Manila. On their arrival in Manila, they'd assumed the last name Baguinda. Blessica had chosen it after seeing a reference to Raja Baguinda, a religious teacher from Sumatra who taught Islam on the island of Mindanao from 1390 to 1460. Resorting first to petty theft and prostitution to survive, the teen girls quickly learned to take other desperate young girls in, adding them as prostitutes to what was fast becoming a gang.

The sisters quickly promoted themselves to bosses and stopped taking clients themselves. Both girls were now hard as nails. Sadly, Mahalia developed a sociopathic lack of concern for anyone besides herself and her sister. Blessica had even begun to believe that her sister enjoyed killing, and Mahalia had become quite good at it. Because of this, they had few problems handling clients who became abusive or refused to pay. Over time, young men attracted by free sex and easy money began to serve as muscle for the sisters. As a result, the gang grew and expanded.

Despite the nature of their business, Blessica and Mahalia fiercely protected their girls. It became understood on the streets of Tondo that if a girl had to work as a prostitute, Dalawang Mga Ate Na Mafia was the gang they wanted to work for.

Of course, there were always those who caused problems. Those girls disappeared, sold off, and shipped to brothels in other corners of the globe. As more politicians and celebrities became clients of girls run by the gang, their wealth and influence grew. Eventually, the sisters were approached by a powerful government official from Vietnam named Trán.

"Mahalia, if you can pry yourself away for a few minutes, I just got word from Tony. They have the two girls from the airport and are headed to the warehouse with them now. Three of his men are taking care of the girls' bodyguard; they will dispose of the body."

Mahalia kicked the girl away and sat up in bed. "That is wonderful news. I will get dressed, and we can go to the warehouse. I want to get a look at these two. It is not very often we have such important visitors. I'll be just a minute."

Blessica sat in the oversized chair near the balcony window as her sister ran into the bathroom to shower.

163

She looked over at the girl, who was now covered and lying on the bed. She had once asked her sister what she did with these girls when she grew tired of them.

Mahalia smiled. "I set them free."

Blessica did not know exactly what her sister meant by that, but she doubted Mahalia's ability to let them go. It was not in her nature.

A few minutes later, Mahalia emerged from the bathroom and started pulling on some clothes.

"Have you heard about your American fighter? Taylor?" she asked, pulling on a pair of tennis shoes and bending over to tie the laces.

"I heard they beat him to death in an alley behind that old club in Mabini. Nobody has seen him since that night."

Mahalia looked up from tying her shoes. "You didn't go watch?"

"No, I did not go."

"I would have loved to see that!"

Blessica turned away. *I am sure you would have, sister.*

The ride in the van took about twenty minutes. Both girls remained silent as they lay on the floor in the back. The men had used zip ties to bind their hands and ankles. Still in pain from the blow to her abdomen, Jum Y had her eyes open, glaring at the man sitting, leaning against the van's side. Xuan fixed her eyes on Jum Y. She was terrified but somehow seemed to draw strength from the look on Jum Y's face. If Jum Y could be brave, so could she.

Or at least I can try, Xuan thought.

The van made a final turn and came to a stop. There were voices, and something sounded like a big garage door sliding open. The sound stopped, and the van drove forward several more yards before it again rolled to a stop. The girls heard the door closing.

The driver killed the engine, and the two men in front got out. The van's side door slid open, and both girls were pulled out, then dragged across the concrete to a small room where they now lay on the floor. The door slammed shut, followed by the sound of a bolt sliding into place. The two were finally alone.

It was dark. Precious little light passed through the two filthy windows high on the wall behind them. Xuan could barely distinguish Jum Y's form on the floor a few yards away.

"Jum Y," Xuan whispered. "Are you badly hurt? What is going to happen to us? Are they going to kill us?"

"No, they are not going to kill us. But I am afraid we might wish they had."

Xuan gasped, and Jum Y instantly regretted her words.

"Do not worry, Xuan. Sirichai and the others will come for us. You must be brave. We must stay alive. Hana and Dish will look for us, and they will find us. They have Quan and Carlos, too. They will find us because they are good at what they do. So, we must be strong and survive until they get here."

Xuan could not help herself; a quiet sob escaped her. "They killed Sirichai."

Jum Y closed her eyes to concentrate. Her mind could not see it.

"No, they did not. Chai killed them, and he is looking for us now. Xuan, you must be brave. I have survived this before, and I can do it again. You must do the same."

There was silence for several seconds. Then Jum Y heard Xuan's voice, quiet but determined.

"Yes, I will be brave."

The driver nosed the C-Class Mercedes-Benz 180 out of the condo's parking level and into traffic. Once on the street, he headed toward the warehouse near where the Pasig River opened into the Bay of Manila. In the back seat, the two sisters quietly rode for several minutes. Finally, Mahalia spoke.

"I am sorry. I know you liked that American, Taylor. But he has no place in our world. You know that, sister. I cannot pretend to know what you saw in him, but you are my sister, and I care about you."

Blessica nodded but said nothing. *What did I see in him?*

He was a good fighter, even destroying that monster, Garcia. She also enjoyed the pleasure he gave her. She would miss that. But there was more than that. She knew Taylor was ex-military, and she had decided some time ago not just any military—some special operations branch or something. Despite his drinking, he had a way about him.

What had happened to him? How had he come to live like he did—hiding in the gutter?

He must have done something terrible.

Blessica had seen the pain and self-loathing in his eyes. Once, she accidentally dropped her guard and asked Taylor what had happened to him. He only shook his head and pulled her back over on top of him.

Blessica realized there was much more to the American than he wanted people to know, which intrigued her. And yet, she lived in her world; he lived in his; there was no way for the two to coexist. She knew that, of course. Perhaps at another time, in another place.

Things could have been different?

Finally, Blessica spoke. "It doesn't matter now, does it, Mahalia? Taylor is gone, and we continue. It is life."

Mahalia nodded. "Yes, sister, it is simply life." Mahalia turned to look out the window at the passing city. They had not yet found the body of her sister's American lover. She was taking no chances. She had people out looking. She would find him if the American was alive and rectify that situation. Her sister was too soft sometimes. She needed to be protected. Reaching over, Mahalia grabbed Blessica's hand, slightly squeezing it.

"Everything will be okay, sister."

Blessica nodded, then turned to gaze out the window at the city from her side of the big black car.

Finally, the Mercedes turned down a side street near the river and stopped at a large door. The driver sounded the horn twice. A few seconds later, the door began to rise, and the driver pulled the sleek Mercedes into the warehouse. Once inside, he cut the engine.

When the big door opened again and a second vehicle entered, Xuan sat up against the wall. The big door did not close this time, and the room was a bit lighter.

Glancing around, Xuan noticed Jum Y was no longer lying on the floor near her.

"Jum Y?" Xuan whispered—the reply came from shadows to her left.

"I am here."

"What are you doing?"

"Just checking out our accommodations."

The attempted levity was not lost on Xuan.

"Well, they suck."

It was clear to Jum Y that Xuan was terrified. Searching her feelings, Jum Y realized that, for some reason, she was not afraid. That surprised her. Instead, she realized that she was furious. She had been given a second chance at life, and these people, whoever the hell they were, were not going to take that from her.

Jum Y half-crawled and half-slid over to where Xuan was sitting against the wall.

"They will find us, Xuan. Hana will find us. She will bring Dish, Quan, Vivas, and others. Maybe JD will come. Sirichai will know who took us. We must be strong until they can find us."

"But, what if Sirichai is dead?"

Jum Y paused to consider this, only for a moment. "Chai is alive."

"How do you know?

"Trust me, Xuan. I know. I feel it in my heart; he is alive. He will make one of them talk, and he will get help. They will find us."

"I hope you are right, Jum Y. I am so scared."

"I'm scared too, Xuan, but stay strong. Don't let them know you are afraid. Our friends will come."

Hearing the bolt slide in the door's lock, the girls shifted to see who was coming in.

As the door was flung open, their eyes struggled to adjust to the sudden light. Two figures stepped into the room, followed by a third. As Jum Y's vision cleared, she saw that the first two were female. The third was the leader of the men who kidnapped them—she'd heard someone in the van call him Tony.

The two women approached the girls on the floor while Tony remained close to the open door. The women gazed down at the girls. The expressions on their faces gave nothing away. To Jum Y, they looked to be not much older than she and Xuan.

"Well, well, what do we have here?"

"Two frightened little girls, Blessica." Mahalia glanced over at Xuan. "And that one is adorable."

"You already have one."

Mahalia smiled. "I can always set her free."

Blessica shook her head. "Trán wants these two alive and untouched."

"Oh, I won't damage her."

While neither Jum Y nor Xuan spoke Tagalog, they had both heard the name Trán. They looked at each other, shocked and wide-eyed.

"No need to worry, at least for now." It was Blessica, who spoke in English. "Trán wants you both unharmed. He wants you both back in Vietnam, where he has plans for the two of you."

Xuan shivered but struggled to keep her face looking calm.

Jum Y forced herself to laugh. "I am not worried. Our friends will come for us. You are the ones who should be worried."

Mahalia laughed. "You have no friends here. And your bodyguard is dead."

"Are you sure?" Mahalia did not answer right away. Instead, she was gazing at Xuan, who was trying to appear brave.

Blessica turned toward the door. "Tony, call your men. Make sure their friend is dead."

Tony nodded and retrieved his cell phone from his hip pocket. He called Aldo. The phone rang, but there was no answer. Then, he tried two more crew members with the same result.

Mahalia did not look happy. Glaring at Tony, "Go find out what those idiots of yours are doing. They better not be screwing around on my time. If they are, they'll all wish they were dead."

Tony turned and left right away.

Mahalia saw Jum Y smiling. "It is nothing. Tony's men are just having some fun after killing your friend."

"Maybe."

Blessica spoke up. "Should we send these to the island?"

The gang kept an active holding area on Mindanao, where they stored troublesome girls before sending them off to other buyers in Asia and Mexico. The camp had formerly belonged to the gang that had kidnapped them. A couple of years after their escape, they returned with some hired help and exacted terrible revenge, taking the camp for themselves. There had been no survivors.

"No, we will keep them close by. Trán will be ready for them in a few days."

Blessica looked at her sister. "Why are we keeping them here? That is not a good idea. It will be too risky, too tempting for some of the men in our gang."

"No, our apartment has a spare bedroom with a bath. We can keep them there. It is much nicer." She smiled at Xuan. "And they will be handy should we need them for some reason."

Blessica rolled her eyes and shook her head, then turned to leave the room. Mahalia pulled a butterfly knife from her hip pocket and cut the zip ties binding the girls' ankles, first for Jum Y and then for Xuan.

"Can you walk?"

Xuan nodded. The ties hadn't been tight enough to cut off circulation; just sufficient to prevent them from attempting to escape.

Reaching down to grasp one of Xuan's hands, Mahalia helped her to her feet. Then, keeping her grip on Xuan's hand, she pulled her toward the door. "You, too; let's go."

Jum Y struggled to her feet and started toward the door after Mahalia and Xuan.

Mahalia led the two girls toward the sleek black Mercedes where Blessica waited. She glanced back at Jum Y, who was following. "This way, now. If you two girls don't mind sharing a bed, we do have some much better accommodations for you. At least it's a king-sized bed. You will have plenty of room."

Leaning in, Mahalia pressed her lips close to Xuan's ear. "You don't mind sharing your bed with another girl, do you?"

Keeping her eyes pointed straight ahead, Xuan did not answer. However, she could not stop the involuntary shudder running through her body.

Feeling Xuan's reaction, Mahalia laughed as she shoved her down and into the back seat of the Mercedes.

.

CHAPTER 18
Thailand

Quan sat at his desk in Club Obsessions' security office. Hana had confided in him that she wanted to sell the club. She had then asked him to run the Thai branch of Spring Lotus. He'd spent the last forty-five minutes reviewing paperwork that would make him the director. There was a lot of work to do.

Dish and Chanmali were already working for the foundation. Dish would locate kids needing help and get them to Thailand. The network he'd created during his many years as a gun smuggler was a tremendous asset. Chanmali ran the dormitory where the kids would stay during their time in Bangkok; she also covered the front desk. Unfortunately, Hana had not found the time to hire a replacement for Benh. Nobody talked about it much, but her death still haunted them all.

Quan had immediately accepted Hana's proposal. He liked the idea. Sure, he loved his work at the club, but he also had to admit that he was not getting any younger. Besides, the idea of helping kids like Jum Y, Xuan, Hao, or Behn, appealed to him. It was something that would be truly meaningful. He'd certainly always protected the dancers at Obsession, but this was something more, something better.

The cell phone on his desk rang. Quan glanced down and recognized the number.

"This is Quan." He listened briefly before cutting off the man on the other end. "Hold on, just a second." He grabbed a legal pad and pen, shifting the phone to his left hand.

"Sirichai, slow down. I want you to start from the moment you stepped off the plane. Leave nothing out."

As the tuk-tuk navigated the streets of Manila, Sirichai collected and organized his thoughts, then started over, relaying what had transpired in painstaking detail. Quan listened intently and started jotting down essential information on the legal pad, only occasionally asking a question for clarification.

When Sirichai was finished, Quan spoke. "This is not your fault, Sirichai. None of us suspected trouble during the flight to America. If you had not left the airport, they would have had to do something there and probably had orders to kill you and the girls—quicker, cleaner, and easier to get away with." Quan paused, letting his brain process the information Sirichai had given him. "What's done is done. Now, we must decide what we will do next. Are you injured?"

"No, I am okay."

"Good. Have the driver take you to the Manila Hotel. We know that place. Wait in the bar. Have a drink. I will discuss this with Hana and call you back within the hour. Meanwhile, I want you to get a map of Manila and begin laying out what happened and where; familiarize yourself with the city as much as possible.

As you said, the van's tag was probably stolen, but we have some contacts in Manila. I will have them dig up what they can.

The incident at the Korean restaurant will most certainly be on the news. Watch the local news reports and look for any possible identification of the men you eliminated.

Also, I want you to gather as much information about these Baguinda sisters as possible—facts, theories, gossip, rumors, anything. Got that?"

Sirichai affirmed that he did.

"Okay, I will talk to Hana. I am sure some of us will be headed that way soon. Wait for my call."

"Yes, sir." The call ended.

"Hung!"

Hung stuck his head in the door to Quan's office. He had taken to hanging around the lobby as a precaution against further trouble. "Yes, Boss?"

"Are Vivas and Hana back from the US Embassy yet?"

"Vivas just checked in. They are on their way. Is something wrong?"

Quan looked up at Hung. "Xuan and Jum Y have been kidnapped."

Hung suddenly felt sick inside. Then, just as suddenly, the feeling was gone, and Hung was all business. "What do you want me to do?"

Have Chanmali call Hana's father and ask him to get over here as quickly as possible. If Slim is still around, have him bring Slim with him. Then, go get Dish."

Hung nodded, and his head disappeared from the doorway.

Quan met Vivas and Hana in the lobby of Spring Lotus with the bad news. Both listened as Quan explained the situation Sirichai had relayed to him.

"Shit!" It was all Vivas could say.

Hana remained surprisingly calm. "Where is Sirichai now? Is he alright?"

"Sirichai is okay. He is waiting for further instructions at the bar in the Manila Hotel. I told him I'd call him back within the hour. That was twenty minutes ago."

Hana nodded, thinking. "Where are Dish and my father? Is Slim still around?

"Chanmali called your father. He and Slim are on the way. Hung went to get Dish. They should all be here shortly."

"Okay, good. Have Chanmali call the Manila Hotel. Have her talk to the manager and use my name. I have stayed there several times on business trips. It is a clean location, and my father has some connection with the owners. Have her reserve," Hana did a quick calculation, "eight rooms. If I remember right, that should give us an entire wing on one floor. If it's more than eight, that's okay. Just have her get an entire wing. They typically keep a few wings open for large private business groups, even when they say they are booked. Have them move people to other rooms if necessary; we will pay for any inconvenience. Have Chanmali put Sirichai in one of the rooms closest to the elevators."

She turned to Vivas. "Does that sound okay?"

Vivas nodded. He saw Hana's look. "We're heading to Manila." It was not a question.

"I will call the airport and book a charter flight." She turned to Quan. "Will your old friend let us use his airstrip?"

"No problem." Quan had an old comrade from his days in the Thai Special Forces who, now retired, ran a charter air service, flying tourists to surrounding islands from a small airstrip about forty-five minutes from Manila.

Vivas spoke up. "I'll start getting things ready." He turned to Quan. "You will fill me in on anything I need to know?"

"When everyone is here, we will all meet in the conference room. I will send Hung up to get you."

"Right." Vivas started toward the elevator and the small apartment he and Hana shared on the building's third floor."

Hana completed the call to the charter airline service, and there was no problem. She was, after all, a frequent customer. She leaned back in her chair and let her head rest against the wall behind her.

She could not believe the girls had been taken. *These people don't know when to stop. How much is enough?*

Hana had lived on the edge for many years, but there were lines she would never cross. Since meeting JD and helping him get his mother out of Vietnam, she'd been reevaluating aspects of her life. The words JD had spoken to her that night, sitting on a bench in Dish's remote little mountain village, had changed her perspective in ways she couldn't have imagined. Then, meeting Carlos had been another game changer.

There was a quiet knock at her door.

"Come on in."

It was Dish. "Can we talk now, Hana? It is something important."

"Of course. Have a seat."

Dish looked tired. Hana figured he had to be at least in his late seventies, but even Dish was unsure how old he was. The Jarai and other Montagnard tribes had very few records of anything since the war in Vietnam. "What's on your mind, my friend?"

Dish was three times Hana's age, and the two had a long history going back to her father and Major Anurat, smuggling guns to anti-communist rebels in Vietnam.

Dish sat down. "You are okay, Hana?" He could see the pain and anger in her eyes. "I will be quick. I am happy here. Chanmali is happy here. Spring Lotus is our home."

"I am so pleased you and Chanmali are here. You are both like family to me."

"Thank you. All the time, I think about poor Benh. She was a good person. She was also … family."

Hana understood how the old warrior felt. Dish had never gotten over Benh sacrificing her life for his. Benh had died in his arms, referring to him as "uncle" and telling him that God—a God Benh had never believed in—had told her to go back and save him. It was the first time Hana ever saw the stern old man with tears in his eyes.

Dish continued, speaking in his usual quiet manner. "I think this will not stop while Trán and Fong are alive. I must go to Vietnam and kill them."

Hana was stunned. "Dish, you mustn't. You are getting too old for this kind of thing. Think of Chanmali."

Dish lifted his hand to stop Hana. "Chanmali and I have talked. She agrees. It is to protect her as well. I hope to return, but I must do this. I have thought this since Benh died; it is the only answer. I have talked to people in my village. They are already watching Fong, asking questions, and preparing. I have the beginning of a plan. It should succeed with help from two good men, and maybe a little help from the God who talked to Benh." A great many Montagnard people were Christian, but Hana had never heard Dish even mention God, not before Benh's death.

"Two good men?"

Dish nodded. "I want to ask your father and his friend, Slim, to help. I believe we will succeed, and they will come back." Dish looked down at his hands, which he held out before him. "They have the skills I no longer possess at my age. My hands are too old. Of course, Mai's son or your Carlos could help, but Mai's son is in America, and Carlos will go with you to rescue the girls, as he should."

Dish smiled. "You are his woman. He is your man. It is good. Like Chanmali and me."

Hana sat back. She had not expected this. She'd figured Dish might want to go to Manila with her and Carlos, but she'd not expected he'd hatch his own solution to the continuing problems created by Trán.

"You are telling me you want to go to Vietnam to kill Trán and Fong, and you want to take my father and Slim with you?"

Dish shook his head. "No. I am going to Vietnam to kill these two criminals. I am only asking you if I can ask your father and his friend, Slim, to help. If not, I can ask Anurat for help. But I think your father and Slim are more, how you say, professional."

Hana sat in silence for a few seconds before answering. "I believe you are right, Dish. My father and Slim are professionals, like JD and Carlos. I will not tell you not to ask them. They will do what they think is best, regardless of what I think. They can speak for themselves. I only ask that you do everything possible to ensure you all return here safely, unharmed."

Dish nodded, then stood to leave.

"Dish."

He turned back.

"I will talk to my father for you. But I think Major Anurat can also help with a few extra men if you think they are needed, or maybe assistance getting the three of you back out of Vietnam. That extra support might not be a bad idea."

"Yes, Hana. That is so."

About thirty minutes later, Hana sat with Carlos, Quan, and Dish in the small conference room, each lost in their own thoughts. Finally, Chanmali poked her head in long enough to inform them that Hana's father had just called. They were close and would be there in a few minutes.

About ten minutes later, Hana's father, Rick, entered, followed by Slim. Both men took seats at the table.

Rick spoke first. "What's happened?"

Quan looked up from the fingernail he'd contemplated for several minutes and answered. "I received a call from Sirichai about an hour ago. It is not good. Jum Y and Xuan have both been taken captive in Manila."

"Shit!" Rick glanced over at Hana, then back at Quan. "What do you know?"

"They had a five-hour layover at the airport in Manila. The girls wanted to go into the city to eat rather than dine at the airport. Jum Y talked to a man at the taxi stand who recommended a nearby place. He advised them to use one of the official airport taxis because they were safer. Sirichai was against it at first, but the guy seemed honest and offered sound advice, so they went." Quan paused, then continued. "Somehow, they were waiting for the girls."

"Son of a bitch!" Rick exclaimed. He and Carlos looked at each other.

"The kid at the airport?" Vivas asked.

Rick nodded.

"We can worry about that later," Quan stated. "The guy Jum Y spoke to at the taxi stand showed up at the restaurant while Sirichai and the two girls were eating. He had two men with him. Sirichai started the girls toward the kitchen and moved to cover their exit, but three more men, one of whom appeared to be their leader, came in through the kitchen and cut them off. At least one, the man who appeared to be the group's leader, had a handgun. He took the girls."

"Damn!" Slim muttered. "This was certainly a planned grab."

"The leader ordered the other three to kill Sirichai, ditch the body, and call in once they'd finished."

Rick sat back in his seat. "It sounds like Sirichai is not dead?"

Quan shook his head. "Sirichai killed two of them; another wet his pants, dropped his knife, and ran off. Before Sirichai killed the last kidnapper, he extracted some information from him."

"What do we know?" Rick asked.

"There is a gang run by two sisters. The two go by the last name Baguinda. They had the girls snatched on the orders of someone in Vietnam. The girls are to be unharmed and held until someone comes from Vietnam to retrieve them."

Hahn looked over at Vivas, who nodded. "Trán"

Dish spoke up. "It must be this Trán." He glanced over at Slim. "You were right, my friend. We must kill him and Fong if we want this to end."

Slim nodded. "So, what's the plan now?"

Hana answered. "I got Sirichai a room at the Manila Hotel. He is uninjured and, at Quan's direction, is digging up all he can on these Baguinda sisters and the men he took out during the kidnapping.

I've chartered a flight for Quan, Carlos, and myself. We will be in Manila later tonight. Quan has a former associate with a small airstrip out in the provinces, not too far from Manila. We will land there and then join Sirichai at the Manila Hotel. We will take those girls back."

Hana was wearing an expression none of them had seen before. Both her father and Vivas were concerned.

"Hana? Are you alright?" Rick asked.

"No, Dad. I am not fucking alright! I am terrified for Jum Y and Xuan. I am scared for all of us. But more than that, I am furious. We would have let it go after Trán's failed attempt at the club, but this Trán is either too evil or stupid to let this end. So, now we will end it for good. I want to start a new life with Carlos without this shit hanging over us." Hana paused, then added in a quieter tone, "Hell no, I am not alright…!"

Vivas reached over to take Hana's hand in his. "It's okay, Hana. You know I am with you to the end."

Rick considered his next words carefully. "I understand what you're saying, Hana. I do. But this is serious business. People on our side could get hurt too."

"I know that, Dad. But people on our side are already getting hurt. We can't just close our eyes and run away from this. These people must be stopped." Her tone was grim and determined. "Maybe now I understand why men like you, JD, Carlos, and Slim do what you do. I guess I am my father's daughter."

Slim turned to Hahn, laughing purposefully to break the tension. "That she is, boss. Okay, what do the rest of us do?" From Dish's earlier comment, he already suspected what was coming.

Hana turned to Slim. "Dish is going to talk to our old friend, Major Anurat. He plans to go to Vietnam to kill Fong and Trán. He asked me for permission to ask you, Slim, and you, Dad, to go with him. I guess I am asking for him."

Shocked, Hahn looked at his daughter; Hana met his gaze. "These people murdered thousands during the Vietnam War, including Mai's family and Dish's entire village. Then, years later, these same people kidnapped Mai. They prey on kids like Hao and Jum Y, and poison their people for profit. Finally, they tried to kill Dish and me, and murdered a harmless, mixed-up kid like Benh, who would not have harmed a soul."

There were now tears running down Hana's cheeks.

"Benh stopped dancing and was trying to make a better life for herself, working with us at Spring Lotus." She used her hands to wipe tears from her cheeks. "I'm sorry."

Nobody said a word.

Hana finished wiping her eyes. "These animals do not deserve to live. Their victims deserve justice, but we all know they will not get it from the Vietnamese government - or any other government for that matter. These animals will continue to enslave kids, poison people with drugs, and murder anyone who gets in their way. We cannot let them get away with all this. This is not about revenge. I believe that while they are alive, they will continue to come after us. The action we take now is for self-preservation."

Rick leaned back in his chair, silent. After a moment, he looked over at Dish. "Are you up to this, old man?" he asked quietly.

Dish nodded, his mind returning to Benh and how she died—taking a bullet meant for him—saving his life. He could not get her last words out of his mind. "You and Slim, just try to keep up with me, okay."

Slim leaned forward in his chair, resting his hands on the conference table. "I'm in."

Hana stood. "Okay, I have something to do. Then let's put our heads together and figure out how to make this happen."

"Where are you going, Hana?' Vivas asked.

"I am going to call Mai. She will be expecting those girls at the airport. Someone must tell her what has happened." She left the conference room and walked down the hall to her office. They heard the door close.

The men at the table remained quiet for several long moments. Nobody envied Hana having to make that call.

Finally, Vivas broke the silence. "Okay, then. How will you guys eliminate Trán and Fong without getting yourselves killed?"

CHAPTER 19
Knoxville, Tennessee

JD finished his last repetition of Seishin No Tomodachi. He was gaining immense respect for this kata. Developed by an old friend of his instructor, Sensei Tokumura, the kata demonstrated its creator's mastery of elegantly executed blunt-force trauma. Unfortunately, the kata's creator died several years ago, defeated by perhaps the one opponent he could not beat, even with his remarkable skill: cancer.

JD bowed out and whistled for Sophie, who was resting in the shade of a giant oak tree. The two started for the Jeep Wrangler parked in the gravel area about twenty yards away. JD brought Sophie to Lakeshore Park a couple of evenings each week, where they would play catch until she'd had enough. Then, JD would work on his Isshin-ryu kata or the Largo Mano Escrima he had picked up from his friend and former SEAL teammate, Vivas.

With her usual enthusiasm, Sophie loped to the Jeep, carrying her favorite squeaky ball.

"Place," JD commanded, pointing to the Jeep's cargo area. Sophie leaped up into the back and JD closed the gate. He had been working with Sophie for some time, although he'd decided to use English rather than Dutch. Ajax, his former SEAL K9 partner, had been trained to respond to commands in Dutch.

While JD still missed Ajax, he and Sophie had developed a terrific bond. Sophie was a German Shepherd; not quite as agile as Ajax, a Belgian Malinois, but she was equally intelligent and just as loyal as Ajax— and perhaps a bit stronger because of her size.

JD was now working with a local trainer to certify Sophie as a search-and-rescue dog. He felt this would be an excellent way for them to do some good together. Sophie loved the training and was making fantastic progress. They both had a great time doing it.

The top was off the Jeep, and JD reached in to give Sophie a scratch behind the ears, which she received with appreciation.

"Okay, girl. Let's have some supper. Ellen will be looking for us."

It was Friday, and that meant date night. JD knew Ellen had planned to make fried rice and homemade egg rolls for dinner. Then, the two planned to walk down to the Riviera Theater, share a large tub of buttered popcorn, and watch Marvel's newest movie release.

JD climbed into the driver's seat, turned the key in the ignition, and pointed the Jeep toward the loft he and Ellen shared on Gay Street. Leaving the park, he turned right onto Lyons View Drive and his mind turned to Jum Y and Xuan. If he remembered correctly, they should be getting into McGhee Tyson Airport sometime tomorrow. His mother was very excited to see both girls again.

Fifteen minutes later, JD parked the Jeep in his rented spot at the State Street Garage. He killed the ignition and, getting out, opened the back gate. Sophie jumped out, squeaky ball in her mouth.

"Heel." Sophie fell in at JD's left side. There was no need for a leash. Pressing the button on the key fob to lock the doors, JD led Sophie out of the garage and crossed State Street to enter the Woodruff Building from the backside. A few minutes later, the man and dog were in the elevator on their way to the apartment.

Unlocking the door, they entered. JD hung the keys on a hook as Sophie headed straight for her water bowl in the kitchen corner. JD followed behind to discover Ellen sitting at the kitchen table, talking on her cell phone.

"How's dinner coming, babe? Need any…?"

He stopped short, seeing Ellen's look. Something was very wrong. "What's wrong, Ellen?"

Ellen didn't respond right away. She was almost in a state of shock. Finally, she seemed to notice JD standing there, speaking to her. She extended the phone to him, her hand shaking. "You need to talk to your mother."

From Ellen's voice, JD knew that whatever it was, it was terrible.

Stepping closer to his wife, JD placed his left hand on her shoulder, and with his other hand, he took the phone. "Mom?"

While JD talked to his mother, Ellen got up and walked over to where Sophie was sitting, her soulful, brown German Shepherd eyes intently focused on JD. Sophie whined, also sensing something was wrong. Ellen stood and stroked Sophie's head, watching JD's demeanor transform for the second time in the last few days. A minute ago, he was a carefree young man walking happily into the kitchen. Now, Ellen watched as her husband slowly transformed back into the man she had seen that day in Niger, the man who'd risked his life as a member of the SEAL team who'd rescued her from Islamic terrorists. JD was again the stern, seasoned, professional warrior. It was a startling transformation that always scared Ellen a little. He set the phone down and slowly turned toward her.

"Mom told you?"

Ellen nodded. "What do we do, JD? Those poor girls."

JD took Ellen in his arms. For the moment, he did not know what to say.

Ellen already knew he was heading to the Philippines as soon as possible. "We have to do something."

"I know, honey. I know. Hana and Vivas are already on their way to Manila. One of Quan's men is already there. It will do no good to go charging in there half-cocked. This thing is outside my area of expertise. We need more information. We'll be no help to them charging in without a clue, but time is of the essence with something like this. Damn, I've got to think."

Now, who do I know that might be able to help? I could call General Ellington, I suppose.

Ellen sat down at the kitchen table and spoke, her voice quiet but firm. "Your mother is going to Manila. Hana has chartered a flight for her tomorrow. She didn't ask your mother to bring you, but I am sure she hopes you'll come."

"Yes, I will be on that flight as well."

"I know that, JD. And I'm going with you."

"What? No way, Ellen. It is way too dangerous, and you're…"

"Pregnant? Yes, you're damn right I am. So don't you mess with me! I waited here when you went to Vietnam, which was the hardest thing I have ever done. I know you are good at what you do, but I still worried about you every second you were gone, that maybe you'd get killed and I wouldn't see you again. I am not going through that again."

JD started to protest, but the look on Ellen's face stopped whatever he'd been about to say.

"Honey, I understand that you want to protect me, and I love you for that. But it would be best if you wrap your head around the fact that I am going. Hana has reserved a block of rooms at the Manila Hotel. I will stay there with her and your mother while you men do whatever you need to do. We can provide logistical support, strictly behind the scenes. And if something happens to one of you, I won't trust you to some Filipino doctor we don't know. I am sure there are good doctors there, but you won't know who is safe. I happen to be a damn good doctor, so I will be there—end of discussion."

JD didn't know what to say, so wisely, he said nothing. He instead set his mind to processing this turn of events, finally deciding Ellen might be right. She could stay at the hotel with Mai and Hana. It would be safe there, with security. Besides, having a doctor on the team could be beneficial, and anyway, he realized this was a battle he would not win.

"Okay, Ellen, you are right. Staying with Mai and Hana will be fine. I'm sorry."

Ellen nodded, saying nothing. She was frightened but determined. She'd decided on this course of action while she was still talking to his mother, before JD walked in the door. Ellen had realized she couldn't keep JD from going, and truthfully, she wouldn't have tried. This was the only viable course of action. She wanted to help.

Sitting quietly for a few minutes, Ellen studied her belly, now showing signs of pregnancy. She looked up at JD as he moved to stand behind her, placing his hands on her shoulders.

"It will be alright, Ellen. I promise. We just need a plan."

But what …? JD thought silently. He hated to admit it, but he was coming up empty. Of course, they would still head to the Philippines with Mai, but he hated being unprepared.

Just then, Ellen sat up straight. "Oh my God. I have an idea! Vicky!"

"Vicky?"

"Vicky Davis. She's a nurse in our office at the medical center. She knows your mother. I talked to her a few weeks back, and she told me how her church helps women start a new life. Your mom approached her about sponsoring Jum Y. She and her husband agreed. Vicky was so excited about meeting Jum Y."

"Okay. That's great, babe. But I am not sure this Vicky would have the needed information."

"Wait, JD. Listen. She was telling me about an organization called SIAM. This organization is a group of retired SEALS, special forces, police detectives, and other law enforcement folks who volunteer to find and rescue trafficking victims. Vicky was telling me this group has a pretty good track record. Her church has helped several women and children rescued by SIAM. Maybe they have information that can help."

"They just might."

Ellen grabbed her phone from the table. "I am Googling them right now. They must have a phone number."

A few seconds later, JD punched the number Ellen gave him into his phone.

A female voice answered. "SIAM, Jenny speaking. How can I help you?"

"Hello, Jenny. This is JD Cordell. I need some help. Two young ladies just went missing. Is there someone I can talk to right now?"

There was a short pause before Jenny spoke. "JD Cordell. I know that name. You are the SEAL with the dog who was in the news?"

"Ah, yes. That was me. Look, Jenny, this is kind of urgent. Two young ladies, one a good friend and one related to my mother, have gone missing in Manila. I need some information. Is there somebody there who might be able to help? I am looking for any background details I can get."

"Oh my God. I am sorry, and yes, you need to talk to my dad. Hold on, just a minute."

A few seconds later, another voice came on the line. "JD, this is Ed Weaver. How can I help?"

"Thanks, Ed. These two young ladies were flying from Thailand to the US. They're part of a pilot program to help kids rescued from bad situations start a new life. These two, Xuan and Jum Y, are from Vietnam. One is a relative of my mother's. The other one helped get my mother out of Vietnam when she was kidnapped. They disappeared during a layover on their flight, from the airport in Manila."

"Damn, JD. I'm sorry to hear that. I heard about your mother through some buddies of mine. I'm glad that the situation worked out as it did. I'm sorry to disappoint you, but we focus on rescues in the US. We've had several successes in Mexico and a few others in Canada, but unfortunately, the Philippines is a bit outside our area of operations."

"Understood. Can you tell me anything at all that will help?"

"Maybe. We do a prodigious amount of research. Several large gangs control most of the human trafficking in that part of the world. In the Philippines, most girls trafficked go to Asia and the Middle East; although lately, some have been coming into the US across the border from Mexico. Many end up in South Korea, where they are forced to work in clubs frequented by off-duty soldiers. Recruited as bartenders, mama-san takes their papers away once they arrive, and they quickly discover they will be serving up their bodies along with the alcohol. Typically, they live in rooms above the club and are only awarded a day off if they sell enough sex and booze. They are not allowed outside the bar unless escorted by Mama-san until they have learned to comply."

"Shit! How do you know all this?"

"It's an often-repeated tale. We have helped a few girls get a fresh start in the States. Twenty-two Filipino and seven Russian girls have escaped from bars in South Korea this year alone. Sometimes, soldiers marry them to help them get away. Most soldiers are ignorant of the trafficking. They're young, horny, away from home for the first time, and commanders do not educate their troops well."

"Damn, Ed. You're not kidding. I didn't know about this, but SEALs have a different operational model than most."

"Most people don't know, JD. This situation with these two girls sounds outside the typical trafficker's MO. They didn't recruit these two ladies; they were grabbed at the airport, correct?"

"That's right."

"This sounds like it may be something different," Weaver observed. These gangs have systems that help them stay under the radar, and they rarely stray from them. It helps them stay in business. Do these girls have anyone who would want to harm them? Someone in Thailand, perhaps?"

"No, I wouldn't think … Shit! Not Thailand, but maybe in Vietnam. We killed a nasty criminal rescuing my mother. He would have been well-connected. Damn it! That could be it."

"JD, that may be a good thing. If someone ordered them to be grabbed for revenge or leverage, that might keep them safe for a while. And you know, as I do, that

Asians have a lot of patience. They can take their sweet time with revenge. They like to savor it. You may yet have some time to help those girls."

"Perhaps."

"Listen, JD, I do know someone who might help. I'm a retired Green Beret. I served with this younger guy for a while and we became pretty good friends, but he shot a little girl in Afghanistan. He had no choice; it was an extremely fucked up but righteous shot. The problem is that it fucked him up badly inside, and he lost it. I tried to help, but …"

JD understood.

"Anyway, he's slowly killing himself in Manila. I still check in on him occasionally. He got tied into some underground fights and some bad people. One of them is a woman who calls the shots for one of the bigger gangs in the Tondo area. Two women run it—twin sisters, I've heard. I don't know if it's true or not. Anyway, I do know that this gang runs prostitution rings, which are, of course, tied to human trafficking. I am pretty sure he doesn't realize all that, not in his current state. Or maybe he is beyond caring. But, if you can get to him and convince him to help, he'd be a real asset. He would know exactly where to go and who to see. He was solid once. I think he's still a good man, just lost in a terrible place."

"What's his name?"

"William, William Taylor, but he goes by Bill. The last time I was there, he was living in Tondo, in a one-room

197

shithole behind a seedy little bar. I bet he's still there; he'd have little motivation to move. I have the address here somewhere. Let me find it and I'll text it to you. Is this number good?"

"Yes, it is. Thanks, Ed. You've been a big help."

"Wish I could do more, but coincidentally, I am leaving today, flying to Texas. I've been asked to assist with a task force created to stop some of this damn trafficking across our southern border. Hell, if it weren't for that, I'd damn sure go to Manila with you. Anyway, good luck, sailor."

'Thanks, Ed. I appreciate that. And good luck in Texas." JD hung up the phone. "Well, we know more now than we did. And we may have another asset in place—at least if we can find this Bill Taylor, and he's willing to help."

Sophie came up and pressed her nose into Ellen's lap. JD stroked the dog's head. Suddenly, an idea came to him.

"You know, it's a chartered flight into a private airstrip. We can take Sophie. She can stay at the hotel with you, Mom, and Hana." JD grinned. "Extra security. And she's becoming quite the tracker. So, she may come in handy as well."

"That's a great idea."

"What do you say, Sophie? Want to visit the Philippines?" Sophie wagged her tail and whined, as if to say, "Just try to leave me behind."

CHAPTER 20
Del Rio, Texas

Pallie collected his bag from the overhead bin and made his way off the aircraft, through the sky bridge, and out into the main concourse of Del Rio International Airport. He was traveling light, informed by Commander Elliot that everything he needed would be provided once he got where he was going.

Pallie's eyes scanned the crowd and spotted a man with a small hand-printed sign. The man had ex-military written all over him, and the sign he held had Palazzolo's name on it. He headed that way. The man saw him coming.

"You Palazzolo?"

"Yep. Who the hell are you?'

"The name's Riordan. I got orders to pick up some big lummox who'd be getting off this plane."

Pallie grinned. "Fair enough. Who told you that?"

"You'll find out soon enough. Follow me; I arranged some first-class transportation for us."

Pallie followed Riordan through the airport exit and into the short-term parking lot, where Riordan led the way toward an old, beat-up 1980s model Ford Bronco.

"You came in that?" Pallie asked incredulously.

Riordan laughed. "Don't let her looks fool you. Despite her rough exterior, she's a highly tuned beast. We will blend in with the cartel crowd, and she will kick their asses when needed. We've got several more just like her. Different makes and models, same idea."

Pallie nodded. As they got closer, he noticed a large decal on the passenger side of the rear hatch window. It was Wile E. Coyote, flashing his middle finger at anyone who happened to be behind them. It made him smile. "So, it's a camouflaged coyote insult vehicle."

Riordan laughed. "Yeah, you could say that."

Throwing his bag into the back seat, Pallie climbed in on the passenger side as Riordan fired up the engine. Pallie had to admit, the engine sounded badass.

"Where are we based, Laughlin?"

'That would be sweet, but nope. We're using some old private airstrip in the desert, about seventy-five miles out of town. From the looks of things, whoever owned it abandoned it some time ago. We bunk in the old office areas and have a hanger for storage. There's another building we will use to house anyone we can rescue. They've made it as comfortable as possible. And hopefully, any kids we rescue will be transported out quickly."

"What about any shitheads we capture?"

Riordan shrugged. "I doubt many will surrender, but if they do, we can truss them up and throw them in the corner of the old hanger."

"Sounds like delightful accommodations."

"Could be worse. The boss finally fixed the AC unit in our building. It got damn hot in there during the day; not too bad at night, though."

"We're getting spoiled as we get older. Comfort is suddenly important."

Riordan grinned. "Isn't it, though."

The two-hour ride passed quietly, with only occasional comments about the desolate nothingness that quickly surrounded them. Eventually, Riordan turned the Bronco onto an old dirt track that continued into the desert scrub. Twenty minutes later, some old buildings appeared on the horizon.

As they drew closer, Pallie could make out a hangar, then an office building off to the side. A few seconds later, he spotted what was once probably a large storage building behind the office structure. Several cannibalized aircraft of various makes and models lay abandoned along the runway.

Riordan pulled the Bronco up in front of the abandoned airstrip office building and killed the engine. Pallie opened the passenger door and climbed out. He stood there for a minute, gazing at the scrub brush stretching out for miles. The heat was stifling.

"Who in the fuck would build an airstrip out here in the middle of nowhere?" Pallie asked.

"The CIA, that's who," came a voice behind him. "It was once used as a base for clandestine operations in South America."

"Chief?" Pallie turned to see Chief Whitley in the doorway to the old airstrip office. Beside him stood a wiry, tough-looking older man wearing sandals, faded jeans, and a Batman T-shirt. The man's face reminded Pallie of old shoe leather.

Whitley grinned. "Good to see you, Pallie."

"What are you doing here, Chief? I thought you retired."

"I did, but Admiral Spence asked me to come down here and run this little chicken-shit outfit, so here I am."

"Who's the old guy in the Batman shirt?"

"This is Nantan Lupan."

"Who?"

"He's an Apache Indian. It means Grey Wolf or something like that. He goes by Tony."

"Okay, then." Pallie smiled and nodded in Tony's direction.

Whitley went on. "Tony is a former Delta operator who retired and then worked ten years for the border patrol. He knows this area like the back of his hand."

Pallie noticed the older man's eyes. They were dark, almost black. Pallie would have guessed the man was in his late fifties, but it was hard to say. Despite his age, those eyes were sharp and clear—the kind of eyes that miss nothing.

He sure looks like one tough old son of a bitch, Pallie thought.

So far, Tony hadn't uttered a word. His sharp eyes focused on Pallie, who found the man's silence irritating.

"Does Tony ever say anything?"

"Wise old Apache once say, it is better to have lightning in hand than thunder in mouth." It was Tony.

Pallie glanced back at Tony and chuckled. "I can't argue with that, Chief. Nice to meet you."

"You met Riordan, your chauffeur, of course," Whitley confirmed.

"Yep. He seems solid. Who else do we have?"

"It's a small team; all top-notch operators. We've got Ed Weaver, who's retired from Special Forces. Weaver runs his own private security company. His specialty is finding lost and abducted kids. The POTUS recommended him personally. Weaver is in the hangar, working on one of our trucks; you'll meet him soon enough."

Whitley turned back toward the office door and yelled, "Hey, WP, get your ass out here and meet our Sicilian connection."

A few seconds later, a well-muscled black man wearing jeans, flip-flops, and a white sleeveless T-shirt stepped out through the office doorway and walked toward the three men.

"Pallie, this is WP. One of those East Coast SEALs—a volunteer, just like you."

Pallie grinned. "WP, huh? What does that stand for?"

"Walter Pickle," the man replied without a grin. "I go by WP. So, if you insist on calling me Walter, Pickle, or Walter Pickle, you and I will have a 'come to Jesus' meeting."

Pallie laughed. "If you think you're tough enough. I do like a good scrap."

"Shit, growing up in Chicago's Washington Park with a name like Walter Pickle, you better be tougher than everyone else."

"Fair enough. How about just plain Walt?"

WP shook his head. "Nope."

Pallie extended his hand. "Okay then, WP. I'm Pallie."

Pallie then walked over and shook hands with Tony. Then he turned back to Whitley. "Is that it? You, me, Tony, Riordan, WP, and this Weaver guy?"

"We got one more guy coming tomorrow. His name is Eric Dewald. He's with Homeland Security, a drone and electronic surveillance expert. He's going to help us find these bastards. Go and get settled in. It will take a day or two to get used to this damn heat. Yesterday it got up to 102 fucking degrees! Once this Eric guy arrives, we'll start laying out an operational plan and go to work."

"Be nice to have Vivas and JD here."

"Yeah, well, Vivas is in Thailand getting married, and JD is probably still learning to cope with being married. I talked to JD several weeks ago. Ellen is pregnant."

"No shit? How about that, a junior JD."

"Scary," Whitley laughed.

As Whitley and Tony wandered off toward the old storage building, Pallie followed WP into the office building and dropped his bag near an empty cot. Then, deciding to check out the hangar, he left the air-conditioned comfort of the re-purposed airstrip office and crossed a sizeable sand-covered concrete area. As he entered the open bay door, a solid-looking guy was dropping the hood on a Chevy K5 Blazer. From its appearance, Pallie guessed it was an early 90s model.

"You Weaver?" Pallie called out.

"Could be. Who wants to know?"

"Name's Palazzolo. I go by Pallie."

Weaver looked up. "I've heard the name. You helped Cordell get his mother out of Vietnam."

"How do you know that?" Pallie asked, surprised.

Weaver shrugged. "Special ops is a small world, and I have connections."

"You know JD?"

"Not really. But JD called my office yesterday right before I drove out here. How's that for crazy? He needed some information about Filipino trafficking gangs in Manila."

"I wonder what that was about?"

"Two girls he knows got snatched in Manila on a flight layover. They were flying to the US from Thailand. I understand one is somehow related to his mother. I suspect he's headed to the Philippines as we speak."

Pallie stopped dead in his tracks. "What the hell did you just say?"

At that moment, Whitley stepped into the hangar. "I see you two have met." Then Whitley saw the look on Pallie's face. "What's up, Pallie?"

"Weaver here just said that he talked to JD yesterday. Mai's cousin, Xuan, and another girl got kidnapped in Manila. They were on their way to the US. Part of Hana's new project, I'd guess."

"Shit."

Weaver looked over at Whitley. "Sorry, Chief. I didn't connect you with Cordell, or I would have said something. The other girl's name was Jum Y or something like that."

Pallie's face said it all. He remembered Jum Y well. She was a brave young lady with a real scumbag for a father. So now the girl has a second chance, and this shit happens? Pallie stood there shaking his head. He needed to call JD and wondered how fast he could get to the Philippines.

Not fast enough, he thought. He'd have to get ahold of his commander and get permission or something. *What the fuck can I do?*

"Damn, Pallie! I can see it on that ugly mug of yours. You're ready to jump on the next flight to Manila."

Pallie stood there with his brain churning, saying nothing, as Xuan and Jum Y's smiling faces flashed across his mind.

Those poor kids. And here I am, stuck in damn Del Rio, Texas.

After a few seconds, Pallie shook his head. "You're right, Chief. I am. Or at least, I was. But this thing will be over, one way or another, before I can even get there. I would not want to be the sons of bitches who grabbed those two girls when JD gets a hold of them. If they hurt those girls, he'll take out every scumbag that was involved. I'm guessing Vivas will be with him, probably Hana's father, Rick. Maybe even Quan. That's quite a team right there."

Whitley nodded.

"Much as I want to be there, I know JD will handle it. So, I guess I'll stay here. We've got kids right here in the same damn boat, and if I can eliminate some of these trafficking shit birds, by God, I'm going to do it."

Ed Weaver spoke up. "JD thinks they've got some time, at least a few days. I agree with him."

"What do you mean?" asked Whitley.

"I just talked to JD yesterday. This kidnapping is a different situation. It falls outside the usual trafficking pattern of these gangs. JD thinks someone had these girls grabbed for revenge, maybe leverage, probably ordered by somebody in Vietnam, pissed off by the rescue of his mother. JD thinks these girls will be held and then returned to Vietnam."

Pallie and Whitley both wrapped their minds around this new information.

"Maybe…" Pallie had been on that rescue mission in Vietnam. It might just mean that Xuan and Jum Y would be okay, at least for a few days. "That does make sense."

Chief Whitley shook his head. "I hope so, man. You'd know better than I do."

"Shit!" Pallie exclaimed, turning and heading for the hangar entrance.

"Where you headed?" Whitley called after him.

"Got to call JD and wish him luck … and pray for those two girls."

Weaver and Whitley exchanged glances. They both understood exactly how Pallie felt.

CHAPTER 21
Thailand

Hana left her office and found Quan in the lobby talking to Chanmali, who now also worked at the front desk. After Benh's death, Xuan and Jum Y had offered to fill in until they left for the US. Since the girls' departure, Chanmali now split her time between the old hotel, which served as a dormitory, and the front desk at Spring Lotus.

Both Chanmali and Quan looked up as Hana approached. "How's it going, Chanmali?"

Chanmali smiled. "Just fine, Hana. I like to stay busy and I enjoy helping here."

"Well, I am glad. Let me know if it gets to be too much." Hana turned to Quan. "Do you have a minute? I want to discuss something with you."

"Sure, I want to talk to you as well."

Quan followed Hana into her office, and each took a seat. "I have a favor to ask you."

"What is it?"

Hana didn't answer immediately. She had a feeling he was not going to like it.

"We need someone to stay here and watch things at Spring Lotus and the club. We don't know what this Trán is planning, but we know he was behind the attack on the club, and if Trán had Xuan and Jum Y kidnapped in Manila, he must have a lot of connections."

"I agree."

"I also want someone here who can support my dad, Slim, and Dish if they need it in Vietnam. That can be handled much easier from here than Manila."

Quan nodded. He knew where this was going.

"I am asking you to do this for me. I understand you want to go with us, and we could use your help, but after what happened to Benh, I don't want anyone else hurt. I can't risk Dish, Slim, or Dad left hanging in Vietnam. Hung is very good, but he does not have the connections and organizational skills you have. Nobody else here can do that as well as you can. Carlos could, maybe, but he doesn't have your local connections. He would be at a real disadvantage."

Quan looked down at the floor, turning this over in his mind. He did want to get his hands on the thugs who had taken Jum Y and Xuan. Like everyone else, he had grown fond of the two girls. But Hana's request made sense, and he knew she was right. She was a great boss who had earned his respect long ago.

"I do want to go to Manila with you." Hana could tell he was struggling to keep his emotions in check. "I have grown very fond of those two young ladies. But, at the same time, I know you are in excellent hands with Vivas, and your plan makes sense. So yes, I will stay here to protect folks at Spring Lotus and the club. And I would be the person best able to help Dish and your father from here, if needed."

Hana had to smile. "And Slim, too?"

Quan grinned. "Okay. Slim, too."

"Thank you, Quan. It means a lot to me. And I know Dish will feel better knowing you will be here. He worries about Chanmali."

The sleek white Audi sedan pulled up at one of the charter terminals at Suvarnabhumi Airport. A Gulfstream G700 waited on the tarmac, its twin jet engines warmed up and ready to go. Dish climbed out of the passenger side and opened the door for Hana. Quan had popped the trunk, and he and Vivas were at the back getting their luggage. Quan grabbed two duffle bags and carried them toward the waiting jet. Vivas grabbed a third duffle and a suitcase, and moved them to the front of the car, where he set them down and waited for Hana, who was talking to Dish.

"Dish, you be careful, and watch over my father and Slim."

"Everything is good. I talked to Anurat. He will help if we need anything."

"Okay, just be sure you all return in one piece, please."

Dish smiled. "Yes. I promise. Chanmali will not be happy if I come back in many pieces."

Hana hugged the old Montagnard warrior tight, then turned and walked over to Carlos, who was waiting a few yards away.

"Are you ready, Hana?"

"Yes, Carlos. I am ready."

"Okay, let's see what this cool-looking jet can do." He picked up the suitcase and the third duffle bag. Hana stopped long enough to hug the surprised Quan, as well.

"Take care of things, Quan. Keep everyone safe."

"Yes, do not worry, Hana. We will all be here when you get back. I promise."

Hana slipped her arm into Carlos's, and the two quickly climbed the airstair to board the G700.

CHAPTER 22
The Philippines

When Mahalia finally ended the call with Salonga, she was furious. It was not the news she had wanted to hear.

That idiot, Aldo, was a pretty boy. He was too slick and too sure of himself. Then, when the time came—nothing. He let the girls' bodyguard get away, and worse, he'd gotten several men killed. He was lucky he was already dead.

I'd skin that little bitch alive.

Slipping her phone into the pocket of her jeans, she went looking for Blessica and found her sitting on the balcony of their apartment, sipping a glass of wine.

"That pussy, Aldo, fucked up. The bodyguard got away. He killed Aldo and two others. Tony's fourth man is missing; he probably ran away when the fight started. There's no sign the girls' bodyguard even had a scratch on him."

"That's certainly not good, but what can the bodyguard do? He is one man, alone in Manila. He does not know who or where we are. He could call people in Thailand, but what can they do?" Blessica paused, thinking. "He may try to leave Manila. Have our people watch the airports for him. We know what he looks like. Aldo got a picture of him at the airport before approaching the girls."

Mahalia nodded. "Yes, we will watch. I'd love to get my hands on him. He will pay dearly for what he has done."

"Well, if he so easily killed three of our men, he is very good. We must be careful. Or perhaps our men were no good, and maybe he did us a favor."

"Maybe. I don't care. I want blood for what he did. If I get my hands on him, I will have it."

"Maybe you will... I haven't seen that girl you had in a few days. Is she gone?"

"Oh, her? I set her free. I was getting tired of her."

"Well, I have seen you eyeing the one named Xuan. Remember, Mahalia, Trán does not want her injured. She is to be left alone."

"I won't hurt her."

"You know what I mean, sister. Leave her alone. We don't need any problems with Trán. He has been good for our business, but the man is ruthless. Trán is powerful; he has a long arm. We have seen this."

"I am not afraid of Trán. He is just another man. I can handle him."

"Perhaps. All the same, Mahalia, I am telling you to leave that girl alone."

Mahalia turned to face her sister and her voice turned cold. "You are not my boss, Blessica."

Jum Y lay on her side of the king-sized bed. Xuan was in the bathroom taking a shower. So far, they'd been well treated. They were well-fed and pretty much left on their own. Not long after being placed in this bedroom, their luggage showed up, so they even had clean clothes.

Jum Y did not like Mahalia's apparent interest in Xuan and had been waiting for something to happen. So far, it had not. She knew Xuan was also aware of Mahalia's interest, which frightened her.

Growing up in a tiny Vietnamese village, Xuan had not seen much of life in the broader world. In so many ways, she was naïve and innocent. It was one of the things Jum Y loved about her friend. Xuan reminded her of a happier time, when her mother was still alive, before her father sold her to a brothel to pay off his gambling debts.

So far, Mahalia had kept her distance. But Jum Y had seen the look in Mahalia's eyes when she looked at Xuan, and did not trust that predator to hold off much longer, especially if Trán's men were coming for them soon.

Xuan came out of the bathroom and put on clean clothes. She forced herself to smile.

"Well, I am still terrified, but I feel better."

"That's good. I think I will take a shower as well. I will only be a moment."

Just then, the door to the bedroom opened, and Mahalia entered.

"Ah, there you are, my little cutie. And freshly showered, as well. My timing could not be more perfect."

Xuan backed away, a mixture of fear and disgust on her pretty face.

Mahalia laughed. "Don't be frightened; I won't bite you, at least not that hard. I am in the mood for something sweet, and you are certainly sweet."

Xuan found her voice. "I will not go with you."

Mahalia laughed again. "Of course you will; you have no choice." A lascivious smile danced on her face. "You are quite pretty. I watched you shower. I have cameras, you know, for security. I must know what my guests are up to, after all."

Xuan gasped, taking another step back. "You are sick."

Mahalia grinned. "Oh, I don't think so. I know what I like. And I like you. I may tell Trán to go fuck off and keep you for myself. If you're good, eventually, I'll set you free." She was enjoying herself like this was some secret joke to which only she was privy.

"Now, come with me. You have nothing better to do for the next hour or so."

"Stay where you are, Xuan." Jum Y interrupted, speaking in a tone Xuan had never heard her friend use.

Mahalia turned to face Jum Y. "If you know what's good for you, you will shut your mouth, you little whore. Yes, I know what you were. If Trán didn't want you, we'd ship you to Mexico or South Korea."

Jum Y did not back down. She took a bold step towards Mahalia. "If you know that, then you know I survived on the streets of Ho Chi Minh City, you sick bitch. You will not touch my friend. I'll rip your eyes out and stuff them right down your nasty throat, right here and now. I may die but you will too. I promise you that."

Used to having the upper hand, Mahalia was stunned by Jum Y's threat. She reached for her hip pocket, then realized she'd left her knife in her bedroom. She'd not expected to need it in her apartment, where members of their gang guarded her and Blessica.

"Brave but stupid threats. I hold both of your wretched lives in my hands. Now, Xuan will come with me, and you will sit down and shut your mouth, or you will both be dead before this day is over."

Xuan was shocked by the look on her friend's face as Jum Y took another step toward Mahalia. It was the look of a lioness, ready to die to protect her young.

"MAHALIA!" Blessica stood in the doorway. One of the gang members was with her. "Mahalia, you need to leave now. I mean it. Right now."

Mahalia looked over her shoulder at her sister and scowled. Then her gaze returned to Jum Y. She smiled. "Another time, perhaps?"

"I'll be right here."

Before turning to leave, Mahalia looked over at Xuan and smiled pleasantly. "See you soon, my little dove." Then she left the room without glancing at her sister.

Blessica paused in the doorway for a moment, looking embarrassed. Finally, she turned to face both Jum Y and Xuan.

"I apologize for my sister's behavior. A guard will be posted outside your door until this is over." Then she turned and walked away, and the door closed.

Xuan stumbled over to the bed and sat down. She was shaking.

"Oh, Jum Y. What are we going to do? I was so scared. But you - you were so brave. I have never seen you like that."

"It is a part of me I haven't needed in a while, but we need it now."

Xuan shook her head in amazement. "I do not think I could have done that ... face her as you did. That woman is pure evil."

"Oh, I think you could, Xuan. You are braver than you think. You had the courage to leave your home in Vietnam for an unknown future in America. That took real courage too. I know you will do what must be done."

"Maybe, I am not so sure. Any courage I have is because you are here with me. I'm glad I was not alone with her. So, what do we do now?"

"Well, I am going to take my shower now."

"What? That crazy sister might be watching!"

Jum Y smiled a sad smile. "It won't be the first time a stranger has seen me naked."

CHAPTER 23
Knoxville, Tennessee

JD's phone began to vibrate on the kitchen table. He and Ellen were getting things together for their trip to the Philippines. In an hour, they'd leave to pick up his mother and drive to the charter terminal at McGhee Tyson Airport, where a jet was being fueled and prepped for the eighteen-hour flight.

JD grabbed the phone but didn't recognize the number. He pressed the green answer button. "Hello?"

"JD, it's Pallie."

"Pallie? What the hell, man! Sorry. I'm afraid you called at a bad time."

"Yeah, JD, I know. I volunteered for a mission hunting traffickers down here on the Mexican border. This guy, Ed Weaver, is here as well. He told me what's going on."

"I see. Then you know about Xuan and Jum Y."

"Yeah! That is fucked up. Listen, man. I figured you'd have this straightened out before I could even cut loose of this shit and get to Manila. So, I guess I'll leave it to you. I'm sure Vivas and Quan will be there too. Maybe even Hana's dad. You guys should be able to handle it."

"I hope so. I believe we can do this, that is, if we get there soon enough."

"Hey man, if anyone can, it's you. I know that. But look, if you need me, holler. Do you hear me? I'll go AWOL if need be. You get those two girls back. Do you hear me, JD? And the assholes who did this … take down a few of those lowlife savages for me. Okay?"

"I got you, Pallie. I got you. And Pallie…"

"Yeah?"

"Thanks."

"Shit. You're my brother, man. You need me, you call. That's the straight shit."

"I know, Pallie. Thanks."

"Well, I'm sure you have plenty to do. I'll get off here and see if I can help even the score. Stay cool, JD. I've seen what you can do."

"You too, Pallie. You stay cool as well."

The call ended just as Ellen came into the room.

"Who was that?"

"Pallie."

"Pallie? How is he?"

"He's worried, but okay. He heard about Xuan and Jum Y from Weaver, who I spoke to at SIAM. Pallie called to say good luck and told me to call if we need him."

"I doubt the Navy would let him come."

"They couldn't stop him if he thought we needed him."

Forty-five minutes later, they were loaded up and ready to go. They decided to take Ellen's Volvo XC90 to the airport. It had more cargo space than his Jeep because Ellen had ordered a car-top carrier when she bought it. JD would use it to secure his two duffle bags.

Ellen had quietly watched as JD went to the closet and retrieved a locked Pelican storage case. Opening the case, he first unloaded his Glock 19 G5 and checked the action. JD placed it, several magazines, and four boxes of ball ammunition in a ballistic nylon range bag. He slid the range bag into one of the duffle bags along with his Flesheater 9 in its specially designed mylar sheath. It could be carried in several configurations using several carrying systems. Ellen was familiar with the duffle bag JD referred to as his bug-out bag, and she'd teased him about it. He would smile and say, "Better to have it and not need it than to need it and not have it." Now, she understood.

She knew the duffle bag contained several bottles of water, a water purification system, and a collapsible water bottle. It also included protein bars, MREs, eating utensils, a small metal cooking pot, a P-38 can opener, and a compact cook stove. Finally, there were changes of utility-style clothing, gloves, a hat, a poncho, extra socks, shelter and bedding, fire-starting kits, and a well-equipped first-aid kit. It was an expert warrior's survival kit, the last item JD hoisted onto the car-top carrier. Sophie was already in the back of the Volvo.

JD turned to Ellen. "Are you ready, babe?"

Ellen nodded and got in on the passenger side, letting JD drive. He started the vehicle and headed toward his mother's house, about twenty minutes away. The ride was quiet, with both of them lost in their thoughts.

JD was simultaneously worried and amused. He had never started a mission like this, bringing his wife and mother along. It almost seemed surreal, and would be funny if it weren't so damn serious. He would have scoffed at the possibility of such a situation ever occurring. Yet here he was, doing precisely that right now.

Ellen, for her part, was trying not to throw up. She was suffering from a severe wave of morning sickness.

Oh great, she thought, *this couldn't have come at a worse time. If I have to throw up, JD will just have to pull over. That is all there is to it.*

When JD and Ellen pulled up, Mai was ready and waiting in the driveway with her two bags. JD had stopped once for Ellen on the trip, and she felt much better. As he loaded Mai's two bags into the car's trunk, Mai climbed in on the rear passenger side, where Sophie greeted her enthusiastically.

Managing a quick neck ruffle and hug for Sophie, Mai turned to Ellen. "Are you alright, dear?"

Ellen smiled. "I am now. I had some morning sickness earlier, but we got that settled on the way over."

Mai leaned forward to kiss Ellen's cheek as JD lowered himself back into the driver's seat.

"Everyone all set?"

Ellen and Mai both nodded.

"Okay, let's go."

Twenty-five minutes later, they were boarding the jet. The luxurious interior was unlike anything they had flown in. Mai made herself comfortable on a plush sofa in the forward club section of the cabin. Ellen and JD took adjoining seats across the aisle from her, and they all buckled up for take-off. There was no seat belt for Sophie, who had never flown before and was anxious, panting up a storm.

The take-off was smooth, and the Gulfstream G650 climbed quickly to its assigned cruising altitude of 36,000 feet. JD held Sophie's collar, petting and whispering until the jet leveled off and the ride was steady. At that point, Sophie relaxed, and JD released his hold on her collar. The dog immediately found a comfortable spot on the floor near Mai's feet.

All three stayed quiet for some time, each lost in their thoughts, worried about Xuan and Jum Y. Finally, Mai spoke up.

"I am so glad you are coming, JD. You and Carlos will be a big help to Hana and me in rescuing our poor girls."

"Thanks, mom. I am only coming along to keep you and Hana out of trouble. You two make quite a rescue team yourselves."

Sitting there, JD was thinking about their odds for success. He figured they weren't that good. However, JD never paid much attention to the odds. Odds did not matter in a situation like this. You did what you had to do to complete the mission.

His mother did not doubt they would get Xuan and Jum Y back. He had to admit, she was like a force of nature. When she set her mind to something, it usually happened, so there was a chance they might pull this off.

JD was reminded of a line by Louis L'Amour, one of his favorite authors, "There's no stopping a man who knows he's in the right and keeps a-coming." JD chuckled to himself. *I wonder if Louis L'Amour ever met my mother.*

He only knew of one time his mother had not achieved her goal: yesterday, when Mai tried to convince Ellen not to go to the Philippines with them. After all, she had the baby to consider. His mother had about as much success as he did, and eventually, Mai gave her efforts at persuasion up.

"What are you thinking about, JD?" Ellen asked.

"Nothing important, honey. Just letting my mind wander a bit to relax. Are you okay?"

"I've been thinking about men like you and Carlos. I am beginning to see what drives you. This thing with Xuan and Jum Y - what kind of people do things like this? I understand what you meant when you said the Navy could not stop Pallie if he thought we needed him. In a way, it is why your mother and I are also on this flight. I just hadn't looked at it that way before."

"Well, I never started a mission accompanied by my mother and my pregnant wife before, that's for sure."

Ellen laughed. "You've never had a pregnant wife before."

"True enough. You got me there. I admit it worries me, but I'm glad you're here."

Ellen leaned against her husband, resting her head on his shoulder.

When the travelers disembarked the Gulfstream after landing, it was raining hard. The runway was deserted except for one turboprop plane about thirty yards away.

Despite the rain, it was pretty hot. JD decided the rain felt good under the circumstances.

A large passenger van parked a short distance away, near the private airstrip's small office. A young man hurried toward them carrying a large umbrella and held it for the two women as they rushed toward the van. JD made several trips up and down the airstairs and was soaking wet by the time he had all the luggage offloaded. The man ran back and helped him carry the suitcases and duffle bags to the back of the van. After emptying her bladder, Sophie trotted over to the vehicle. Another figure stepped out and opened the door to let Sophie jump into the back. It was Hana.

With the luggage loaded and everyone in the van, the young man slid behind the wheel and started the engine. Hana sat in the front passenger seat and turned to greet everyone.

"Sorry about the weather, but the rain does help make the heat bearable, at least until it stops. I am so glad to see you. I wish it were under different circumstances."

Mai nodded. "We do too, dear. But we are here to help."

"Thank you, Mai. Ellen, it is nice to see you again. But you should not have come. You're pregnant."

JD cut Hana off. "Don't go there, Hana. It's been tried twice with no success. Besides, we may need a good doctor on our team. I certainly hope not, but you never know."

"I am here to help in any way I can. Being pregnant does not get in the way of that."

"Certainly not," Hana agreed. "I do understand and appreciate it."

Lastly, Hana turned to JD. "JD, thank you so much for coming. We can use your help. Carlos is here with me, but I asked Quan to stay behind to ensure the folks at the club are protected and to assist your uncle, Slim, and my father if they need it. This is Sirichai," indicating the young man behind the wheel. "He was escorting the girls on the trip. He is one of Quan's men and really quite good."

Sirichai scowled and barely glanced at the passengers. "Not good enough, it seems."

Mai and Ellen both saw the disappointment in the young man's eyes.

Mai spoke first. "Sirichai, I know what happened, and it is not your fault. You did your best, and you got two of those horrible men. And because you are here, we know who has them and why, which is a big help. You will help us get Xuan and Jum Y back. So, we are in your debt."

"I agree," JD added. "From what I understand, you had no reason to suspect an attack like that. It was a tough situation, and you were badly outnumbered. I don't know if anyone else could have done any better. And we are better off because of what you did and the information you got from that gang member." JD paused. "Put that guilt shit behind you and focus. We will need you to get those two girls back."

Sirichai glanced at JD in the mirror, then returned his concentration to the road before him. He knew how much his colleagues respected JD, and there had been no accusation on his face. Suddenly, the young man felt a little better.

JD turned to Hana. "I may have another asset for us. A former green beret here in Manila. He knows the local scene and has connections that may help us. I don't know if this man will help, but if he will, it may be a game-changer for us."

"That's great! Then, we must convince him to help. Carlos is out rounding up some equipment and supplies we may need. The man who owns this airstrip is with him. He is an older man, a friend of Quan. He knows his way around Manila and has worked with my father before. They should be back at the hotel by the time we arrive."

Finally finished cleaning the rainwater from her coat, Sophie sat up and whined.

Hana grinned. "And this must be Sophie!"

Arriving at the Manila Hotel, Hana motioned to a bellhop to transport their luggage to their rooms.

"We have the entire east wing of the seventh floor to ourselves. You must be tired and hungry after the long flight. The restaurant here is pretty good, unless you want to rest first."

"I don't know about Ellen or Mom, but I am more hungry than tired. We slept most of the flight," JD replied. Ellen and Mai both nodded in agreement.

"Okay, get some dry clothes, and we can meet in room 705. Carlos and I are in that room. Mai, you are in 707, and JD and Ellen will be in 708. Sirichai is in room 701. The other rooms on that wing are empty, and we are setting up our operations center in 704. Sophie is good to go. I have taken care of everything. Just let the bellhop know who gets which bags. No need to tip. That is also taken care of."

"Damn, Hana. You haven't changed a bit," JD laughed. "I see you have everything under control. But there is one bag I will take myself." He reached down and grabbed his bug-out bag. "Just some personal stuff."

Despite her smile, JD could tell that Hana was anxious. He knew she wanted to get the rescue operation underway. "What do you say we meet in your room in thirty minutes?"

"Yes! That sounds perfect. Thank you."

"Yes, that sounds great," Ellen added. "I am quite hungry." Ellen was looking forward to a decent meal.

"That's because you are eating for two, my dear," Mai observed before turning to Hana. "Did Dish come with you?"

Hana paused, unsure how to tell Mai what her stepbrother was doing. Dish was not a young man; she knew Mai would worry about him. JD, seeing the hesitation in Hana's manner, caught her eye and nodded. It was better to put all the cards on the table.

"Mai," Hana began. "Dish decided to return to Vietnam and his old mountain village, to talk to some of his folks. Do you remember Poh and Hai? Hoa has been staying there as well. He has devised a plan to take care of this other Trán and that corrupt policeman, Fong. Dish thinks that as long as those two are alive, this nightmare will not end."

Mai was shocked. "But Dish is much too old. You shouldn't have let him do this."

"Hana would not have been able to stop him, Mom," JD interjected. "You know Uncle Dish."

Mai was silent for a minute. "You are right, JD. I am sorry, Hana. I should not have said that. I do know my brother."

"You have nothing to be sorry for, Mai. I understand, and I am worried about him too. However, my father and Slim agree with your brother, and you will be happy to know they went with him. I trust they will keep each other safe."

JD tried to reassure his mother. "Uncle Dish is old but can still run circles around most men half his age. And I know how good Hana's father and Slim are. I'm sure they will be fine, especially with help from Uncle Dish's friends. Mom, Uncle Dish is probably the only one who can pull this off and get away. He has all the connections."

"I also told Quan to give Dish any assistance or backup he may need," Hana added. "Quan is very competent as well."

Mai felt better. "My brother will succeed. I am sure of that. I will pray that God watches over all of them."

Thirty minutes later, JD and Ellen knocked on the door to Hana and Vivas's room. It was 3:00 pm local Manila time, which meant 3:00 am back in Knoxville. JD didn't know if he wanted breakfast, lunch, or dinner. Ellen had already stated she wanted dinner. They knocked on the door and heard Carlos's yell, "Enter!"

Mai was sitting on the couch, talking to Hana. Carlos greeted JD with a huge grin. "Man, Am I glad to see you. But shit, you're going to be a father. You and Ellen should be home, especially with Ellen in her condition!" He then wrapped Ellen up in a big hug. "No offense, Ellen."

"None taken, Carlos. But I am only pregnant, not dying."

"Fair enough."

JD stepped up, placing his hand on Vivas's shoulder. "Hey man, I can't let you have all the fun. Besides, you helped me get my mother out of Vietnam. Me helping you now is just reciprocity.

"Pallie called me right before we flew out of Knoxville. He is tied up hunting human traffickers on the southern border. He learned about Xuan and Jum Y by talking to Ed Weaver, who is helping with that mission. Coincidentally, I'd spoken to Weaver the day before about this situation. Ed is retired Special Forces; and runs a private business rescuing victims of human trafficking. Ellen heard of his group through a lady who worked in her office. That lady and her husband also know my mother and had volunteered to sponsor Jum Y. I called Weaver to see if he had any wisdom to share, and then he ended up working with Pallie."

Vivas was amazed. "That's just crazy, JD. What are the odds?"

"Slim to none. Pallie sends his regards and says if we need him, yell."

Vivas laughed. "Good old Pallie."

"There's more. Weaver told me about a guy named Taylor, also ex-Special Forces. Taylor served with Weaver. He lives in Manila, where he's been slowly drinking himself to death. Weaver said the guy's head is in a pretty bad place."

"What happened?"

"Taylor was providing overwatch during some mission in Afghanistan and had to shoot some little Afghan girl. The girl's mother had put a couple of hot grenades in the girl's hands and sent her toward the other members of Taylor's team. I guess it screwed him up bad."

"Oh shit. That's tough. Not sure how well I would handle that myself. But how can this guy help?"

"Long story short, this Taylor has been screw…" JD remembered his mother only a few feet away "…ah, dating one of these Baguinda sisters. Weaver says if we can get him to help us, he will know where we need to go and who we need to see."

"No shit?"

"No shit."

"How do we find this guy?"

"I have an address."

"For real?"

"For real."

"After we eat, let's go talk to this Taylor guy."

"I think that's a great idea."

CHAPTER 24
San Francisco, California

Fifteen-year-old Latoya Jenkins walked briskly along the sidewalk, heading home from a friend's house after a long Wednesday night study session. They had a big test coming up on Friday, and Latoya wanted to do well. She had plans for her life.

A pretty girl, Latoya had inherited her mother's flawless dark skin and her father's green eyes. It was a striking combination. Latoya wore her hair in the neat braids her mother had worked hard at for what seemed like hours. She was a friendly girl, popular with her classmates. The boys loved her, and Latoya maintained casual friendships with several young men at school. However, she would not let herself get drawn into any relationship that might derail her goals.

After graduating from high school in two years, she planned to leave the stinking cesspool San Francisco had become. Her hometown was no longer the destination of tourists excited about the streetcars, Fisherman's Wharf, and sampling the many excellent restaurants with every kind of ethnic cuisine. Instead, because of incompetent local politicians piling one terrible decision on another, it was a city of homeless, needy, and desperate people. San Francisco's once-beautiful parks were now rag-tag tent cities, and far too many streets were strewn with rotting garbage, drug addicts' used needles, and human feces. As a result, businesses were leaving in droves. Latoya was getting out.

She had chosen to enlist in the US Navy, and wanted to get into intelligence. While in the Navy, she would get her degree in Cyber Security. Latoya knew it was a growing field and would be wide open for the foreseeable future.

That will be my ticket out of here.

She did not notice the nondescript white Dodge panel van turning the corner behind her, slowly keeping pace with her.

"Excuse me, can you tell me where the closest gas station is? We are just about out of gas."

Latoya stopped and looked. A young Hispanic girl was speaking to her from the open passenger window of the van. Latoya's father and mother had repeatedly warned her about talking to people she did not know. She hesitated, but the girl seemed friendly enough.

"Sure," Latoya responded. "About three blocks down, on your left is a BP station and convenience…"

She never completed the sentence. Grabbed from behind, someone huge lifted Latoya off her feet. One big hand covered her mouth. She tried to scream but could not. A second later, she was in the back of the van, where a hard blow to her stomach forced the air from her lungs. As she struggled to regain her breath, duct tape was quickly wound around her head, covering her mouth. Next, someone jerked Latoya's arms violently behind her back, forcing her down on her stomach on the floor of the van. Duct tape quickly secured her wrists and ankles. Terror set in, and she began to cry. A moment later, the Hispanic girl was beside her on the floor.

"I'm sorry! I'm so sorry! I had to—they said they'd kill me."

"Shut your mouth, bitch." The heavily accented voice did not reveal any human decency in its tone.

Latoya lost all sense of time. A while later, she and the Hispanic girl were dragged from the van by two men and dropped on a warehouse floor. Latoya noticed the other girl was similarly taped and gagged. Three evil-looking, armed men played cards at a nearby table while ensuring the captive girls remained where they lay. Eventually, they cut the tape around both girls' ankles, and they were led out through a door and then shoved into the back of an eighteen-wheeler. Latoya caught a glimpse of many other girls sitting in the truck before the door slammed shut, and she found herself in total darkness. The truck started up and began to move.

Hours later, they stopped. The door opened, and there were more men with guns. The men ordered the girls from the van, then stood by and jeered while a few of the girls, having no choice, relieved themselves in the desert. When they finished, the men herded them through a warehouse door. Latoya guessed there were about twenty in the group and was surprised to see a few young, terrified-looking boys in the group as well.

The captives moved into one corner of a large, open room where the men ordered them to sit and remain silent. Latoya caught the eye of the young Hispanic girl who'd spoken to her from the van window. Shaking her head, the young girl looked away; her face was a mixture of terror and sorrow. Tears were streaming down her cheeks.

Latoya heard someone call one of the guards, Miguel, and he remained in the building, sitting in a chair against the wall where he could see the entire group. Latoya thought the rifle across his lap looked like one of those Russian AK rifles she'd seen in movies.

Miguel wore torn jeans and old, western-style boots. His sleeveless shirt was stained and filthy, his hair long and greasy black, his face unshaven. To Latoya, he looked like he hadn't bathed in some time. She shuddered.

CHAPTER 25
Del Rio, Texas

Riordan entered the hangar, where Pallie and Weaver were busily checking some of their equipment. Before they found themselves in a situation, it was essential to be sure everything was in good working order.

"Hey, you two miscreants, come over to the head shed. That new guy, Eric Dewald, is here, and it sounds like something may be up."

Pallie looked up. "Don't get your panties in a wad. We're on our way." Pallie set the pair of night vision goggles he'd just finished checking on a crate and turned to follow Riordan. "Are you coming, Weaver?"

"Right behind you."

A few seconds later, they joined Riordan, Tony, and WP in the head shed, as they had taken to calling the old airstrip office that now housed their sleeping quarters and operations center. Right behind them, Whitley walked in followed by another man, a civilian sporting a longer hairstyle. He appeared in pretty good shape and was dressed in jeans, tennis shoes, and an Ozzy Osbourne 'Diary of a Madman' t-shirt.

"Okay, ladies, listen up. This is Eric Dewald. He just arrived a few minutes ago. Eric is a former CIA operative and currently works with Homeland Security. He is going to serve as our team reconnaissance expert and computer geek. He also brings news from the boss. It seems we have our first actionable intelligence, but this mission is different. I will let Eric fill you in." Whitley moved over to sit on one of the nearby cots. Eric remained standing and stepped up to address the small group.

"Alright, thanks for the introduction, Chief. I haven't met any of you, but Chief Whitley has given me a brief rundown on each of you. I know who and what you are, and since you are here as volunteers, I'm grateful. You don't know me either, but I can assure you I am damn good at what I do. We have solid intel that a team of cartel thugs has a group of young ladies stashed about one hundred and fifty miles south of here. The word is they will be shipped out tomorrow night. That means we will go in at zero dark thirty this morning."

"Exactly how do we know this?" Weaver asked.

"I can't exactly tell you. But suffice it to say that we have an informant within the cartel responsible for most of the trafficking in this area. This informant's intel has consistently proven reliable over the last few months."

Pallie spoke up this time. "Where are these kids being held?"

"They are in a large storage building belonging to a now-defunct oil company. The old oil field is close to the Mexican border; it's been abandoned for almost ten years."

Whitley stood. "I have talked to Tony about this location; he knows the area well. He was on this site a few months ago and saw this storage building up close. There is only one window in what is a small office area. There are two loading docks with large shipping doors at the other end."

Weaver and Pallie both glanced over at Tony and nodded. "So, how do we get there?"

"Very flat country," Tony responded. "Helicopter no good. Too loud. We drive, then walk."

"Okay, I got that part," Riordan commented. "How do we know what awaits us when we get there?"

"That's my job," Dewald answered. "I have that part covered."

Pallie raised his hand. "I have a question. You said this mission is different. What did you mean by that?"

"These aren't illegal immigrants smuggled into the US from south of the border. These are American kids— girls being smuggled across the border into Mexico."

"Son of a bitch!" Weaver exclaimed. "I suspected that was going on."

Pallie cursed softly under his breath. "I don't see how it's any different. It doesn't matter whether they're smuggling kids into or out of the US, the people doing this are evil as fuck. If any of those sons-of-bitches line up in my sights, they're going down."

There was a general murmur of agreement.

"Okay, we are leaving here at 1900 hours." Whitley checked this watch. "That gives us time to get ready, drive as close as possible, get in, and set up well after dark. We'll hit them about 0300. Got it?"

Each replied in the affirmative.

"Good. Pallie, you and WP help Eric get his gear checked out and loaded into one of the trucks. That's all for now. Let's get on it."

"Yes, Chief."

Pallie grabbed a rather large pelican case from the back of Dewald's Nissan Xterra. It wasn't as heavy as it looked.

"Careful with that, Pallie. That's Red Wing you're tossing about there."

"Red Wing?"

Eric laughed. "Can I help if I'm a huge Avengers fan?"

"Oh, yeah. I haven't seen the movies, but I read those comics when I was a kid." He paused and looked down at the case he was holding. "What does this Red Wing thing do?"

"She's my eyes in the night skies. I designed her myself and built her with some friends from MIT."

"Okay, but what does she do?"

Eric looked slightly hurt by Pallie's repeated question, but brushed it off and continued. "She's a drone, but not just any drone. She has three camera systems: infrared, night vision, and a hi-powered HD camera with a 100x zoom lens. Red Wing is nearly silent in flight and just about invisible in the night sky. I can carry the whole setup on a specially designed backpack." He paused to shift some equipment in the Xterra. "With her control console, I can spot a field mouse hiding in the grass anywhere in a two-hundred-and-fifty-mile radius. I can also relay the camera feed nearly anywhere in the world, but due to the nature of these missions, they will be recorded locally and handed over to the boss. We wouldn't want the wrong people to see them."

Pallie nodded. "Okay then, Red Wing sounds impressive."

Eric grinned. "Oh, you'll be much more impressed after tonight."

It was precisely 0100 hours when four vehicles stopped about five miles from the old oil field. The men exited the vehicles and set about their tasks. Most of the team wore outdoor sportsmen's clothing and lightweight hiking shoes. Pallie and WP were geared up in desert camouflage fatigues and gooney hats. Tony wore faded blue jeans, leather moccasins on his feet, and a shirt of some indescribable brown color. Weaver jokingly referred to it as shit-brindle brown.

Weaver, Riordan, and Chief Whitley carried Glock 19 9mm pistols with spare magazines. In addition to their Glocks, Pallie and WP carried silenced M4 rifles with three full ten-round magazines. Both Pallie and WP had their preferred combat knives as well. The old Apache warrior had a Winchester lever-action 30-30 slung across his shoulder and a massive bone-handled Bowie knife on his right hip. With the clear skies and a full moon overhead, they did not need night vision goggles.

Still dressed in his jeans, Ozzy Osbourne t-shirt, tennis shoes, and sporting a custom Wilson Combat Arms 1911 pistol holstered at his right hip, Dewald retrieved the large pelican case from the back of the Ford Bronco. Setting the case down on the hard-packed desert sand, he removed the top and put it carefully to the side. Next, Dewald lifted a large black drone from the case and placed it on the case's lid. Then, reaching back into the case, he came out with a console covered with various knobs and switches and an eight-inch diagonal LCD. Lastly, Dewald pulled an antenna array from the case attached to a tripod base, much like a photographer would use. Extending the tripod's legs, he stood it in the desert sand a few yards from the truck and, unwinding a cable attached to the antenna, plugged the end into the console several yards away. Satisfied, he flipped a switch on the console and the unit came to life. After running a few quick checks, Eric approached Chief Whitley, standing with the rest of the team near the old K5 Blazer.

"Red Wing is ready."

Chief Whitley nodded. "We're all set then."

The plan was to send Red Wing in first to scout the situation and determine the number of possible combatants guarding the girls. Then Tony would lead Pallie and WP to the old oil field and storage building. Riordan, Weaver, and Chief Whitley would follow shortly after, with three vehicles to offer support and transport the girls out. WP and Pallie, being Navy SEALS, were well suited to this kind of mission. With the tough old Apache, they figured they could quickly eliminate any guards the cartel might have on hand, especially if Dewald could use Red Wing to tell them exactly where they were.

Dewald returned to the console he'd placed on the fourth vehicle's tailgate, an older Ford F250 pickup truck. As the rest of the team moved around to view the LCD screen on the console, Eric worked the controls, and Red Wing lifted silently into the desert night.

"Damn," Pallie whistled. "A fucking mosquito makes more noise flying than that drone."

"Red Wing is over the site," Dewald announced moments later. The night vision camera painted the scene unfolding on the LCD in an eerie greenish hue, but they could see the compound. A few seconds later, the large storage building came into sight."

"How high is your drone flying?" Chief Whitley asked.

Dewald glanced at a gauge on the console. "One hundred and forty-four feet. Switching over to Infrared."

He guided the drone over the building. Bright reddish-yellow images appeared on the LCD. They could see about twenty heat signatures gathered at one end of the building.

"Those must be the kids," WP observed.

Dewald nodded. "It looks like there are five guards. Four are outside, two are patrolling around the building's perimeter, one is stationary by the loading docks, and one is near the office entrance. The fifth is inside, sitting against the wall a little back from the girls."

Whitley nodded. "That's it then. Tony, you guys may as well get going. Let us know when you're in position."

Tony grunted.

"We're all on the same comms, and Eric will keep the drone overhead. We'll let you know if anything changes." He paused. "I know I don't need to say this, but keep the frequency clear except for mission-critical comms. I don't want any slip-up. I don't want these girls to suffer one bit more than they already have. Got it?"

There was a collective affirmative response.

Tony turned and silently faded into the desert night. Without a word, Pallie and WP disappeared right behind him. It was 0145 hours.

Tony led the way, settling into a steady mileage-eating trot. Pallie fanned out to the old Apache's right about fifteen yards away and slightly behind, matching Tony's pace. WP was on Tony's left. Twenty minutes later, their comm units clicked.

"Radio check, over." It was Chief Whitley.

All three acknowledged good communications and continued trotting through the desert. On a clear night, there was little to interfere with their radio signal in the vast open expanse. Pallie estimated they must be about halfway to their destination at the pace Tony had set. The three continued in silence.

Another twenty-five minutes passed before Tony raised his hand, signaling the other two to stop. Spry for his age, Tony crouched and slowly continued forward several more yards, then stopped, concealed behind some low desert scrub growth. For several minutes, he just crouched there, watching. Then he signaled WP and Pallie forward. WP went to the left and into a slight depression beside an old work shed near the loading docks. Pallie worked his way around to the right, toward what appeared to be a tool shed a short distance from the office entrance. Tony low-crawled his way to a position where he could watch the front of the building and keep track of the two roving guards.

Once they were all in place, Tony would signal. Pallie would take the two guards at the front entrance, the stationary guard and the one circling his end of the building, with his silenced M4. At the same time, WP would take down the two guards at the loading dock end. Once the door guard was down, Tony and WP would go straight in and remove the single guard while Pallie provided cover from outside. Tactically, it was a piece of cake.

As Pallie approached his position behind the smaller storage building, WP's voice came over the comms.

"In position."

They were set. Suddenly, their comms units clicked. It was Eric. "The guard inside is moving."

Pallie dropped to the sand behind some desert brush and waited. He was still about twenty feet from the small storage shed.

A few seconds later, Eric's voice came again. "Oh shit. This is not good. He grabbed one of the girls and is moving toward the front office exit. Pallie, you're on the right. He'll be coming toward you."

There was a momentary pause; then Eric was back.

"The girl is fighting him; he's hit her several times. He has her at the door now; they're coming out."

"Shit," Pallie muttered. He couldn't see the door from where he lay in the sand. "I have no eyes on."

He began low-crawling toward his right, trying to shift to a position where he could see the guard with the struggling girl.

Eric said, "Pallie, I will be your eyes."

Lighting a cigarette, Miguel leaned back in the chair and began to study the girls in the group with interest. When his eyes fell on Latoya, he caught her looking at him. She looked down immediately, but it was too late. A malicious grin formed on his face, revealing several missing teeth.

Miguel took a final drag from his cigarette and flicked it to the floor.

Now, that's one sweet little puta. I'll take that one behind the small shed; break that little bitch in right.

He and his fellow guards often availed themselves of the merchandise they were paid to watch. It was simply a fringe benefit.

Miguel stood to stretch. Then, slinging his rifle across his shoulder, he walked toward the group of kids huddled in the corner. It was no problem; the kids were too terrified to do anything and could go nowhere. Guards were at the doors, and they were in the middle of the desert. In the four years that Miguel had done this, there had never been a problem.

Latoya looked up and saw him coming, his gaze locked on her. The look on the man's face told her everything she needed to know. Suddenly, she felt nauseated and, if possible, even more terrified. While they all still had gags and their wrists taped, their ankles were free. Latoya struggled to her feet, looking wildly around her. There was no place to go. Miguel was close; he reached for her hair, grabbed several of her braids in his right hand, and began to pull her toward the other end of the warehouse. Shaking her head, Latoya struggled. The open-handed slap that struck the side of her face was brutal. She staggered, but the man did not loosen his grip.

"Come, my little chica. Come with me now."

Again, Latoya struggled. The rest of the group watched, terrified, as Miguel struck the side of her head with his fist.

"You must come with me, chica, or I will beat you until you do. But you be good to Miguel and save yourself much pain, no?"

He grinned nastily and began pulling Latoya toward the door at the front of the warehouse.

Dragging the helpless girl through the door and into the desert night, Miguel made his way toward the smaller storage shed about thirty yards away. All hope suddenly left Latoya; she wanted to die right then and there. Feeling the girl give up and no longer resisting, Miguel quickly covered the distance to the building, his anticipation growing.

Eric reported in a whisper, "Fifteen yards, coming right at you, Pallie. He's dragging the girl behind him. Ten yards now and closing."

"Got the asshole," Pallie responded. Miguel had just entered his line of sight, still dragging the girl behind him. Finally, the man stopped not five feet from where Pallie lay in the desert scrub and turned to face the girl. He roughly ripped the duct tape from around her head, uncovering her mouth, and then pushed her to her knees in the sand.

"Alright, my little chica, first …" He stopped. The girl's eyes were open wide with shock, but Miguel realized she wasn't looking at him at that moment. He started to turn his head.

Pallie rose from the desert floor like an avenging angel. A strong hand closed on Miguel's mouth, jerking his head violently back. Pallie thrust the blade upward into the man's kidney, the cold steel of his combat knife reaching up into Miguel's lower abdomen. The pain Miguel felt was intense but short. Pallie violently twisted the blade to the right and jerked it free. Miguel dropped to the desert sand and lay still.

Latoya screamed.

The three men all tensed, ready for the guards to react to the sound. They did not. The cries of a girl from behind the smaller storage building were nothing for them to concern themselves with; they had heard it before.

Wiping the blade of his knife on the dead man, Pallie slid it back into its sheath and knelt beside the sobbing girl.

"Do not move from this spot. Do you understand me? Do not move. You are safe, and I will be back for you shortly. You must not move!"

The girl looked up at Pallie, but there was no response.

"Do you understand? Nod, so I know you can hear me. You must not move. Stay here; I will be back for you."

This time, the girl nodded.

Pallie touched the comms unit at his throat. "The girl is safe. The inside guard is down. Go. Go now."

As Weaver, Riordan, and Whitley started toward the abandoned oil field, WP gently squeezed the trigger of his M4, which emitted a quiet cough. The 5.56mm round struck the guard seated by the loading dock door squarely in the forehead and the man tumbled out of his chair.

Pallie approached the warehouse building in a crouched run, heading directly toward the guard at the front door. Bringing his M4 up to his shoulder, he fired twice, the two 5.56mm slugs striking the man in the chest. The man sagged back into his chair and did not move.

WP's M4 coughed twice more, and Pallie knew the roving guard to his left was no longer a threat.

Where is that last asshole?

Pallie's eyes scanned his immediate area. There was no sign of him. Then, sensing a movement behind him, Pallie spun around, dropping to one knee. The last man was already bringing up an old double-barreled shotgun to fire. Pallie heard a quiet thud, and the man's eyes bulged as his back arched. The man dropped his gun and tried to reach around to his back. He failed, collapsing forward onto his stomach, where he lay still. A large, bone-handled Bowie knife protruded from his back. About thirty feet away, the old Apache chief straightened up, unslinging the lever-action rifle from his shoulder; he started toward Pallie.

"Chief, you and WP get the rest of the girls out here. I'll get the girl by the shed."

Tony nodded and started toward the door to join WP, who was already moving in that direction.

As Pallie walked past the man on the ground, he yanked the bone-handled knife from his back. Then, cleaning the blood from the blade by wiping it across the dead man's shirt, he slid it carefully into his belt. It was very sharp. Turning, he returned to the shed, where he found the frightened girl still lying where he'd left her. She had not moved an inch.

"Shhhh. It's okay, honey. You're okay now. Don't be scared."

Pallie could see that the girl was in shock or at least too scared to move. He knelt next to her.

"Can you sit up, honey? You are safe. No one will hurt you now."

The calm, quiet, reassuring voice slowly registered, cutting through the fog in Latoya's brain.

Can I sit up? What?

Comprehension was slow in coming. Finally, the girl nodded and struggled into a sitting position.

"My name is Palazzolo. You can call me Pallie. I'm going to cut the tape on your wrists, okay?"

Latoya nodded.

Pallie moved around behind her and, using his knife, carefully sliced through the tape binding the girl's wrists. Then he moved back and knelt in front of her again.

"What's your name?"

"La … Latoya."

"You're a brave girl, Latoya. Very brave. Can you stand?"

Latoya wasn't sure if she could. Pallie stood and offered her his hand, helping her to her feet.

"Take a few seconds and get your legs under you. We have vehicles on the way. They will be here in a few minutes."

Latoya's eyes found the man lying in the sand a few feet away and gasped, suddenly fearful again.

"He can't hurt you. I'm sorry you had to see that. It must have been awful."

She looked up at Pallie. "It was … uh, yes … awful. But, if you had not come, if you had not … done what you did …" Her voice trailed off.

"Don't think about that. It's over now. If you can, let's walk to join the others. There are a few more bodies out there, I'm afraid. Just don't look at them. Instead, look at the desert sky. We'll be out of here shortly."

Latoya nodded and followed Pallie around the shed. She kept her eyes on the desert sky as they walked toward the group of kids standing with WP and Tony.

Reaching the group, Pallie turned to Tony. Carefully sliding the Bowie knife from his belt, he handed it to the old Apache, handle first.

The old chief nodded. "Thank you. Good knife. I'd hate to lose it."

"I guess that was some of that 'lightning in hand' you talked about the other day."

Tony just smiled.

A few minutes later, three vehicles pulled up, stopping a few yards away from the huddled group of kids. Chief Whitley jumped out of the first vehicle.

"What's the situation?"

Pallie shrugged. "Five dead assholes. Twenty-three rescued kids. Eighteen girls and five young boys. They are pretty dirty and hungry, but otherwise, I think unharmed."

"Five boys?"

"There are sickos of all kinds in this world."

"I guess so."

Ten minutes later, the vehicles returned to the desert with all the kids on board. It was a bit crowded, but nobody complained.

Eric Dewald waited, still monitoring the situation from overhead. He kept Red Wing in the air, keeping a sharp watch for possible other cartel members traveling in the area.

After linking back up with Eric twenty minutes later, it took only a few minutes for Red Wing to be back in her Pelican case and loaded up. Pallie, Tony, and WP switched to the Toyota Land Cruiser with Eric to give the kids more room. The convoy pulled up in front of the old airstrip's office just four hours later, and everyone began to unload.

Weaver and Riordan led the kids to the building designated to house them while they waited for transport. The building was air-conditioned, with two bathrooms and twenty-five cots already set up. If needed, more were stored in the hangar.

Weaver and Riordan worked their way through the group, talking to each kid and assuring them they were safe now. Pallie and WP showed up a few moments later, carrying several cases of MREs for distribution to the hungry kids.

Weaver got up on a chair near the door and began to speak. "We know you've been through a lot, but you are safe now. There are clean bathrooms behind you. Have something to eat. MREs are not quite like mom's home cooking, but we eat them and we're still alive." He smiled.

Pallie thought he saw a couple of the kids smile. *That's a good sign*, he thought.

Weaver continued. "In a little while, a plane will fly you all to a military base where doctors will check you out and make sure you're okay. There will be folks to talk to if you want to talk. They will get your information, contact your parents and family to let them know you are safe, and arrange to get you all home. Eat, clean up a bit, and rest if you can. One of us will be right outside if you need anything. You will be home soon."

Weaver stepped off the chair and left the building, followed by the rest of the team. Riordan volunteered to take the first watch and sat on the bench beside the door.

Back inside, Latoya sat on one of the cots and opened her MRE package. Sensing she was being watched, she looked up to see the young Hispanic girl standing there looking at her, clutching her unopened MRE.

"What do you want?" Latoya asked.

"You have every reason to hate me, and I have no right to ask you to forgive me. I want you to know that I wish I had never spoken to you. I was so scared those men would kill me if I did not do what they said." She started to cry. "I am so sorry. It would have been better if they had killed me."

Latoya considered the girl's words, saying nothing. Finally, the young Latina turned to walk away.

"What is your name?" Latoya asked.

"Maria … Maria Gomez."

"How old are you, Maria?"

"I'm thirteen."

Latoya felt her eyes start to water. "Sit down next to me, Maria. We both need to eat."

Reaching over, Latoya took Maria's MRE pouch, opened it, and handed it back.

"Where are you from? Where is your family? We will be going home soon."

Maria looked up from her MRE pouch. She had been exploring its contents. "My mother sold me to the coyotes. They use me to cross the border. The men say they are my father." The girl paused. "My father is dead. He died when I was nine."

"You have no family?"

Maria shook her head.

"Stay close to me. I will be your family now."

The military cargo carrier landed smoothly on the short airstrip. Martha Knopp was the first one down the loading ramp.

She spotted the kids coming out to see the plane that had landed. They were all in a deplorable state.

Oh my God. These poor kids.

Chief Whitley immediately approached and gave Martha a rundown of all that had transpired.

Listening carefully, Martha only had one question. "And the five dead traffickers?"

Whitley shrugged. "We left them as they lay. WP thought it might send a message to their business partners."

Martha nodded. "It might at that, but we can't leave dead bodies rotting all over the southwest desert. I'll have local law enforcement discover the bodies and put out a press release stating that the circumstances are under investigation—suspected rival cartel ambush, or something like that."

Whitley smiled. "You're the boss."

"Right now, I just want to see these poor kids. I also want to meet the rest of your team and thank them. It looks like this mission was very successful. I hope these prove to be reproducible results."

"They are if the intel is good."

"We have the best people working on this and a reliable inside source. It should be."

"Okay, what's next?"

"Well, we are flying these kids to Ft. Campbell. It's all low-profile. We don't want to further traumatize the children by exposing them to the media. Air Force doctors will check them out, and we have counselors ready. Once we know who they are, we'll contact their families and get them home. I want to talk to your team..." She glanced at her watch. "...in twenty minutes?"

"Yes, ma'am. I'll have them gather in the hangar. At least there is shade."

"Sounds great." Martha walked toward the kids huddled near the building where they'd been resting.

An hour later, Pallie stood off to the side, watching as the crew of the military transport plane began preparing to load the kids.

"Mr. Palazzolo? Pallie?"

Pallie turned to see Latoya coming up behind him, holding the hand of a young Hispanic girl.

"Hey there. Latoya, right?"

"Yes. This is Maria, my new sister."

"Your new sister?"

"Well, I just adopted her." Once she explained the situation, she could not see her parents turning the girl away.

"Well, nice to meet you, Maria." Pallie winked at the young lady, who smiled shyly.

"Mr. Palazzolo, I wanted to tell you something."

"Please, call me Pallie."

"Okay, Pallie." She paused a minute, looking at the ground. "Pallie, when … uh … all this happened to me, I could not believe it. I kept thinking it was a bad dream and that I would soon wake up at home in bed. But I never woke up. Then, when that man took me, I knew what he would do. I fought as hard as I could, but he kept hitting me, and I gave up—I gave up, I wanted to die." She stopped. Tears were streaming down her face, and she didn't try to wipe them away. "Behind that building, I realized what the rest of my life would be … but then you were there."

Pallie started to say something.

"Please, Pallie, let me finish. What happened behind that building was awful, but I am so thankful you were there. I will never forget what I saw, but I also know what would have happened to me if you had not done what you did. I will always remember you, and I will always be grateful. I want you to know that."

Pallie nodded his head, not knowing what to say.

Latoya turned to walk away, then stopped.

"I am going to join the Navy when I finish high school. I want you to know I will never give up again."

Pallie stood there, searching for something appropriate to say. Then, finally, he smiled. "Always in the fight."

Latoya stood there quietly, gazing back at him. Finally, she reached up and wiped tears from her cheeks.

"Always in the fight," she repeated.

Quickly, before Pallie could react, she wrapped her arms around him.

"Thank you, Pallie." Then, taking Maria's hand, she led the girl toward the plane.

Pallie stood there a few minutes, lost in his thoughts. Then, his mind turned to Jum Y and Xuan, whom he'd never met."

Dammit, JD. Please get those girls out of there.

"Pallie, you okay?" It was Chief Whitley, now standing beside him.

"Yeah, Chief. I'm fine. What's next?"

.

CHAPTER 26
The Philippines

Taylor awoke to the sun streaming through the split in the simple flowered curtain hanging in the open window. He sat up slowly, testing how his body felt and how his injuries were healing. He was feeling more rested than he had in a long while. Last night was his second night free from the horrible nightmares that had haunted his sleep for years.

Ruby's thoughtful words from the other night had been on his mind. Taylor had even tried to put himself in the little girl's shoes, to decide how he would feel in the same situation. Of course, that experiment's results were hardly conclusive. Still, Taylor's mental condition had improved since his talk with Ruby; he now felt a sense of hope.

Careful examination showed that the injuries from his recent beating were healing well. He was still quite stiff, with some sore, tender spots. As of the previous day, he'd still not recovered much of his old stamina; he tired quickly. That would continue to improve. For the most part, he felt much better. Taylor figured it was high time that he started contributing to his upkeep.

I have been a mooch long enough. I doubt Ruby will take payment from me, but she must at least let me cover my room and board.

That afternoon, Taylor caught Amado as the young boy returned from school. "Hey Amado, how are you doing?"

"Okay." Amado went to the refrigerator to get some cold water.

"Listen, I have a small favor to ask. I know it costs your mother money to care for and feed me, and I want to help."

Amado returned with the glass of water and took a huge swallow. "Okay."

Do you know the Tondo Uptown bar or the Tattoo You tattoo parlor?"

"Yes, they are not far. Maybe a twenty-minute walk from here."

"I rented a room behind the bar. It is the only door at the back of the building. It's locked, but there's a key hidden. It's hanging on a hook in a crack behind the window shutter on the left side of the door. It is hard to see, but it is there if you look."

"Okay, I understand."

"A picture of old army buddies in Afghanistan is hanging near my cot. You will find some money if you take the photo down and remove the cardboard on the back. I want to help pay for the food I eat and replace some of the money your mother has already spent taking care of me."

"I think my mother will not take your money."

"I know. I will have to work on that. Will you get it for me?"

Amado thought about it for a few seconds. "I will get it tomorrow on my way home from school."

"Great. But please be careful. Try to avoid being seen if you can. There may still be people looking for me."

"I will be careful."

The boy returned to the kitchen and began rummaging around for something to snack on until his mother came home from work to prepare dinner.

Taylor settled back into the couch. *Maybe tomorrow, I'll try to take a short walk.*

For now, he could do laps around the small courtyard. He needed to regain his strength and endurance, especially if people were still looking for him.

The cab pulled to a stop in front of a seedy-looking tattoo parlor. JD and Vivas climbed out of the back seat and took a minute to survey their surroundings. JD's mind flashed to the one tattoo he had allowed himself to get, a SEAL trident on his upper left arm. He chuckled.

"Wow! I wouldn't have my trident tattoo now if this had been the only tattoo parlor available. Man, this place looks like a case of hepatitis waiting to happen."

"Yep. That is one nasty-looking joint."

JD spotted the bar; it was just as Ed Weaver had described it to him. Nodding at Vivas, he walked toward the entrance.

"This looks like the place, alright."

They passed by the disreputable-looking bar and continued down the alley beside it. As the two men rounded the corner, they discovered a young Filipino boy retrieving something from behind a shutter on the right side of the apartment's single window, near the door.

JD spoke. "Hello."

The boy nearly jumped out of his skin.

"Uh, Hello."

"Are you a friend of Bill Taylor? My name is JD. This is Vivas. We are looking for him. I understand this is where he lived."

Still recovering from his surprise, Amado did not quite answer the question. "Are you Americans? Are you friends of his?"

"Well, honestly, we've never met. But a friend of Bill's told me I could find him here. I need to talk to him because we need his help. It's important."

Amado considered this. These were Americans like Taylor, not Filipino gangsters, and looked like soldiers. Finally, he decided: "Taylor is not here now."

"Do you know where he is?" JD asked.

"You need his help? You will not hurt my mother?"

Vivas spoke this time. "We are not here to hurt Taylor or your mother. We are trying to find two missing girls. Taylor's old friend told my buddy here…" Vivas pointed at JD, "…that Taylor might be able to help us." Vivas paused as the boy absorbed this. Then he added, "We don't have much time."

"There is no need to be afraid. What's your name?" JD asked.

"Amado."

"Well, Amado, we will not harm you or your mother. You can trust us."

Amado decided he believed these men. They did not look like men who would lie. "Taylor is at our home. Some gangsters beat him after he won his last fight. He was hurt very badly. My mother found him in the alley when she came home from work. I helped her get him to our house with a cart. He sent me here to get his money - to give to my mother to help pay for food because she cares for and feeds him." He paused, then added, "My mother is a good lady."

Vivas glanced over at JD. "Sounds like our guy."

JD turned to the young boy. "Amado, will you take us to him? There will be no trouble. Like I said before, it is crucial."

"It is about twenty minutes to walk."

"I can pay for a taxi."

"It will still be twenty minutes. Taxis must take good roads, and there is much traffic. I know shorter ways."

JD glanced over at Vivas, who shrugged.

"Okay, Amado. We will follow you."

"I must get Taylor's money first. Then I will take you."

"That's fine. We'll wait right here."

Amado unlocked the door to Taylor's apartment and went in.

It was hot, but the breeze made the heat bearable. Taylor sat on the couch, letting the light wind cool his body. Earlier, he'd done ten laps around the courtyard and was quite tired, but it felt good. Tomorrow, he would try for fifteen.

Ruby was outside hanging some laundry on the clothesline. She washed their things by hand in the kitchen sink, which surprised Taylor at first. He used a local laundry service. He just dropped it off and picked it up.

It dawned on Taylor that he made pretty good money winning his fights despite his situation. Lately, he'd spent most of his earnings on whiskey. Ruby did what she needed to do for herself and Amado. Taylor found his respect for Ruby growing. He closed his eyes and relaxed.

Suddenly, he heard Ruby cry out and he was wide awake. She had just finished hanging the last shirt on the line when five tough-looking gangsters entered the courtyard. They fanned out, putting themselves between Ruby and any means of escape. One slightly older man stepped forward.

"Okay, lady. We don't want to hurt you, but we will if we must. Where is the American? We know he's been staying here."

Ruby backed up a few steps. She was frightened, but tried not to show it. "He left. Taylor is not here anymore."

The leader of the group laughed. "I don't believe you, lady. Don't make me cut you up; tell me where he is." The thug's hand shifted to his right hip and returned with a butterfly knife. Ruby's eyes grew wide at the sight of the knife. The man flipped it open casually.

"I think you won't enjoy this, puta."

"That will not be necessary." Bill Taylor stepped through the door out into the courtyard. "I'm right here, you little punk." He was in no condition to take on five street thugs, but he could not stand by and let Ruby get hurt.

Ruby looked at Taylor, the fear in her eyes obvious, but nothing could be done about it now.

"Ah, there you are," the thug smirked, "the great American fighter. We have been looking for you, and our information was right. You have been hiding behind this woman's skirts, but now we have you. Mahalia Baguinda will pay me a lot for your ugly head. I will gut you like a pig."

Taylor forced himself to laugh. "Well, come on, you little chicken shit, give it your best shot. I take out punks like you for fun."

Taylor caught Ruby's eyes. He nodded toward the door and mouthed, "You go."

Ruby shook her head. *No.*

He jerked his chin toward the door again, mouthing to her, "Go." He could not win this fight, but maybe he could buy Ruby time to escape.

Taylor took a couple of cautious steps toward the leader. He could not afford to trip or stumble now.

"Okay, asshole. Let's do this."

Grinning, the gangster started to circle right with the knife held loosely in his grip, goading Taylor into coming closer. Taylor waited, preparing for the attack he knew was coming and hoping he was up to the challenge.

"Is there a problem here?" All eyes turned toward the courtyard entrance. Just inside the doorway stood two Americans. Behind them stood young Amado, a scared but determined-looking boy.

The gangster leader turned to face JD. Vivas moved to stand to JD's right, placing himself closer to Amado's mother.

Amado was already at his mother's side. Ruby wrapped her arms around her son and tried to push him behind her. Amado shrugged her arms off and placed himself squarely between his mother and the gangsters.

"Well, look at this. Now we have the mother and her little bastard." He glanced back to JD. "And who are you? Why is this any of your business?"

"Well, I don't like chicken-shit twits who threaten injured men, women, and children. So, I am making this my business. You and your buddies can leave now if you like, or stay and get hurt. I'm okay either way."

"Do you know these people?"

"Nope, I've never met them. But I know I don't like you."

"I don't like you either, asno. I think I will cut you up, real bad."

JD smiled. "If you think you can, you are welcome to try. One more time, I strongly suggest you and your friends leave."

The thug hesitated only an instant, pretending to consider JD's suggestion. Then he lunged, coming in hard and fast with a wicked slash at JD's midsection. Pivoting to his right, JD used his left hand to guide the knife past its target. Almost simultaneously, the hard knuckles of his right fist slammed into the gangster's left temple. The man dropped to the ground like a sack of potatoes. He did not move.

A second goon ran at JD, slashing wildly back and forth with his blade. JD caught the backswing with his right arm, sliding down to trap the wrist in an unbelievably powerful grip. His left shin slammed into the man's right lower leg, causing him to fall back and expose his throat. JD immediately brought his left arm down, and the hard knob of bone on his left wrist slammed into the man's carotid sinus. The second attacker dropped to the floor beside his boss.

The now wild-eyed third gangster, hoping to use the boy's mother as protection, made a desperate dash to grab Ruby. Taylor saw it coming and launched himself into the assailant's path, driving the heel of his right palm into the opponent's chin, attempting to force him back. Vivas reacted as well, sliding a small throwing knife out of its sheath in the waistband of his jeans. He hurled it at the man and the blade entered his back low on the right side, burying itself to the hilt and slicing through the upper kidney. The man collapsed at the feet of wide-eyed Amado.

The boy had not moved, bravely keeping himself between his mother and the oncoming attacker. Taylor now stood between the three of them, the sudden surge of adrenalin helping him remain on his feet.

The two remaining gangsters, seeing their three buddies dropped so quickly, stood frozen, unable to run. They wanted no part of what these Americans had to offer.

After ensuring the two men he had put down would not get back up anytime soon, JD walked over and knelt near Amado. The boy was shaking, but still standing his ground.

"That was a courageous thing you did, Amado, protecting your mother. Are you okay?"

Slowly, the boy nodded. JD then turned his attention to Ruby, who had moved over to help steady Taylor.

"I'm alright," Taylor insisted as she tried to examine him. Finally, Taylor looked up as JD approached. "Thanks for the help, but who the hell are you?"

"My name is JD Cordell, and my knife-throwing buddy here is Carlos Vivas." Vivas stood, watching the two very nervous gangsters standing in the courtyard corner. He nodded a greeting, keeping his eyes on the gangsters.

"Damn, Vivas! Where'd you get that great little throwing knife?"

"Got it this morning while I was out shopping."

JD turned back to Taylor. "And you must be Bill Taylor."

"That's me."

Satisfied that Taylor was okay, Ruby stood and turned to face JD.

"You are Amado's mother? Your son is a fearless young man. You must be very proud of him."

"Yes. He is brave and a good son. I am always proud of him. My name is Ruby Damilo."

"Nice to meet you, Ruby."

Taylor frowned. "That's great. Now that we all know each other's names, I still have no idea why you're here. How do you know me?"

"We are here because Ed Weaver told me you might be able to help us."

"Ed Weaver?"

"Yes. You do come very highly recommended, Mr. Taylor."

"Ed recommended me?" JD could hear the surprise in his voice.

"Yes, he did. He said you were in a tough spot but you're a good man. And if anyone can help us, you can."

"Ed Weaver said that? How do you know him, and how did you find me?" Taylor paused. "Help you with what?"

"Well, that will take some explaining. First, let's secure this courtyard and discuss it." JD turned to Ruby. "Ma'am, I suggest you gather a few things; it will be best if you and Amado come with us. It is unsafe for you here now, but I promise you will be safe with us."

Ruby did not know what to make of the situation, but she agreed it was unsafe for her and Amado to remain in this apartment. These two men had just stopped three evil men from hurting her, her son, and of course, Taylor, a man it seems they had not met before. It was not a difficult decision to make.

"Give me a few minutes." She disappeared into the apartment.

"What do we do with these two?" Vivas asked.

JD considered that for a moment, then turned to the boy. "Do you have any duct tape or good rope, Amado?"

Amado pointed at the clothesline. "Just that rope."

Vivas nodded, retrieved his knife from the gangster's kidney, and headed toward the clothesline. JD followed to help. A few minutes later, the two thugs were securely tied up in the courtyard corner.

"They'll get loose or be set loose sooner or later, but we'll be long gone by then," Vivas observed.

"Can you keep an eye on the street? I want to have a little chat with our friend here."

"Got it covered." Vivas re-sheathed the throwing knife and moved to the gate. Spotting a bench near a food stall across the street, he went over and sat. He could now see anyone approaching the courtyard entrance from any direction.

JD moved over to where Taylor sat on the apartment's small porch. "Mind if I sit?"

"Cop a squat. Plenty of room."

JD cautiously leaned back against one of the rickety-looking posts holding the porch roof. He glanced up to make sure it was safe.

Taylor grunted. "It should be fine. I've leaned against it several times over the last few days."

Taking a second, Cordell glanced around the small courtyard. Despite its age and not being in a particularly good state of repair, he could tell someone was keeping it as clean as they could.

"Ruby seems like a nice lady."

"She is a good woman. Saved my life."

JD understood what that meant because he knew what it would mean to him. His mind was adjusting to the circumstances, which were not what he had expected to find. While certainly a little worse for the wear, JD saw that Bill Taylor was indeed a warrior; weak as he was, he hadn't hesitated to step up when the situation demanded it.

JD decided to be direct. "From what Weaver told me, I thought we'd find you curled up with a bottle. But that doesn't appear to be the case."

"That's also thanks to Ruby. No booze in just over a week. When she and Amado carted me here, I was damn near dead. When I came to, she didn't have any alcohol to drink, and I was in no condition to get anything. Besides, she's a kind, decent woman and a single mom. I won't drink in her home. Beyond that, I can't say. Right now, it's one day at a time."

"Amado told us Ruby found you beaten and left for dead in an alley, and he helped her get you here in a cart. Can I ask what happened?"

Taylor shrugged. "I guess I pissed off the wrong people and won too many fights. Shit, I've lost track of how many, exactly. I only lost two, mostly because I was too drunk to stand, never mind fight.

I fought some tough fighters; some were very good. I guess it's a key advantage if you don't give a fuck about living." Taylor looked down at the floor. JD stayed quiet and waited. "I guess some pretty bad people lost a lot of money betting against me."

"I suspect that's not what happened this last time?"

"No. It was a setup. Somebody brought in a damn monster. I figure he was supposed to kill or at least maim me. He was good, but it didn't work out as they had planned. He was certainly kicking my ass, but I got lucky and shattered the guy's jaw. He went down like he was dead. I still don't know what became of him."

Shifting a bit to get comfortable, Taylor went on. "When I went to collect my winnings, somebody sapped me from behind. They took me out into the alley and beat the crap out of me. I was just short of dead. That's where Ruby found me." He changed the subject. "You and that other guy, what's his name? Vivas? You do alright yourselves."

"We're both former Navy SEALS."

"Shit, I don't know about Vivas, but you're a lot fucking better than alright. I saw what you did, and it was effortless. Those punks never had a chance. What you did took many years of serious martial arts training. I'd say Okinawan karate from the looks of it, and not that stupid sport karate crap. I know because I am damn good myself."

"I've had some terrific instructors."

"Who'd you train with?"

JD laughed. "Oh. My dad, my mom, and this old Okinawan guy who lives in Knoxville, Tennessee."

It was Taylor's turn to laugh. "Your mom?"

"She's Vietnamese. My dad met her in Vietnam during the war. Her father was very skilled in a Vietnamese martial art called Nguyen-ryu. My dad learned some and was pretty good, but mom was much better."

"How about that? My dad studied Uechi-ryu most of his life, starting in seventh grade. Then, he served in

Vietnam. He also spent time in Okinawa, and trained with some top Okinawan instructors. He was tough, and he had skills, but he always was a bit too cocky. He got his ass kicked by an orangutan in some Montagnard village."

"What? No way! Was your dad Steven Taylor? My father knew him. I know all about the orangutan story. It's a family favorite."

"No shit, your dad knew my dad? That's wild. Small world, isn't it?"

"Yep," JD chuckled. "And my mother knew that orangutan."

Both men realized it was time to get to why JD was in Manila.

"So, why did Ed Weaver give you my name?"

"Well, he did more than that. He also gave me your address and some good information. The short version is that we are here to rescue two kidnapped young ladies. It's a long story, but it started in Vietnam. There is an evil son of a bitch who wants them returned to him there. We know who has them, but we don't know how to find them, and time is of the essence."

"I'm sorry to hear that, JD, but I'm unsure how I can help."

"It's the Baguinda sisters who took them."

"Oh! Shit."

"Yep. That is why I'm here."

Taylor shook his head. "And Weaver knows I was messing with Blessica. He sometimes checks in on me and even stopped by once when he was in Manila on business."

"Sounds like he tries to keep tabs on a brother."

"Yeah. Maybe so. Understand, this thing I had with Blessica, we weren't in love or anything like that. She just likes screwing tough guys, I guess. She is something else. We had some damn good chemistry. But she and her sister, Mahalia, run one of the biggest gangs in Tondo, and I was just a fucked up ex-soldier who won a lot of fights. There's no way she ever really cared about me."

"Sounds like you might have cared about her."

"Maybe, a little … who knows. But I'm not that guy anymore."

"What happened? Weaver told me what went down in Afghanistan. That was some heavy stuff, man; tough to carry around. It would have messed with anyone's head."

Taylor jerked his chin toward the apartment door. "Ruby happened. She is one hell of a woman. She didn't just save my life after the beating. I was one fucked up dude. I don't know if it was PTSD or just old-fashioned guilt, but I battled my demons every night since I took that damn shot. I know I had no choice, and the brass cleared me, but that doesn't make it okay. I saw that little girl's face every damn night. I took that same shot night after night and watched that poor girl's brains blow up in my face every time. The booze helped sometimes, but not enough." He paused to collect himself. "I haven't had that dream in three or four nights now."

"What changed?"

Taylor looked back through the open door into the small apartment. He saw Ruby move from Amado's room back into the main room, carrying a small bundle. Not knowing what had happened, Taylor was unsure how to explain it, but he knew when it started.

"Ruby told me I didn't kill that little girl; her mother did. And because of what I did, that little girl went to meet God without the blood of my team staining her soul. Ruby said that if that little girl could talk to me now, she would not blame me. She said the girl would thank me."

"Interesting. Do you believe that?"

Taylor thought about it. "I'm not sure. But I guess at least some part of me does."

JD nodded.

"Would you believe it?" Taylor asked.

"Honestly, I'm not sure either. But I think I can see my mother believing that."

The five piled into a taxi for the drive to the Manila Hotel and, upon their arrival, made their way through the lobby, where Vivas waved over a helpful bellboy. They piled into the elevator and JD pressed the button for the seventh floor. When the elevator stopped, they headed across the small common area to the hotel's east-wing rooms.

Vivas led the way, followed by Ruby carrying two shoulder bags, then Amado toting a third. Taylor limped along behind Amado. He offered to take the bags for Ruby, but she refused. Cordell brought up the rear, carrying a large, heavy suitcase. It was unclear when—or even if—Ruby and her son could return to their small Tondo apartment. Ruby had packed as much as she could.

They found Sirichai sitting in a chair outside the door of his room at the beginning of the hallway. He greeted Vivas and JD, then smiled and nodded at Ruby and Amado as Vivas led them to a room. They found Hana and Mai sitting on a couch, bent over a map of Manila they'd spread out over the coffee table. Ellen was seated with a laptop at the small business desk against the wall across from the queen-sized bed. Sophie lay sacked out enjoying the cold air from the air conditioner below the room's window, which offered a spectacular view of the city.

All three ladies looked up as the group entered the room. Sophie lifted her head as well. Then, seeing all was well, she thumped her tail twice and settled back into her nap.

Mai spoke first. "Hana and I are trying to get a feel for the area. Manila is a big city. Ellen is researching the nearby medical facilities, just in case."

Looking up from the map, Hana spotted the newcomers. "You must be William Taylor. I guess JD and Carlos were successful in finding you. Thank you for coming." Turning, she smiled at the woman and the nervous young teen beside her. "You must be friends of William? You are both welcome here."

Ruby nodded.

Taylor spoke up. "This is Ruby Damilo and her son, Amado. I am alive and able to be here now because of what they have done for me. But please, for God's sake, call me Bill, Taylor, or anything else. I hate William."

"Then we are in their debt." Hana approached Amado first, smiling at the shy boy, and offered her hand. Amado glanced up at his mother before he extended his hand to shake. "What a nice young man," Hana said, turning to Ruby. "It's nice to meet you as well, Ruby."

Ruby took Hana's offered hand and shook it.

"Let me introduce the rest of us. First, you passed Sirichai in the hall, of course, and have already met JD and Carlos. You may have only heard Carlos referred to as Vivas."

"I answer to either one."

"Carlos is my fiancé, but things keep getting in the way of us completing the marriage. Hopefully, once we have resolved this problem, that will be next on our list."

"I'm sure we can find a man of the cloth in Manila," Vivas offered.

Letting the comment pass, Hana continued. "This is Mai, JD's mother."

Mai stood. "So nice to meet both of you."

"The lady at the computer is JD's wife, Ellen. They are soon-to-be parents. Ellen is a medical doctor.

Hopefully, we won't need her skills, but hey, better safe than sorry."

Ellen came around the couch to greet Ruby and Amado before sitting beside Mai.

Hana turned to JD. "I assume there must be a good story here?"

"Well, as a matter of fact, there is." JD quickly described the events, beginning with meeting Amado at Taylor's apartment and ending with the fight at Ruby's. "I could not leave Ruby and Amado there alone. After what happened, it would not be safe for them. We are in their debt, and I am pretty sure Taylor wouldn't have come without them, not after what they've done for him. So, here they are."

"You did exactly the right thing. We have room for them until we get this sorted out. I believe room 708 has two queen-sized beds that Ruby and Amado can use. Will …uh, sorry … Bill can use 702, across the hall from Sirichai."

"Sounds good." He went over to Ellen on the couch and knelt beside her, speaking quietly. "Hi there, beautiful."

"Are you alright, JD?"

"Just fine; Vivas too. They were street thugs. It was no big deal. Listen, babe, can you check Taylor out? He had the crap beat out of him about a week ago and was pretty much on death's door when Ruby found him. We need to make sure he's okay."

"Of course, I'll get my bag. It's in our room. I'll be right back."

Sophie got up and trotted to where Amado stood with his mother. She began sniffing his fingertips, and Amado seemed nervous.

"It's okay, Amado. Sophie is my dog. She's friendly. It's okay to pet her if you want to."

Reassured, Amado slowly extended his hand. Sophie gave it a quick sniff and then a welcoming lick. Amado grinned and started to pet her gently on the head.

Ellen returned moments later, carrying a blue ballistic nylon bag that contained her medical equipment.

JD turned to Taylor. "Bill, my wife is a pretty darn good doctor. Would you mind letting her check you out? We just want to make sure you're okay."

"I'm fine. I need a bit more rest, but I feel much better since our little brawl earlier."

"Let's just make sure, okay?" Ellen insisted. "I'll take you and Ruby and Amado to your rooms. You can settle in, and I'll give you a quick once-over."

Taylor started to protest, but then thought better of it. *It won't hurt to have a real doctor check me out.*

Ellen motioned for Amado to come along. "Sophie can come too."

"Wait!" It was Ruby. "I don't understand. Why are all of you people here? What are you here for?"

Hana turned to face Ruby.

"Well, Ruby, the quick version is that the six of us and a few others met during an incident in Vietnam. The events leading up to that incident go back to the Vietnam War. I will let the people here fill you in as time permits on whatever they want to share about their parts in the story. For my part, I met JD and Vivas on a mission to rescue a woman kidnapped in Vietnam by an evil man, a drug lord. I have connections that helped them succeed in their mission. That adventure had a significant effect on me, and as a result, I started an organization to help rescue kids from terrible situations and get them to a better place.

Two young ladies—one a distant cousin of JD's mother, Mai, whom you just met, and the other, who aided us in that Vietnam rescue—were the first two girls in my program. They were flying to America to start new lives, but were grabbed by thugs while on a layover here in Manila. We have learned that the kidnapping connects our missing girls to what happened in Vietnam, as another corrupt Vietnamese government official wants these two young ladies back there. We have also since learned that the Baguinda sisters kidnapped them."

Startled, Ruby stared at the people around the room. "Dalawang Mga Ate Na Mafia? Those are terrible people, very bad."

"Yes," Hana continued, "I'd say they are. We are here to rescue our two friends."

"This is crazy," Ruby exclaimed. "You do not understand who these people are!"

"Well, Ruby, you are half right," JD agreed. "We do not know them but we do know what they are. Vivas and I are retired US Navy Seals, and your friend, Taylor, is ex-Army Special Forces. Sirichai, out in the hall, is a former Thai Special Forces operator. We do not know where they are holding our two friends, but we can rescue those girls if we find out soon enough. That is why I needed to find Taylor."

"But I do not understand," Ruby said, looking at Taylor and then back at JD. "How can Bill help?"

"Because I, ah ... I know Blessica Baguinda."

Ruby looked at him. Shock and then pain registered in her eyes. She looked down at the floor. The room went quiet.

"Okay, that's enough of that," Ellen broke the awkward silence. "Come on, Bill. Let's get you checked out. You too, Ruby and Amado. We'll get you settled in. I've got the keys to your rooms; follow me. You too, Sophie!"

Slowly, Ruby turned and picked up her bags. Amado had stopped petting Sophie and was now looking back and forth between his mother and Taylor. He retrieved his bag as well. Without a glance at Taylor, Ruby took Amado by the hand and followed Ellen out the door with Sophie leading the way.

JD looked over at Taylor. "Shit, man. I'm sorry."

While he tried to hide it, they could all see the look on Taylor's face. "It's not your fault, JD. Besides, it had to come out sooner or later." He turned and walked out the door to catch up with Ellen.

"That ended well," Vivas observed quietly.

"Shit!" JD replied.

"Taylor was right." Hana moved to stand close to Carlos, who reached up to put his arm around her. "It was going to come out sooner or later. It was better that she heard it from him. At least now it is out there, and Ruby will have time to adjust."

"Adjust?" Vivas inquired.

"She likes him," Hana replied.

Mai offered, "I think it will work itself out."

"What will?" Vivas asked.

Mai stood and began to fold up the map of Manila. "He likes her too."

JD frowned. "How do you know that?"

"A woman knows," his mother replied.

Taylor stepped out into the hallway just in time to see Ruby follow Amado into their room and shut the door. Ellen had started back down the hall toward him with Sophie at her side.

"Okay, Mr. Taylor. Let's get you checked out." She handed him the key to his room. "After you."

Once in the room, Ellen sent Sophie to a corner and told the dog to lie down, which she did. Then, Ellen faced Taylor.

"Can I get you to strip down to your shorts?"

Taylor hesitated, and she smiled to put him at ease. "Don't worry. I am a doctor. I have seen it all."

Taylor nodded and did as she asked.

Ellen stifled a gasp. His body was covered with bruises, most of which had now become yellow-green, indicating they were healing. She gave Bill a short but thorough examination, with some poking and prodding that brought a wince or two from her patient. Digging a stethoscope out of her blue bag, Ellen listened to his heart and lungs and checked his pulse. Finally, she had Taylor follow her finger back and forth with his eyes. In a few minutes, she had finished.

"Well, JD is right. Somebody beat the hell out of you. I suspect you have a few broken ribs. I can't be exactly sure how many without an X-ray. The good news is they seem to be healing well, along with your rather extensive contusions. Your lungs sound good. In short, I think you'll live."

"Thanks, Doc."

"Don't mention it. But … what have you been eating this last week?"

"Nothing at first. Then chicken soup. I eat rice, vegetables, and a little meat when Ruby has it."

"Okay. Let's get some red meat in you. I am prescribing a few hotel steaks. I think a little more animal protein will go a long way toward helping you regain your strength. I can tell you were drinking a lot for quite a while, but I suspect not for the last week or so. Am I right?"

Taylor nodded.

Ellen smiled. "I hope you will continue in that current direction. Keep up with how you were previously drinking, and you'll soon have cirrhosis of the liver. Keep it casual. Now, I am going to wrap your ribs. Then, I will see if Ruby and Amado need anything. After that, I'll see if Amado will help me take Sophie for a walk... It's none of my business, but if I were you, I would take advantage of the opportunity to have a little heart-to-heart with Ruby."

"I'm not sure she wants to see me right now."

Ellen moved toward the door. Sophie got up to follow. "A part of her doesn't, but I think there is a bigger part of her that does. Anyway, it's certainly up to you."

With Sophie at her side, Ellen opened the door and left, closing it behind them. Taylor heard them start back down the hall.

Taylor took a few minutes to mull over Ellen's comments. He could see little point in trying to talk to Ruby now. Then it dawned on him that his few belongings were in one of the bags Ruby had carried into the room she and Amado were sharing.

Hell, I need to go down there anyway. I might try to explain.

Ruby and Taylor had never discussed being more than a kind woman and a man desperately needing help. There was nothing more to it than that. Or, was there? Taylor had to admit; he found her quite attractive.

But what in the hell do I have to offer her? I don't even have a job, and my fighting days are over. Besides, she would never put up with that. Now that Ruby knows the truth about me, that will end any chances of anything else. I'll do what I can to help JD rescue these two girls, and see that Ruby and Amado are safe. Then maybe I will make my way back to the States and find a way to start over. Probably better for Ruby and her son as well.

He sat down in a chair to wait. The compression bandage Ellen had wrapped around his ribs really helped. A few minutes later, he heard Ellen stop just outside the door with Amado and Sophie. Ellen seemed to be arguing with Sirichai, who insisted he should go with them when they walked Sophie.

"It's alright, Sirichai. Sophie will protect us."

Sirichai was not having it, and asked Ellen to wait while he let Vivas know he would go with them to walk the dog. After what happened with Xuan and Jum Y, he would take no chances. He was back a moment later, and Taylor heard the four of them walk off toward the elevators.

Taylor left his room and started down the hall. The door to room 704 was half-open. He heard JD and Vivas talking, but couldn't make out what they were saying. Passing by them without being spotted, a second later he was standing at the door to Ruby's room.

Shit. Taylor had no idea what to say.

After several moments of hesitation, he finally knocked on the door.

"Just a moment."

A few seconds later, the door opened, and Ruby stood looking at him.

"Sorry to bother you, but my … uh … stuff is in one of your bags."

Ruby nodded but didn't say anything. She stepped back to let Taylor pass and pointed to one of the chairs where his few belongings were stacked neatly. "They are there."

Taylor picked up what was there and then turned back to Ruby. She stood with her back to him, looking out the window at the city of Manila.

He fidgeted with the things in his hands. It wasn't much, just a few things Ruby had scraped together for him while he was recuperating—a change of underwear and socks, a toothbrush and toothpaste, a bag of Bic disposable razors, and shaving cream. There was also the money Amado had retrieved from his apartment. Of course, he had more money and belongings at his apartment, but it did not seem wise to try and get anything from there now.

It certainly wasn't much to show for thirty-five years of life.

"Ruby?"

She did not respond.

"Okay, please listen. I'm not good at this sort of thing. I'm just going to do my best. When you found me, I was a different man. I have no excuse for what I became. I think I was dead inside. Part of me wanted to die because of what happened in Afghanistan and what I did. But another part of me, I guess, at least at some level, refused to quit. So, I drank … a lot. I fought, and I fell in with some bad people. One of those people was Blessica Baguinda. She didn't love me, and I didn't love her. She used me, and I guess, I used her too. I can't change any of that. I can only change what I do now and going forward."

Ruby stood like a statue, still with her back to him. She still did not respond. Taylor could not see her face.

"I know you are a Christian woman. I respect that. I have never been what you might call a religious man. But I can't shake the feeling that you were meant to find me in that alley. I should have died that night. I've thought about it over and over this last week. It is the only thing that makes any sense to me. You did not only save my life, Ruby. You saved who I am; maybe you'd call it saving my soul. I don't know what a priest would say about all that. I am certainly no expert. But that is the honest truth, the best I can explain."

Taylor started to step toward her, then thought better of it.

"I guess in my state, it didn't register with me just how bad Blessica and her sister are. I knew about the gang and the fights, of course. I knew they ran a prostitution ring, because I occasionally ran off some unruly clients for them. I guess that all just proves how far I had fallen."

Taylor couldn't tell if Ruby was even listening to him.

"I can't change anything in the past, but I hope you can forgive me. I was lost; I had forgotten who I was.

Now, because of you, I remember. I will do whatever I can to help these folks get these two girls back and then focus on putting my life back together. You and Amado have had a lot to do with me feeling like a man again and why I care about life again. I owe you so much, and I will never forget what you've done for me."

He slipped out of the room and shut the door behind him. He did not see Ruby reach up to wipe the tears streaming down her cheeks.

Returning from their walk with Sophie, Amado and Ellen passed Taylor in the hall. He nodded but said nothing. Ellen could tell the smile on his face was forced, and that was not a good sign.

Sirichai sat in his chair in the hall and spoke to Taylor as he got to his room. According to Hana, Sirichai would stay there until they were all secure in their rooms, and only then would he go to bed. JD had told Sirichai not to worry and that Sophie would let them know if anyone was prowling around. But JD knew that Sirichai felt he needed to redeem himself.

Amado slid his key through the slot and opened the door. They entered to find Ruby sitting in a chair. Ellen could tell she had been crying.

"Are you alright, Ruby?"

"Yes, I am okay. Amado, it is time for your bath. Everything is in the bathroom, ready for you. It is getting late."

"Okay, mom. I am tired." Amado headed into the bathroom and shut the door.

Ellen was not surprised the boy was tired. Amado looked to be about fourteen. It would have been quite an exhausting and emotional day for anyone, never mind a young teenager.

"Are you sure you're alright, Ruby? I saw Taylor in the hall. He looked horrible."

Ruby started to speak, then shrugged. She did not know what to say.

"You know, Ruby, this is none of my business. We have just met, and I guess I've already inserted myself into this situation more than I should have. It is just that this is a critical time for us, and we need everyone to be focused."

Ellen paused, trying to decide how much to say.

"I have met a lot of men like Taylor. He is so much like my husband and Carlos. They are hard men who have seen things most of us, thankfully, never have to see. They do it to protect us."

Ellen moved to sit on the edge of the bed. "Would you mind if I sit down?"

"No, please sit. Please."

"I met JD in Niger. He was part of the SEAL team that rescued me. I was kidnapped by radical Islamic terrorists while working for Doctors Without Borders. He had another dog then, a SEAL K9 named Ajax. He was an amazing dog. Ajax got hit by shrapnel from a grenade when he took down a terrorist who was getting ready to throw it at Carlos and JD, who were helping me get into one of their vehicles. If it weren't for Ajax, we would have been killed.

When JD saw Ajax was down … well, I couldn't believe the change. One second, he was an iron-hard warrior who had just killed several men. The next second, he was tender, worried about his dog's life. Ajax is dead now, but he was much more than JD's dog. He was his partner, like a brother. I had never seen anything like that before.

Carlos was on that same SEAL team. I know he and JD killed several men that day. They did it to save me."

Ruby looked at Ellen, who had become quite emotional in recapping her rescue. Ruby was surprised at the extent of her feelings.

"I never tried to understand men like that, until that day. Even then, I didn't understand, at least not until this gang kidnapped Jum Y and Xuan a few days ago. I think I do understand now, at least a little. That is why I am here, too."

Ellen paused, trying to put her final thoughts together.

"These men live by an extreme code. It is certainly not for everybody. There isn't any room for gray areas in their actions. They live right on the edge, yet each has a strong moral compass. I guess when they fall, they fall hard.

I know Taylor has been in a tough place and has done things many people would condemn. He is now coming to grips with those things. But before that bad stuff happened, Taylor put his life on the line every day to keep people like you and me safe, not just at home but all around the world, in horrible places you and I will never see.

Taylor is coming back to himself now. You and Amado have both played a huge part in that. He is becoming whole again, and we need him. I don't know how you feel about him. Women are better at hiding our feelings. But it is as plain as the nose on your face that Taylor loves you and thinks the world of your son. I just wanted to make sure you can see it as clearly as I do."

Ellen stood and started toward the door, with Sophie following.

"I'll say good night. It's getting late, and we may have a busy day tomorrow."

"I understand. Thank you for sharing your thoughts. You've given me much to consider. Goodnight, Ellen."

Alone again, Ruby got up from the chair and moved over to sit on the bed. Amado had chosen the one closest to the door, probably thinking again about protecting his mother. Ellen's story circled through her mind. When she found Taylor in that alley, she'd had no idea that he'd lived such a life before.

Ellen's story must have been some of what Hana referred to earlier. But what happened in Vietnam? What else have these people seen and endured? What else has Taylor seen and survived to protect others?

"Mom?" Amado, finished with his bath, had come out of the bathroom. He was wearing the clean underwear Ruby had left in the bathroom for him. "Are you okay, Mom?"

Ruby smiled. "Yes, Amado. I am okay. You worry too much for a little boy."

"I am fourteen, Mom."

Ruby looked at her son. "Why, yes. Yes, you are. I guess you are not a little boy anymore."

"Mom?"

"Yes?"

"Are you mad at Mr. Taylor?"

"Why do you ask that?"

"I saw your face when he said he knew that mafia lady, Blessica Baguinda."

"You know about her?"

"Yes. Everyone knows about her. I even saw her once."

"You saw her? How?"

"It was when I snuck in to watch a fight. It was when I saw Mr. Taylor fight. I climbed up on the roof of a building and snuck in through a window. I saw the whole thing."

"Amado, I don't want you ever to do that again. It is dangerous, and we are better people than that."

"I know, Mom. I won't ever do it again. Will you forgive me?"

"I already have, you silly young man. Now, come over here and kiss me before you go to bed."

Amado leaned over and kissed his mother's cheek, then spun around and, in one giant step, leaped into bed.

"Amado?"

"Yes, Mom?"

"Was she pretty, Blessica Baguinda?"

"Yes, Mom." Amado crawled under the covers and adjusted the pillows. He had never slept in such a bed. "But she is not as pretty as you, Mom."

"Salamat. Thank you, son. Now, go to sleep."

CHAPTER 27
Vietnam

At precisely 1:10 pm, Ahn walked through the door of the Saigon Spa for her weekly massage. Her appointment with Chau was scheduled for 1:15, and she looked forward to it. The visits to the spa were one of her few chances to get away and do something nice for herself. Over the months she'd been coming here, her masseuse, Chau, had become a good friend. Ahn did not have many friends.

They often talked about what it would be like to live in America. It was something Ahn constantly dreamed about. Chau, however, was less enamored with getting away. She was content with where she was, probably because Saigon Spa was a legitimate business, catering to well-to-do clients and traveling professionals. They offered a variety of massages, baths, and therapies but no 'happy endings'. Ahn always got the full treatment: a complete body massage. It was expensive, but she earned it. Besides, Fong paid the bill.

Ahn was just about to sit in the waiting area when Chau entered the lobby, greeting her client with a smile.

"Ahn, how are you today? So good to see you."

"I am fine, Chau. I hope you are well. I need full treatment. I feel like my muscles are tied in knots."

"We can fix that. First, a cup of tea, then a hot bath, and then your massage. Okay?"

"Okay."

Chau led the way down the hall to a private waiting area with comfortable seating and a small coffee table. The dimmed lighting was easy on the eyes. Fresh-cut flowers were always beautifully arranged in a vase on the table, and incense burned on a small shelf mounted on the wall. It was a pleasing aroma; simple, not overpowering. The waiting room was clean and the atmosphere was designed to be pleasant and relaxing.

Chau motioned Ahn to sit on the small sofa near the coffee table, then poured two steaming cups of rice tea from a porcelain teapot on the corner counter. She took the two cups of tea and sat down next to her friend, handing one of the cups to Ahn.

Chau knew Ahn was Fong's mistress. They had talked about it a time or two, and Fong made no secret of it. Ahn figured it was his way of warning everyone to keep away from her. It was one reason she had so few friends. Many people were frightened of the corrupt lieutenant colonel with the Vietnamese mobile police force.

Chau smiled, then took a sip of the hot tea.

"You should find another job, Ahn. Then maybe you will not always be so tense."

Ahn looked down at the cup of tea in her hands and nodded with a sad smile. "If only I could, Chau. I know my fate, and it is not good for me to think about it too much. I am stuck until Fong decides to find someone else. Then, I will be in the streets." She sighed. "I think sometimes I will not let that happen. When it is time, I will kill myself. I cannot go back to that life."

Chau reached out and put a hand on her friend's shoulder.

"Do not talk like that, Ahn. It hurts me to hear you. You shall go to America and start a new life, and Fong will get what he deserves. You will see."

"That is not likely, my friend, but thank you for saying so. That is why I like to come here. You always cheer me up. But let's be honest. I'm never going to America. Vietnam is where I am, and it is here I will stay."

"Let's drink our tea, and then you can shower while I prepare your bath. After that, we can talk more while I work the knots out of your muscles."

Forty minutes later, Ahn lay covered with a towel as Chau began to work on her neck and shoulder muscles. Chau's hands and fingers were unbelievably strong and dug deep into the soft tissue, finding each knotted muscle fiber and working it until the knot dissolved. Sometimes it was painful, but when her hands moved on, the relaxation they left behind was wonderful.

Chau focused on her work, and Ahn, happy to remain quiet, did nothing to distract her friend. A soft knock on the door to the massage room startled Ahn.

"It is okay, Ahn. This man is an old friend of my father. I want you to listen to him."

Ahn started to roll over, trying to get up.

"Do not worry, Ahn. Please trust me. This man will help you. Trust me and listen to what he has to say. Nothing will leave this room. I promise you."

Ahn settled back onto the massage table but was far from relaxed.

"I am going to let him in, Ahn. Don't be afraid. Just listen, please. You can trust me."

Chau adjusted the towel covering her friend and then opened the door. An older man stepped in. He was neatly dressed in the clothing of someone who lived in the mountain region to the Northwest. His hair was white, and his face resembled wrinkled shoe leather. The man sat on a stool in the corner of the room but said nothing as Ahn studied his face. Finally, he smiled.

While the man certainly was old, his eyes were clear and bright. Ahn noticed that the smile lit up his whole face and there appeared to be kindness in those eyes. She had not seen that from a man in a long time.

"Hello, Ahn, my name is Hai. I am an old friend of Chau's father, and I have watched Chau grow from a little girl into a fine woman. You have a good friend in her. "Ahn, I must tell you that I have been watching you for a few days now."

"Watching me? Why? What am I to you?"

"You are a woman able to help me solve a serious problem. And I, in return, can help you get what you desire."

"Get what I desire?"

"Quite so."

"And what is it that you think I want?"

"Chau tells me you wish to be free of Lt. Colonel Fong, and hope to travel to America to start a new life."

Ahn looked at Chau. Had her friend betrayed her?

Chau saw fear register in Ahn's eyes. "Trust me," Chau repeated. "Listen to what Hai has to say."

Ahn looked back at Hai, forcing herself to speak. "What kind of magic do you possess that you can help me?"

"I have no magic but I have good friends, friends in many places. I have Vietnamese friends and friends who are Degar. I have friends in Thailand and in America.

Ahn, Fong and his boss, Minister Trán, are sinister, evil men. They prey on our people, poisoning our children with drugs and selling young girls and boys into short, wretched lives as prostitutes."

Hai paused, and Ahn noticed that his eyes had changed. They were dark now, filled with something. Was it anger or pain?

Yes, she thought. *I see anger and pain in those old eyes. But something else as well. It is worry.* She saw genuine concern in Hai's eyes.

"Recently, they tried to murder some old friends of mine who are now living in Thailand, friends who work to help people like you start a new life. One of these is a very old friend whom I have served many years, since fighting with American soldiers against the communists. These are evil men who must be stopped."

Ahn could not detect any hint of deceit in the older man's tone or face. And she had gotten pretty good at spotting just that. After all, it was a matter of survival in her line of work. "Who is this old friend of whom you speak?"

Hai smiled and the anger and pain seemed to vanish from his eyes, but the concern remained. "His name is Dish. You may have heard of him."

Ahn gasped. Indeed, she had heard this name. She'd heard many stories about the Montagnard named Dish—stories often shared in hushed voices and dark places by those who'd sided with the Americans during the war, those whose families had suffered the wrath of the communist regime ever since. Dish was the Montagnard, the Jarai warrior who had never surrendered and who, to this day, still had a bounty on his head. Many times, she'd heard Fong curse that name under his breath.

Ahn remained silent for several minutes. Chau said nothing the whole time, standing beside Ahn, her hand resting reassuringly on her friend's shoulder. Ahn shocked herself when she heard her own voice ask, "What do you want of me?"

It was pretty simple. Hai explained what he needed. Through his contacts, he'd learned that after his cousin's death, Trán Ngô Sang had assumed ownership of the old Michelin rubber plantation about sixty kilometers northwest of Ho Chi Minh City. Dish had killed Trán's cousin, a former Viet Cong colonel turned drug lord, while rescuing his sister, Mai, who Trán had kidnapped in a plot to trap the old Montagnard gun smuggler.

Ahn nodded. She already knew a good deal about this. She knew Fong had been on the drug lord's payroll and now reported to his cousin, Minister Trán. She also knew he'd led the investigation into the attack on the old plantation.

It is funny how many men seem to believe that because they "own" someone, that person can't have a mind of their own and excellent ears.

Fong often spoke to associates on the phone in her presence, as if she did not even exist. Ahn shuddered at this realization.

Maybe because, sooner or later, she would cease to be?

Fong had discovered that Americans were involved in Mai's rescue. He'd managed to track Dish to his current location in Thailand, where his spies learned of the roles the woman named Hana and a retired Thai army major had played. However, after digging into the major's background, Fong knew better than to go after the old army officer or mention him in his report. Fong had discovered that Major Anurat Detphong was a very dangerous man in the gun smuggling world. Therefore, only Dish and the woman named Hana became the primary targets for revenge.

Hai continued to describe what he wanted from Ahn. Trán Ngô Sang had replaced the old plantation house, which had been burned to the ground during Mai's rescue, with a modern structure that served as a residence and office space while Trán was there, typically several days each month.

After the attack on the nightclub in Thailand, Dish had asked Hai to keep an eye on Fong and learn what he could of this other Trán, the cousin of the man he'd killed. Hai had done that, putting Dish's former gun-smuggling network back to work. Dish was still a folk hero to many Degar and South Vietnamese people, plus anyone who still suffered under the brutal oppression of the communist government. There were always those willing to help.

Ahn listened as Hai explained that he'd learned Trán held young women at the plantation until he'd completed arrangements to ship them off to work in brothels around the world.

Ahn wondered if Fong knew of this and then, finally decided that he must. After all, he'd protected the pimps and drug dealers who worked the red-light districts of Ho Chi Minh City for Trán, the drug lord. Furthermore, that was where Fong had first encountered her.

Why would he not now be a part of this cousin's scheme? Fong would see it as a promotion, moving from the employment of a drug lord to the payroll of a high-ranking government official.

Finally, Hai came to the crux of his plan. "I need you to let me know when Fong will be at the plantation with Trán in the next few days. Or if he will not, somehow arrange a meeting between the two at the plantation."

Ahn's eyes widened as she listened to Hai's request.

"How you do this is up to you, but they cannot suspect any trickery. Trán and Fong are cunning men who have survived this long because they are always on alert, and suspicious. You must be very careful, Ahn."

Ahn immediately understood the risk involved.

Hai saw the look on the young woman's face. "These are bad, dangerous men, and I know it is a frightening thing I am asking you to do. It is not without risk. But if you can arrange a meeting or let us know when such a meeting will occur, I promise you that neither Trán nor Fong will leave the plantation alive. You will be safe with my friends. They will guide you to my village in the mountains near Cambodia. From there, we will get you to Thailand, where my friends will help you get to America."

Ahn had some difficulty processing all this. It was indeed a terrifying proposition; so much could go wrong.

But what if it could work? Ahn had to think about it. *Could I arrange such a meeting? Under what pretext? I must be there, and they must not suspect anything. Hai is right; they will kill me if they suspect I am plotting anything.*

305

In that moment, another thought pierced the turmoil in her brain.

I am already as good as dead—maybe I have a few years left before Fong will want a younger girl, and I know too much.

She felt her friend's grip on her shoulder tighten as Chau leaned over to whisper, "Ahn, this is your chance. Please, take it. You can trust these people, and you are smart. I know you can make this happen. Hai is a good man and will do what he says." Chau paused, then leaned in closer. "Ahn ... Hai, my father, and Dish go back a long time to when the Americans were here. You are my friend. Because I trust you so, I will tell you this. It would be dangerous to my family if this became known."

Shocked, Ahn turned to look up at Chau. She saw only sincerity and concern on her friend's face. Ahn was still surprised when she turned back to Hai and heard herself say, "I will do it."

Hai smiled with gratitude and relief. "Thank you, Ahn. It will work out. We know Minister Trán will arrive at the plantation tomorrow evening. He usually stays three or four days. You must get them to meet during that time for this to work. If not, we must wait for his next visit, which could be a problem."

Hai handed Ahn a slip of paper. "This is a phone number you can call or text when you know you and Fong will be at the plantation. Nobody will answer. Just text or leave a message. You should memorize the number and then get rid of the slip of paper. If you cannot contact us, it should still be okay. We are watching the plantation day and night, and will see you arrive. Do not put yourself at unnecessary risk trying to get us a message."

Ahn nodded. She was already trying to figure out how to get Fong to the plantation to meet with Trán in the next few days, and take her with him.

.

CHAPTER 28
Thailand

Three men left Bangkok in a rented Toyota van and drove nonstop for twelve hours to Sisaket. Using contacts developed over his years working with the CIA, Rick Hahn provided Dish and Chanmali with new identity papers when they arrived in Thailand. It seemed prudent, especially since Dish was still wanted for a rather large reward in Vietnam.

Dish was now traveling under the name Keej, a common enough name among the Hmong. The Hmong were another tribe living in various Southeast Asian regions, including the Vietnamese central highlands. They were often lumped with the Jarai and other Degar tribes called Montagnards. While some Hmong sided with the North Vietnamese, most had sided with the United States during the Vietnam War.

Dish laughed at the choice of name, which in Hmong means 'capable'. Chanmali stated she thought it entirely appropriate. Dish preferred his real name and only used the name Keej when necessary, such as when sneaking back into a country where his real name carried a sizable bounty—either dead or alive.

The trip was mostly quiet, with Rick and Slim taking turns driving while Dish was the navigator. Although all three had been over this route several times, Dish had never bothered to learn to drive. Rick tried several times to pry some of Dish's plan out of him, but he would shake his head.

"You will know soon. Good plan. Little trouble for three men. First, I talk to Hai in my old village. Then I will tell you my plan." After that, he said nothing more.

Finally, Hahn gave up and relaxed back into his seat. Slim was at the wheel. He was sitting in the back. *Might as well take a nap*, he thought. *Dish will fill us in when he is damn good and ready*. Rick closed his eyes and quickly dozed off.

They pulled the van over once for gas, something to drink, and to stretch their legs. Hahn relieved Slim at the wheel and they soon returned to the road. Slim settled into the back and was quickly asleep. In their line of work, you became pretty adept at grabbing whatever shut-eye you could when you could.

Once in Sisaket, they went directly to Major Anurat Detphong's home. The security detail let them through with a mere glance; Dish was well-known to them. When the van stopped, Major Anurat was already descending the stairs from his veranda, and the three men got out.

The old gun smuggler enthusiastically greeted his visitors. "Dish, my old friend. It does my heart good to see you again."

Dish bowed his head in greeting. Anurat returned the bow.

"Rick, it is good to see you, too. I told your beautiful daughter some time ago that we should get to know each other better. We have done business for many years, but I think we should be friends, yes?"

"Sure, Major. Can't have too many friends in this line of work." Rick indicated Slim, who stood just to his right. "You remember Slim? I believe you two have met before. Slim has been with me for years, and we've been through many tight spots together."

"Yes, I certainly remember Slim. You are most welcome in my home. Come, I have dinner prepared. You can rest here tonight. We will discuss what I can do to help after eating."

CHAPTER 29
Vietnam

Ahn sat at the small table in her kitchen. As she sipped her tea, she returned to the shocking event at the Saigon Spa.

Hai left quietly after they finished talking, slipping out the door with a reassuring smile. Chau wanted to complete the massage, but Ahn's brain would not let that happen. She was too excited and scared to lie still. She got up, dressed, and hugged Chau.

"I am sorry, Chau, but I must go. My mind is crazy now, and I must think. I cannot thank you enough. And never worry, my friend. Your family secret will always be safe with me. I will guard it carefully until my death."

Chau kissed her friend's cheek. "I know that, Ahn. That is why I told you. I may not see you again, so I will say goodbye now, and good luck to you. I will always remember you, my friend. Do not forget about me when you are in America."

Ahn felt a tear run down her cheek. "I will never forget you, or what you have done for me. I know there is risk, but this is a chance. I must try."

Chau hugged her friend once more. "It will work. I know in my heart it will work." With that, Chau released her hold on Ahn and watched as her friend turned and hurried from the room.

In her kitchen, Ahn's mind shifted to the problem before her. How would she get Fong to the plantation and, just as important, take her with him? She knew that he would never do that himself.

Minister Trán will have to tell him to bring me. How do I make that happen?

She would have to call Trán and talk to him. She had to give him a reason to contact Fong and tell him to come to the plantation and bring her. Fong would visit her apartment later that evening, but his phone was password-protected. She could not get Trán's number from his phone. Then she remembered his little green book. Fong was just old-fashioned enough not to trust modern technology entirely. He kept important contacts in a little green book he carried in his suit jacket pocket, a backup should something happen to his phone.

Suppose I can get my hands on that book for a few seconds. Trán's number will surely be in there. Ahn's mind was forming a plan.

Ahn was ready when she heard Fong let himself into her apartment. Smiling, she greeted him as he entered.

"Ah! You are just in time. I have dinner prepared. Some of your favorite dishes."

Fong was a bit surprised, but then Ahn did this occasionally. Most often, when she'd had an enjoyable day combined with a trip to the spa. At first, Fong had been unsure about allowing her trips to the spa, but Ahn had done nothing to abuse the privilege, and those same evenings were always highly satisfying.

Fong smiled. "You have been to the spa today, Ahn?"

"Of course. You know it is my day for the spa. I have prepared pho with chicken, steamed rice with ground pork, and your favorite, Chinese broccoli. There is steamed fish, as well."

"Everything smells so good, Ahn. You spoil me."

Ahn gave the pho a last stir and, setting the spoon on the counter, walked over to Fong. "Here, let me take your jacket. I will place it right over there on the chair," indicating a straight-backed chair in the corner near the door to her bedroom.

Fong seemed to pause, and for a moment Ahn was afraid he would not let her take his jacket. But he shrugged out of it, handing it to her.

"Have a seat. I will get dinner on the table." Ahn hung the jacket neatly over the chair's back, then returned to the kitchen and began setting dishes on the table.

She waited, trying to appear unconcerned as she went through the motions of enjoying her dinner. She was too nervous to have much appetite, but forced herself to eat a fair amount. Fong enjoyed the meal immensely, having second servings of steamed fish, pho, and broccoli.

When they were through, Ahn stood and cleared the dishes from the table. As she reached to take Fong's plate, she smiled.

"How about some dessert."

Reaching up with his arms and pulling her down close, Fong pressed his face into her hair.

"You smell very good, Ahn. I think you will be dessert."

Ahn forced herself to laugh. "Wherever is your mind?" Pulling back, she let her long hair brush across his face and shoulder. "I took a bath before dinner. Why don't you bathe and relax while I clean up the kitchen? I will be in bed when you are through."

Fong sighed lustfully and reached up to stroke her back. "You will wear the black negligee I got you a few weeks ago?" She looked ravishing in it.

"Yes, I will. Now hurry and bathe. I will be ready."

Fong stood and headed toward the bedroom and its attached bathroom. Holding her breath, Ahn waited to see if he would take his jacket with him. Instead, Fong walked right past it. He had other things on his mind.

Moments later, Ahn heard the water turn on. Swiftly, she moved to the chair and felt the jacket, finding what she sought in the left breast pocket. Retrieving the little

314

book, Ahn quickly began scanning through it. She found Trán's name and two phone numbers on the third page. Crossing to the kitchen counter, she wrote the numbers on a pad she kept for grocery lists. Her heart raced in her chest, terrified Fong would reappear and catch her in the act.

Tearing the page with the numbers she'd just written from the pad, she slid it under a vase holding an arrangement of flowers. She quickly returned the book to its pocket, returned to the kitchen, and began to clean up.

I did it.

Ahn's heart began to slow its rapid pace. Satisfied, she made her way into the bedroom and quickly undressed. Tossing her dress, bra, and panties into the laundry basket, Ahn slid into the nightgown she'd already stashed under her pillow. She knew how much he loved seeing her in it. Arranging herself comfortably, Ahn waited for Fong to finish in the bathroom.

Fong left the apartment a little after 9:00 p.m. His unofficial duties required him to be around during business hours, which meant late evenings circulating among the nightclubs and brothels of Ho Chi Minh City's District One.

Ahn was scared. Sitting alone at her kitchen table for almost an hour, she'd been trying to devise a plausible story to tell Trán while working up the courage to make the call. The paper on which she'd written the two numbers sat on the table before her.

I don't think I can do this.

Then Ahn thought of her friend, Chau, and the risk she had taken on her behalf. "This is your chance; take it," Chau had said. "You can trust Hai and his friends."

Suddenly, Ahn picked up her phone and dialed the number listed as Trán's cell phone before she could change her mind. It began to ring.

On the third ring, a voice answered. "Hello, who is this?"

"Minister Trán, this is Ahn, a friend of Fong. We have met a few times in the past."

Trán Ngô Sang searched his memory. Then he remembered her. He'd seen her once when he'd been to Ho Chi Minh City to see Fong. She was a beautiful girl, and young. But how did she get his number?

"Yes, Ahn. I do remember you. Why are you calling me? It's very late."

"Minister Trán, I know it is late. I am so sorry to bother you at this hour. But I am worried about Fong. He just left here, and he's deeply troubled by something. I told him to call you, but he will not. He is terrified. I don't know what it is about, but I heard him mention Americans. I wasn't trying to listen, but I heard anyway."

Trán considered this. Fong had always been loyal, but frightened people could do stupid things. "Why are you telling me this, Ahn? Aren't you Fong's woman?"

"It is true, Colonel, I am his mistress, and he has been good to me. I wanted him to call you and get your advice, but he was scared to talk to you. I don't want to make trouble for him, sir. I know he is loyal to you, but if he has trouble, I will have trouble also."

"I see. What would you have me do, Ahn?"

"Please, Colonel, talk to Fong. I know he fears something, but he respects you. Maybe together you can fix whatever bothers him. If not, I don't want trouble for something Fong has done. I thought maybe if I help you, you will help me? I would be in your debt."

Trán did not immediately respond, and Ahn feared he would hang up. Then he spoke.

"Ahn, it took a lot of courage to call me like this. You are either very brave or stupid. I have not decided which. I will consider what you have said carefully. However, if this turns out to be some deception on your part, I will be very unhappy. Do you understand?"

"Yes, yes, I understand, Colonel. Please don't tell Fong I called you. I am just trying to help and look out for myself. That is all."

"We shall see." The phone went dead.

With a shaking hand, Ahn placed her phone down on the table. She did it. Now, all she could do was wait. A sudden chill ran down her spine as Ahn realized she had probably just signed her death warrant.

Oh, Chau. Please be right about Hai and his friends.

Trán set his phone down and leaned back in his chair. *Interesting. What kind of game is Ahn playing?*

He certainly did remember her. She was a striking woman, the kind of beauty a man doesn't forget. And she was still young, maybe in her late twenties.

What has Fong gotten himself into? Or maybe Ahn was trying to better her position.

Now that, Trán could understand. It made sense. After all, a girl like that would be ambitious and want to climb as far as her looks would take her. It might be a pleasant distraction to have her around for a while. If she became troublesome, he could easily ship her off to South Korea or the Philippines.

Trán's mind turned to Fong. The man was undoubtedly a good detective, but Fong had failed in Thailand. It was true; he had provided the men. But it had been Fong's plan.

Fong's plan was too complicated. How hard was it to kill two people?

Perhaps it was time for Fong to go. The man knew too much. Maybe it was time to recruit a replacement. There were always cops looking to make more money. Being a Vietnamese police officer, even a lieutenant colonel with the mobile police force, did not pay all that well. The problem would be finding one as good as Fong had been.

But it was not impossible.

Yes, Trán decided. He needed to talk with Fong. Not tomorrow, however. Tomorrow, he had a new shipment of girls coming in from Laos; it would be busy. The day after would work nicely. Then, he could fly back to Hanoi.

Right now, it was time for bed. He would call Fong tomorrow morning, invite him to a dinner meeting, and tell him to bring his charming mistress. It would be nice to have some company. Only he, his driver, and the disgusting brother and sister team were currently at the plantation. Unlike his cousin, Trán Ngô Sang believed that the fewer who knew of his private business, the better. He preferred to do his own dirty work and keep a low profile. People couldn't tell what they did not know.

CHAPTER 30
Thailand

Major Anurat was not kidding when he said he had dinner prepared for his guests. There were skewers of chicken satay, fresh spring rolls, and Miang Kham—fresh chaphlu leaves filled with roasted coconut shavings mixed with chopped shallots, chili peppers, ginger, garlic, lime, cashew nuts, and dried shrimp. The main course consisted of a fantastic shrimp curry, simple Pad Thai noodles, and Jasmine rice. Their host provided a selection of fresh fruit and colorful flavored rice cakes for dessert. Simple rice tea complemented the savory meal. It was a feast, and all three travelers were quite hungry.

Once they finished eating, Anurat's housekeeper cleaned away the dishes and the major turned to his guests.

"My friends, we have fought the evil of communism that has taken over Vietnam and threatened other countries for too long. We have killed many communists. I wish it were not so, but men like us who refuse to live under an oppressive yoke have little choice. It is forced upon us because we choose to be free. This evil gives too much power to small men; corrupt men who prey on their people, and we too often find ourselves in a situation such as this one. Again, I wish it were not so."

A general murmur of agreement came from the other three men seated around the low table.

"I agree, Major," Slim commented. "But then, I'd be out of a job. I'd have to retire." Slim chuckled. "Not that retirement would be so bad."

Hahn chuckled, "Slim, I just can't picture you sitting in a rocking chair in a retirement home."

Both Dish and Slim laughed, and even Major Anurat smiled before going on.

"I know little of Dish's plan, but I know his mind. If he has designed a plan, it will be sound. Please tell me what I can do to help. The world would be better off if men like this Lt. Colonel Fong and Minister Trán were not in it."

Dish settled back onto his cushion. "It is a simple plan, relying on human nature and the distrustfulness of evil men; this is why it will work. This meal tonight and a place to rest are more than enough help, old friend. I greatly appreciate both.

"Tomorrow, we will drive to Xayden, crossing the Mekong River on the ferry at Muang Champassak. Once in Xayden, we will hike to my old village, where Hai will be waiting for us. He's been in contact with Fong's mistress, a young woman named Ahn. Ahn has agreed to arrange a meeting at the old plantation where my sister was held. It is a private place in the countryside that Trán has taken over since I killed his cousin. Ahn will arrange to get Fong there for a meeting with Trán."

"We know Trán will be there?" Hahn asked.

"Hai has had men watching, and we know Trán holds young girls there for shipment to other countries, where he sells them to work in brothels."

Slim and Hahn both looked up. The more they learned about Trán, the more they agreed the world would be better off without him.

"Then what?" Slim asked.

"Hai has arranged a truck to take us close to the plantation. My village has weapons— pistols, a few AK-47s, and a few M16 rifles. I also have a good Barrett .50 caliber rifle. JD used that rifle to save his mother from Trán's cousin. And sitting here. I have a former Special Forces sniper to shoot it, and his old friend to be his spotter," Dish grinned.

"Well, it is a simple enough plan," Hahn agreed. "But what about the other girls? We can't just leave them there. How will we get them out? I think we should sneak in quietly, get in close and neutralize any guards, and set those girls loose. We can take them to Thailand, or they could go home if that is an option for them. It might be better to take them to Thailand … safer for them."

Dish nodded. "We can do that, no problem. It should be simple enough to get to the two guarding the girls. Hai says they are from North Korea, a brother and sister. He says they are evil, filthy people. And, how do you say— not very bright? We will sneak in quietly to kill Fong and Trán. After that, we all will leave in the truck with Poh and drive close to my village. One of Hai's men will drive the truck back to Lai Khe, and we will hike the rest of the way to the village, then rest. In the morning, we walk back to Xayden."

Slim looked over at Dish. "Why is Ahn helping us? What does she get out of this? Can she be trusted?"

Dish leaned back and sighed; his face suddenly looking old and tired. "It is the same sad story. Ahn is trapped in a bad life with no way out. It is better than being on the streets, but eventually, she will be older and no longer pleasing to Fong's eyes. He will want a younger mistress and will probably kill her because she knows too much about his business. Ahn knows this. In exchange for her help, I promised to get her out of Vietnam and into Thailand. Ahn wants to go to America, and Hana can help her start a new life there."

"Hana knows of your plan with Ahn?"

"No, but she will help."

Slim glanced sideways at Rick. "Yes, Hana will help her. She's a chip off the old block. And it seems we have a plan! I suggest we all get some rest."

Rick nodded, still thinking about Hana's role in all of this. He was very proud of his daughter. She'd become one hell of a woman. He'd told her he was happy she decided to sell Obsession and go to the US with Vivas. It would be a much better life for her, and she deserved it.

Dish mistook the look on Hahn's face. "Do not worry, my friend. I promised Hana I would bring you back to Thailand safe and in one piece. Slim also."

Rick looked up, returning from his thoughts. "Okay. That's good to hear."

"That's for sure," Slim agreed.

Major Anurat stood. "It sounds like things are as set as they can be. My housekeeper will show you where you can sleep. Please know you only have to ask me if you need anything more. It is getting late now, so I will say goodnight.

CHAPTER 31
Vietnam

Fong was ordering his breakfast of scrambled eggs, fried rice, and black coffee when the cell phone in his jacket's breast pocket began to chirp. Frowning, he retrieved the phone and verified the caller, then pressed the green icon to answer.

"Good morning, Minister. What can I do for you?"

"Good morning, Fong. I am out at the plantation for a couple of days, conducting business."

Fong knew what that meant.

"I have a few things I wish to discuss with you while I am here. Would you make yourself available tomorrow evening? We can discuss our business over dinner. I grow rather weary of my assistant's company and could use a change."

"Is there a problem, Minister?"

'No, Fong, no problem at all. It is just some routine business and a chance to talk to someone besides Phoc. He is a loyal and hard-working assistant, but not too much for intellectual conversation. Perhaps you could bring your mistress … what is her name?"

"Ahn?" Fong was shocked.

"Ah, yes. That is her name. Bring Ahn. I seem to remember her as quite a pleasant young woman. It will be enjoyable to have both of you join me for dinner. Shall we say about 7:00 p.m.? That will give you time to get out here, and it will not be too late when you head back to the city."

Fong was not sure what to make of this, but he knew better than to refuse.

"Yes, sir. 7:00 pm. We will be there, and thank you for the invitation."

"Not at all, Fong. Do you think I am too old to enjoy dinner and a quiet evening of conversation with one of my loyal associates and his lady?"

"Not at all, Minister."

"Good, good. Then I will expect you both at 7:00 sharp."

The call ended and Fong sat there, stunned. This had to be a trick. There must be something wrong. He could not think of anything, at least not since the failed attack on the club in Thailand. But those things happen, and truthfully, though it probably would not matter to Trán, that was not his fault.

I used the men Trán himself provided. It was not my fault they were not up to the task.

Since then, everything had gone as smoothly as silk. The collections were good. Everyone paid on time, fearing Fong's heavy-handed retaliation if they didn't. Trán should have nothing to be concerned about.

Maybe that's it; maybe Trán is happy with my work. This dinner could be a good thing. Or maybe Trán wants Ahn. That, too, is possible. Yes, that is indeed a possibility.

Fong decided he needed to talk to Ahn. He needed to know if Trán had ever approached her. Fong would hate to give her up now; she was his most prized possession. Perhaps Trán was just happy with his work. Maybe his time had finally come to move up in the world.

Ahn set the teakettle back on the burner. She waited a few minutes for the tea to steep in her cup, then removed the teabag. Picking up the steaming cup, she walked over to the couch in her apartment's sitting room. Her stomach was in knots; she hoped the rice tea would help her relax.

She had just taken the first sip of her tea when Ahn heard the key turn in her apartment door lock. Fong walked in.

Ahn struggled to appear calm. "Oh. You are here early. I was not expecting you until later this evening. It is only mid-morning."

"Something has just happened,"

"What has happened? Not something bad, I hope."

"I am not sure. I got an unexpected call from Minister Trán."

"Unexpected? How so?" Ahn set her tea down and stood to take Fong's jacket. "Please sit and tell me. I will get you some tea."

"Minister Trán has invited me to the plantation for dinner tomorrow evening, and he requested I bring you as well."

"Me?"

"Yes. Trán said a pleasant evening of dinner and conversation with the two of us would be nice. However, that does not sound like Trán."

"I would not know. I only remember meeting Minister Trán once, when he was in Ho Chi Minh City and you introduced me. I think that was about two years ago."

Returning from the kitchen, Ahn handed Fong a steaming teacup and he sat down on the sofa.

"He has never approached you since that meeting? You are such a beautiful woman, Ahn."

"No. He has not approached me in any way. We both know what I am, or what I was before you helped me." Ahn knew she needed to put Fong's mind at ease. "Besides, Minister Trán is a very powerful man. I am sure his world is full of beautiful young women."

Fong, taking a sip of the rice tea, considered this.

"Maybe it is good news for you. I know how hard you work for him. Surely, the minister requires loyal and hardworking men. Perhaps he has a better position for you, a promotion."

"I have considered this possibility. But why invite you?"

Ahn shrugged. "Perhaps it is just what he says. Maybe the minister wants a pleasant evening and a break from the usual business. Having a woman's voice at dinner can help with that, I would think."

Fong took another sip, then set the teacup down on the end table near the sofa. "Do you think that is all this is?"

Ahn noticed Fong's eyes were focused intensely on her face. She smiled, willing herself to relax, but her nerves felt taut, like a bowstring.

Taking her seat on the couch, she folded her legs under her and took another sip of her tea.

"I can't think of why it shouldn't be that. Surely, someone as smart as Minister Trán would want to keep his best employees happy, and he knows I am your woman. He would understand that trying to take me away would not be good for business, and besides, there are so many other women he could easily have." Ahn forced herself to look into Fong's eyes and smile. "I sense things are going well for you … a woman knows these things. I suspect he wants to reward you for keeping his operations running smoothly. He wants to keep you happy and working hard. That is all."

Fong relaxed back into his chair and, retrieving his teacup from the end table, took a sip of tea. Ahn's words did make sense. Things had been running smoothly for months.

Finally, Fong nodded. "Yes. I think perhaps you are right. That does seem to be the most logical explanation." His eyes moved from Ahn's face to the gentle swell of her breasts just visible under the silk robe she was wearing.

Sensing the change in Fong's mood, Ahn shifted her legs, allowing the robe to part below the sash and exposing more of her legs to his gaze—anything to divert his mind from tomorrow's meeting with Minister Trán.

Some men are so predictable.

She needed to make Fong happy and get him out of her apartment. She had a message to send.

CHAPTER 32
The Philippines

"Okay, what's the plan?" Vivas asked.

"It seems to me the first thing we need to do is find out exactly where the Baguinda sisters have the girls stashed."

JD took a sip of the coffee Ellen had just set down on the table for him. She placed another cup before Vivas, then sat next to Mai on the couch.

Hana moved the small office chair from the desk close to the couch. She'd passed on coffee. "And how exactly do we do that?"

"We grab Tony Salonga." Bill Taylor was standing near the window that looked out over Manila. "He will know. He's the sisters' top lieutenant."

"You know this Salonga?" JD asked.

"Yes, I know him. And I know where he hangs out, and who he hangs with. He shacks up with a woman who lives in Tondo. If he's not working, he will be with her or at a pool hall just down the street from her place. It would be better to grab Salonga at her place. We can sweat what we need out of him there. His lady friend is also a member of the Baguinda sisters' gang. She's no better than he is, maybe worse, so I wouldn't lose any sleep over her."

"Okay then," Hana cut in. "JD, why don't you, Taylor, and Sirichai grab Salonga and find out where they're holding the girls? Carlos, I'd like you to stay here while Sirichai is gone. We're a tough bunch of ladies and have Sophie, but I'd like someone here just in case."

Vivas nodded, but he could not hide the disappointment on his face.

JD saw the look. "Don't worry, buddy. There will be plenty for you to do before this is over. We both know Sirichai will want to get his hands on this Salonga character for grabbing the girls."

"Yeah! I get it."

"Okay then, we should leave here about 9:00 p.m.," Taylor advised. "Salonga will be at the pool hall or his girlfriend's place by then. If he's at the pool hall, we'll watch and wait until he heads to her place. Sound good?"

Everyone agreed. Taylor continued. "That gives us some time to kill. I want to return to my old room and retrieve some of my belongings. It's probably not smart to go by myself. Thanks to the doc's advice," Taylor smiled at Ellen, "I am feeling much better, but not quite one hundred percent yet."

Vivas looked up. "I'll go. If I have to sit here tonight, I want to get out and do something this morning."

Hana glanced over at him. "Okay, on one condition, Sirichai and I will also go with you. We'll take a cab, get Taylor's stuff, and return here."

Vivas grinned. "Yes dear."

Everyone laughed.

"Grab a couple of rolls of duct tape while you're out," JD suggested.

"Roger that."

Mai, followed by Ruby, entered the room. Amado appeared a few seconds later with Sophie at his side.

Hana stood up. "Good morning, Mai, Ruby. There is coffee. Would either of you like some? I have nothing for Amado, but we can order something from room service."

"Coffee sounds great." Mai walked over to get some.

Ellen stood. "Sit down, Mai. You too, Ruby. I'll get you both coffee, and then Amado and I will order something from room service. I'm famished. Amado, do you like pancakes?"

Amado's eyes lit up.

"Thank you, but I will pass on coffee for now." Ruby seemed uncomfortable. "If you have finished your meeting, I would like to talk to Bill, if he doesn't mind. It won't take long."

Surprised, Taylor looked up at Ruby. "Uh … sure, Ruby. There's time. I don't mind."

As he stood to join Ruby, Taylor turned to Hana and Carlos. "Will you two be ready to go when we're finished talking, or are you ordering pancakes? The earlier, the better. I want to get my stuff and get back here."

Vivas stood. "Yep, we'll be ready when you are. I'll let Sirichai know. See you in a few minutes."

Taylor followed Ruby down the hall to her room.

"Please, Bill, sit down." He looked around, then sat on the edge of the closest bed. Ruby sat in the chair by the desk, turning to face him.

"What's on your mind, Ruby?"

"I want to apologize for how I acted yesterday."

"You don't owe me an apology. I understand. I know who I am—well, who I was. It would be hard for anyone to look past that."

"No, that is not so. And I do owe you an apology. I have heard a lot about what you did here in Manila. I do understand that is not who you are, not inside."

Taylor started to stand.

"Please, Bill, sit … let me finish."

Taylor sat down again.

"I talked a long time with Mai this morning. She is a nice lady and very wise. We talked about many things—how she grew up in Vietnam, and when the Viet Cong murdered her family. She told me of her life with the Jarai people and her brother, Dish. Mai also told me about meeting her American officer husband in Vietnam, and going to America. I know about her life and her son, JD; how, when her husband died, she returned to Vietnam to look for her brother and was kidnapped by a very bad man. She told me about Dish, Vivas, this man Pallie, and the others who helped rescue her, including Hana."

Ruby paused. Taylor did not know what to say or where this was going, so he waited quietly for Ruby to continue.

"At first, I did not understand what Mai was trying to tell me. I know the world has bad people; my mind understands that. But then, I understood what Mai was trying to say. I have never had to look upon such evil with my own eyes, to try and stop it myself, or protect someone I care about from such people. Mai asked me what I would do if people like that had Amado." Ruby started to cry.

"My husband was not a good man, but not truly evil. He was not like the people that JD, Carlos, Mai, Hana, or you have seen. When caring for you, I could see you were troubled by your past. I knew you had ghosts, but I was not afraid because I could see you are also a good man. Then you told me what you did, and my heart broke for you. I understood why you lived as you did. Then I saw you start to change; it was so good, Bill, to see you returning to your true self.

"I do understand now what Mai was telling me. Sometimes, good men must do bad things to protect good people and those they love. And because they are good men, doing those things sometimes haunts them, even to the point where they lose hope…"

She stopped, seeing the look on Taylor's face. Ruby looked down momentarily, unsure what to say, but she had to finish.

"I must say one more thing, Bill. I forgot all this when I heard you talk about the Baguinda woman. I was hurt. I was angry and jealous. But I know that you are not now who you were then. And we did not know each other then. You did not know me, and I did not know you. It was wrong of me, and I am sorry. Can you please forgive me?"

Taylor sat still for a few seconds, afraid to say anything.

Shit! he thought. *Don't be a damn pussy!*

"You are right, Ruby. I had lost hope and forgot who I was. I was dead inside, and I guess, just waiting for my body to die as well. Then you found me in that alley. What you did for me gave me hope. And what you said to me gave me a reason to fight my way back. Because of what you saw in me and said to me, I discovered that I wanted to live again. I cannot change what is in the past. I can only control what I do now. I never wanted to cause you pain or jealousy. I never wanted to make you angry."

Ruby smiled. "I am a Filipino woman, Bill. We are known for getting angry and jealous. We have a word for it here; it is tampo."

Taylor chuckled. "Yes, I think I have heard of that. But seriously, Ruby, I have seen the kind of woman you are, how you care for your son by yourself, how hard you work. I am pretty sure you saved my life in more ways than one. You are amazing, Ruby Damilo. I owe you so much." Suddenly, Taylor knew how he felt, what he had to say. "And, I want to tell you," he smiled, "since we seem to be baring our souls to each other here … I love you, Ruby."

She looked up at Taylor's face, which had just turned a little red. "You love me?"

"Yes, I do."

"Bill, that is why I got so angry and jealous, because I love you too."

Taylor smiled, and Ruby could see the relief on his face. "Whew. I am so glad. I was really worried after yesterday. I was sure I had blown it."

He stood up and offered Ruby his hand as she got to her feet. Once his hand closed around hers, he knew everything would be okay.

"There is one more thing I have wanted to ask for the last few days, but I guess I was too chicken."

The thought she could do anything to scare this man seemed funny to Ruby, but she kept a straight face. "What is it, Bill? Please, you can ask me anything."

Taylor suddenly felt like a giddy, young kid on a first date. He decided it was an amazingly wonderful feeling. "Would it be okay if I kiss you?"

"I hoped you would."

Ruby stood on her tiptoes as Bill leaned forward, meeting her halfway.

The trip to Taylor's apartment was uneventful. Sirichai and Vivas opted to wait outside near the idling taxi; however, Hana asked to go in with him.

"Why?" Taylor looked puzzled. "It's not much to look at."

Hana shrugged. "Just curiosity, I guess. I can wait outside if you prefer."

"Come on in if you like. There's not much to see."

Everything looked like he'd left it, except for the picture Amado had taken off the wall on his earlier visit. The photo, still in its frame, was lying on his cot.

"Not very fancy, Bill. But it's certainly neat and clean."

"I guess I wasn't concerned with fancy. The neatness is just old army habits."

Walking over to the cot, he picked up the picture in its frame, opened a footlocker at the end of the cot, and placed it inside. Then, grabbing the one chair at the small table, he moved it to a spot near the front left corner of the room and climbed up. Reaching into a crack between the joists and the floorboards of the building's second story, he retrieved the wad of cash he'd stashed there, slipping it into his pocket. Hana saw Taylor's eyes shift to several whiskey bottles on a shelf near the sink. He secured the lid on the footlocker and hefted it onto his shoulder. With a quick nod to Hana, they went through the door, leaving the whiskey bottles where they sat. Hana smiled and followed after Taylor; he was already loading the footlocker into the cab's trunk.

Since JD had suggested they pick up a couple of rolls of duct tape, they had the cab driver stop at a hardware store long enough for Vivas to run in. He came out with four rolls.

Hana laughed. "JD said a couple of rolls, Carlos."

"Better to have it and not need it than not have it and find you do."

"Exactly," Taylor agreed.

Sirichai nodded. It made perfect sense to him.

The three were back at the hotel in time for lunch, and the entire group, except for Sophie—who was assigned sentry duty in the room Hana euphemistically called their operations center—headed down to the hotel restaurant for a decent meal. Except for Taylor's steak diet, most had lived on snacks for two days.

After lunch, the team gathered again and JD laid out his plan for the rescue mission. It was simple enough, but it all depended on them getting the girl's location from Salonga and immediately acting on it. Vivas, Hana, and the others would remain at the hotel, prepared when JD called with the location of the girls.

At JD's suggestion, Hana had rented two Toyota work vans. The team's equipment, including their weaponry, mostly personal sidearms, would be ready to go in the van for the rescue. Once they had the girls and reassembled at the hotel, the second van would transport the rest of the party and their luggage to the airstrip.

With the assistance of Ruby and Amado, Mai would ensure their gear and luggage were packed up and loaded. Earlier in the meeting, Hana suggested that Ruby and her son leave with them. Then, once everyone was safely out of danger in Thailand, they could discuss any additional needs or plans. Ruby, after a glance at Taylor, agreed to Hana's proposal. She had Amado to think of, and she knew they would probably not be safe in Tondo after this business with the Baguinda sisters.

Once Salonga talked, Vivas would meet the other three men at the girls' location with the van and their gear and assist with the rescue. When they had the girls back at the hotel, they would immediately go to the private airstrip where the jet waited. Their pilot had stayed in a surprisingly comfortable room at the airstrip, compliments of Quan's friend. Hana had already notified him to prepare the jet for a quick take-off.

Since they were departing from a private airstrip near Manila and landing at the private charter section of the airport in Bangkok, Ruby and Amado did not need passports or other papers. However, if the rescue team could locate them quickly, Jum Y and Xuan would have travel papers. Once everyone was safe, anything else could be sorted, including Ruby and Amado's legal status.

At precisely 9:00 p.m., three men climbed into a taxi. Taylor, riding shotgun, gave the driver an address for a billiards parlor in Tondo. The driver nodded, turned the meter on, and pointed his cab into traffic. JD and Sirichai sat quietly in the back, each man alone in his thoughts, preparing for what would happen shortly.

Not caring for the silence, the driver turned on the radio. The sound of Fourth Impact, a popular Filipino girl band, singing their cover of 'Bang Bang', a pop song currently getting a great deal of airplay, filled the cab. Both JD and Taylor frowned. JD thought he detected a slight smile on Sirichai's face as the younger man sat straighter in his seat. JD smiled.

There is no accounting for musical taste.

"Stay focused," JD leaned over to whisper.

Sirichai nodded.

After twenty minutes of battling insane traffic, the cab turned left onto a dimly lit side street and, a few seconds later, pulled up in front of a seedy-looking storefront. Once a market of some kind, the sign over the door now announced BILLIARDS. The establishment did not look friendly or inviting, with dingy windows covered in dirty, aging signs and posters. Telling the driver to wait, the three men climbed out of the cab to talk. The driver did not need to be privy to their discussion.

"It's my kind of place," Taylor commented, "or at least, it was."

"Okay, we need to see if Salonga is in there, but if you go in, Taylor, and he recognizes you, would that be a problem?"

"Perhaps," Taylor acknowledged. "I am not sure."

Sirichai offered, "I will recognize the man. I got a good look at Salonga back in the restaurant when his men took the two girls."

"Are you sure? Salonga might recognize you too."

"I don't think so. He did not pay much attention to me, only to his men and the girls. He certainly knows Taylor much better than he knows me."

"That's for damn sure," Taylor agreed.

"Okay then. Taylor, stay out here and watch things. We don't need anyone sneaking up behind us. Sirichai and I will go in and see if Salonga is in there. I guess we may be a few minutes. After all, we'll not want to draw more attention to ourselves than two strangers already will, so we may need to order a beer or shoot a game of pool." JD paused, turning to Sirichai. "How's your game?"

"I was my ranger battalion's 8-ball champion for two years."

"That will help. Okay, champ, let's go." JD and Sirichai started for the billiard hall's door.

Taylor moved to the other side of the narrow street to get a better view of the storefront and anyone approaching.

"If you need backup, just holler!"

JD reached for the handle and pulled the door open before he and Sirichai disappeared inside.

The pungent smell of stale beer, cigar smoke, and sweat permeated the air. It was larger inside than it looked from outside, with a dozen nine-foot billiard tables. A bar ran halfway down the left side of the hall, with a few tables and chairs scattered in the corners. The billiard tables were all in use, and the clientele fit nicely with the atmosphere. All the dining tables and chairs were full as well. Sirichai discretely scanned the room as JD strode to the bar and spoke to the bartender.

"No open tables? My buddy and I just wanted to shoot some billiards, and the taxi driver knew this place."

The bartender shook his head. "We're full; tournament tonight. Come back tomorrow, okay?"

"Tournament, huh? Can we watch? Maybe have a cold beer?"

"Better you come back tomorrow. Too busy. It's crowded tonight. Now, only warm beer."

"Well, shit! Warm beer? That doesn't sound so good."

JD glanced over at Sirichai, who nodded.

"Okay, maybe we'll come back tomorrow. Thanks!"

The two left the billiards hall and walked over to stand near the rear of the taxi, which was now parked across the street. Taylor joined them.

"Salonga is not in there," Sirichai reported.

"Are you sure?" JD asked. "It's pretty crowded for such a dumpy-looking place."

"I am sure. I looked at each man's face. He is not in there."

"Then he is about three blocks up the street at his woman's apartment."

JD mulled the situation over. Even though Taylor had assured him that Salonga's girlfriend was an equally unsavory character, he was uncomfortable with involving the woman in this mess.

Taylor seemed to read his mind. "JD, I'm not kidding; that woman is no prize. Her name is Tala, and she is as bad as they come. I know she helps run the girls working for the gang, and I am sure she is personally responsible for much of their pain and suffering."

"Yeah, I get that. But it still goes against my grain. I don't want to hurt any woman."

"I get you, but Salonga doesn't have to know that. He wouldn't hesitate if the situation reversed; he will probably expect the same treatment from us."

"Would he talk to protect his woman … this Tala?"

Taylor considered that for a moment. "I'm not sure. Filipino mafia goes way back in his family to his father and grandfather. He might not. Honor among thieves, I guess you could say."

"Maybe she will talk to save him." It was Sirichai. Both JD and Taylor looked over at the young Thai.

Taylor nodded. "You may be right there, Sirichai."

"Let's hope so," JD commented. "I am not keen on this sort of thing, but damn it, we're going to get those girls back, so I sure as shit hope you are right. The question is, how do we do this quietly?"

"I have an idea," Taylor said. "Let's knock on the door. I can speak enough Tagalog to say I have a message from Mahalia. Of the two sisters, she's more likely to communicate with a scumbag like Salonga. When he opens the door, we go in."

"He had a handgun at the Korean restaurant," Sirichai added.

JD nodded. "Okay, good to know. I'll cover him." He patted his right hip. "I came prepared. It's risky carrying here, but I figured the situation might warrant taking that risk."

Taylor nodded. "The explains the long, baggy shirt. Okay. Sirichai and I will restrain Tala. If we can keep her quiet while you get the information from him, we can leave the two trussed up, phone Vivas, and rescue the girls. We won't have a lot of time. When Salonga gets free, he'll notify Mahalia immediately, and the jig will be up. She will not hesitate to kill the girls."

"We need to be ready to move fast. Give me a minute to call Vivas and bring him up to speed. Hopefully, the four of us can handle whatever we find, free the girls and get the hell out of there. The ladies will have everything loaded up, and we can make a beeline to the airstrip. We will be safe once we get in the air on our way back to Thailand."

JD grabbed the burner phone in his back right pocket, one of several purchased by Vivas earlier, to make the call.

"Everything is ready on our end," Vivas said. "Give me a shout and I'll be there. The girls should be nearby if the Baguindas expected a quick transfer to Trán's lackeys. They're not likely to have them stashed in the jungle or on some remote island somewhere."

"That's what we're counting on, Vivas." JD ended the call. Three grim-faced men started up the street a moment later, walking toward Salonga's girlfriend's apartment.

"That's Salonga's van parked in front," Taylor noted.

Sirichai nodded. It was the same van he'd seen pull up at the Korean restaurant a few days earlier, when Xuan and Jum Y were grabbed.

Taylor calmly walked past the van and up to the front door, followed by JD and Sirichai. Once JD and Sirichai were in place at either side of the doorway, he knocked.

"Hey, Salonga, open up, katropa! I have a message from Mahalia."

A voice from inside responded. "Sandali lang, just a moment."

JD unholstered the Glock 19 concealed by his shirt at his right hip and stood ready on the right side of the door. Seconds later, the door cracked open and JD exploded through it, pressing the Glock into Salonga's face, forcing him up against the wall.

Taylor and Sirichai were right behind him, intercepting Tala as she came around the corner into the living area. Sirichai wrapped her in his arms, pinning her arms at her side. Taylor placed his hand over her mouth and spoke.

"Katahimikan, silence. We do not want to hurt you. Nod if you understand."

Tala's eyes flashed angrily, recognizing Taylor. Then, sullenly, she nodded.

"That's good," Taylor confirmed. "Nobody needs to get hurt. Just stay quiet, and everything will be okay."

Salonga leaned against the wall, the barrel of JD's Glock pressed against the back of his head. JD had the thug's legs back and spread, his arms wide, palms against the wall. Salonga was going nowhere.

JD spoke. "You are Tony Salonga, and you work for the Baguinda sisters. You both do. And I think you probably speak pretty good English, so listen carefully. First, let me be clear; I am not in a mood for any games. I want to know where they are holding two young women who are very important to me—Xuan and Jum Y. You grabbed them at a Korean BBQ restaurant two nights ago. One of you will tell me where they are."

"I will tell you nothing, butas! You are all dead men!"

"I had a feeling you might say that." JD signaled to Sirichai, who nodded and dug into the large cargo pocket on his right hip. His hand returned holding a roll of duct tape. Moments later, the three had Salonga taped to a chair Taylor had retrieved from the kitchen. Utterly immobilized, his ankles, knees, shoulders, and arms were taped securely to the chair's legs, arms, and back. One more piece of duct tape covered his mouth. Taylor stood next to Tala, who sat on a small sofa, her ankles and wrists bound securely with duct tape. No duct tape covered her mouth, but she remained sullenly silent.

JD spoke again. "Tala," he paused, ensuring she was looking at him. "I hate this sort of thing. I do. But I have little time, and those two young women mean much more to me than your boyfriend there." JD nodded at Salonga.

Tala remained silent.

"My friend over here," JD nodded toward Sirichai, "was there when your friends grabbed these two young ladies. He killed two of your boyfriend's men, so I suspect he will not be opposed to killing your boyfriend, if necessary. You can save Tony a lot of pain and suffering by telling me what I need to know. If you do, I promise neither of you will be harmed. However, we must ensure you do not get a warning to the Baguinda sisters before we rescue the girls, so you will be securely bound and gagged. We won't hurt you; and eventually, you will get free or be freed."

Tala glanced at Salonga, who shook his head and mumbled into the duct tape gag. For a minute, JD was afraid she would tough it out and not say anything. He turned and nodded at Sirichai, who took a step toward Salonga.

"They have the two girls at their Vista Towers condo. They are keeping them in a spare bedroom. 1200 Benavidez Street, in Tondo."

"What's the apartment number?"

"They are on the twelfth floor, number 1250. It is near the service elevator."

"That's handy," Taylor commented.

"Do they have security? Someone guarding the two girls?"

Tala nodded.

"How many?

"Usually one, but maybe two or three now. No more than that. One guards the girls to keep Mahalia away from them."

"What?" JD asked.

"Mahalia likes girls," Taylor said. "I've heard the rumors."

Tala nodded.

"Okay. Thank you, Tala. Hopefully, your boyfriend will appreciate what you just did for him."

JD and Sirichai secured Tala's bindings and gagged her with more duct tape, leaving her on the couch.

"Well, the worst she can do is roll off onto the floor, and then she'll just be stuck lying there." Taylor turned to the bound woman. "You'll be more comfortable, Tala, if you stay on the couch."

JD, who had disappeared into the kitchen area, returned. "I called Vivas. He's leaving now. I told him to bring Sophie. She's not a combat dog, but her rescue dog training might come in handy if we need to track anyone, and there is the German Shepherd intimidation factor." He checked his watch. "With traffic, Vivas figures it will be about thirty minutes. It looks to be about the same for us."

Sirichai looked up. "How do we get there? Taxi?"

"We'll take Salonga's van. I figured he'd have a vehicle. I also found his gun on the kitchen table. We'll keep that as well."

JD tossed Sirichai the keys he'd picked up from the kitchen counter. "You drive, Sirichai. Taylor, you're the navigator. Let's go."

CHAPTER 33
Vietnam

Hai showed the men to Dish's old longhouse. To Dish, it looked exactly like he and Chanmali had left it.

"Is no one using it?" Dish asked.

Hai shook his head. "No. We keep it for you if you and Chanmali need it again."

Dish set his small pack down on the floor.

"My wife has made sleeping mats ready for each of you," Hai continued, pointing toward the back of the longhouse. "She will have food ready soon; you must rest for tomorrow. I will tell you everything after we have eaten."

Slim turned to Hai. "Thank you. I would appreciate a little food. I worked up quite an appetite on that little stroll up into the mountains."

Hahn nodded in agreement. "Yep. We're all hungry after the hike up from Xayden."

Hai laughed. "Okay. I will go see how much time before we eat."

Without a word, Dish turned and walked out of the longhouse to cross the small village center. Hahn and Slim followed him. There was nothing much else to do for the moment.

Stepping across a small stream that ran from the base of a ledge and disappeared over the cliff to their left, Dish moved on, finally stopping near a small cluster of water pines. Hahn and Slim caught up to him and found him standing near a pile of carefully placed stones. Freshly picked flowers lay on the well-cared-for grave.

Hearing the two men approach, Dish turned and spoke before they could ask.

"It is the grave of my nephew's dog. JD's ... how do you say ... K9? Ajax was the dog's name."

Both Hahn and Slim nodded. They'd both heard the story from Hana some time ago.

"Good dog, brave dog. Ajax gave his life to save my sister, Mai. You know my nephew's mother?"

Both Hahn and Slim nodded. While they had never met Mai, they both knew the entire story. The fact that everyone concerned thought so highly of her was enough for them.

"It makes me happy to see the people in my old village take such care of this grave. It is the resting place of a true warrior."

"Indeed, it is," Slim agreed quietly. He'd seen Ajax in action in Niger.

Rick nodded. He knew Hana had become quite attached to Ajax during their earlier trip from Thailand to this same village. She'd been heartbroken over the dog's death and JD's loss.

Hai approached. "Food is ready."

"Okay. I just wanted to see. Thank you, old friend, for keeping this so."

"My wife and I take care of the grave. It is our honor. We know what this dog meant to many good people."

The four men followed Hai in silence, returning to his longhouse, where dinner waited.

The sun was peeking over the farthest mountain ridge when Hahn and Slim joined Dish on the veranda of the longhouse. Both had slept well. After splashing cold water on their faces from a basin provided by Hai's wife, they were ready to get on with the task at hand.

"What's the plan, chief?" Slim asked Dish as the old Montagnard turned to greet the two men.

"Hai's wife fixes breakfast. Then we, uh, as you say, load up. We hike fifteen kilometers to where a truck meets us. It is the same as we did to rescue my sister. This time, the truck takes us to the other side of the plantation. Then, a short walk to an excellent place Poh found to watch who comes to the plantation."

Slim nodded.

Hahn spoke up. "I'm not leaving any girls in the hands of that brother and sister team you described. When we take out Trán and Fong, we need to get those other girls out of there along with Ahn. We'll give Hana's Spring Lotus Foundation its first real test. I hope the dorm rooms are ready."

Slim added, "I believe Hana will handle it just fine."

Hahn agreed. "I think you're right, Slim." He turned back to Dish. "You told us you have a good sniper rifle, but we need weapons better suited for close-quarter combat. Maybe those M16s you mentioned? Or, some handguns?"

Dish grinned. "First, let's eat breakfast. I am hungry. Then, you can see what weapons we have."

Hai's wife prepared a breakfast of scrambled eggs, rice, and vegetables. It was a pretty hearty meal. The eggs were fresh, with the many laying hens roaming freely throughout the village. The vegetables were spicy enough to cause a bead of sweat to break out on both Slim and Hahn's foreheads, though both tried valiantly to appear undaunted.

All three men thanked their hostess for the meal and hospitality. Then Hahn and Slim followed Dish to his longhouse, where several village men placed two wooden crates on the veranda. Dish opened both containers. Each contained a selection of armaments of various makes and models, including Chinese-made AK-47s, four M14A1 rifles, two early M16 rifles, and several of the improved M16A1 rifles. There were also several AR-

15s, three M2 Carbines, and even an M3 submachine gun, often referred to as a 'grease gun'. All looked recently cleaned. As Slim inspected the weapons, he found several Colt M1911A1s and a Smith & Wesson Model 12 .38 Special revolver hiding under some rifles. The crates included several magazines for each gun.

Hahn looked at Dish. "Impressive collection."

"You should find what you need. Once you choose, Hai will provide ammunition."

"Do you have holsters for the 1911s?" Slim asked. "I'd take one of those and an M16A1 rifle."

"We have older holsters for web gear, but a man in the village fixed them to work with belts."

Hahn nodded. "Great. Then an M16 and a Colt 1911 work for me as well. Of course, we'll also need water and traveling rations."

Hahn grabbed a pair of binoculars from one of the crates. "These should come in handy."

"Yes. Hai will have our supplies ready for us when we leave. Then, Poh and three of his men will meet us with the truck. I have two radios and will give one to Poh. That way, he will know when it is time to go, and to come and pick us up."

"Sounds good," Hahn replied.

"It is a twelve-hour ride to the plantation," Dish continued, "and maybe not so smooth in the back of the truck."

"Slim and I are tough old birds; we'll survive. So, when do we leave?"

"When you are ready," Dish replied.

Hahn looked over at Slim. "Thirty minutes?"

"That works."

"Good," Dish confirmed. "I will let Hai know."

CHAPTER 34
The Philippines

Carlos turned to Hana. "The guys found out where the Baguinda sisters are holding the girls. They're keeping them at their condo, Vista Towers, in the Tondo district. I'll meet JD there in about thirty minutes. He wants me to bring Sophie."

"Sophie?" Ellen asked. Lying on the rug in front of the room's air conditioning unit, Sophie perked up when she heard her name.

"Just for intimidation purposes. German Shepherds have that effect. JD thinks her presence might keep someone from doing something stupid."

Hana stepped up and hugged Carlos, then kissed him. "You be careful. I don't want anybody hurt."

"We'll be careful. According to Salonga's girlfriend, there are maybe two or three guards and the two sisters.

We have four highly trained combat veterans and hopefully, the element of surprise. We'll be fine. Will you ladies be ready to move?"

Mai nodded. "Yes. The other van is loaded. We are all set. Amado has been a great help. He's a fine young man. You should be very proud of him, Ruby."

Amado, sitting on the rug next to Sophie, blushed and smiled at the compliment.

Ruby smiled as well. "Yes. I am very proud."

Vivas grabbed Sophie's leash from where it hung over the back of one of the room's chairs. Sophie jumped up and trotted over to him expectantly.

"Hey, Sophie, let's take a ride."

Hana caught Ellen's worried look. "Carlos, please make sure Sophie gets back unhurt. I want everyone back the same way you left."

"Yes, dear. Just be ready to leave when we return. Let's go, Sophie."

Vivas made his way out into the hallway and toward the elevator, Sophie trotting along right beside him. A few minutes later, he opened the van's side door in the hotel parking garage and Sophie jumped in.

"Okay. Let's get going, girl; JD's waiting for us."

Sophie's ears perked up at the mention of JD. She tilted her head and let out an anxious whine.

Vivas chuckled. "I know, girl. He's fine."

Vivas started the van, checked the directions on his phone, backed out of the parking spot, and drove toward the garage exit.

CHAPTER 35
Vietnam

Hahn shifted the M16 slung on his right shoulder and checked his watch: 1705. The three men squatted, concealed in the scrub brush about forty yards from the building where the girls were being held.

Slim shifted over beside him. "We have about two hours before Ahn and that bastard, Fong, are due to arrive."

Hahn nodded.

Dish also squatted in the brush, about twenty yards to their left. It never ceased to amaze Hahn how that old man could squat like that for hours with no signs of discomfort. Bringing the binoculars up, Hahn surveyed the two structures and the surrounding area for the fourth time since their arrival.

A door opened in the newly constructed building that served as Trán's office and living quarters at the old plantation. The new building had replaced the old plantation house that Dish burned to the ground during Mai's rescue. Based on Colonel Anurat's description, Hahn decided the man must be Trán's assistant.

"Trán must be getting ready to receive his guests," Hahn whispered to Slim.

Slim grunted affirmatively.

The man carried a box to the second building. He knocked on the door and waited. The door opened and a squat, shabbily dressed man stepped out, took the box, and went back inside without so much as a word spoken. The door closed. Trán's assistant turned, returned to the new structure, and went inside.

"Must be tonight's dinner for whoever is being held in the barn," Slim observed.

"Yep."

They planned to wait until Fong arrived with Ahn, then give them time to settle and finish dinner. Hahn would enter the building where Trán entertained his guests while Slim and Dish would move to the other structure. Once Slim and Dish were in place, Hahn would move inside to take out Trán and Fong.

They had no suppressors, so Hahn's shots would signal Slim and Dish to neutralize the brother and sister guarding the captive girls, and get them out of the building. They would not kill the two guards unless given no choice.

Once Hahn had Ahn safe, Dish would signal Poh, who was waiting just off the plantation on the main road, pretending to have engine trouble. When Dish called, he would start their way.

Three of Poh's men sat hidden in the back of the truck as backup, if needed. Once Poh arrived at the plantation buildings, they would load up in the truck, drive to Dish's village, hike back to Laos, pick up their van, and drive back to Thailand. The girls who wanted to leave Vietnam would stay at the village with Hai until Hana and Dish could arrange to get them to Thailand and into the Spring Lotus program.

Hahn checked his watch.

It wouldn't be long now.

CHAPTER 36
The Philippines

Taylor returned to Solanga's van, now parked in an alley behind the Baguinda sisters' condo. Being familiar with the building and to its residents, JD had asked him to go in and scout the situation.

"Everything is quiet. It's a typical day in paradise. Once Vivas arrives, we can take the elevator to the Baguinda's apartment. I don't think the service elevator is used much—I can't remember anyone ever using it. But we still need to watch it, just in case."

JD nodded. "I agree." He glanced at Sirichai. "You watch the service elevator while Taylor, Vivas, and I, along with Sophie, take the elevator up. No one gets on or off the service elevator until we are ready to leave the building with the girls." Sirichai nodded.

"What about the guards Tala told us about?" JD asked. "What will we be up against?"

"The few times I have seen any of their thugs there, they usually sat on a couch in the front room. According to what Tala said, I suspect one is probably sitting outside the guest bedroom door. When you go in, the kitchen is off to the right of the front living room. There is a small dining area as well. It is pretty damn fancy. To the kitchen's left is a hallway that leads back to the bedrooms. Blessica's bedroom is the first door on the left. The guest room is across the hall. I know because Blessica had me wait in there once while she and Mahalia met with someone in the kitchen to discuss business. I think each bedroom has a full bathroom. Mahalia's bedroom is at the end of the hall. I have never seen it."

JD listened attentively, then, for a few seconds, mulled over the floor plan Taylor had described.

"Okay, first we will handle anyone sitting in the front room. Then, one of us, you, Taylor, will secure that area while Vivas and I clear the hallway and the bedrooms, grabbing the girls. When we have the girls, we pull back to the front room and exit, hustling back to Vivas's van and straight back to the hotel. Sound like a plan?"

"Sounds good," Taylor replied.

Just then, a vehicle pulled up behind their van. It was Vivas.

CHAPTER 37
Vietnam

While he rarely used it, Fong's position with the Vietnamese Mobile Police Force allowed him to use a government-provided car. Fong enjoyed driving and considered himself a good driver, but he rarely had the need. He decided to use the dark gray Toyota sedan tonight rather than take a taxi to Trán's plantation.

Pulling up in front of Ahn's apartment building at precisely 5:30 p.m., Fong got out and took the stairs up to her door. Ahn, opened the door looking positively ravishing in a black cocktail dress and matching shoes. A white silk scarf adorned her neck. She'd put her hair up in a neat bun and added just the right touch of makeup. The sight of her caused Fong to catch his breath.

"I hope that isn't all for Trán's benefit." He was only half joking.

Ahn smiled, pleased. "No, it is for you. I want to look nice and help you impress Minister Trán."

Once at the car, Fong opened the door for Ahn and then walked around to the driver's side. It was about an hour's drive to the old Michelin rubber plantation; the first twenty minutes passed quietly. Ahn could tell Fong was deep in thought.

"I am sure it will be fine. I know you are worried, but things have been going well. I know your business is good. I am sure Trán is pleased, and there is nothing for you to worry about."

Fong nodded. "I think you are right. But still, it is hard not to have some doubt, especially with a ruthless man like Trán."

Ahn said nothing. Her palms suddenly felt sweaty. She knew she was playing a dangerous game that could quickly go very badly for her. Then she remembered Chau's words.

"Trust Hai and his men. Trust Dish. They are good men, and they will get you away safely. You will be okay."

It's not like I have much choice now. Tonight's events had already been set in motion.

I have to see this through to the end, no matter what that end might be. Ahn decided to change the subject.

"It is pretty out here in the country. I have never been out of the city."

"Well then, another first resulting from the minister's dinner invitation. It looks like tonight will be quite the night for you."

365

Ahn shifted in her seat to suppress an involuntary shudder. She glanced at Fong, hoping he hadn't noticed.

"Yes." She forced a smile onto her face. "That is true. It will be a pleasant dinner and the beginning of good things for you."

"Maybe so."

Fifteen minutes later, Fong turned down the hard-packed dirt road onto the plantation grounds, winding his way to the newly built office and remaining outbuildings. He noticed a truck parked alongside the road near the turn-off. A man bent over the front bumper, peering into the engine compartment. He looked up and waved as they drove by.

"It looks like that man has trouble with his truck. Should we stop?" Ahn asked.

"No. The village of Lei Khe is just up the road; he can get help there. We do not want to keep Trán waiting."

Bringing the sedan to a stop, Fong turned off the ignition. "We are here."

Trán's assistant came out to meet them, moving around the sedan to open the door for Ahn, a welcoming smile on his face.

"Good evening, Miss Ahn, and to you, Lieutenant Colonel Fong. Colonel Trán is looking forward to visiting with you both over dinner. Please follow me to the dining room. Your host will join you there momentarily."

"Thank you, Mr. … uh."

"My name is Li Phoc."

"Thank you, Mr. Li. It is an honor to be here."

Taking Ahn by the arm, Fong nodded at Li. "Shall we?"

They followed Li into the building, across the foyer, and into a modern, well-appointed dining room. The table was set for three and could seat six, with comfortable-looking chairs, two on each side and one at each end.

"Please, take a seat. I will tell the Colonel you're here. Would either of you care for some wine?"

"Please," Ahn nodded. "Perhaps a Chardonnay? Something light?" Her mouth was dry.

"The same for me," Fong said. "Thank you, Li."

Li smiled, nodded, and went back through the dining room doorway.

Fong motioned Ahn to a table chair and sat beside her. They had just taken their seats when Trán entered, followed by Li carrying a bottle of an excellent Australian Chardonnay. Fong started to rise.

The old colonel grinned. "Fong, Miss Ahn, it was so good of you to come. Please, please don't get up." Trán moved down the table and took the seat at the end. "That is a good Chardonnay, Li. I will have a glass as well."

"Excellent, sir." Li poured three glasses and set them before Trán and his guests, then placed the bottle in a waiting ice bucket beside the table and left the room.

CHAPTER 38
The Philippines

JD, Taylor, and Sirichai climbed into the back of the work van and began sorting through the gear Vivas had loaded before leaving the hotel. Each had a paddle holster and Glock 19. There was also a package of large black zip ties. Each man shoved several into a pocket.

"So, what's the plan?" Vivas asked, slipping into the shoulder rig harness that carried his Flesheater combat knife. JD finished briefing him on the information they'd gotten from Salonga's girlfriend, Tala.

"According to Taylor's layout description, we must watch the service elevator. The access is right near the Baguinda sisters' apartment. If any alarm is raised before we gain entry, they may try to slip the girls out that way, and we also don't want any surprise visitors. Sirichai will handle that."

Sirichai nodded, and JD continued. "Anybody comes down that elevator once we go in, you stop them, Sirichai, and I mean anyone. Anyone trying to go up gets stopped as well. Once we have the girls, we can sort out any inconveniences or ruffled feathers."

"Got it," Sirichai agreed.

"The rest of us will take the main elevator to the condo. We'll take Sophie with us. She's a trained search and rescue dog, not a combat dog, but she is intimidating and may help keep things from going south."

Vivas reached over to scratch Sophie behind the ears. The dog whined in appreciation. "You'll do fine, girl."

Taylor spoke up. "I suggest quietly picking the lock and going right in. Speed and surprise will be in our favor."

JD agreed. "That is precisely what we are going to do. Vivas, do you have your pick set with you?"

Vivas grinned. "Never leave home without it."

"Then, Vivas will pick the lock. Taylor, you enter first; you know the layout. I'll follow with Sophie. Vivas, you bring up the rear. We've got to subdue any front room guards as quickly and silently as possible."

Taylor will secure the front living area as I take the lead with Sophie; she will help make the Baguinda sisters think twice about doing anything stupid. Vivas will move down the hall with us to the bedrooms, and we will secure the girls and the two sisters as needed. We'll back out the same way we came in."

Taylor pointed out, "The guards most likely won't have firearms; that's too risky here in the Philippines. But they will certainly have knives; they carry knives from birth!"

Vivas grinned. "I could use a little knife practice. It's been a while."

JD shook his head. "We don't want to hurt anyone unless we have no choice, and any dead bodies could cause problems we want to avoid. Mostly, it will be up to these guards and how they react to us. Remember, our primary focus is quickly grabbing the girls and returning to the airstrip."

Taylor spoke again. "This is a very upscale condo; the no-loitering policy is strictly enforced. Very few residents, if any, will be wandering around this time of night. There should be no innocent bystanders around.

I can't see Blessica causing any real problem. She's smart; she will play it cool and sit tight. Mahalia, on the other hand, is another story. She's the only real wildcard. There is no telling what she will do. If we can subdue the guards quietly and get control of Mahalia and Blessica, we should be in and out quickly with nobody any wiser."

JD looked at the other men. "We all know that even the best-laid plans can go to hell quickly. We don't know for certain what we'll find when we get in there; it's possible that we may stir up a hornet's nest. Let's remain focused but flexible."

Vivas, Taylor, and Sirichai all nodded. Each man understood what JD meant.

"Okay, then. Let's get geared up. We'll go in ten minutes.".

CHAPTER 39
Vietnam

Fong cleared his throat. "It is a nice surprise to be invited to dinner, Colonel Trán. Ahn rarely leaves the city; she enjoyed the drive to your plantation."

"How nice. It is a pleasant drive, isn't it?"

"Oh yes. Very nice. It is quiet and so different from the city. Thank you, Colonel, for your kind invitation."

"It is my pleasure, Ahn. Li is an excellent assistant, but it is nice to have someone new to talk with occasionally, and a lovely young lady such as yourself certainly brightens up the room. Don't you think, Fong?"

"Yes, of course."

"All your hard work pays off, Fong. You work hard, and you are loyal." Trán paused for a sip of wine. "Things seem to be going well in Ho Chi Minh City business-wise."

"Yes, Colonel. Collections are on time, and the clubs are all doing well. I hope you are happy with how things are going."

"I certainly am. Now, Fong, is there anything that needs to be brought to my attention, anything I can help with while I am here?"

Just then, Li announced dinner was being served and began to set food on the table. First, a whole poached fish, quickly followed by a large bowl of rice, several vegetable dishes, and a platter of spring rolls. Trán indicated that Ahn and Fong should help themselves. "We can continue our discussion after dinner. Now is not the time to discuss business."

Ahn placed a large piece of the poached fish on Fong's plate. It smelled delicious. He reached for the bowl of rice.

Dinner passed with polite small talk. Ahn, her stomach in one big knot, forced herself to smile while she ate and chatted pleasantly about the weather, life in Ho Chi Minh City, and the history of the old Michelin rubber plantation before the war in Vietnam. Trán, as it turned out, was quite knowledgeable about the plantation's history.

Finally, Li arrived to serve them each a cup of French coffee. Ahn was starting to relax just a bit.

"Is everyone full?" Trán asked.

"Most certainly," Fong replied. "Thank you for such an amazing dinner."

"Yes," Ahn agreed. "It was delightful."

"I am glad you both enjoyed it." He took a sip of the sweetened coffee.

"Why don't we take a short walk to settle our dinner? I can show you around the plantation while Li cleans up. It is an interesting place. Then we can come back here and finish our discussion before the two of you return to the city."

Doing her best to appear calm and at ease, Ahn forced a delighted smile. "That sounds wonderful, Colonel Trán. A short walk would certainly help settle our meal."

Fong was still uncertain how to read the situation. "Why not?"

Hahn crouched beside the front passenger quarter panel of the gray Toyota Fong had driven to the plantation. He was about ten yards from the door. He spotted Slim and Dish as the two quietly slipped from some scrub brush and quickly crossed to the building into which the squat Korean had carried what they assumed was dinner a short time before. The two men were now out of sight, waiting around the corner.

Glancing around, Hahn could not see any security cameras. This surprised him, but it was consistent with the information Dish's people had provided when scouting the location at the old Montagnard's request. Either Trán felt safe here, or he did not want any video evidence of what was happening at the plantation.

Carefully and quickly, Hahn moved to the door. Flattening himself against the wall to the immediate right side of the door, he reached for the doorknob and gave it a tentative turn. It was locked.

His ears picked up the sound of voices approaching. One was female. That has to be Ahn. He moved swiftly back to the cover provided by the gray Toyota and, crouching beside the passenger-side rear wheel, brought the M16 rifle he was carrying up to a ready position. Moments later, the door opened, and a beautiful young lady stepped out, followed by a man in his early fifties. Hahn decided that had to be Fong, who was followed by a still older man in his late sixties or early seventies. That man could only be Colonel Trán.

Trán spoke, motioning toward the building that concealed Slim and Dish around the corner—the same building the Korean had entered earlier. "This is one of the original buildings from the old plantation. Of course, you can see the new building we were just in. The original plantation house was burned to the ground not too long ago, by an old Jarai criminal named Dish."

Ahn nodded. "I have heard of that criminal. Some people in Ho Chi Minh City consider him a hero."

Fong scowled. "Just a common criminal who has been lucky to avoid capture."

"Common criminal?" Trán chuckled. "I am not sure 'common' would describe him, but he is a criminal, nonetheless." Trán referred to the building again. "There are some interesting things stored in that older building. Why don't we start our tour there?"

Ahn suddenly became wary. She would not have thought it possible to be more afraid, but she did not like the look of that old building. Still trying her best to appear calm, she smiled. "Wouldn't you prefer to show us the grounds? It is so pleasant and cool out here this evening. Much better than a dusty old building."

"I am afraid I must insist." Trán's tone had changed. His face was no longer that of a gracious host; it was now a blank mask, his eyes cold and empty. They were looking directly at Ahn. "The circumstances leading up to our little dinner were quite unusual, and I distrust unusual circumstances."

At that moment, Li stepped out holding a Mauser C96 pistol pointed directly at Fong. The door to the older building opened, and a squat, powerfully built Korean man holding an old Arisaka shotgun stepped out into the open. The man looked brutal; his mouth twisted and scarred from some past horrible accident, his eyes showing little in the way of intelligence. Behind him in the doorway stood a Korean woman holding a rusty old machete. By her look, clearly related to the man, probably his sister. Except for the man's disfigured mouth and jaw, she had the same dull, unintelligent look in her eyes. They were almost twins. The man had the shotgun aimed directly at Ahn.

Trán's phony laugh was not a pleasant sound. "Fong, did you know that Ahn called me to arrange this little dinner party? She called me claiming to be concerned for you and wanted to help you solve this problem with Dish and his American friends."

Fong stared at Ahn, shaking his head. "You stupid little whore. You have killed us both."

"Ahn should not have had my phone number, Fong. That was very careless of you. I do not tolerate carelessness. I am sure her real motivation was to advance her own position at your expense. I believe this little whore is ambitious; she has goals of her own. I have special plans for her. Seven young women are currently locked in that building under the careful watch of my two guards. Ahn will now make eight. I will sell these girls to my contacts in the Philippines. You, Ahn, will spend the remainder of your days servicing men in a brothel in Manila, or maybe Mexico."

Ahn gasped as a choking, frightened sound finally escaped from her lips.

Trán turned his attention back to Fong. "You, Fong, will be dead. I can easily find a replacement for you. Greedy, underpaid policemen are a dime a dozen." Trán nodded to Li.

The Mauser in Li's hand tilted toward Fong's lower abdomen and barked once, the bullet striking him just to the left of his navel, ensuring a prolonged and painful death. The Korean man, his wreck of a face twisting into what must have been an evil grin, started toward Ahn.

Ahn screamed.

Hahn stood and fired twice with the M16; both bullets struck the advancing Korean in the head. The man took a few more staggering steps before collapsing dead at Ahn's feet.

Li pivoted at the sound of the shots and spotting Hahn standing near the Toyota, brought his Mauser up to bear. Slim stepped out from the cover beside the building and fired a three-round burst, the bullets tearing into Li's chest. The Mauser dropped from Li's hand as he fell back onto the gravel driveway and lay still. Dish stepped forward as both Hahn and Slim turned to bring their rifles to bear on Trán.

"Don't you even blink, asshole!" Slim growled. Even if Trán did not understand the words, he understood the intention.

A mournful wail, hardly recognizable as coming from a human being, broke the sudden stillness. The Korean woman dropped her rusty machete and ran forward, flinging herself onto the dead body of her brother. She lay there, sobbing.

Dish moved forward to face Trán and stopped ten feet away from him. His right hand held the old Colt 1911 he'd carried through the Vietnam War when he fought the communists, a gift from one of his American Special Forces friends. Trán stood still, waiting.

"Are you going to kill me now?" Trán asked. "You should think about that. I can make you very rich."

Dish paused, then—almost sadly—shook his head. "I am very rich in the ways that truly matter. You have much to answer for, Trán. You ordered Fong to kill me and the daughter of my old friend. You caused the unneeded death of Benh, a young kid who died to save my life. You had people in the Philippines kidnap my sister's niece and her friend, a young woman under my protection. You poison our people with your drugs, and you sell our children into slavery. You bring too much pain to many people in our world." Dish paused, but Trán remained silent. "Killing you brings me no pleasure. I am an old man who has seen too much death in my time. Yet, my young friend, Benh, asked me to help other kids like her, Jum Y, and Xuan, and those poor women you have locked up here. I know this will not end until you are dead, so…"

Dish lifted the Colt and shot Trán in the center of his forehead. Trán fell over backward and lay still on the gravel. Turning, Dish fired again, this time at Fong, sending a bullet into the dying man's head, ending his suffering. Sliding his old 1911 back into its holster, Dish moved to where Ahn stood silent. She was in shock.

Placing a hand gently on her shoulder, he spoke quietly. "Ahn, it is okay. You are safe now. I am Dish. These are my friends, Slim and Rick Hahn, and we will help you."

Ahn spoke, her voice carrying a sound of disbelief. "It is really over? Trán and Fong are…" Her voice trailed off.

Slim poked at Trán's still body with the toe of his boot. "Dead as can be. Well-deserved, I'd say."

Ahn's legs gave out and she started to collapse. Dish caught her and held her up as she buried her face in his chest and sobbed.

Hahn moved into the building and reemerged a few moments later, followed by seven young women, all hungry and dirty, desperately needing a bath and some fresh clothing. The women blinked as their eyes adjusted to daylight. Seeing Fong, their loathsome guard, and Trán lying dead on the ground, excited chatter quickly rose among them.

Slim watched the seven women, as comprehension slowly took hold, and then confusion began to set in. Their joy and relief at being freed clashed with doubt as to what lay in their immediate future. Slim's attention turned back to the Korean woman still lying over the body of her dead brother, moaning and sobbing in anguish. "What about her?"

Dish looked down at the woman, feeling only pity. "We will leave her alone. We don't know what her story is. I suspect she has suffered much in her life. There are villages close by. People who will help her. She will be okay."

Hahn moved over to stand beside Dish, who was still holding Ahn as she struggled to get herself under control. "I guess we should get the heck out of here. We now have eight new candidates for Hana's Spring Lotus Foundation."

Dish nodded. "Yes. It is good. I will tell Poh to bring the truck." He reached for the small radio at his belt.

D.C. Gilbert

Having partially recovered from the shock of the sudden violence and resulting deaths, Ahn stepped back from Dish and gazed around the area, as comprehension began to take hold. She felt suddenly frightened of all the unknowns ahead of her. "Where will I go? What do I do?"

"First you go to my old village in the border region, and then to Thailand. We will ride and then walk a bit, but you are safe and can go to America if you wish. You are free, Ahn."

With that, Dish led her across the clearing toward the truck that had just pulled up. Ahn walked beside him, feeling her first real hope in many years. After one last check of the area, Slim and Hahn shouldered their rifles and followed them toward the truck.

CHAPTER 40
The Philippines

Exiting through the van's sliding side door, the four men moved casually towards the condo's main entrance. Taylor and JD walked side by side, with JD leading Sophie on her leash. Vivas and Sirichai followed just a few steps behind.

Once through the double doors and inside the lobby, Vivas and Taylor followed JD and Sophie to the main elevator. Sirichai peeled off to the left toward the hall to the service elevator, stationing himself by the entrance to a stairway that led to the lower parking levels. From this location, he could easily observe the front entrance and service elevator doors.

Taylor pressed the up button, and the three waited for the elevator. A few seconds later, it arrived, and the door opened. They stepped inside.

"Sophie, sit," JD commanded. Sophie sat. He knew it was essential to give her familiar commands so she would stay focused. He could tell from the dog's manner that she sensed something serious was happening; she was excited.

Vivas reached over and pressed the button for the twelfth floor. The elevator started up. They remained silent until the chime announced they were on the twelfth floor.

"Well, gentlemen, here we go," JD murmured. The door slid open.

Taylor stepped out first and started down the hall toward the suite occupied by the Baguinda sisters. JD, leading Sophie, followed closely. Vivas came last, covering the hallway behind them. Seconds later, they were at the door. JD and Vivas stationed themselves on either side of the door as Taylor pressed his ear to the door, listening.

At this hour of the morning, the Baguinda sisters would probably be sleeping in their bedrooms. If their guards knew their business, at least two would be awake—one in the living area and one guarding the door to the guestroom where the girls were probably sleeping. If there were another guard, he would likely be asleep after his last shift, or in preparation for his next one.

Taylor took his ear away from the door. "All quiet," he whispered. They could hear no sound from anywhere on the floor. At this early morning hour, everyone should be sleeping.

Swapping places with Taylor, Vivas pulled a small locksmith's tool kit out of his pocket and moved to the door. Motioning Taylor to get ready, Vivas worked at the lock. There was a barely audible clicking noise. Vivas nodded at Taylor, who reached up, turned the doorknob, and gently pressed on the door, which swung open.

Inside, the room was dark. Taylor paused just inside the doorway. They waited a few seconds, listening. There was little sound from within, just a gentle snort made by a sleeping man. Taylor signaled, and JD, leading Sophie, stepped into the room. After glancing up and down the hall to ensure all was well, Vivas quietly followed the other two through the door, quietly closing it behind him..

Sirichai glanced at the watch on his left wrist. It was just a little after three in the morning. His eyes swept the lobby and then returned to the service elevator. So far, he had seen no one. It was, he reflected, almost too quiet. Then he caught a movement near the lobby entrance with the corner of his eye. He turned just as Tony Salonga came through the swinging double doors. Salonga immediately headed toward the elevators. Sirichai quickly stepped out, moving to intercept him. Salonga spotted Sirichai immediately and turned to face him.

Sirichai stood quietly waiting, a slight smile on his face. He'd wanted a chance to get his hands on this man. He spoke in English.

"Where's your girlfriend? Where is Tala?"

Salonga sneered. "I killed that stupid little bitch for talking. Mahalia does not tolerate traitors or snitches, and neither do I."

"That's too bad; she probably saved your life. But then, I figured you were not very smart. Besides, you are too late. JD already has the girls."

"Then I'll have to settle for killing you." Salonga moved toward Sirichai, sliding an Italian-style stiletto out of his back pocket, the blade springing out as he closed the distance between them.

Calm and relaxed, his feet shoulder-width apart, Sirichai stood waiting with his hands at his sides. Salonga closed the gap, lunging in low with a wicked slash at Sirichai's midsection. Rotating his body to move with the slash, he deflected it to the left with his right hand, which suddenly changed direction, backhanding Salonga across his face with enough force to send the man staggering back, blood now dripping from his nose and mouth.

Shaking his head to clear it, Salonga moved in more cautiously this time. Feigning a second upward slash at Sirichai's midsection, Salonga suddenly brought the knife down in an arc toward Sirichai's forward right leg. Sirichai quickly shifted his right leg back, but not fast enough. Salonga, Sirichai had to admit, was fast, and the blade cut a painful gash across his right thigh. Sirichai could feel the hot blood wet his pants as the blade swept on.

Not giving Salonga a chance to recover from the movement, he slammed the calloused edge of his right hand into the tendons just above Salonga's right elbow. Salonga's right hand involuntarily flew open, and the stiletto skittered away across the floor. Instantly, Sirichai reached up with both hands, grabbed his attacker around his neck, and drove his left knee upward into Salonga's midsection. There was a loud crackling noise as the powerful knee strike cracked several of the man's ribs. Setting his right leg down as Salonga began to drop forward, Sirichai shifted his left leg out to widen his base and catching the falling man across his left thigh, brought his right elbow down to strike Salonga hard in the spine between his two shoulder blades.

Sirichai straightened up as Salonga collapsed to the floor, where he lay still, breathing but unconscious. Taking a minute to collect himself, his eyes moved over the lobby. It was still quiet. He examined the cut across his right thigh. The gash was bleeding but not too deep. Reaching down, Sirichai tore a strip from the prone man's shirt and tied it tightly around the wound. The unconscious man was not in any condition to object.

The wound tended to for the moment, Sirichai turned his mind toward what to do with the still unconscious Tony Salonga lying on the floor. He'd better stash him somewhere. They didn't need early risers tripping over him first thing in the morning.

A man lay on the couch, sound asleep. As JD and Sophie moved to cover the entrance to the hallway, Taylor clamped the palm of his left hand over the sleeping guard's mouth and pressed the muzzle of his Glock to the side of the man's head. The guard's eyes flew open. Taylor shook his head, indicating the man should remain silent. The shocked guard decided it was in his best interests to comply.

Vivas secured the man's wrists and ankles with zip ties, whispering softly. "If this one was sleeping, there may be another one awake. He could be in the bathroom."

Taylor nodded as he peeled a strip of duct tape from a small roll and used it to gag the zip-tied guard, who was now sitting on the couch.

Suddenly, a flushing toilet disturbed the quiet. A door opened, and they heard a muffled exchange of words in Tagalog between male voices. Someone was coming down the hall toward them.

Vivas moved silently to stand beside JD and indicated he should step back. Sliding the Flesheater from its sheath under his left arm, he waited as the second guard came around the corner into the living area. Vivas clamped a powerful hand over the man's mouth, pulled him around the corner, and pressed the razor-sharp blade of his Flesheater against the guard's throat. There was no mercy in either the hand clamped over his mouth or the knife blade pressing against his jugular; the guard froze. JD stepped forward, holding a finger to his lips, indicating that the guard should remain quiet. The frightened man quickly nodded his head.

Well, JD thought, *so far so good*. With these two guards secured, that leaves only the one at the door to the room the girls are being held in, and the two Baguinda sisters.

Mahalia Baguinda opened her eyes, instantly awake. Something is wrong!

Quietly rising from her bed, she slipped into a pair of red shorts she'd tossed on the floor earlier and pulled on a light blue sleeveless T-shirt hanging over a bedpost at the foot of her bed. Crossing the room to the dressing table she used as a desk, she first slid open the top left-hand drawer and picked up the butterfly knife she kept there. She slid it into her shorts at the small of her back, where the T-shirt concealed it quite well.

Opening the lid to her laptop computer, Mahalia began checking the security cameras she had scattered throughout the condo. All seemed quiet. The two guards were sitting calmly on the couch in the living room.

Something bothered her. She looked at the guards again. They were not sitting normally; they were sitting very upright and still … rigid … almost like they were … Prisoners, she thought.

Someone is here. Why? The two girls in the guest room? What else could it be?

She switched to view the camera feed showing the hallway. The guard was still sitting in the chair outside the guestroom door. He shifted his position, trying to get more comfortable, so clearly, he was awake. Then, Mahalia was shocked to see a man coming down the hall toward the guard. A big dog, a German Shepherd, walked beside the man on his left side. She noticed the man was also armed; carrying a semi-automatic pistol in his right hand.

JD signaled silently to Taylor and Vivas, then rounded the corner into the hallway with Sophie close on his left side. Vivas moved to follow JD while Taylor shifted to cover the two zip-tied and gagged guards sitting on the couch. The guard stationed by the guest room door, trying to find a more comfortable position, did not see JD or the dog at first. He shifted the chair forward and then tilted it, leaning back against the wall.

Keenly aware of growing tension and in full protector mode, Sophie emitted a low warning growl. The guard looked up to see JD, gun in hand, and the German Shepherd beside him. The guard was instantly wide awake.

"Hey! Who the hell are you?" the man shouted in Tagalog.

JD did not answer the question. Instead, he leveled the Glock in his hand at the guard's head.

"I suggest you stay very still."

Vivas had quietly moved up to stand beside JD, gun in hand. The guard swallowed hard, looking at the two men in amazement. He did not make a sound.

There was a noise from the room directly across the hall, and the door opened. Blessica Baguinda stepped out in a bathrobe and looked around. She was shocked to see two armed men and a dog standing in her hallway.

"What the fuck is going on here?"

JD replied. "You must be Blessica. We are friends of the two girls you have locked away in your guest room; we are here to take them home. We are not here to harm you or your sister, so nobody needs to get hurt if things stay quiet. Do you understand?"

Blessica paused, then nodded. "I understand."

"Where is Mahalia?"

"Still in her room, I'd guess."

Suddenly, the door at the end of the hall swung open, and Mahalia stepped into the hall. Her calm expression masked the nearly uncontrollable rage within her. Sophie shifted her focus, sensing instinctively that Mahalia was a threat.

JD spoke. "This is what is going to happen. One at a time, Blessica first, then this guy," he indicated the guard at the door, "and finally, Mahalia, will move to the living room. My friend here will escort you. Once in the living room, you will sit, and another of us will watch over you to ensure nobody tries anything stupid. Understood?"

Blessica and the guard nodded. Mahalia scowled and glared at JD, who remained calm and unaffected. Eventually, she also nodded.

One by one, Vivas escorted each in turn to the living room. Blessica was shocked to see Taylor with a 9mm Glock in his hand, covering the guards on the couch.

"Taylor?"

When he did not reply, she looked down, saying nothing. Vivas guided her to a chair across from the couch. The third guard had his hands and ankles zip-tied together and was sitting on the couch between the other two, his mouth similarly duct-taped shut.

Finally, Vivas escorted Mahalia into the living room and seated her in a chair beside the one occupied by her sister. He and Taylor could now easily cover all five of their captives. Only then did JD knock on the guestroom door.

The shout from the startled guard in the hall woke Xuan. She could not tell what was happening. Shaking Jum Y awake and motioning her to stay quiet, the two huddled together and listened intently for clues as to what was happening outside their room. They heard a male voice telling the guard and the Baguinda sisters what to do, but they couldn't tell who it was. Jum Y thought the voice was vaguely familiar, but try as she might, she couldn't place it. Some minutes later, after things had again quieted down, there was a knock on the door.

"Xuan, Jum Y, this is JD Cordell. I am Mai's son; Dish is my uncle. I know you've never met me, Xuan, but I met Jum Y in Vietnam when she helped rescue my mother. I guess, Xuan, I am your uncle … or something like that. Don't be frightened. You are safe now. I am coming in."

JD holstered his gun and stepped inside. Jum Y recognized him immediately and started to cry. A moment later, Xuan was also in tears. Sophie followed JD into the room and whined. "This is Sophie, my dog. Vivas is here, too. He is watching the Baguinda sisters in the living room."

"Vivas is here too?" Jum Y exclaimed. "Is Chai here as well?"

"Chai? Oh, you mean Sirichai? Yes, he is here as well. He is watching the lobby for us. We need to get going; we need to get you both out of here."

"Chai is here too," Jum Y repeated.

Jum Y threw herself at JD, giving him a big hug. "I knew you would come. I knew you would find us."

"Of course we would. We can talk about everything later. Right now, we need to get out of here, okay?"

Both girls nodded. They could not stop smiling.

Within minutes, the girls' luggage was collected, and Blessica—at JD's insistence—returned the two passports taken from them when the girls were first kidnapped. The three guards were securely bound and gagged with duct tape, lying on the floor in the guest bedroom recently vacated by the two girls. Everyone else was assembled in the living room. They were ready to leave.

Sophie sat very still; the German Shepherd's eyes remained fixed on Mahalia as JD moved to grab Xuan's suitcase. Vivas already had Jum Y's suitcase in hand. Mahalia remained seated and silent in her chair, the blank expression on her face hiding the fury she felt inside.

Blessica also sat quietly, mostly staring at the floor. Her eyes would occasionally stray toward Taylor, then quickly look away. Finally, she turned to face him.

"Taylor?"

Taylor turned to meet her gaze.

"I am sorry, Taylor. I am so sorry. I know my sister paid to have that monster, Garcia, kill you. I know there is nothing I can say to you. I cannot undo what has been done."

Taylor stood, silent and impassive. "I understand."

Suddenly, as if a dam had broken, tears were streaming down Blessica's face. "I wish I met you at another time or in another place. I wish … I wish my life were different. I did care for you, Taylor; I did. But I could not see any way around … any way things could work out for us. I really wish things could have been different."

Taylor said nothing at first, then he shrugged. "I guess I cared for you, too, at one point. Things might have been different at another time and place, but I don't know. However, that man is gone now. I wish you good luck, Blessica. I hope life gets better for you."

She turned away and looked at the floor again, tears rolling down her cheeks.

Mahalia laughed out loud. It was an evil, almost maniacal cackle. "Garcia should have killed you, Taylor. Maybe I should have killed you myself. I know you wanted me. You wanted us both. I could have easily killed you in my bed." She straightened up in her seat and spit at Taylor. "You will all feel my pain … you will feel my wrath."

Xuan waited beside Jum Y, about fifteen feet from where Mahalia sat. The two girls were anxious and ready to leave. Vivas turned toward the door with Jum Y's suitcase, motioning the girls to follow him. Sophie's low growl of warning was followed immediately by Blessica's scream, "Mahalia, no!"

Mahalia came out of the chair with the butterfly knife open, blade held low, gleaming wickedly. She lunged for Jum Y. Vivas turned, but it was too late. Taylor and JD were both caught flat-footed. Neither could reach Mahalia or Jum Y in time. Xuan, seeing Mahalia coming, shoved Jum Y out of Mahalia's path. As Jum Y tumbled to the floor, Mahalia spun toward Xuan with a malicious grin. "You little bitch…"

Sophie sprang forward with a deep-throated growl, her eighty-seven pounds of canine muscle colliding with Mahalia. Sophie's jaws clamped down hard on Mahalia's left forearm. The dog's forward momentum carried her past Mahalia, the woman's forearm still clamped in her jaws, causing her to spin and lose her balance. Mahalia fell hard, her head striking the corner of the end table beside the couch. She lay still.

JD's voice rang out. "Sophie, sit!"

Releasing Mahalia's arm, Sophie sat, her body quivering, still intently focused on Mahalia, whose still form remained sprawled on the carpet.

"Oh, shit!" Vivas murmured. There were a few seconds of total silence. JD moved to get his hand on Sophie's collar. Setting the suitcase down, Vivas moved to help Jum Y to her feet.

Xuan rushed to Jum Y. "Are you okay?"

Still stunned, Jum Y took a second to answer. "Yes, yes. I am okay. Thanks to you, Xuan." She glanced down at Mahalia lying on the floor. "Is she…"

Taylor stood up from where he knelt to check on Mahalia. "She is dead."

"Damn it," JD muttered. He turned to Blessica. "Why did she do that? This did not need to happen. I am sorry, Blessica. Sophie was only protecting the girls."

Blessica stood stone still, not answering. Her beautiful face flashed with fury, grief, and, finally, sadness. When she spoke, it was in a carefully controlled voice. "I don't blame your dog. It was not the dog's fault. My sister caused this to happen; her actions killed her. It was a tragic accident," she sighed.

Blessica looked directly at Jum Y and Xuan. "My sister has not been right since we escaped from a terrorist camp many years ago. I don't think she ever set any other girls free. I am almost certain she kept them around and then killed them … all of them. I don't know how or where." She shook her head sadly. "Or maybe she just shipped them off. I don't know."

Jum Y and Xuan looked at each other, horrified.

"She would have murdered both of you. Maybe I was also a little afraid of her. I know you will not understand; I don't expect you to. But she was my sister, and I loved her." She looked up at Taylor with a sad, tired face. "Who knows? One day, she might have killed me. I am as much to blame for what happened here as she was. Now go.

Take your friends and go. Get out of here. You will have no trouble from me."

Taylor nodded. Vivas, saying nothing, quietly led the two girls out the door, now carrying a suitcase in each hand. At JD's command, Sophie fell in on his left side. JD glanced briefly at the young woman kneeling by her dead sister, now very much alone.

"I am sorry," JD started in a quiet voice. Blessica did not look up. "I did not start this mess and certainly didn't want your sister killed. That was unfortunate." He turned and followed Vivas through the door, Sophie at his side. Taylor started after them but paused in the doorway and turned to look back.

"Blessica, I am very sorry all this happened. I'm sorry about Mahalia. She was your sister, even if she did try to have me killed. Sometimes life deals us a shitty hand to play. You and Mahalia got dealt one, and maybe I did, too. But I have a new life now—new friends, Ruby and her son. I know this will sound strange coming from me, but Ruby is a good woman; her faith in me probably saved my life." Taylor paused. "Blessica, maybe this is your chance. I know you are tough. You are a strong woman. Look at where you came from and where you are now. It may not have been a happy path, and you may not have chosen it, but you made it. Despite all the bad things you have done, hidden deep inside, you still have a good heart. It would help if you listened to it. If Ruby could find a way to have faith in someone like me, I should find a way to have faith in you. If you need a friend, you have me. I can't say where I will be, but you can reach me through the Spring Lotus Foundation, which my friends are part of. They will know how to find me."

Blessica stood up from where she had been kneeling beside Mahalia. She looked at Taylor, her face tear-streaked and grief-stricken. "I am pretty messed up right now, Taylor. I am angry and sad. But somehow, I am also relieved. I should hate all of you for the death of my sister; instead, I am only saddened by it." She took a deep breath. "You need to go. Get out of here. But I will never forget you or what you said just now. Thank you for saying it."

Taylor nodded, then turned and walked out.

Sirichai watched as Taylor stepped out of the elevator and into the lobby. A quick scan to make sure the coast was clear, and Taylor motioned the others to follow.

Jum Y and Xuan stepped into the lobby followed by Vivas, who carried two suitcases, and JD, with Sophie on her leash. Sirichai moved to meet them, and the group exited the condo lobby. A few minutes later, with Taylor at the wheel, the van quickly disappeared into traffic. It was time to link up with Hana and the rest of the team before getting to the airstrip.

Sophie, JD, and Sirichai sat in the back with the girls, making themselves as comfortable as possible on the cargo van's floor. Sirichai sat between Jum Y and Xuan, who were both very quiet. Xuan was busily stroking the dog's neck.

Riding in the shotgun seat, Vivas helped Taylor navigate the narrow, busy streets.

"Trouble in the lobby?" JD asked, spotting the makeshift bandage on Sirichai's right thigh. "We'll get Ellen to check your leg out as soon as we return to the hotel."

"Tony Salonga showed up," Sirichai replied. "He claimed he'd killed Tala for talking to us. He came after me with a knife."

Vivas turned back to inquire, "Is he dead?"

"Did you kill him?" Jum Y asked, shuddering. "I hope not. Too many people are already dead."

"He was breathing—alive, but unconscious. I hid him in the lobby utility closet. He did go down hard. I do not know if he is okay."

Jum Y sighed, and suddenly seemed to melt into a startled Sirichai's side. She closed her eyes, murmuring, "Please, Chai! No more killing, okay?"

Xuan looked away, hiding her grin as she saw Sirichai's arm move to encircle Jum Y's shoulders.

CHAPTER 41
Vietnam

Hai hurried to greet the weary travelers as they trooped into the mountain village high in the border region between Vietnam, Cambodia, and Laos.

"You are back!" he exclaimed, greeting Dish with a huge grin. Slim and Hahn nodded their greetings and, setting down their weapons, moved toward Hai's wife, who brought up a wooden bucket of fresh water and an odd collection of drinking cups and old tin mugs. Leaving the water distribution task to the men, she moved on to the eight young ladies, seven of whom were quite dirty and dressed in rags. Still in her black cocktail dress, white scarf, and modified heels, Ahn looked around, amazed by the village and the warm welcome. Slim had hacked the heels from Ahn's shoes so she could navigate the forest trails without risking an ankle.

Hai excused himself and headed toward his longhouse as his wife's gaze turned to the group of young ladies.

"Oh my, you poor things. "We don't have much to offer, but we can get you cleaned up, give you some food, and maybe we can find something better for you to wear than you have now."

During their trek into the mountains, the seven young women had come to understand that Dish and his friends were not just another criminal gang, that they were not going to be sold into slavery, and that they were free. Eventually, a few began showing signs of life, talking to Ahn and Dish, and smiling shyly at Slim and Hahn. Now, meeting Hai's wife in the village, several began to cry.

Seeing tears on several of the girls' faces, Slim poked Hahn in the side and surreptitiously pointed in their direction. "I hope those are tears of happiness."

Hahn nodded. "There's probably a lot of different emotions wrapped up in those tears, but I'd suspect happiness is certainly a part of it."

"Yup. I need a beer."

"Me too, my friend. Me too. Let's get back to the world."

Both men turned on hearing someone approach. Dish grinned. "Not a bad day for an old mountain warrior."

Hahn chuckled. "Not bad at all, old friend. But I am exhausted. Maybe it is time for old men like us to retire; let the younger pups have it."

"And do what?" Slim snorted. "Hang around on the damn porch and do nothing? I'm not one to sit around and play pinochle. And I hate fishing."

Dish laughed. "Maybe doing nothing is good! But maybe fishing is also good, I think. I do not know this pinochle. But I have good news. Hai has been in contact with Quan, as you requested. Quan will meet you all in Xayden with transportation two days from tomorrow. So, we eat, sleep, and rest here for a day; the girls need rest, too. In two days, we will start down to Xayden. Okay?"

Both Hahn and Slim nodded.

"Say, Dish," Slim started. "You wouldn't happen to have a cold beer hidden around here somewhere, would you?"

Dish smiled. "I think maybe Hai has thought of that for you."

Slim grinned. "Now that's what I needed to hear!"

EPILOGUE

The Gulfstream G700's twin Rolls-Royce turbofan engines hummed quietly. The cabin lights were dimmed. JD stirred restlessly in his seat, the accidental death of Mahalia still weighing heavily on his mind. While it often came with being a US Navy SEAL. JD never enjoyed killing. It was sometimes necessary, and he accepted that, but the death of Mahalia was simply an unfortunate accident.

She probably deserved it, especially if she killed all those young ladies like her sister suspected. Still, we didn't have to be the ones to do it. Oh well, her death may save a few poor girls from horribly short and terrible lives.

JD decided he could live with that; besides, he had little choice now.

Ellen shifted, and JD listened to her quiet steady breathing as she slept beside him, her head resting on his shoulder. Sirichai and Jum Y sat in the seats across the aisle, both sleeping. Jum Y hadn't left Sirichai's side since they left the Baguinda sisters' condo. Nearer the rear of the cabin, Taylor and Ruby sat chatting quietly, their voices indiscernible over the hum of the jet engines.

JD glanced at his mother, who sat on one of the couches. Sophie was curled up at her feet while Amado lay sleeping, his head in Mai's lap. She smiled at her son and nodded; no words needed to be spoken. Xuan sat at the other end of the couch, sleeping with Amado's feet in her lap. Vivas and Hana slept side-by-side, wedged together on the cabin's other couch. JD grinned. If the jet banked hard to the left, both would likely tumble onto the floor.

Suddenly, the phone in JD's right hip pocket began to vibrate. Carefully, trying not to wake Ellen, he fished it out. He did not recognize the number.

"Hello?"

"JD, it's Pallie. Did you get the girls out? Is everyone safe?"

"Hey, Pallie, I didn't recognize the number."

"Sorry, my phone's battery died. I'm out here in the middle of the damn Texas desert; electrical outlets are scarce. I borrowed the chief's cell phone."

The chief?"

"Yeah. His name is Gray Wolf but he goes by Tony; he's a genuine Apache Indian. Shit, JD. We can talk about that later. Did you get the girls out? Is everyone okay?"

"Yep. Both Jum Y and Xuan are fine. We're on a plane headed back to Thailand right now, and we'll be back in Tennessee in a few days, maybe a week."

"Excellent. When I get a chance, I'll come out for a visit and bring Kathy."

"That would be great. How are you, Pallie?"

"I'm good, man. But I gotta say, JD, this child trafficking is some tough shit to handle. These are some purely evil assholes. We just rescued about twenty kids being smuggled across the border into Mexico. There was this girl, Latoya, a great kid … she almost got … Anyway, she's okay. I talked to her a bit. Tough kid. She says she wants to join the Navy when she graduates high…"

JD heard Pallie's voice break. "Pallie, hey, are you okay?"

There was a long pause before Pallie's voice returned. "Yeah! I'm fine. I must be gettin' old. This shit gets to me. Like I said, these are some evil sons of bitches. Listen, man, I got to go. I am so happy to hear that the girls are safe. Give everyone my regards, and I'll talk to you soon." The call ended.

Ellen stirred. "JD, honey, who was that? Who called?"

"It was Pallie. He wanted to know about the girls and if they're alright. I told him we had them, they're fine, and we're returning to Thailand. I told him we'd be in Knoxville in about a week."

"Is Pallie alright? What did he say?"

JD looked at his wife and realized how truly blessed he was. He placed his arm around her shoulder.

"Pallie's alright. His team just rescued a bunch of kids at the border. He sounded a little shaken up. I guess he talked to one of the kids, and seeing this trafficking stuff up close was tough on him. Hell, I don't care who you are, seeing this stuff … it's hard on all of us."

Ellen squeezed his hand.

ABOUT THE AUTHOR

Darren C Gilbert was born in Ilion, NY, but grew up in North Adams, Massachusetts, a small town in the heart of the Berkshire Mountains.

An avid reader, Darren particularly enjoys military history, epic sagas, spy novels, and historical fiction. In addition to serving in the U.S. Army from 1979 to 1983, Darren has 40+ years of martial arts training, including managing a traditional karate dojo for 12 years.

Darren earned undergraduate and graduate degrees from the University of Tennessee and Western Governors University. He is also an Executive Security International Executive Protection Program graduate and a Certified Protection Specialist. He currently resides in Knoxville, Tennessee.

Darren continues to teach karate and self-defense in the Knoxville area and does what he can to support OUR Rescue in their efforts to end the trafficking of children.

Reviews are critical to the success of any author. If you enjoyed Reciprocity, please take a moment to leave a review.

https://www.amazon.com/review/create-review?asin=173460235X

www.ingramcontent.com/pod-product-compliance
Lightning Source LLC
Chambersburg PA
CBHW071642260626
47170CB00001B/201

* 9 7 8 1 7 3 4 6 0 2 3 5 7 *